Praise for Susan Krinard

"In an intriguing departure
from her popular werewolf romances,
Krinard takes readers to a realm where
the Faerie and mortal worlds intersect
and spins a darkly magical story of love,
betrayal, and redemption.... A cast of
exceptionally well-done secondary
characters (most notably a villainous aunt
and a wise, enchanting child), the
excellent use of language, and an intricate,
nicely unfolding plot add depth....
The Forest Lord's compelling characters
and the universal nature of their
underlying conflicts should guarantee
an across-the-board appeal to general
fantasy fans and other readers."
—*Library Journal* on *The Forest Lord*

"*Touch of the Wolf* is a mystical,
enthralling read, brimming with
lyrical prose, powerful emotions,
dark secrets, and shattering sensuality.
Susan Krinard brings the world
of the werewolf to life
in a riveting and believable way."
—Eugenia Riley, bestselling author

"Magical, mystical, and moving,
Krinard's book has a surprise villain
and a nice twist at the end
Fans will be delighted by this
and its underlying ecological r
—*Booklist* on *The Forest*

SUSAN KRINARD

HADDON

SHIELD OF THE SKY

LUNA™

www.LUNA-Books.com

LUNA™

First edition October 2004

SHIELD OF THE SKY

ISBN 0-373-80211-0

www.LUNA-Books.com

Printed in U.S.A.

I'd like to give special thanks for the generous assistance that made this book possible: to C. J. Cherryh, for being a constant source of inspiration and for information about ancient Greek language; to Sondra Schlotterback and Nancy Varian, for support and valuable suggestions; to my agent, Lucienne Diver, for encouragement and expert advice; to Markus, the Fighter Guy, for detailed instruction on ancient fighting techniques; to Arja Hartikainen, curator of the Siida Museum, for patiently answering my questions about Sámi vocabulary; and to my husband, Serge Mailloux, who never once expected me to cook.

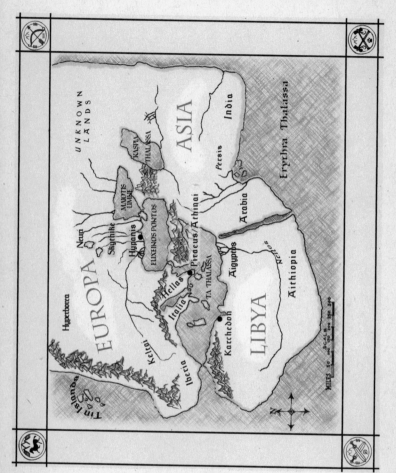

PHILOKRATES'
MAP
OF THE
KNOWN WORLD

Prologue

Forbidden.

It was a word Rhenna had heard seldom in her childhood. Until she was six, she had gazed at the snow-capped peaks of the Shield of the Sky and known the great mountains only as protectors, home of devas, guardians of the lands of the Free People that stood in their shadow.

But when she reached the age of first testing and the Earth-speakers found that she bore no special gifts to belie her common parentage, she was taken to the foot of the Shield by her mother's sister and told what she must never do.

"The Shield is forbidden to you," said the blacksmith, whose arms were broad as oak branches. "Only the Chosen climb the hills, at the appointed time, to meet with the Ailuri."

Many years passed before Rhenna knew what her aunt had meant by her cautious words, the small warning gestures and

averted gaze. Pantaris was afraid of nothing, not longtooth cats
nor brutal steppe storms nor barbarian raiders.

Yet her aunt's warning burned deep, scarring her with curiosity, and Rhenna could not remember a day since when she had not
looked up at the Shield and longed to discover its secrets.

Today is the day.

Rhenna shifted in her crouch behind the boundary stone and
gazed up the broken slope over which her sister had passed. The
world had altered much in fourteen years. Pantaris's hair had
gone gray as the iron in her forge, and Rhenna no longer saw the
world with the eyes of green youth. Her arms were strong, her
aim true, her skill respected among the Sisterhood. She wore her
brown hair in the braids of a woman grown.

Only her desire had not changed. No one would believe that
the devas spoke to *her*—yes, even to a mere warrior—that they
came as breaths of air or gentle breezes or howling winds, wordless and strange. Always they bade her look to the mountains.

Now Rhenna, daughter of Klyemne, Sister of the Axe, gazed
upon the path of the Chosen and knew she would risk everything
to see that which was forbidden.

She glanced behind her, past the carved axe handle that stood
over her shoulder. The others had all gone: the sisters and aunts
and mothers weeping at the honor bestowed upon their kin; the
Earthspeakers who presided over the ceremony of leave-taking;
the warriors standing guard as they had always done, silent and
stolid.

Not one of them had seen Rhenna linger. Even if they had,
they would not have guessed her purpose. It was unthinkable.
Inconceivable.

Forbidden.

She lightly touched each of her weapons, whispering a prayer
for luck, and removed them one by one. First was the great double-bladed axe, which she laid on the bear pelt she had spread be-

side the stone. Her gorytos, the side quiver with its precious burden of bow and short arrows, joined the axe. Then came the belt knife, longtooth-hilted, and both of her boot daggers.

Last of all she removed her cap. She folded the leather neatly atop the pelt and unbraided her hair, letting it fall loose about her shoulders.

Kneeling beside the pelt, Rhenna chanted the song of preparation for battle. She touched her forehead to the boundary stone and begged its favor, spread her fingers against the soil and did the same. She opened her heart for all the devas to see.

Then she rose to her feet and trod the winding path among the oaks, ascending as a hundred Chosen had done before her. Soon she was in the pines, and still the way led up and up. If she looked back, she would see the steppe spread out below like a map painted on rough skin.

She did not look back. The single path began to separate, sending faint strands hither and yon like an unraveling skein of wool. She knelt and studied each branching and followed that which bore her sister's boot print.

Soon.

The air of summer was warm even here, where deva winds caressed the hillsides. Red deer grazed in lush meadows, unafraid of ordinary predators.

Rhenna stopped to swallow the sudden thickness of fear. She loosened her jacket to let the breeze flow freely under her shirt and dry the sweat on her skin. If the devas were against her, surely they would have made themselves known by now.

Once more she climbed. The path did not branch again. After half a league she found a pile of abandoned clothing, discarded with no semblance of order. Rhenna almost smiled. So like Keleneo, who had been chosen for the Seekers because she could never keep her thoughts on the work at hand....

A strange scent came to Rhenna, and she lifted her head. The small hairs rose at the back of her neck. She walked more slowly, listening. Great boulders rose like sentinels. She sucked in a breath and rounded a giant, pitted rock burnished silver by the elements.

There, in the shadow of a twisted pine, lay a wedding bower. Keleneo stood beside it, repairing a hole in the curved, willow-bough wall with deft fingers. Wind blew her transparent shift against her body, picking out the tight buds of her nipples and the long lines of waist and thigh. She didn't so much as shiver. The devas would not allow her to suffer. She was Chosen.

Rhenna closed her eyes and imagined herself in Keleneo's place. She would not wait so calmly. She would stand facing the peaks, watching, alert for the first rustle of leaves or padded footfall. Her pulse would race like a yearling colt. She would imagine him coming to her from the heights, imagine what it must be like to couple with the descendant of a god....

No sound, no scent tore Rhenna from her dreams. All her senses shouted as if she had walked through fire and jumped into an icy torrent.

The Ailu flowed down the hillside like an obsidian river, seemingly boneless, his black coat agleam in the waning sunlight. Huge, disk-shaped paws wove noiselessly among the rocks. His golden gaze struck sparks from the earth.

Mother-of-All, he was magnificent. No whispered tale could do him justice. And Rhenna knew true fear, that she should look upon this magnificence without paying a terrible price.

Keleneo was not afraid. She moved gracefully away from the bower and waited for her lover, arms raised in a gesture of welcome. The Ailu covered the remaining distance almost daintily, as if with one misstep he might send her tumbling.

He touched the point of his black nose to Keleneo's outstretched fingertips. She fell to her knees among the flowers she had gathered, dipping her forehead to the ground at the Ailu's feet.

That was when the miracle happened. Rhenna blinked, and in the space of a moment the Ailu was panther no longer. He stood before his bride a naked man, rampant with desire, fully as magnificent as the great cat he had been. Black hair spread across his shoulders and spilled nearly to his waist. His face was beautiful. He laid his broad hand on Keleneo's head.

Keleneo didn't speak. She pressed one hand to her breast and then brushed the Ailu's erection with a featherlight caress. He flung back his head and shuddered.

Rhenna's throat ached with unshed tears. *You were not Chosen,* the Sisters exclaimed. *Shame,* cried the Earthspeaker, pounding her oaken staff into the ground. But there were other voices like wind in Rhenna's ears, and they told a different tale.

Here you belong, they said. *Here…*

Something moved at the corner of Rhenna's vision. She spun, hand reaching for the knife she no longer bore. Startled eyes met hers—yellow eyes in a brown, masculine face much too old for one of the village children.

Not a child, but a boy on the very edge of manhood. He was naked, shivering, his thin body strung with muscle that could not keep pace with his bones. He tossed black hair out of his face and grimaced in alarm.

An Ailu boy. The thought had scarce taken shape in Rhenna's mind when she heard the roar behind her and followed the boy's terrified gaze.

Keleneo shrank into the shadow of the hut, hands pressed flat over her mouth. Her Ailu mate screamed in rage. He changed from man to beast in a heartbeat and crouched to spring.

Rhenna flattened herself to the boulder and swung back to the boy. She never knew what she might have demanded of him, for he was already gone.

She clenched her fists and stepped out to meet her fate. Blood drummed behind her ears. *The devas led me here. They will protect me.*

Black flashed across Rhenna's vision. No deva appeared to intercede. Her belly tightened in anticipation of the killing blow.

"*No!*" Keleneo's voice, riven with horror.

The blow never came.

Rhenna opened her eyes. The Ailu crouched an arm's length away, tail lashing, fur stiff along his spine. His teeth gleamed in jaws that could crush a woman's skull in a single snap.

Death, Rhenna could have accepted. But his glorious, golden eyes conveyed punishment beyond bearing…all the scorn, the utter contempt of the Elder-Council judging the blasphemer.

Forbidden.

Rhenna didn't even have time to flinch when the Ailu reared up upon his hind legs and lunged, striking at her head. Searing pain came only long counts after the blow, as if the claws had torn the skin of some other face.

Someone wept. The Ailu spun on his haunches and sprang away, not toward the bower but back into the mountains. His pads left a trace of red on pale stone.

Rhenna lifted her hand to her right cheek. Her fingers came away washed in crimson. She fell to her knees.

"Sister!" Keleneo stumbled toward her, tripping over the shift in her haste. "Rhenna—"

Calm settled over Rhenna, the peace that was said to come to a warrior before death. But she would not die from such a wound. Nor from what must follow.

"Keli," she said, "we should not speak. Go back."

"To *that?*" She knelt before Rhenna and grasped her bloodied hands. "Your face—oh, Rhenna, your face!"

Rhenna struggled to her feet, pulling her sister with her. "Go back. He will return. I must go…home."

Keleneo gripped Rhenna's arms, her lovely features twisted in dread. "They will punish you."

"But not you, Keli." Rhenna felt blood pooling under her jaw and trickling beneath her collar, thick and warm. "They'll never know we met."

"I can't leave you—"

Rhenna took a deliberate step away. "Mother's Blessing, Keleneo. Forgive me."

Keleneo wept silently as Rhenna picked her way down the trail, half-blinded by the blood. She let it spill unhindered and unheeded over the front of her shirt and jacket.

The devas had lied. They had mocked her with their inscrutable promises, but in the end they had made their meaning clear enough.

Rhenna came to the boundary stone with no memory of how she had traveled there. Her weapons lay untouched. She knelt beside the bearskin and waited.

Just at sunset a girl-child came to the Place of the Chosen, bearing flowers in memory of one who had gone. She saw Rhenna's face and let the bundle fall. Then she ran back to the village as fast as her skinny foal's legs would carry her.

Sun set. The blood dried on Rhenna's face. When the first flickering blaze of torchlight emerged out of the darkness, Rhenna rose to meet it.

Part One

Shield of the Sky

Chapter One

Rhenna's scar was throbbing.

She touched it with absent fingers and scanned the horizon. The horses were quiet. Mares grazed contentedly, heads buried in the rich fodder of oat, rye and feather grass that stretched in every direction as far as the eye could see. Each foal tested its new-found strength and speed against that of the others. Ears quivered and tails twitched, but none raised the alarm.

Far to the east and west lay the well-guarded borders of the Shield's Shadow, the land of the Free People. To the north stood the snow-capped peaks of the Shield itself, and to the south…

Rhenna frowned, shifting her weight on Chaimon's broad back. To the south were the Skudat tribesmen, Hellenish merchants and the empire—barbarians who entered the Shield's Shadow at their peril. No, there was no danger in the south.

Chaimon stamped and snorted, jingling the tiny bells on his bridle. "Forgive me, my friend," Rhenna murmured, scratching the gelding between his ears. "I'm restless today."

Rhenna echoed Chaimon's snort. For nine years she had watched the herds, far too long to begin starting at shadows. Too wise to regard the dubious warnings of phantoms and memory.

Chaimon jingled his bells again. The mares paused in their grazing, and Rhenna heard the muffled drum of hoofbeats.

A horse and rider galloped out of the tall grass. The girl's pale hair was bound in the tail of a novice, and her ears were bare of the double-axe studs worn by every initiated Sister.

Rhenna wound her fists in Chaimon's mane. The Elders had sent someone at last: an apprentice to take under her wing and prepare in the ways of the Sisterhood. The long exile was over.

She swallowed her eagerness and assumed the cool reserve that befitted one of her age and experience. She expected the girl to bring her mount to a decorous halt, but the rider—surely no more than fourteen or fifteen years—charged headlong at Rhenna. Her gelding's flanks were mottled with sweat. The girl sawed on the reins and fell back into her saddle with an ungainly *thump* as the horse skidded to a stop.

Rhenna dismounted and took up a warrior's stance. "What can be worthy of such great haste, Little Sister, that you ignore the good health of your mount?"

The girl braced her hands on her knees and looked down on Rhenna as if *she* were the Elder. Her dark eyes settled firmly, inevitably, on Rhenna's disfigurement.

"Rhenna-of-the-Scar?"

"I am Rhenna of the Sisterhood," Rhenna corrected, the bright spark of hope dying in her breast. "Dismount at once."

With a scowl the girl obeyed. Rhenna moved past her and examined the exhausted horse, running her hands up and down the legs to check for swelling. "You pushed him hard," she said, "but he should recover if he's given enough rest."

"You—" the girl sputtered. "I—"

Rhenna slipped the bit from the gelding's mouth and unfastened the bridle, tossing it to the girl. "You will care for your mount before you take rest, food or drink. Then we'll talk about the proper use of horses."

The girl caught the bridle and glared at Rhenna, thrusting out her narrow chest. Her iron-studded leather coat was at least a size too big. "I have come..." she began, and let out a short, sharp breath. "I was sent to deliver a message from the Elders. You are summoned to Heart of Oaks with your herd, as quickly as you can move it."

Rhenna stopped halfway to the small tent where she stored her supplies. *No apprentice,* she thought. Not her task, after all, to break this filly of her bad habits and teach her the folly of arrogance.

"You are summoned to Heart of Oaks," the girl repeated. "Didn't you hear?"

Rhenna continued on to the tent, where she collected a brush, a waterskin and a shallow bronze vessel. "What is your name?"

"Deri...Derinoe."

"I heard you well enough, Derinoe. You may begin by watering your horse—lightly—and walking him until he cools. Then you may rub him down and tell me why the Elders have called in the herd."

Rhenna's quiet words seemed to diminish a little of the girl's self-importance, but her lips remained twisted in contempt. She snatched the waterskin and vessel from Rhenna's hands as if the merest shared touch might corrupt her.

Rhenna left the girl to her work, mounted Chaimon and rode a circuit of the herd, turning Derinoe's message about in her mind. Never had she been ordered to deliver a herd to Heart of Oaks. When yearling foals were ready to leave their dams, warriors came to take them away for first training. Healers journeyed

across the steppe from pasture to pasture, caring for ill or injured
beasts. Once a year the animals were tallied, stallions exchanged,
bloodlines recorded. The herds remained free except in the harsh-
est winters or in times of severe drought.

Rhenna's scar ached with renewed urgency. She completed her
ride and loosed Chaimon, who trotted to the new gelding and nuzzled his damp neck. Derinoe had rubbed the animal's coat until
it shone like a bronze mirror.

Rhenna nodded approval and provided Derinoe with fresh
springwater and salted meat preserved from her last hunt. She and
the girl crouched beside Rhenna's fire pit, where last night's ashes
still shed some lingering warmth. Derinoe's eyes sought Rhenna's
scar with unconcealed fascination.

"The stories you've heard are undoubtedly true," Rhenna said
softly, "but dishonor is not an illness to be passed by a touch. Eat."

The girl shivered. Her haughty mask crumpled. "You...you
truly saw the Ailuri?"

"What has that to do with your message?"

"I don't know. Everything is changing."

"I have not had news in half a year. Tell me."

Derinoe's eyes flooded with something very like panic. "The
Earthspeakers and Elders are always in the Council Hall or the Sacred Grove. The warriors who guard the eastern and southern
borders are being recalled. I have seen them myself. They say it
is because of the new attacks on the western border—"

"Attacks?"

"The settlements have been raided. Our people have been taken
by *men*." She reached toward Rhenna and stopped, her hand flexing in midair. "When has such a thing ever happened before?"

Rhenna couldn't remember. Every year Earthspeakers rode the
borders, invoking the devas to protect the Shield's Shadow. The
man-tribes who coveted more abundant pastures were turned
aside by howling winds or fierce storms brought by devas of water

and sky. The Sisters of the Axe excelled in the arts of war, but seldom were they forced to test their skills against real enemies.

Now they had been summoned home to defend settlements that should never have been vulnerable to the barbarians.

What had become of the devas?

"How many villages have been attacked?" she asked.

Derinoe scrubbed her face with shaking hands. "They told us…we novices who have not yet won our honors…only what we had to know to gather the herds. No one else could be spared." She met Rhenna's gaze. "Do you know, Elder Sister? Do you understand why these things are happening?"

The girl's naive question slashed at Rhenna's heart, and she saw herself as she had been nine years ago, tumbling from pride to terror in a single day.

"No," she said, granting the girl the respect of an equal. "But the answers lie in Heart of Oaks. We'll rest tonight and take the herd north in the morning. Until then——"

Chaimon jerked up his head. Deri's mount did the same, and every horse in the herd turned toward the south. Nervous whickers rippled among them; ears flicked back and forth like blades of grass in a high wind.

"What is it?" Derinoe asked. "I see nothing. Is it wolves?"

Rhenna held up her hand. At first she, too, saw nothing. But then a hot wind rose, gusting hair into her face, and a dark smudge appeared on the southern horizon.

"No," she said slowly. "Not wolves."

The smudge rose higher, altering its shape with each passing moment. No cloud had ever taken such a form, nor moved so swiftly.

"It must be a storm," Derinoe offered.

She meant one of the black storms that blew out of the east, driving hot, dry winds into the steppe. But Rhenna always knew when they were coming.

"Birds," she said, startled by her own certainty.

Birds. A massive flock of them, greater than any Rhenna had seen.

"I don't understand," Derinoe said. "All the birds that winter in the south have already passed over our land."

She was right; Rhenna had watched them fly overhead by the hundreds in early spring. This was not the same. The mass grew ever larger, accompanied by shrieks and the whirring of myriad wings. The horses bunched, lunging and biting.

Rhenna leaped onto Chaimon's back. "Ride to the flank, Derinoe," she said. "Keep the horses together, whatever happens."

Derinoe caught her nervous gelding, mounted and circled to the opposite side of the herd. The flock cast its own shadow, clattering like a hailstorm. Individual birds darted in and out, smashing into their fellows. Fragile shapes plummeted to shatter on the ground. The air was rank with the smell of excrement. A steppe eagle, king of the sky, dove screaming out of the cloud's relentless path.

Rhenna seldom sang to her horses, for she had no gift for music. Now she reached into memory and found a chant the oldest warriors sometimes used to quiet restive herds. She raised her voice above the birds' dissonant cries.

The leading edge of the shadow raced across the plain. Rodents and insects boiled up from the grass under the horses' feet. A single brown bird, no bigger than a sparrow, darted past Rhenna's ear.

Chaimon trembled. Rhenna used her knife to cut a long strip of cloth from her sleeve and secured it over the horse's eyes.

Then the wave hit. A clap of thunder deafened her, and a blast of hot air threatened to peel the skin from her face. She called out to Derinoe, but her voice was lost in the clamor of panicked horses and the shrilling of the flock.

Light vanished. Feathers fell like rain, covering the horses' backs and filling Rhenna's mouth. Tiny bodies thumped into her padded jacket and tumbled under Chaimon's hooves. Working blindly, Rhenna tore another strip from her shirtsleeve and tied it over her own mouth and nose. The stench was unbearable. And the cries—they were like those of lost souls condemned to endless torment in the Southerners' pitiless underworld.

Time lost its meaning. If the sun still warmed the earth, Rhenna had no sense of it. She murmured in Chaimon's ear, praying that none of the herd would be lost.

The devas should have stopped such an abomination before it crossed into the lands of the Free People.

"Rhenna?"

Derinoe's voice was faint, but it was proof that she was alive. Rhenna opened her eyes. Weak shafts of sunlight danced in the tiny spaces between beating wings. The cloud was breaking up, birds scattering to east and west as the largest portion surged ever northward.

Chaimon blew feathers from his nostrils. Rhenna removed her makeshift scarf. Derinoe hunched over her gelding's back a hundred paces distant. She seemed unhurt. Rhenna turned anxiously to the herd.

Death had followed in the wake of the flock's passage. Thousands of small brown carcasses covered the grass, but not a single horse had been lost. A few had sustained small injuries and many trembled from the shock. They behaved much the same after a violent thunderstorm.

But thunderstorms were natural, born of earth and sky. There was nothing natural about the birds.

"It was an omen," Derinoe said, riding up beside her. The girl's eyes were strange and staring, her cheek streaked with blood as if she had faced her first battle. "The devas are angry."

Rhenna's laugh escaped before she could silence it. Derinoe swung upon her with a zealot's glare.

"You mock them," she said. "I heard…I heard them say that the devas never forgave what you did. You brought this curse upon us."

"Perhaps you're right," Rhenna said. "But the horses need our care, and there's no use bewailing what can't be changed."

Derinoe deflated like a pierced waterskin, wincing as she moved her left shoulder. Over her protests, Rhenna sat the child down and made a thorough examination. Derinoe set her jaw and refused to show any sign of discomfort. A warrior didn't weep in the face of pain.

Just as a warrior didn't question, and never dreamed.

Rhenna returned Derinoe's shirt and remembered how to smile. "Only a pull," she said. "Try not to use it overmuch, and it'll work itself out in time. I'll see to the horses."

Not greatly to her surprise, Derinoe disregarded her advice and insisted on helping to salve cuts and bind bruised legs. After the worst of the injuries had been tended, she and Rhenna gathered the herd. They moved at a slow pace to fresh pasture two leagues from the path of the birds. The horses forgot their fear and settled to graze and rest, comforting one another with gentle nudges.

Derinoe fell into a deep sleep as soon as her head touched her blanket. Rhenna tended the fire, rising occasionally to check on the horses. Only the small, ordinary sounds of dark-loving creatures broke the tranquillity. The night brought its own kind of peace that erased the day's horror, turning it into a dream without substance.

She lay back on her blanket and closed her eyes, dozing in the half sleep she had adopted over the years of solitude. If evil came again she would know, and be ready….

Chaimon's soft lips brushed Rhenna's forehead. She snatched at her axe and sprang to her feet. The smell of dawn was in the air, and Rhenna realized she had slept far more soundly than she'd intended. Derinoe lay still, one arm flung over her face.

Rhenna sheathed her axe and leaned her head against Chaimon's. "You kept my watch for me, old friend."

The gelding's eyes glinted with secret wisdom. Slowly he turned about, facing north, and bobbed his head.

"Yes, home. Heart of Oaks." The place she had longed to go—under any circumstances but these. "Only a few days—"

She broke off, feeling a sudden puff of wind on her face. It was not the hot gust from the south that had presaged the birds; it came from the north and west, from the forest and the outlying settlements of the Free People.

Chaimon nickered. The other horses stirred, a faint rustling and shifting of powerful bodies. Rhenna's scar caught fire. Not so much as a breeze fluttered the edge of Derinoe's blankets. But a mass of air lifted from the ground at Rhenna's feet, wound between her legs and lapped at her fingertips like an affectionate hound.

She knew those winds as she knew her own dishonor. Nine years ago they had befriended an ignorant child, stroking and caressing and feeding her naive pride. They had made many promises—oh, not in mortal words, but in a tongue well-known to the ambitious hearts of rebellious young girls with forbidden dreams.

They had led her to the very edge of ruin, and let her fall.

"I do not hear you," she whispered.

Chaimon stretched his neck and whinnied. The wind clung to Rhenna, dancing about her head, teasing her hair loose with a Sister's license.

"I will not."

Threadlike currents of air worked inside Rhenna's jacket, under her shirt, shivered along her skin. The wind knew her more intimately than any lover. Whorls and eddies curled around her neck and tugged at her lobes, set up a deep humming in the bronze of her ear studs.

Come. You are Chosen.

Rhenna covered her ears with her hands. "Be silent!"

The wind mocked her, lifting Chaimon's mane so that it stood almost erect. Rhenna crouched beside the fire and stabbed viciously at the embers. Abruptly the fire went out, extinguished by a precisely aimed blast of air.

She threw down the stick and stood, legs braced to face her enemy. "You have had your way. Let me be!"

Her shout should have been enough to wake the Skudat dead in their burial mounds. Still Derinoe slept. Dust stung Rhenna's eyes and scoured her cheeks. She felt her way to the tent and knelt to search the pack just inside.

The wind nearly tore the finely woven scarf from her fist. She fought to tie the cloth over her ears and head, knotting the ends so tightly that only a knife stroke could cut it free.

The air turned still.

Blood. One word, voiceless. It filled Rhenna's head as if the wind had driven inside her skull.

North. A current rose at Rhenna's back, pushing at her shoulders. She stiffened her arms to keep her balance. Chaimon reared. Three veteran mares from the herd broke away from the others and came to stand behind her.

North, the wind said. *But not to Heart of Oaks.*

West.

Rhenna struggled to her feet. It had been many years since she had felt real fear. She remembered what it was to dread the stares of her people. She had often worried for sick horses, and spent sleepless nights tending them with many a desperate prayer.

Derinoe's message and the coming of the birds had awakened something greater than alarm. But terror—that had not touched her since she had looked into the eyes of an Ailu shapechanger, had felt in her own ravaged flesh the truth of the ancient stories.

She had sworn then, and a hundred times since, never to seek beyond a warrior's life. But now the devas called to her in portents of blood and death.

She made one last attempt at defiance, turning into the wind. It sealed her eyes shut and stole her breath.

"If I go," she shouted, "will you let the others pass? Will you protect them on their journey?"

Wind became a breeze again, almost playful. Rhenna yanked her loose hair into a knot at her neck and tied it with a leather cord.

Quickly she chose one of the three mares, a seven-year-old of sound wind and stamina. The breeze murmured approval. Rhenna bridled and saddled Chaimon and the mare, and stuffed her saddlepack with provisions, leaving Derinoe the greater part. Sweet springwater filled two fat waterskins, which she secured to her saddle. As an extra precaution, she bound her breasts with a thick winding of cloth and tied a leather girdle about her hips to protect her inner parts from the jarring of an extended ride.

The wind had not revealed her destination nor how long it would take to get there. The devas required her to act on faith.

"I will not risk the horses," she said aloud, tightening girths and examining hooves. "Guide me well."

Chaimon stamped and butted her chest, eager to run. The first light of dawn had crested the horizon by the time Rhenna was ready. She crouched beside Derinoe and shook her awake. The girl blinked and rubbed her eyes, dismay crossing her face.

"The birds—" she gasped. "Is it my watch?"

"It's dawn," Rhenna said. "I have a grave task for you." She helped the girl to her feet. "Can you handle the herd alone?"

"I... Alone?" Derinoe threw back her shoulders, but the tremor in her lips ruined the effect. "I am to take you to Heart of Oaks—"

"You were to find me and send the herd home. You've accomplished the first, and now you will complete your duty."

"Without you? What of your duty to the Earthspeakers?"

Rhenna abandoned the last remnants of discretion. "The devas...have sent a message."

"They *spoke* to you?"

Only another dreamer could lend the question such fearful resonance. The girl needed every encouragement Rhenna could give her now. "As you said, everything is changing. Will you do what must be done?"

"But I...I am not—" Derinoe bit her lip and looked away. "They sent the youngest," she said in a low voice. "The smallest, the ones who weren't ready to fight."

"They sent the strongest and the swiftest," Rhenna said. She seized Derinoe's good arm. "You can do this, Little Sister. I'll teach you what you must know, and the horses will do the rest."

The girl raised her head, fragile pride creeping back into her eyes. "Where are you going?"

"I must learn—" All at once Rhenna understood why she would go, and why the devas had won. "I need to know if these terrible things are happening because of me."

Derinoe flushed. "I didn't... I never meant—"

"I know." Rhenna touched Derinoe's sunburned cheek. "Trust in the devas," she said, filling the declaration with a child's unquestioning conviction. "Trust in yourself."

"I am..." The girl clenched her teeth on the word she wouldn't speak. *Afraid.*

Rhenna gazed across the steppe, far to the north, where the western margin of the Shield melted into the horizon. *Fear teaches. Fear keeps you alive. Never forget to be afraid.*

"You are strong, my Sister," she said, clasping Derinoe's wrist in a warrior's grip. "Sharpen your axe and bind up your hair. It's time to become a woman."

Steppe ponies were neither beautiful nor elegant, but they were built to travel at a steady pace without faltering. Rhenna's horses proved the worth of their bloodlines that day.

She settled Chaimon into an easy lope that he could maintain for hours at a time. When he began to show signs of stress, she dismounted, walked to cool him, and then mounted the mare. Every few hours she watered both horses and allowed them to graze. By nightfall they had covered thirty leagues.

The wind was ever at her back, pushing north and west. It sighed in her ear as she rubbed down the horses and made her evening camp; it crouched beside her meager fire like a loyal Sister. Rhenna didn't expect to sleep, but the devas sang to her, and she woke to Chaimon's gentle nudging just before dawn.

The second day was much like the first, but Rhenna's sense of urgency doubled. The premonitions of blood and ruin grew stronger with every passing league, yet the Shield of the Sky and the verdant rim of forested hills seemed no nearer.

On the third day both horses were weary and Rhenna swayed in the saddle. Stops for rest grew longer and more frequent. Only at sunset did the distant trees rise from a faint green line on the horizon.

By mid-morning of the fourth day, Rhenna reached the edge of the forest. Open woodland of oak, linden, beech and poplar crept onto the grassland, sheltering birds whose songs echoed from branch to branch. Small cultivated fields appeared among the trees.

"Not far now," Rhenna whispered to the mare, who gamely nickered in answer. Chaimon broke into a trot. Rhenna began to recognize landmarks, stands of ancient oaks and the weblike tracings of streams that reminded her of a childhood visit long ago. Boggy earth gave under the mare's hooves, releasing the rich scent of fertile soil.

Sun's Rest, this place was named. The settlements near the western border produced the finest weavings, woodwork and metalwork in the Shield's Shadow, goods used in trade and to create beauty for the People. But the villagers weren't fighters; they kept small livestock and raised crops for their own tables. The man-tribes had so long been quiet that few warriors remained in permanent residence.

If Derinoe was right, all that had changed. The border was a mere dozen leagues to the west. Sisters sent to fight would leave clear evidence of their passage.

Rhenna dismounted and found the tracks of many riders moving at a swift pace toward the west. But something seemed amiss. She lifted her head and listened for the sounds of village life, the everyday murmur of women working at looms and forges and in the fields.

Silence. No frantic scurrying of small animals dodging the tread of hooves and human feet; no querulous chatter of sparrows and thrushes in the undergrowth, nor even the hum of insects. No breath of wind stirred the soft hair at Rhenna's neck or rustled the oak leaves overhead.

Rhenna increased her pace, following a winding and well-worn path through the wood. Snapped branches littered the ground. A chaos of hoofprints trampled the shallow indentations made by the soft boots of artisans.

Trees gave way to a clearing and the first of the pretty wooden houses. Chaimon and the mare stopped and would go no farther. Rhenna continued on alone. She came upon the remains of a fat sow beside the house. A horde of glossy black ravens started up from the nearby pen, circled with raucous cries and returned to their meal.

There were enough bodies to feed a thousand scavengers. Every beast that could not be stolen had been slaughtered and left to rot. Tears leaked from Rhenna's eyes. She drew her axe and held it ready, though she knew there would be no one to fight.

She knew what she must find.

The women had been herded together in the village green. Some had fallen still locked in embraces, others shielding sisters from attack. A few had bravely faced the enemy; one old woman had died with a goatherd's staff in her hand. Its tip was bathed in blood.

Rhenna clenched her fingers around the handle of her axe. Her legs carried her past the mounded corpses. She forced herself to enter each lodge or workshop to search for survivors.

All were empty, weavings and woodwork torn and hacked to pieces. Vegetable gardens had been trampled, plants uprooted in an orgy of destruction. The brightly painted door of one lodge stood open as if in cheerful welcome. A raven flew out, struck Rhenna and dodged skyward with a prize of red meat in its beak.

Step by heavy step Rhenna trudged to the doorway. Her body lacked all sensation, but her eyes continued to search, her ears to strain for any sound of life. The scent of corruption smothered her like a storm of ravens' feathers.

She reached the door. The axe dropped from her fingers.

The children.

Rhenna fell to her knees. Her mouth flooded with the remains of her last scanty meal. Her heart thudded once in her chest and stopped. To breathe was to die.

Oh, the children.

Rhenna flung back her head and wailed. She seized her axe in both hands and ran, stumbling, past the last few houses and into the Sacred Grove.

There were no woman-made boundaries or marks in the earth to show where ordinary woodland ended and the Grove began. Yet Rhenna knew when she crossed the threshold. She had not entered such a place in nine years. Now, as then, it was as if a thousand angry wasps converged upon her body and drove their stings through cloth and leather. Bitter, irrefutable punishment.

And power. Centuries of chants and prayers and invocations saturated the earth under the roots of the venerable trees. It gilded every twig and leaf, infused the very air with the unnameable odors of sanctity. If any villagers had escaped the massacre, they would have fled to this last place of sanctuary.

Rhenna ran blindly for the center of the Grove. Pain ceased as abruptly as it had come. Its absence seemed to have lifted her from her feet, pulled her axe high above her head and dropped her like a child's wooden doll at the roots of the Mother Tree. Her hands sank into ankle-deep mud.

The ground was red.

They had spilled blood in the Sacred Grove. The Earthspeakers had not stopped them. The devas had remained silent. And the Mother Tree...

Every branch within human reach had been cut or torn or severed by merciless iron. Stripped bark hung like flayed skin from the trunk. The great arched roots were buried knee-deep in skeletal leaves.

Rhenna's scar became a patch of numbness that spread across her face, into her shoulder and down her arm, until her fingers could no longer grip the handle of her axe. The weapon fell. With a moan, Rhenna felt among the curled leaves and hewn branches. Every sweep uncovered lifeless hands and staring faces.

The axe blade sliced into Rhenna's palm as she searched the ground. She snatched it up and scrambled from the place of slaughter, leaving a trail of her own blood behind.

Instinct led her to the horses. They flung up their heads with wild eyes, smelling death. Rhenna bound her slashed palm, calmed the animals as best she could and led them upwind from the village, where they would be undisturbed by the stench of smoke and burning flesh. For the span of an hour she composed her thoughts, letting the numbness expand until it made hard, cold lumps of her head and heart. Then she returned to Sun's Rest.

She didn't leave again until her work was done. At dawn she saddled the horses and turned toward the west.

The raiders could not be far ahead. Rhenna had seen no Earthspeakers among the dead. The barbarians must have taken prisoners. Captives would slow them. They would never expect an attack from a single warrior.

Rhenna rode out of the woods and kept riding until the vast column of smoke behind her became a pale gray banner tattered by the wind.

Chapter Two

Tahvo of the Samah stopped at the edge of the cliff and looked down, down and down again, past gradually descending hills and into the vast expanse of the valley below. The world she had known all her life—forest and fell, hills and fields of ice—ended there in the Southlands, where men had only a few words for snow.

She shivered and sat on a stone beside a stream. Her shaman's robe lay heavy and stifling on her shoulders. Not even the eldest and wisest noaiddit, who called the salmon and the reindeer and knew the spirits by name, had ever ventured so far.

They had no need, for all the Samah required lay within their borders. The spirits spoke through the drums, and shamans carried their blessings to the people. Noaiddit healed the sick, forecast weather and sometimes spoke to the dead. A very few could see what was to come.

Tahvo's visions were different. No other female had been shaman for a thousand seasons. From her birth, her family had kept her apart from the other girls, for she had received the spirit-gifts that should have gone to the stillborn boy who had emerged from the womb before her.

You will be a healer, predicted her grandfather, a great noaidi in his own right. And so she had become. She tended the ill, child-bearing women and sometimes the dying. The spirits lent her strength in her work; they were always with her.

But she had never truly understood them. She could not see them or hear their voices or tell one apart from another. She did not summon them to send game to the hunters or keep the heaviest snowfall away from the siida. She had not asked for the visions, yet they visited her instead of more worthy noaiddit. After the fits passed, people looked at her as if she had lost the snow-sense or fallen into madness.

They did not know that the visions had shown her the meaning of an idea for which the Samah had but one word.

Evil.

Tahvo opened her sturdy deerskin pack and carefully pulled her drum from the down padding within. Six years ago, when she had become a woman in fact if not in custom, she had constructed the frame of birch and stretched the reindeer skin she herself had prepared. With alder juice she had painted every mark upon its face: symbols representing each of the four directions, the spirits of Nature, and the three realms of existence.

She had drummed many long nights alone, praying that the spirits might ease this burden. But the answers they put in her heart were as relentless as they were inconceivable.

South.

She put the drum back inside her pack and made sure her small hunting bow was secure in its case. The descent was not difficult, though Tahvo's boots sometimes slipped on the bare earth and mats of needles. She drank from the cold stream and ate what the spirits placed in her path. The snow disappeared. Trees changed their shapes. Unfamiliar birds remarked upon the passage of a stranger.

The next day Tahvo came to another cliff, this one surmounted by a waterfall. At its foot, all was green as far as the eye could see, rolling plain laced with a hundred streams. On the plain lay what the traders called a town, far bigger than any siida. The town's high walls rose from an empty space where trees had been cut to the ground and soil overturned with tools of iron.

To that strange and terrible place she must go.

Stones and gnarled roots gave Tahvo purchase to descend the steep face of the cliff. She paused on a small ledge halfway down, clinging to the rock as she drank from her waterskin. Spray from the waterfall splashed her face, but by the time she had reached the bottom she longed for the kiss of a gentle snow.

All she saw was endless grass. The strength went out of her legs. She lost her balance and fell at the base of the cliff, struggling against the sudden, crushing weight of fear.

For as long as she could remember, since long before the visions came, Tahvo had perceived the spirits as a formless, blended presence inside her, sure as the rising of the sun. Now she felt nothing. The spirits had melted away with the snows, leaving a great void in her chest.

They had abandoned her. But that was not possible. The spirits had set her on this path. Why had they chosen one so blind to receive their warning?

She closed her eyes, remembering everything Grandfather had tried to teach her. *Samah move according to the seasons, but most spirits belong to a place, just as each has its element—earth, air, water or fire. Some, like the winds, range across the open fells. Others reside in a single stand of pines, or in the smallest of ponds. Yet even we who name them do not know all the spirits of the Samah, far less of those beyond.*

Noaiddit never had cause to call upon spirits outside Samah

lands. But the traders invoked what they called their "gods" even when they were far from home.

Tahvo's heart beat fast with hope. She hurried to gather a bundle of twigs and leaves fallen from the top of the cliff and used her flints to coax a small flame. Then she removed her drum, the pouch of precious dreambark and one of the small bronze bowls from her pack. She crumbled a little of the dreambark into the bowl and set it on the fire.

The bark burned with a pungent, intoxicating odor. Tahvo took a deep breath of the smoke. With each inhalation came the blissful release of fear, melting like snowflakes on a reindeer's back. The green expanse of grass broke into pieces that floated up into the sky. The whole world shrank to the size of a pebble.

Tahvo began to sing, tapping the rim of the drum in time to the words. The spirits answered. She could not see or count or name the beings that gathered around her, but she felt at once that they were not those she had known. The skin on her face prickled with moisture, a cooling breath to counter her weariness. The air hummed. She dropped her hands into the grass and felt the life flowing between her fingers, part of an endless web that extended on every side as far as her imagination could reach.

Then the vision came, and she was home again. A stream flowed out of the forest, pure and swift beneath its covering of ice. The spirits of these waters knew the call of the noaiddit, but the stream did not belong to a single country or people. It journeyed ever south, fed by other streams, blessed by innumerable spirits until it became a great river in lands that had never known the Samah tongue.

Tahvo was part of that mighty river. It rushed through and around her, lifting her in a loving mother's arms. She glimpsed wide lakes and mountains of fire, vast waterless plains and forests thick with leaves like green leather. Spirits lived on every shore the river touched. They spoke to each other, but still Tahvo did not understand their words.

Her ignorance did not trouble her. She wished the wondrous vision to last forever. It did not. Suddenly she was back in the forest, standing on the bank of the little stream. The ice cracked and dissolved. Hideous red stones, twisted like animal entrails, appeared in the water, turning it the color of blood. Roiling bubbles surged up around the misshapen lumps. Branches bent low over the stream caught fire. Flames leaped from tree to tree.

The forest burned.

Tahvo gasped for breath, running toward the siida. The flames turned her away. Only the cliff offered escape.

She reached the cliff's edge and leaped.

The vision released her before she hit the ground. She exhaled the last of the smoke and opened her eyes, trembling with relief. Sweet water whispered in the pool beside her. She made a cup of her hands and rinsed the foul taste from her mouth.

That was when she felt the spirit in the pool. She snatched back her hands, belatedly remembering the prayer she had forgotten to offer. She reached dizzily for the cliff wall at her back and felt the life within it, touched the earth and knew that it teemed with spirits who blessed the soil with richness and danced to the drumming of the world's heart.

Tears of joy blurred Tahvo's sight and cleansed the terror of the vision from her mind. The spirits had not deserted her. They were no longer a vague, undefinable presence in her mind. She still could not name them or summon their powers, but they had granted her what she had never possessed: the ability to recognize them not only in the work of healing but in all of nature's elements.

She was not alone, and she knew she never would be, as long as she heeded the spirits' message.

South.

Tahvo stretched cramped muscles, washed the bowl and returned it to the pack. She strapped the drum against her chest, concealing it beneath her coat without knowing why she did so.

She could not reckon the distance to the town; the valley stretched on and on to faraway southern mountains whose white peaks gleamed like teeth against the sky. She crossed creeks and rivers, removing her boots to wade through currents still icy with the memory of winter. Wildflowers thrust above the grass, bowing as she passed. Large hoofed animals with sharply pointed horns—cattle, the traders called them—paused in their grazing to stare at Tahvo with limpid eyes.

The air continued to warm. Tahvo longed to take off her coat, but a noaidi never removed it except in times of direst need. A spirit-wind spiraled about her head and brushed hair from her hot face and neck.

The walls of the village rose higher and more ominous with every hour. Men and women, some afoot and some mounted on the beasts called "horses," converged about the open gate.

Tahvo's heart beat very fast. She fastened her coat and set off for the gate. The grass gave way to a path bordered by fields of stubble and shoots of spring grain. Beyond the fields stood rows of tents and tables spread with goods for trade. The stench of many bodies, animal dung and food overwhelmed the scent of flowers. Naked children darted between the tables. Bright clothing wove a constantly moving pattern impossible for the eye to unravel.

Men argued in tongues Tahvo had never heard before. Their words rattled about inside her head.

"Ah," a voice said at her elbow, "a newcomer to our fair village."

Tahvo turned about to face the speaker. He was taller than Tahvo, with dark eyes and hair on his face cut to a point at his chin. At his belt hung a knife in a sheathe of tanned animal skin.

"Of course you don't understand me," the man said. He looked Tahvo up and down. "From the far North, are you? You'll be needing a friend here, and I've always been too soft-hearted." He smiled with all his teeth. "I am called Beytill."

Tahvo returned the man's smile but did not answer. His mouth moved out of step with his words, yet somehow she made sense of what he said. She gave silent thanks for yet another unexpected gift of the spirits.

Beytill rested his hand on Tahvo's arm, running his hands over the thick fur. "That's a fine coat, my friend, a very fine coat indeed. A handsome bow, as well. What else have you to trade, I wonder?" He clamped his arm around Tahvo's shoulders and pulled her through the gate.

Immediately Tahvo's sense of the spirits dimmed. They did not come within these walls, but she had no doubt that they intended her to enter. Soon they would reveal their purpose.

The village dwellings were built of wood, with roofs woven of dried grasses. Some had open doorways through which many people came and went. Even in this warmth, the women who lingered outside wore too few garments to protect their bodies. Men bore long knives hung from their waists, blades useless for hunting or carving.

The traders carried such weapons. They told tales of war and warriors in the south, of blood shed for reasons the Samah could barely comprehend.

"Nervous, are we?" Beytill said. "I'll wager you've never seen a civilized town. A good draft of beer will set you to rights." He dragged Tahvo toward a house where men stood about drinking from thin metal cups and earthenware bowls. Angry voices escaped the dim interior.

Tahvo braced her knees and stood firm, searching for anything familiar. The high-pitched laughter of children drew her back toward the wall.

A moderate crowd of onlookers had formed a loose circle about a man in a long dark robe of deep red. His face was shadowed by a hood, but his long fingers flashed in motions too swift for the eye to follow, tossing bright objects in circles around his head and shoulders. Children laughed and their elders applauded as he caught the objects one-handed, flourished his wide sleeve and presented a ball of flame in his cupped palms.

The flame looked real. The man might be a noaidi of these people, but Tahvo could not sense the presence of any spirit to help him make such magic.

"The mage interests you, does he?" Beytill said behind her. "I know him. Come." He pushed his way through the crowd until he and Tahvo stood in the front ranks. The noaidi—mage—had already begun another exhibition. He selected a girl child from the audience and stood her before him, resting his hands on her shoulders. She stared up at him, mouth agape. He shaped the air over the child's head, twisting his hands in sinuous gestures like writhing serpents.

The display made Tahvo shiver. She saw no illness or injury in the child that required a healer's attention, and she knew this man was not a healer. Nor was he a shaman in the Samah way. She stared at the black hollow of his hood and suddenly recognized what seemed so wrong.

It was not merely the absence of spirits behind the dark man's working, or even the faint stench of rot he gave off with every breath. His cloak sucked all light into its red folds and snuffed it out, leaving only a kind of shadow where he stood—a void where no living thing could exist.

The mage flung his arm toward the sky, briefly parting the edges of his robe where hood met collar. A small object swung out from a cord around his neck. He smoothed his cloak with an almost imperceptible motion, but not before Tahvo glimpsed the gold-mounted shard of faceted red stone.

She could not move even to snatch the child away.

The onlookers gasped. Fists and elbows jostled Tahvo as peo-

ple shifted for a better view. The child was enveloped in a fever-
ish radiance cast from the mage's widespread fingers.

And the child grew. She began to stretch, pinned like a hide on
a frame of fire, bones visible through skin. The scraps of her thin
clothing melted away. Hips widened, waist narrowed, and her flat
chest rounded into the heavy breasts of full womanhood. Her
parted lips grew lush and moist. When the fire receded, the child
was a child no longer.

Beytill and other men stamped and whistled. The mage stepped
back, hands poised as if waiting for a signal. A woman darted out
of the crowd and began to wail, shaking her fists at the hooded
man.

The mage flicked his fingers. The naked woman vanished, and
the child fell, ashen-faced, into her weeping mother's arms.

Tahvo swayed, lost in a dream not of the spirits' making. Here
was the evil. *Here* was what she had been sent to find....

"See what you can do with this one!" Beytill cried, and gave
Tahvo a great push toward the center of the circle. The people
laughed and jeered, passing her one to another, loosening the fas-
tenings of her coat. She folded her arms against her chest and
stumbled to a halt before the mage.

He raised his head. His features were lost in the depths of
shadow, but his eyes glowed like coals. He extended a hand, and
Tahvo saw that his knuckles were knotted and swollen above the
long fingers.

"Woman," he said in a low, grating voice. "What are you?"

"Woman!" Beytill cried. "That's a female?"

The curious crowd surged forward. Tahvo's heart slammed the
inside of her ribs. The deerskin straps that bound the sacred
drum to her chest grew tighter and tighter, threatening to stop
the air in her lungs.

"A savage from the Northern wastes!" someone shouted. "Who
can tell the difference?"

Beytill waded to Tahvo's side and seized the shoulder of her coat, yanking it open. The drum was exposed, pale as bone laid bare by the slash of a knife.

"What's this?" Beytill demanded.

Tahvo felt the hooded man's gaze fix on the drum. But it was Beytill who plucked at the straps, Beytill who snapped his hand away with a yelp when his flesh turned blue with countless needle-sharp crystals of ice.

Tahvo cried out in shock. A chorus of shouts washed over her, twice as loud as the roar of meltwater racing down from the mountains in spring. Fingers pulled at the thongs and pendants on her coat. Spittle sprayed her cheek. She turned the drum in her arms so that she could tap the rim with two fingers, knelt, closed her eyes and forced all awareness of the villagers from her thoughts.

Help me.

A wind blew out of the North, carrying the scent of snow. Voices raised in anger held a new note of confusion. And fear.

From the place where Tahvo knelt to the village gates spread a wide path of ice. Upon the path trod a white wolf, bigger than any wolf of the forest or fells. It sat on its haunches halfway to the crowd and yawned, revealing long and very pointed teeth.

A spirit-beast. Tahvo had never seen such a creature before, let alone attempted to summon one. She gave thanks and looked for the dark mage. He stood apart from the others, hands tucked into the wide sleeves of his cloak. Beytill pulled the knife from the sheathe at his waist and lunged at Tahvo.

Between one moment and the next the wolf crossed the path and leaped, jaws seizing Beytill's wrist. Beytill screamed. His blade clattered to the ground and broke into a thousand icy shards. The crowd scattered, fleeing Tahvo and the wolf. The mage disappeared.

Warm fur brushed Tahvo's fingers. She met the wolf's blue eyes with confusion and gratitude. He had chosen to make himself visible to her eyes, but he was as unlike the valley spirits as Beytill was unlike Grandfather. Samah spirits never turned their powers against men.

"*Who are you?*" she asked silently, not expecting an answer.

She thought she heard laughter. "*I am Slahtti.*"

Sleet. Tahvo trembled, overwhelmed by the wonder of his voice in her mind. "*Is this the place I was meant to find?*" she asked. "*Is this the source of the evil visions?*"

"*You must save your people.*"

Too many questions thickened her tongue. "*How?*" she begged, clutching his mane in disregard of proper respect. "*Who will hurt them? This man...this mage with the red stone? Why—?*"

The wolf pulled free and shook himself from nose to tail. "*Come,*" he commanded. His breath blew out in a stream of mist that formed a new path of ice in the very air itself. Teeth closed gently on Tahvo's hand.

That was all Tahvo knew until she woke in a bed of wildflowers, her pack beside her and the drum resting on her chest. A handful of snowflakes kissed her face. The walled village was a dark blotch on the northern horizon. White-capped mountains bit the southern sky.

The spirit-wolf had borne Tahvo a day's walk in an instant. He had saved her life, but he was gone. Her questions remained unanswered.

Surely the spirits had meant her to enter the town and witness the evil within it—Beytill's treachery, the cruelty of the people and, most of all, the dark shaman's magic. The threat to the Samah must lie there, if she could only recognize it....

The new vision struck swiftly. This one began with fire. Devouring flame spewed out of the ground like the effluence of some foul and incurable illness. Tahvo saw the exotic lands the valley spirits had shown her—rain forests and deserts, plains and mountains crowned with clouds—reduced to black ash. Vast dark seas boiled and roared.

And there were people…people in numbers beyond counting, pale and dark, short and tall, clothed in furs or naked as babes. They ravaged what remained of the land. They killed for the sake of killing, tearing at each other and hurling themselves into the searing holocaust.

Of spirits there were none. Every one had fled, forsaking the world to this evil thing men had done. But other beings rose out of the desolation, towering above the people who scurried under their feet: eight entities, neither human nor spirit, clad in metal that devoured all light. Each pair of massive hands bore a blade of crimson iron, and each face was hidden behind a mask of bloodred crystal.

Their will was the complete denial of creation, their power that of the spirits twisted into hatred for life itself. They had but a single name.

The Stone God.

Tahvo's body seized in a spine-snapping arc, threatening to burst lungs and heart. Her eyes rolled back, yet she could see.

Above the southern mountains rose a red glow, a grotesque reflection of the Sky Veil that shone in Northern skies. A bloated sun rose, casting fingers of murky light across the plain. From its center exploded a hail of stones—red stones, tossed wide as if by the hands of the metal giants themselves.

Most of the stones struck earth behind the mountains. One tiny chip shot over Tahvo's head and swooped like a hawk toward the distant town. The wooden walls blazed with mordant fire. Children screamed. Sparks shot up to become new stones that flew, swift and deadly, toward the home of the Samah.

Save your people, Slahtti said. Not only the Samah, so isolated in their haven of fell and forest, but the traders and the townsfolk, those who dwelt in the waterless barrens and beside the great sea. All the people in the world.

Tahvo heaved in the grass until she had brought up what little she had eaten that morning. She rinsed her mouth with water from a nearby spring, tucked the drum in her pack and got to her feet.

The spirits had spoken. They had given Tahvo great gifts to aid in the work to come, but the town and its evil were a warning. She still had far to go.

She hitched the pack higher on her shoulders and took the first step.

Chapter Three

The first bright blaze of Rhenna's rage had burned itself to embers by the time she found the captive.

At the end of a day's hard pursuit on the raiders' trail, winding through foothills of oak and ash, Rhenna and the horses paused to rest on a meadow plateau brilliant with blue harebells. Hooves had churned the soft soil in a wide swath across the meadow, leaving a rough circle of flowers unsullied by their passage.

In the circle lay a woman. She had been dead less than a day, for the scavengers hadn't touched her.

Chaimon locked his legs and snorted. The mare rolled her eyes. Rhenna dismounted and fell to her knees beside the body.

The tribesmen had considered the woman too old or too much trouble to carry farther, but they had used her before she died. The labyrinth of slashes on her arms stood testament to her valiant defense. Someone had covered her thighs with a soiled scrap of cloth in a vain attempt to hide the blood and bruises.

But the woman's face was at peace, her features outlined in deepening shadow.

"Pantaris," Rhenna whispered. She touched the closed eyelids, tracing creases scored by sun and wind. She hadn't known that her mother's sister lived at Sun's Rest. How many long years had it been since they had met, let alone spoken?

Is this my doing, Pantaris?

The wise, gentle face was silent. Rhenna smoothed her aunt's shirt over the ugly gash in her chest. The wound was clean of blood. There must be an Earthspeaker or a Healer among the captives. Yet the devas hadn't protected their people from capture and violation. They had let Pantaris die.

The lightest of breezes caressed Rhenna's face. It danced over the harebells, setting their blossoms nodding.

"So you haven't gone," Rhenna said. "You abandon your children and favor the outcast. Why?"

The deva-winds flattened the harebells in a flawless circle about Pantaris's body. Blossoms brushed Rhenna's hand. She snatched it away. "You lead me to a field of slaughter where I can do nothing but burn the dead, and now I must mourn my kin. Punish me as you will, but let me find the others. Let me save them."

Gusts like kittens' paws slapped and buffeted. Rhenna's hair blew free of its bindings and snagged on the ridged flesh of her cheek. She bent to kiss Pantaris's cool cheek, sprang up and caught the horses' reins. She led them west over the trampled earth to the wooded edge of the meadow.

Suddenly her face knocked painfully against an unyielding surface.

But nothing stood in her way. She took another step, and the impact struck sparks behind her eyes. Excruciating pressure drummed in her ears. The air shimmered as if a fine mist hung between her and the rest of the world.

The mare shied and lunged, snapping free of Rhenna's hold.

Chaimon seized a mouthful of her coat and yanked her backward, nearly tumbling her off her feet. At once the pressure eased.

Leaving the horses some distance from the edge of the meadow, Rhenna approached the invisible wall. Her fingertips touched a skin of air that gave and snapped back like a tightly stretched hide. It extended as far as she could reach and well over her head.

She knelt and ran her fingers along the ground. The grass was undisturbed save for a single thin line. Rhenna paced out a hundred strides to the south, testing the wall of air with the toe of her boot. It remained stubbornly solid.

Rhenna strode to the horses, secured the mare's lead and mounted Chaimon. She rode at a gallop straight north for half a league before reining west. Chaimon reared. Rhenna slid from the saddle, released her axe and charged the wall.

Common sense stopped her. She grounded the axe between her feet, closed her eyes and calmed her racing heart.

"Enough. Let me pass."

The devas neglected to answer. They had made their message abundantly clear. She might travel for days to the north or south, but wherever she stopped she would meet that same obstacle, ever to the west.

She was not to pursue the raiders. She was to ride back to Heart of Oaks with a tale of massacre and defeat.

Chaimon blew warm breath down the back of her neck. He knew better than to fight what could not be vanquished. And so did she.

The sun was setting when they returned to the meadow. Pantaris lay untouched where Rhenna had left her. Rhenna rubbed down the horses and built a small fire. She tended the body by moonlight, bathing face and limbs of dirt and blood. The stained clothes she burned. At morning's first light Rhenna wrapped Pantaris in a sleeping blanket and tied her across Chaimon's back.

One last time she attempted to breach the wall of air and was rebuffed. The horses were eager to travel in the opposite direction and set a brisk pace away from the meadow.

As it had done on the steppe days before, the wind held steady at Rhenna's back. She ignored it. Twice during the two-day journey Rhenna crossed the tracks of many horses. The depredations of the man-tribes would not go unavenged.

Weary beyond measure, legs numb and belly flat against her ribs, Rhenna rode into Heart of Oaks almost without recognizing it. A road opened up out of the woods, earth beaten hard by the constant passage of hooves and feet.

Heart of Oaks lay at the crux of forest and steppe, fertile with many streams and rich earth to nurture the crops. Here Healers learned their arts, Seekers delivered their postulants and Earth-speakers from all over the Shield's Shadow came to renew their bonds with the devas in the most sacred of groves.

In ordinary times the road would be busy with warriors and messengers, apprentices and Elders of every trade and craft. Rhenna met no one. For a terrifying moment she feared she had come upon another massacre.

But it was not so. A sleepy girl occupied the sentry post. She shot erect as Rhenna approached, wielding a spear taller than she was. Her presence was proof enough that Heart of Oaks remained inviolate, though she held a position usually given to warriors-in-training.

Derinoe had scarcely left childhood, and the Elders had sent her to cross the steppe alone. Rhenna prayed the girl had arrived safely.

She would know soon enough. Chaimon smelled other horses and broke into a faster walk, carrying Rhenna past the fenced vegetable plots and livestock pens that marked the village's western boundary. Children tended pigs among young oaks and copses of ash, and a carpenter repaired a garden fence. Rhenna rode by the outermost workshops and craft lodges, where women went about

their business with grim concentration. None seemed to notice or acknowledge her.

Rhenna hadn't expected to meet anyone she knew, let alone receive a warm welcome. But she still remembered her only previous visit to Heart of Oaks, and how she had stared with amazement at the riot of activity and noise and color.

Gone were the bustle and the vibrant hum of constant chatter, of horses whinnying and children making mischief. Gone, too, was the easy familiarity of women sure of their places in the world. The few passersby had abandoned the vivid scarves and belts and jewelry that distinguished weaver from potter, field hand from laborer, novice from Elder. Smithies rang with the clamor of metal on metal, but no apprentices gossiped in the welcome coolness outside their doors. The nearest horse pens held only a dozen second-string mounts, most in no state to be ridden.

Rhenna had hoped to discover her own herd well settled under Derinoe's care. She didn't find them, nor did she see more than a handful of warriors. Surely Heart of Oaks would not be left defenseless, no matter how pressing the needs of the Western settlements.

She would soon meet warriors enough when she made her report to the Eldest at the Sisters' lodge. But first she must find a Healer.

The Healers' lodge was located near the Earthspeakers' residence in the center of the village. Rhenna looked for a girl to take the horses, but novices were as scarce as warriors. She patted Chaimon's drooping neck, and urged him and the mare past the last pens and into the very heart of a tempest.

She would have expected the Earthspeakers' lodge or the Council Hall to be gathering places in times of trouble, but at first glance it seemed that every novice and warrior in Heart of Oaks had assembled near the steps in front of the Healers' lodge.

Rhenna dismounted at the edge of the crowd. Chaimon blew out a great snort, and a loose-haired girl spun about in startlement.

"What's happening?" Rhenna asked.

The girl looked Rhenna up and down with wide brown eyes. "You've just returned from the fighting, Elder Sister?"

Rhenna swallowed her shame. "Yes. I seek a Healer—"

"They are inside with the wounded from Sun's Rest."

"Sun's Rest? How many escaped?"

The girl's gaze caught on Rhenna's scar. She seemed to be debating whether or not Rhenna was worthy of an answer. Rhenna spared her the effort.

"This is Chaimon," she said. "He requires water, grain and a good rubdown. See to him at once, and then return for the mare."

Like most novices, the girl was too well-trained to refuse a direct order from an Elder, though she cast Rhenna a resentful glance as she accepted Chaimon's lead.

Rhenna patted the gelding's neck and turned to the mare with her neglected burden. She untied the bindings that held the body in place. No one offered to help. Rhenna eased Pantaris into her arms and carried her mother's sister to the wall of straight backs and braided hair.

"Let me pass," she said.

A few warriors looked. They stepped aside, leaving a narrow path for Rhenna to approach the lodge, then closed in behind her.

Five women sat on the steps. All wore the ragged remains of shirts and trousers, boots in scraps around their feet, hair disheveled and matted with blood and twigs. A young Healer knelt among them, nervously attempting to treat the worst of their cuts and bruises.

The Healer looked up in dismay. "Another?" she began, and then she noticed Pantaris's wrapped body. "Take it inside. There is no one to tend it now."

Rhenna clenched her teeth and drew the blanket away from Pantaris's face. "She, too, was of Sun's Rest."

"Pantaris," one of the wounded murmured. Under her grime the speaker looked much like her fellow survivors, but her voice held the inner calm of rank and experience. She met Rhenna's gaze. "You found her?"

"She was my kinswoman."

The woman's eyes narrowed. "I know you."

"You should not be here, Seeker," the Healer chided, touching the woman's arm. "Go inside. Rest."

The Seeker shook her off. "You are Rhenna. Pantaris spoke of you. I am Iphito of Sun's Rest. We were told that help would come."

A kind of sickness flooded Rhenna's muscles, and she almost dropped Pantaris. "I came too late," she whispered.

"It would have made no difference." The Seeker glanced at her companions. Two of the four were little more than girls. A black-haired woman of middle years sat in rigid silence, her fingers tight around some small object. The last, young and fair, muttered incomprehensible phrases under her breath. A thick bandage had been wound about her forehead.

"There were at least forty of the barbarians," Seeker Iphito said in the distant tone of one relating a tale in which she had no part. "They came just at sunrise, when Laodoke and Orithia were completing the dawn rites. The devas gave no warning."

The fair woman moaned. Iphito patted her arm. "Many of our warriors were scouting at the time," she continued. "They returned only to die. Twenty of us were taken. Pantaris believed, like our Earthspeakers, that we would be saved. She bought us a chance to fight. When she led the barbarians away—"

"You were not with her when she died?" Rhenna asked.

"We did not see her again."

"Enough," the young Healer said. "With respect, Seeker, you

and Earthspeaker Laodoke must rest." She glared at Rhenna. "They have no time for you now."

The pale-haired Earthspeaker flung out her hands. "No," she cried. "The devas, they promised..." Her head darted back and forth like that of a blind serpent seeking its prey. Blank eyes settled on Rhenna. "I saw *you*. The scar. The wind..."

Iphito gathered the young Earthspeaker against her breast. "The barbarians struck her head," the Seeker said. "Did the devas send you to find us?"

Rhenna took a step back and could go no farther. Pantaris's weight drove her legs into the ground like wooden posts. "The devas cannot be trusted," she croaked.

All the small, restless sounds of the crowd stopped at once.

"I remember her," someone said from the back of the throng. "Rhenna-of-the-Scar."

"Was it not she who..."

"...cursed of the devas..."

"*Silence.*"

A warrior had come to stand on the porch behind the wounded and the Healer. Her muscular arms were bare and streaked with blood, her body hardened by battle and the elements. She stared down at the assembly, driving every woman to stillness with the force of her stare.

"Rhenna-of-the-Scar," Alkaia said, her deep voice pronouncing the epithet with cool dispassion. "You are late in obeying our summons." Her gaze dropped to Pantaris's face. "You will bring your kinswoman to the Healers. The rest of you, return to your posts or your lodges and wait for the Council to speak."

Much intimidated, most of the young girls fled at once. The warriors dispersed more slowly, some still muttering of curses and blasphemy. The survivors of Sun's Rest struggled to their feet, Earthspeaker Laodoke leaning heavily on Iphito's arm, and retreated into the lodge. Rhenna carried Pantaris inside.

The main room was filled with Healers and their charges, perhaps fifty women, including the newest arrivals. Most of the injured were warriors. Alkaia gestured Rhenna through a door past the occupied cots and tables. A smaller room had been set aside for the dead awaiting final rites. Most of these, too, were warriors.

Rhenna laid Pantaris on an empty platform. She rearranged the blanket, kissed the cold lips and whispered a prayer for the spirits of the departed.

"You pray," Alkaia said, "and yet you mock the devas."

Rhenna faced the old warrior and stiffly bowed her head. "I ask pardon, Eldest."

"It is not my pardon you need seek." Alkaia blocked the door with her body. "You went to Sun's Rest. Why?"

Though the Eldest's words were uninflected, Rhenna heard her anger. Alkaia had been present on the day of Rhenna's judgment, casting her vote with the other Elders. None had been harsher than the warriors, who had seen one of their own violate the most sacred of injunctions. Perhaps Alkaia had called for a stronger punishment than Rhenna had received.

Rhenna willed the flush from her cheeks. "I will make a full report, Eldest. Did Derinoe return safely with the herd?"

"The herd for which you were responsible?" Alkaia glanced at Pantaris, but her expression didn't soften. "She returned—then left for the western border with half the mares."

To fight, possibly to die. *Brave Derinoe. You are no longer the youngest or the smallest.* "How many of the western villages have been attacked?"

Alkaia sliced the air with her hand. "I asked you a question, warrior. Were you *sent* to Sun's Rest?"

Rhenna had thought herself prepared to admit the truth and suffer the consequences. But what kept her silent was not Alkaia's anger or even contempt, but some unfamiliar glimmer in her eyes that might almost have been called hope.

"I give you this chance to speak privately," Alkaia said, "to spare you worse before the Council. If you can assure me that some mad impulse drove you to forsake your duty, I will intervene on your behalf and moderate your punishment."

Moderate. Had Rhenna committed so great an offense that the Council of Elders would impose the ultimate penalty, banishment from the Shield's Shadow?

"The survivors of Sun's Rest know far more than I," Rhenna said.

The older woman stared at the wooden planks between her feet. "Will you admit that nothing but your own desire to fight drove you to the border?"

"Derinoe... She told you—"

"She told us very little." Ice-gray eyes met Rhenna's. "I am neither without sight nor without hearing, warrior. I heard Iphito's and Earthspeaker Laodoke's words. You can be sure that the Council has heard them, as well." She sighed. "Remember that I gave you the chance to speak alone. Now you will answer to the Council." She turned on her heel and strode to a door in the back of the room, then paused impatiently for Rhenna to follow.

Rhenna made her mind as empty as it had been at Sun's Rest. She let Alkaia lead her from the Healers' lodge, along the stone path winding among herbal gardens and across the courtyard that divided the Healers', Seekers' and Earthspeakers' lodges.

The Council Hall stood apart from the others, a plain structure raised for the sole purpose of hosting the meetings and deliberations of the Elders. Alkaia nodded to the Sister on watch outside the double doors and walked through without stopping. She paused at a wooden table just inside the doors, where she quickly removed the few weapons she carried and laid them on the table's pitted surface. Rhenna did the same, hanging her axe and gorytos from two of the many hooks on the wall.

Like all the permanent buildings of the Free People, the Hall was built low to honor the Earth. Its great room could accommodate as many as a hundred people at one time, but its current occupants huddled about a single table and spoke in hushed and urgent voices.

"Too many of our warriors have not returned from the West," one of the women said. "If we send others, the Eastern settlements and Heart of Oaks will be left undefended."

"It will make no difference if the barbarians come this far," Alkaia said. She moved to an unoccupied seat at the end of the table and braced her arms against its carved back.

"Alkaia." The old woman at the opposite end of the table spoke very softly indeed, but every face turned toward her instantly. "You have word of those who escaped?"

"I have more than that, Earthspeaker."

Rhenna stepped forward, holding herself very straight before the eyes of the Council. Only a few of these women had judged her nine years ago, but every one of them knew her story, and that she had disobeyed their direct commands.

"I see you, Rhenna-of-the-Scar," the old woman said. "You have come to us at last."

Rhenna bowed, well aware of the woman's identity. Euriobe was the eldest of Earthspeakers, her age so great that none lived who remembered the date of her birth. Her fragile neck seemed bent under the weight of her feathered headdress, but her eyes were far more potent weapons than the mightiest warrior's axe.

Euriobe rose. Others hurried to assist her—Kreysa, Eldest of Healers, and a Seeker Rhenna did not recognize. Euriobe waved off their assistance and hobbled toward Rhenna, her polished oakwood cane tapping the floor with every step.

"Is it true," she said, "that you disobeyed our commands and journeyed to Sun's Rest?"

"It is true," Rhenna said.

Euriobe arched a gray brow. "And you do not ask pardon?"

Rhenna knew that she balanced on the blade's edge of decision, and there would be no going back. "I ask pardon," she said, "for listening to what I should not have heard."

Euriobe planted her cane between her feet and released a gusty sigh. "Come and sit. You are weary, and there is much to be explained."

She gestured, and two of the Elders placed an empty chair next to Alkaia's. Healer Kreysa poured water from a jar into a cup and passed it to Rhenna. Rhenna took great care not to gulp the sweet liquid. Her scar had begun to throb and burn.

"Have you need of the Healers' art?" Euriobe asked, resuming her seat.

"No, Earthspeaker."

"The devas have watched over you." Her gaze turned inward, as if she listened to distant voices. "You have seen much suffering, Rhenna-of-the-Scar."

The water turned sour in Rhenna's mouth. "Will you have my report, Earthspeaker?"

"We know what passed at Sun's Rest," Alkaia said.

"The children..." Kreysa whispered.

"I came too late," Rhenna said, staring at the table. "I could do nothing."

"But the devas called you, nevertheless."

Rhenna clenched her fists in her lap. "The winds," she said. "They...spoke of blood and evil."

The Elders stirred and murmured. Euriobe raised her hand to silence them.

"This is nothing new," she said. "Many of us have seen and heard such signs."

"We who were Chosen—" the Seeker began.

"Long ago this child also heard," Euriobe continued, "and we denied her because we feared change. Change is now upon us. The time for denial is past, Marpe."

"Forgive me, Earthspeaker," Alkaia said, "but Rhenna was selected as a warrior. She overstepped her place, and the Ailuri
themselves marked Rhenna for her transgression against the
devas."

"My memory has not yet failed me," Euriobe said dryly. She
compelled Rhenna to meet her eyes. "Why did you follow the
devas to Sun's Rest?"

"They gave me no choice."

"Yet you were forbidden."

Rhenna held the muscles in her face immobile, but the skin
jumped beneath the scar. "I ask no mercy, Earthspeaker."

"And I fear I can grant you none." Euriobe glanced about the
table. "I see what we did not understand nine years ago. Rhenna
was indeed marked by the Ailuri, but not in punishment."

Voices rose again, but this time Euriobe made no attempt to
silence them. She addressed Rhenna. "What do you know of the
Arrhidaean Empire?"

"Only that it lies far south of our borders."

Euriobe leaned back in her chair. "Our personal quarrels have
always been with certain of the man-tribes, yet once we fought
for the wages of petty kings and chieftains in the south. Philip-
pos, father of Alexandros the Mad, conquered many of those
kingdoms. The Elders chose to withdraw our warriors rather
than risk confronting such a powerful force.

"Alexandros continued his father's aggression, but his sole attempt to conquer the Skudat failed. He turned away from the
steppe. His brother Arrhidaeos founded the empire after his
death. We believed that if we did not provoke the emperor's
armies, they would let us be. And so they did. But now the devas
send portents of blood and darkness, and the man-tribes attack
us with impunity."

Alkaia half rose. "The Neuri have always coveted our land.
The empire—"

"—remains almost unknown to us, but not to the Skudat, who sire our children, nor to the Hellenish towns with whom we once traded so freely. Only we have gloried in our ignorance."

"Trusting the devas to protect us," Marpe said, "as they have always done."

"Though they send us so few new candidates to increase, let alone maintain, our numbers," Euriobe said. "Though our borders are breached. Though the Ailuri no longer descend from the mountains to mate with our Chosen."

"And this is not punishment?" Marpe demanded, her glance slicing at Rhenna.

"No. It is something far worse." She turned to Rhenna again. "You cannot know of these things, for we Elders have kept them to ourselves since the changes first began. We did not know how to comprehend them. We had grown complacent and soft in our good fortune. When the devas began to send warnings, we did not listen. Crops failed in the farthest reaches of the Shield's Shadow, and we paid no mind. Warriors reported the peculiar movement of bird and beast out of season, game scarce, foals dropped stillborn.

"Still we considered this only the way of the devas, inexplicable but temporary. Yet there was one sign we disregarded at the peril of our very existence."

"The Ailuri," Kreysa murmured.

Euriobe bent her head. "For centuries our finest young women have gone into the Shield to take Ailuri mates. Never did one return with an empty womb. Until nine years ago."

Rhenna felt blood well in the parallel gashes on her cheek but dared not lift her hand to stanch it. She could hear every heart beating, the whinny of a horse in the yard, the hum of a fly among the rafters.

"Keleneo came back to us untouched," Euriobe continued. "In years that followed, several of the Chosen failed to find mates, and many blamed Rhenna-of-the-Scar. They were wrong. It is not anger that keeps the Ailuri from us. Seekers who have gone into the mountains find none to accept our messages of goodwill.

"The Ailuri have disappeared."

Rhenna's stomach knotted with horror. "Disappeared?"

"Gone. All of them."

Rhenna pushed her chair back from the table and tried to stand. "You do not believe…that this is my doing?"

"Your single rebellious act could not be the source of such a catastrophe. Sit down."

Rhenna obeyed, the muscles in her thighs quivering as her blood dripped onto the table. "Forgive me, Eldest," she whispered. "My face—"

Euriobe reached out to touch Rhenna's cheek with a shriveled finger. It came away unstained. "You feel what we cannot," she said. "The Ailuri did not kill you, but left their brand so that none could forget. The devas led you to witness the terror at Sun's Rest. There is purpose in all these things, whether or not we choose to see."

Rhenna pressed her palm to the scar. No blood. "I don't understand."

"We have sought in vain for the cause of the Ailuri's vanishment. Yet those who escaped Sun's Rest heard the raiders boast of seeking more challenging prey in the Shield."

"The man-tribes hunt Ailuri?" Alkaia demanded, her face drained of color. "How is this possible?"

"I have no answer. As well ask why the Neuri attack us now, after years of minor skirmishes." The skin around her eyes looked thin as parchment. "There is no more time for debate. I have no doubt that the Ailuri's disappearance is in some way connected to the other afflictions our people have recently endured. We may defeat the man-tribes, but they do not work alone. Evil comes from the South…perhaps from the empire we have so long ignored. And without the Ailuri, our people will surely die." Her gaze came terribly, inevitably, to Rhenna. "This is why I have summoned you to Heart of Oaks. I believe you have a bond with the Ailuri, for good or ill. You have been chosen to seek them, no matter how far that quest may take you, or how long it may last."

Rhenna's tongue swelled in her throat. The very earth was crumbling beneath her boots, capricious as the deva-winds.

"You need not speak," Euriobe said, almost gently. "I hear all your arguments. You think you are not worthy. You do not wish to carry a burden that may affect the very future of our people."

"It is too great for one to bear alone," Alkaia protested.

Rhenna turned mutely to the Elder warrior, remembering what she had said in the Healers' lodge. *I give you this chance to speak privately, to spare you worse before the Council.*

But this was no punishment. This was high honor, noble duty, bitter destiny. This was Rhenna's chance to atone for the past.

"I know it is much to ask," Euriobe said. "We selected you, in part, because you are a skilled hunter and tracker, and well accustomed to living and traveling alone. But you have other gifts. You were ever curious beyond your years, observant and intelligent. As a child you were quick to learn foreign tongues that seemed of little use to a warrior who remained in the Shield. You speak the koine of the Hellenes, though only the very eldest remembered enough to teach. Above all, the devas have marked you, Rhenna-of-the-Scar. If anyone can find the Ailuri, it must be you."

Rhenna looked from Alkaia to Seeker Marpe and Healer Kreysa, at all the other faces of wise, accomplished women prepared to judge her once again. Their expressions were closed, offering neither support nor condemnation.

"You will not be compelled to accept this charge," Euriobe said. "You will lose no honor by refusing. If you agree, you will surely face great hardship, even death."

The next Ailu I meet may finish what the first began, Rhenna thought. "What am I to do if I find them?"

"Restore them to us, if you can. Bring word if you cannot."

No one spoke for many heartbeats. Rhenna unclenched her fists and rested her hands on the table. "When must I go?"

The Earthspeaker closed her eyes, and her mouth moved in silent prayer. "You must leave as soon as you have rested, and gathered the mounts and provisions you require."

"What of the attacks on the western settlements?"

"Their safekeeping is not your concern," Alkaia said.

"Then why did the devas send me to Sun's Rest?" Rhenna demanded. "Where are the devas, Earthspeaker? Why do they allow their children to be slaughtered?"

"Be silent," Marpe hissed. "You have no right—"

"She has every right," Euriobe said wearily. "I do not know, Rhenna. The devas are no longer as powerful as they once were. It is strength, not will, they have lost. If I believed they had truly abandoned us, I would don mourning clothes to prepare for the destruction of the Free People." The old woman rose from her chair. "There is one thing more I wish to show you."

The other Elders left their seats and formed a solemn procession behind Euriobe, Rhenna and Alkaia. The Earthspeaker led them out a side door and across the clearing to the eastern edge of the village.

Heart of Oaks' Sacred Grove was twice the size of the one at Sun's Rest, its potency a hundred times greater. Ancient oaks rose overhead, vast trunks forming an almost perfect circle. Bell-hung branches interlaced like clasping hands. Leaves chattered and sighed in a language only the Earthspeakers understood.

The others passed into the Grove without hesitation. Rhenna prepared for the familiar agony. She stepped into the Grove. A strange vibration started in her feet and shivered up the muscles of her calves and thighs. Power rushed into her chest.

But there was no pain. A sudden and violent wind made the tiny bells ring with voices like those of crying children. The Elders stared at Rhenna as if she had shouted some new blasphemy.

"What troubles you, Daughter?" Euriobe asked. "I know your faith has been cruelly tested."

"Perhaps she has no faith," Marpe accused.

"Then she must rely upon what her senses tell her." The Earth-speaker held out her hand. "Come."

Rhenna took Euriobe's soft, wrinkled fingers in hers. The old woman drew her to the center of the circle and the very foot of the Mother Tree.

"See," Euriobe said.

Mother Tree wept tears of blood. Her weathered bark was cracked from gnarled roots to trunk, and from each crevice ran thick red sap. Even as Rhenna watched, a shower of withered leaves, brown out of season, shook loose from the lowest branches.

"She suffers," Euriobe said. "I feel her pain and can do nothing to comfort her."

"Finding the Ailuri will end this?" Rhenna whispered.

"Even the devas cannot say. This I do know—the source of this monstrous evil must be found, or the People will perish."

Chapter Four

Tahvo reached the top of the pass and sighed with relief. These mountains were very much like home. Snow sparkled on every peak. The air froze in Tahvo's lungs, but she offered thanks for the blessed coolness.

The spirits heard. Her sense of them had only grown stronger with each day of her journey; they were numerous in this high place, so far from the dwellings of man.

But they were not like Slahtti. They could not answer her questions.

Tahvo sat on a rock burnished clean of snow and touched her drum. She knew she was selfish to wish for the spirit-wolf's return. Sometimes her fears seemed very large, but she had not faced true danger since leaving the town. She had learned a valuable lesson there: men of the South were not like the Samah.

She had taken care to travel near shelter whenever possible—low hills, stands of trees, riverbanks—and had avoided the scattered villages. She had watched from safety when men on horses followed the roads that crisscrossed the plain from one walled settlement to another.

None of the horsemen had ventured into the mountains. Tahvo had found the pass only by the grace of the spirits. No trail marked the way. The slopes were sharply pitched and hazardous with scree. By day Tahvo rested wedged between rocks, hardly able to move. At night she had slept curled about the trunk of a pine that clung to a cliff with the stubbornness of an old man comfortable in his bed. She had prayed often and fervently.

But then she had seen the first snow in crevice and cleft, and her heart had lightened. After another half-day of climbing she reached a level snowfield of spruce and pine. Mountaintops rose high above her head, but the way between them was easy. Small animals emerged fearlessly to inspect her. Graceful deer pawed through thin-crust-that-melts-away-from-new-green. Golden hawks spread their wings to catch the ever-shifting currents of air. Bear and lynx left spoor in meadow and wood.

Nowhere was there a single sign of man.

Tahvo had not known what to expect. These mountains were a barrier to her final destination, yet still she had no image of what that destination might be. She sensed that she had many more days' walking before she could look down he other side of this range to the mysteries that lay below.

So she continued south, making camp in caves cut into the rocky hillsides. One morning she emerged from her night's shelter to find the tracks of some enormous beast sunk deep in the snow. They were not those of a lynx, nor any animal Tahvo knew.

She knelt and placed her gloved hand over the vast paw print. The tips of her fingers barely reached the ends of the animal's clawed toes. The tracks were fresh, yet she had heard nothing of its passage. It had paused near the cave and continued on its way as if it had noted and ignored the human intruder.

A row of icicles suspended from the cave mouth cracked in a gust of wind. Three sharp points broke off and plunged into the snow to either side of and above the track. Tahvo removed her glove to trace the pattern formed by the shards of ice.

They made the shape of an arrow aimed precisely the way the big cat had gone.

Tahvo brushed off her hand, put on her glove and followed the tracks. The animal had walked at a slow pace, pausing often to rest. It might be ill, or injured, yet it left no blood. Tahvo knew it would not be a spirit-beast, like Slahtti, for such creatures did not suffer from sickness or old age. Perhaps the spirits intended for her to heal it…if it permitted her to approach.

The tracks led Tahvo on a winding path between high boulders and ended at a cliff pockmarked with many caves like black, hungry mouths. The beast had entered the nearest. Tahvo sat cross-legged on a flat rock and waited.

The air was still. The creature must have smelled her long since, but it did not emerge. Tahvo opened her pack and drew out the carefully wrapped portion of cooked rabbit left from her last meal in the valley. She laid it at the cave's entrance.

"Stop."

The voice behind her was low and firm. Tahvo's senses sparked with almost painful recognition, as if new eyes had opened in the back of her head. She turned about on her knees.

The woman was lean and tall, and she stood with her legs braced like one ready for violence. Tahvo held her hands out to her sides so that the stranger could see she was unarmed.

"I mean no harm," she said in the language of the Samah.

"Who are you?"

The tall woman's question formed curious shapes in Tahvo's head, and the spirits gave her the means to answer. "I am Tahvo of the Samah," she said. "I have come from the North."

The stranger said nothing for many heartbeats, did not even

seem to breathe. "How do you know the tongue of the Free People?"

"The spirits have taught me, just as they have brought me to this land."

"Spirits?" The woman's voice cracked, as if with anger. "Stand up."

Tahvo obeyed and studied the woman with keen interest. Her hair, braided close to her head, was brown as earth, her eyes the color of moss or lichen. Under her fur-lined cloak she wore garments of woven cloth and hide much lighter than Tahvo's, some pieces studded with metal. She bore a bow case at her hip and bladed weapons like those carried by the men in the walled village.

Those men had breathed out a miasma of greed and fear, cunning and hatred. They had been ready to kill without reason. This woman might be a warrior in the Southern manner, but Tahvo knew without question that she concealed no ill purpose. Her face was stern, scarred, but unmarked by evil. Her eyes had seen much sorrow. Her age must be near Tahvo's own, or a little older; the woman's body was well-balanced in all its parts and her skin as yet uncreased.

"Your weapon," the woman said. "Throw it down."

It took Tahvo a moment to realize that the woman was referring to the small knife she used for preparing food. She unsheathed it and laid it on a flat stone.

"What are you doing in the Shield of the Sky?" the woman demanded.

The Shield of the Sky. Tahvo was pleased with the name. A shield was for defense, not attack.

"I am traveling to the South," she said patiently, "and there was no other way to reach it from my country."

"Why did you follow these tracks?"

Tahvo sensed more behind the woman's question than curiosity. Here was the heart of her wariness. "I have never seen such

tracks before," Tahvo said. "I believe that they were made by a creature beloved of the spirits."

The woman's eyes widened in astonishment. "What do you
know of the Ailuri?"

"I do not know this name," Tahvo admitted, settling onto her
heels. "I only know that the beast within the cave is ill, perhaps
dying. I wished to help. I brought an offering of food." The weight
of Tahvo's fur hood was suddenly stifling, and she pushed it away
from her face. "The spirits——"

"You are a *woman*."

Tahvo had heard that same tone of surprise among the Samah
of other siidat and in the walled village. The great coat and muffling layers of a shaman's garments disguised her shape, and her
own people never expected to see a female noaidi. But the villagers had been astounded, even angry.

"I do not know your ways," Tahvo admitted. "If I have of-
fended——"

"You do not seek the Free People?"

"I——"

"Give me your pack."

The pack. The drum. Tahvo flexed her fingers and stared into
the woman's eyes.

"I don't bluff."

Tahvo removed her quiver and arrows, her small hand axe and
the pack.

The woman crouched with supple grace to examine them.
"These are a hunter's tools," she said. "You're no warrior."

"Samah do not fight."

The woman set the pack at her feet and untied the flap. She
could not fail to see the drum, but she did not touch it. She peered
inside the pack until she was satisfied, then pushed it back to
Tahvo.

"Are you an Earthspeaker?" she asked.

Tahvo heard two different words stacked one atop the other like tanned hides. "I listen to the spirits and heed their messages," she said. "It is they who have led me to this place, as they send me to the Southern lands."

The woman muttered a curse Tahvo did not comprehend. "There is great danger in the South, Tahvo of the Samah."

"What is this danger?"

"If your people do not fight," the warrior said, "you're not likely to survive it."

"The spirits protect me."

The warrior stood abruptly, brushing snow from her trousers. "You have great faith in your spirits. I hope it's justified." She cast an impatient, worried glance toward the cave.

"You hunt the great cat?" Tahvo asked.

"Hunt it?" The woman hissed between her teeth, and Tahvo realized that the sound was laughter. "I have been searching for the Ailuri this past half moon, and these are the first signs I've found. I would no more kill him than you would...." She raked her hands through her hair, loosening the braids. "Why did you say he's dying?"

"His tracks tell me. I am a healer. I can ease his passage, woman of the Free People."

The woman scowled, waging some fierce battle within herself. "Rhenna," she said at last. "I am Rhenna." The tendons of her neck tensed and released. "I don't know you, Tahvo of the Samah, but I believe you mean no harm. You may stay. But you'll do nothing unless I permit it. Do you understand?"

Tahvo smiled. "I do, Rhenna."

"Then remain here until I call you." Rhenna left Tahvo's bow, axe and knife by the pack, lightly touched her own weapons, and strode into the cave.

For a moment Tahvo simply breathed, letting the tension flow from her muscles. She gathered up her tools and laid her pack against a rock where the snow had melted. Gently she removed her drum, whispering the chants on the back of her tongue.

From within the cave came a groan so loud that it tore Tahvo from her prayers like a winter gale. The cry repeated, softer and full of pain. Tahvo grabbed pack and drum and crawled to the cave's mouth.

Rhenna was crouched beside the great cat, close but not touching. The beast was every bit as big as Tahvo had guessed, his body alone as long as an average Samah. He sprawled on his side, tail curled against his flank and jaws open wide in pain.

But it was his fur that arrested Tahvo. Most creatures of snow-bound lands wore pale colors to better hide from their enemies. Hare and grouse turned white in winter, and the lynx cloaked himself in mottled tan and gray. Tahvo had never seen an animal black as winter midnight.

Rhenna spoke to the cat in a low voice broken with distress. "Please," she whispered. "Stay alive. Tell me where I can find the others."

One huge paw twitched, but the beast's eyes remained closed. Rhenna extended her hand, hesitated, brushed at the prominent scar on her right cheek. "I know that once I intruded into your mysteries. Punish me again if you wish, but do not let my People suffer. Let me help you."

The cat's breath rattled in his throat. Tahvo knew she could wait no longer. She ignored her sudden, piercing desire for the solace of dreambark and entered the cave.

Rhenna hardly glanced away from the dying beast. "I told you to wait until I called for you."

Tahvo stopped, clutching the drum to her chest. "You wish to speak to the Blessed One. Perhaps I can help."

"How?"

Tahvo heard hope behind the terse demand. "He is weak. I can ask the spirits to lend him strength for a time, so that he can answer. May I enter?"

Rhenna released a sharp breath. "Can I stop you?"

Tahvo bent her head and sat cross-legged on the cold stone floor. "Those you call Earthspeakers petition the spirits?"

"When the spirits choose to listen."

"They listen now." *Let them grant me the skill.* Tahvo drummed until she felt the spirits gather near. They showed her what she must do. She set the drum aside and spread her hands above the great cat's body.

"Wait——" Rhenna stared at Tahvo with eyes hard as iron. "If he speaks...you will witness secrets no outlander has ever seen or heard. What will bind you to silence?"

"Healers hear many secrets," Tahvo answered steadily. "I will not reveal them."

The warrior's gaze pushed and pressed and finally relented. Her broad shoulders dropped. "Do what you will."

Tahvo lifted her hands again, skimming them just above the great cat's side. Waves of pain flowed into her fingers: old age, wounds no longer quick to heal...and despair. Emotion was a solid thing under Tahvo's hands, black as the beast's coat but laced with red.

Red like the Stone God.

Tahvo forced herself to look more deeply and saw the withered lungs, the blood flowing sluggishly through constricted vessels. The Ailu's heart lay encased in crystal, a shell that tightened with every beat until the organ had no room to move.

This was no evil magic. This was a disease of the beast's own creation.

"He does not want to wake up," Tahvo told Rhenna, flexing her fingers to relieve the ache. "I will try to reach him."

She lowered her hands to touch fur. Its texture was rough and uneven, bare skin was exposed where the hair had been rubbed away. The Ailu flinched.

"Be at peace," she said, forming the words in her thoughts as she had done with Slahtti. *"I will ease your pain."* She stroked her hands over the length of the cat's body, singing softly to summon the spirits' power. She imagined blood pumping swiftly through the great beast's body like a spring flood released from the slumbering heart of the mountain. *It flows freely. There is no hindrance....*

Flesh quivered. The Ailu's small ears lay flat against his skull. *"Go. Go away."*

Tahvo took more of his pain. It, too, was like water, but it froze as it came. Her joints stiffened, and her muscles groaned with a thousand minute tears. The Ailu grew very still. Rhenna made a sound of denial and lifted the cat's head in her hands.

Then everything changed. A surge of some uncontrollable force rushed up and out, knocking Tahvo back on her heels.

Where the cat had lain was a naked old man. His knees were drawn up to his sunken chest; his wrinkled skin was neither black nor pale, its tawny hue marred with flaking patches and half-healed sores. Thin strands of white hair clung to his scalp. Every breath shook his frame, a stretching of flesh over bone.

Rhenna kept the presence of mind to hold the old man's head above the cave floor. She glanced at Tahvo with guarded amazement and horrified pity.

Tahvo began to understand. The Ailuri were shapechangers. It had been said that the greatest noaiddit could take the true forms of bird and beast. But this old one was no shaman. His changing was as natural to him as flight to an eagle, a twinning of souls only the spirits had mastered.

Yet he was no spirit. He would know true death—and welcome it.

"Forgive me," Tahvo whispered.

The Ailu opened his eyes—tarnished gold dulled to bronze, pupils drawn to needle-points in spite of the dark.

"Why have you done this?" he croaked. "Let me die."

"No." Rhenna eased the old man to the ground, shrugged out of her cloak and bunched it under his head. "Hear me. I am Rhenna of the Free People, and I have been sent to find the Ailuri."

"The…Free People." The Ailu coughed and looked at the warrior without seeing her. "Do they still live?"

"They live. I have come into the Shield to learn why the Ailuri no longer honor our Chosen."

It almost seemed to Tahvo that Rhenna was waiting for some sign of personal recognition from the old man, but he gave none. He turned away.

"You have come…for nothing," he said. Spittle dripped from his mouth.

Tahvo found a waterskin Rhenna had set aside and lifted it to the Ailu's lips.

He refused the offer, slapping at the skin with one feeble hand. Tahvo took up the healer's stance once more. Her arms would not stop trembling, yet she threw all her will into taking some measure of the old one's pain.

"What is your name, Blessed One?" she asked gently.

"Name?" His breath hitched on a laugh. "Once I was called…Augwys."

"Where are the others?" Rhenna asked.

"They are gone."

She lowered her face close to the Ailu's. "What has become of them?"

"Taken. All taken to the South."

Nausea pooled in Tahvo's belly. "The Stone," she murmured.

Augwys jerked violently. "Raiders came. I was too old."

"Raiders?" Rhenna repeated. "You are kin to devas. Where are those who protected the Shield? How could men enter the mountains unbidden, let alone defeat the Ailuri?"

Augwys's eyes rolled back in his head. "Barbarians," he rasped. "Neuri. Only a few at first, then many. They carried——" He reached for Tahvo's hand and clamped it in skeletal fingers. "The red stones. Nothing could stop them." He coughed again. "Too proud. We would not ask help, not even from…those we took as our mates."

Rhenna beat her fist against her thigh. "Why do barbarians want the Ailuri?"

"Too proud——" He began to gasp, his chest rising and falling in short, sharp bursts. Tahvo felt the old man's heart flutter.

"He can answer no more," she said.

"Augwys!" Rhenna lifted the Ailu into her arms. He flopped like a doll made of down and hide.

Tahvo touched Rhenna's arm. The warrior lowered Augwys to the cloak.

"Is he gone?" she whispered.

"Soon." Tahvo hesitated. "Your people have ways of easing the final passage?"

"*I* am no Earthspeaker."

"Then, if you permit…I will drum the spirits to guide and protect him."

"As they've already done so well?"

A blast of icy wind found its way into the cave. "Their ways are not always easy to understand."

Rhenna stood abruptly and paced to the far end of the cave where the ceiling curved down to brush the top of her head.

Tahvo turned to the Ailu. "Blessed One, do you give your leave?"

Augwys hardly moved, but his lids lifted just long enough for Tahvo to glimpse the blemished gold of his eyes. He longed for death.

So Tahvo drummed. The barrier to the otherworld was remarkably thin, not difficult to cross by one who was prepared. Its ever-shifting, shimmering surface resembled the blue and green flames of the Sky Veil, which all Samah knew was its outer manifestation.

Tahvo found the Ailu's soul poised on the threshold, an essence of light caught like a salmon between spear and net. Augwys feared to pass, because of some overpowering guilt, yet he knew he had finished his time on Earth.

Healing souls was a gift Tahvo knew she did not possess. But she reached out with spectral hands, stroking the faint light as she would heal an injured body. She found and shared the good memories Augwys had forgotten: the exhilarating, terrifying day he had left the women and gone to be with his people in the mountains; learning how to take the shape of a great cat in the manner of his ancestors; his first mating. Remembering what it was to be young and strong and certain of the future.

"You have lived well," Tahvo told the old man. *"Others will finish the path you have begun."*

"There are no others."

Tahvo blocked the grim thought and gently pushed Augwys's soul toward the portal. Augwys hesitated; his light took the form of a golden cat. He lifted one paw and touched the Veil. It undulated like a liquid rainbow, myriad colors blending and parting in a joyous dance.

"You are free."

The cat swung his head toward Tahvo, golden eyes no longer dull but lambent with hope. He walked into the Veil. Tahvo remained behind, reaching toward the Veil with a mingling of fear and desire. All the secrets of the spirits lay on the other side.

She touched the Veil as Augwys had done. But there was no beautiful rainbow to welcome her. The Veil seemed to freeze, not in the way of clear water but like half-eaten carrion abandoned by a wolverine. Red streaks spread out from her hand, engulfing every other hue in a sanguine tide. Fire raced up her arm.

Tahvo screamed.

Chapter Five

Rhenna wheeled about, reaching for her knife. Tahvo knelt beside the body of the Ailu, hands outstretched, her mouth wide in a grimace of pain and terror.

Rhenna didn't understand what the Northwoman had done, nor what might happen if she interfered. But the sound of Tahvo's cry was enough to overcome her doubts. She strode across the cave, dropped to her knees beside the pale-haired woman and grasped her shoulders in both hands.

Tahvo convulsed like one stricken by the falling sickness. Her strange silver eyes rolled up into her head.

"Come back," Rhenna commanded, shaking her. "Outlander you may be, but I won't be responsible for your death."

The Northwoman's head snapped from side to side, and then she slumped in Rhenna's arms. Rhenna dragged her to the wall of the cave and propped her against it, pushing the mouth of the waterskin against Tahvo's lips. Tahvo gulped air and water one after the other.

"My thanks," she whispered hoarsely.

Rhenna glanced at the dead Ailu, who had become a cat again. "What did you do?"

"He has...passed over."

Rhenna sank down beside Tahvo and rubbed her dry, aching eyes. "You almost went with him."

"That was not my intention."

Rhenna had no heart to laugh. Weeks of futile search had brought her to this—the company of an odd and solemn little healer who had arrived just in time to steal Rhenna's final hopes.

But Tahvo wasn't to blame. The deva-winds had deserted Rhenna at Heart of Oaks. She had taken Chaimon and her spare mount, Dory, into the Shield of the Sky, moving west day after day as she looked for signs of both Ailuri or barbarian invaders. She hadn't found so much as a single black hair.

No enemies, and no allies. Yet Euriobe's warnings spurred Rhenna on, limning vivid memories of slaughtered farmers and a grievously wounded Tree. She forgot her own exhaustion and drove the horses to their limits. When they could go no farther, she left them in a meadow of new grass and continued on alone, climbing up and up, scraping her hands on rough stone where hooves could never find purchase.

Only there, in air thin enough to sear her lungs, had she discovered the big cat's spoor. Hope had lashed Rhenna beyond hunger and thirst, pain and despair. She'd tracked the Ailu to the cave...and found Tahvo waiting.

Her shock had been great. No ordinary person could have entered the Shield and remained unscathed. Men of the North who ventured into the passes never crossed to the other side.

Yet this woman...this healer...had, bent under a heavy fur coat hung with a hundred tokens of wood, bone and metal. An Earthspeaker not of the Free People. One the Ailu had trusted.

"Did Augwys say more?" Rhenna asked. "Did he leave any message?"

Tahvo licked her lips and braced her arms on the cave wall. "No. I...am sorry."

Rhenna smoothed her face of emotion. "You have done me a service in aiding the Ailu. I would see you well."

"I am not ill." The Northwoman blinked silver eyes in a face as frank as an owl's. "You are going to find the Ailuri," she said. "I will go with you."

Asteria's blood. Rhenna jumped to her feet and backed away. "Your spirits may speak to you," she said, "but they are not mine. You know nothing of my purpose."

"I know these Ailuri are of great importance to your people."

"It is none of your concern."

"The Blessed One spoke of the red stones. I have seen them."

"What?"

"In the visions. And the hooded man..." She shook her head as if to dislodge some invisible binding. "You asked if I sought your people. Why?"

Rhenna weighed her answer. She owed this outland woman a debt, and Tahvo had revealed far too much skill to have lied about her connection to the spirits, whatever they might be. Yet her motives remained a mystery.

The Elders had given the People's fate into Rhenna's unworthy hands. They knew what she was and what she had been. And she had nothing to trust but her own judgment.

So she told Tahvo of the Free People, how they lived apart from men and welcomed any woman who came to them seeking shelter.

Tahvo's mouth grew round as a child's. "If you banish men from living among you, how do you make children?"

Rhenna's cheeks warmed, and she longed for a Seeker's command of outlander ways. "We take mates as we require them."

"What are these 'Chosen'?"

"It is not a thing I can discuss."

"You said that the Ailuri are kin to the spirits who should protect these mountains. By this you mean that your spirits...attack any who are not of your people?"

"You have no devas to guard your land's borders?"

Silver brows drew together. "The spirits of my land...have never been asked to do so. There has been no need...." She hesitated, as if she might add more, and then went on. "Your spirits did not turn me away when I followed the Blessed One. They gave me strength to help Augwys."

"Where were they when the barbarians came?"

Tahvo closed her eyes and seemed to retreat into herself. "They could not fight. They *could* not. They did not have the power."

"You spoke of visions," Rhenna said, grasping at the most fragile of threads.

"The warning they bring comes out of the South, like the raiders who captured the Ailuri. And the red stones." She blinked slowly. "There is a link...."

"What are these red stones?"

"I see a Stone God." Her voice took on the singsong cadence of an Earthspeaker's chant. "He is not one, but many. The red stones are his weapons."

Evil comes from the South. Euriobe's words. Rhenna had heard that Southerners worshiped their devas in images carved from stone. But what outland god had the power to overcome guardians who had stood firm for a thousand years?

Some great evil had provoked the Western tribesmen, had damaged the Mother Tree, had taken the Ailuri. Tahvo gave this evil a name. If it was the same evil.

"What has this Stone God done to you?" Rhenna demanded.

"I do not think it has yet reached the Samah."

"Then why are you here?"

"The spirits remain in our world by choice, bestowing their gifts for the good of men. The Stone God is undoing, unbeing. If this evil grows too great, the spirits will return to their home beyond the Sky Veil and leave us in darkness forever."

"Would that be so terrible?"

Tahvo's eyes grew opaque, like ice-glazed iron. "The trees wither," she whispered. "The village burns."

Rhenna knelt before the Northwoman and seized her arms. "Tell me. Tell me everything you know about this Stone deva and what it has done to my people."

Tahvo's gaze cleared. "They have already suffered. Did your spirits not send you here to prevent the loss of many others?"

"My Elders sent me——" To the Shield, to find the Ailuri. But the cat-men were not here. Augwys had already told her what she must do. Where she must go.

South.

"There is much I have not yet seen," Tahvo said. "But I know the Ailuri are a part of the spirits' purpose. That is why I will go with you. You do not trust the spirits, but you will have need of one who does."

"I said before that your devas aren't mine."

"Once I, too, did not look beyond the spirits of my homeland. Those I knew are not here, yet others have aided me in my journey." She hesitated, forming her words with care. "This evil does not regard the borders and walls men build against each other. Men and women make alliances—the Free People and the Ailuri, the Samah and the traders. Can we not do the same?"

Rhenna thought of the quest ahead of her, a journey alone into unknown lands with only the faintest of trails to follow. She wouldn't return to Heart of Oaks without an Ailu or proof that every last one of them was dead. If she lived long enough.

"The steppe teems with savages who take pleasure in rape and murder," she said harshly. "I cannot protect you."

"I am a healer," Tahvo said. "You may need such skills."

Rhenna thrust her fingers into the hair at her temples, pulling at the braids. "Why should *you* trust *me*?"

"I have seen those who enjoy cruelty and pain. You are not like them. Your anger is not for me, Rhenna of the Free People."

Rhenna turned to kneel at the dead Ailu's side, willing the knots from her fingers. The sleek body seemed younger than before, as if freed of its burden of age. "You do little to convince me."

"The spirits teach me your tongue, but not how to speak it well. What should I say?"

"Say that you'll forget these visions and save yourself."

Tahvo was silent. Icy wind ruffled the Ailu's fur, giving it the semblance of life. Something in the air made Rhenna's skin pucker with more than the chill. She spun to face the cave mouth.

The wolf was white...no, silver, like Tahvo's eyes. The luxuriant thickness of its pelt would have made it an object of avid desire for any tribesman, had such a beast existed in the Shield's Shadow or the barbarian lands. But the animal stood a full handspan taller than any steppe wolf, and its pale blue eyes gleamed with intelligence.

Tahvo got quickly to her feet. "Do not be afraid," she said. "I know this spirit." She approached the wolf, hand extended. The beast sat on its haunches. Tahvo sat, as well, and the two communed in a voiceless hush that almost pulsed with magic.

"This is one who aided and protected me on my journey," she said when they had finished. "He is named Slahtti, or 'Sleet,' in your language. He has agreed that I must go with you."

Rhenna looked past Tahvo's shoulder to the wolf's half-open mouth and its impressive set of teeth. "Does he?"

The wolf rose and advanced stiff-legged into the cave.

Rhenna showed the wolf her open hands. "I'm not your enemy. I have not harmed your Earthspeaker. Go where you will."

The wolf merely stared. Rhenna finally lost her patience. "I must see to the Ailu's body," she said. She sidestepped the wolf, prepared to fight, but he let her pass to the outside. She gathered what scraps of dry wood and kindling she could find in the vicinity, arranged them about the Ailu's body and carefully cleared the cave floor of any other material that might allow the flames to spread beyond the cave mouth. Then she took out her flints and set about starting a fire.

The flints refused to spark. Rhenna felt a heaviness in the air, vapor settling on her skin and the wood.

"Do you and your spirits forestall me, Woman of the Samah?" she asked coldly.

Tahvo shook her head, but after a few moments the damp chill receded. Rhenna struck her spark and coaxed the fire to life. Tahvo backed out of the cave, taking the wolf with her. Rhenna gathered her supplies and left the fire to do its work.

The Northwoman waited alone, watching the smoke drift into the sky. Rhenna avoided her gaze. "Heed my advice," she said gruffly. "Your devas may have no power to protect you in tribal lands. Return to your home, Tahvo of the Samah." And then she left.

Her back prickled as she retraced the path she had taken that morning, but Tahvo didn't follow. Rhenna made the descent with almost reckless haste. Chaimon and Dory had spent the hours enjoying a much-deserved rest, but the day was waning; they lifted their heads and whinnied impatiently as Rhenna drew near.

Rhenna was eager to be gone. She readied the horses and tried not to dwell on the healer, with her quiet, naive conviction and ominous predictions. She regretted the necessity of leaving Tahvo behind, but she couldn't accept the burden of care for an eccentric outlander when her own people's future was at stake.

She'd given Tahvo fair warning. Devas grant that Tahvo had the

sense to return to that gentle place where the spirits had no need
to defend their country's borders.

Rhenna clung to that thought as she led the horses down toward the foothills. Down and south, into the lands of the Neuri,
longtime enemies and now hunters of Ailuri. Deva-beasts,
Southern gods, red stones...such madness was beyond Rhenna's
comprehension.

She continued to lead the horses while the descent remained
steep and strewn with loose rock, picking her path carefully to
avoid injuring the animals. Snow melted on sun-warmed rocks and
in open meadows among the pines. Shoots of green burst from
the thinning white shroud. Spring had finally come to the Shield.

Once she had reached less arduous country, she mounted Chaimon and rode where the ground was relatively level. She had come
out of the Shield many leagues west of the pass by which she had
entered. Foothills gave way to the rolling country of the upper
steppe and the borderlands of the Shield's Shadow. From now on
there would be no true rest, no easing of vigilance.

She made camp beneath an overhang of granite, where the
heavy growth of shrubs and the arrangement of rock hid her
small fire. A fortunate hunt provided a small rabbit for dinner, al-
lowing her to preserve her dwindling store of salted meat and
cheese. She resumed her journey at dawn.

The horses sensed the border before she did. Rhenna hadn't
expected devas to be guarding the frontier after they'd abandoned
the Western settlements. But when Dory and Chaimon stopped
abruptly on to an open stretch of steppe, she, too, felt the hum
in bones and blood that meant she was leaving Shield lands.

Perhaps she only sensed the wild devas, unclaimed by any race
of women or men. Unlike the Free People, the Neuri made little attempt to patrol their borderlands. That lapse in no way lessened the danger.

Several leagues past the border Rhenna intersected the trail of many horsemen. Just before nightfall she found them.

Rhenna left the horses behind the concealment of low trees and waited for darkness to cloak her advance. The moon was nearly full, but any small hillock or thick clump of grass provided cover to one who knew the steppe. Rhenna imitated the viper, stretching flat on her belly, and worked her way close to the camp as swiftly as she dared.

The Neuri had lit a large fire, secure in their strength. Their horses were picketed loosely to one side, unguarded; a dozen men moved in and out of the flickering light, passing skins filled with fermented mare's milk. The warriors had discarded all but personal weapons for the sake of comfort, and most had removed their armor of leather, mail and hammered iron. A clumsily dressed antelope carcass hung on a spit over the fire. Every so often one of the men tossed kumys on the seared flesh and laughed as the liquid sputtered in the flames.

There were no captives. Either this was not the band that had attacked Sun's Rest, or they'd already disposed of their prisoners and were on their way home to their own beaten females.

Rhenna pressed her face to the ground. Anger was a knot in her chest, a desire for blood that would have driven a younger Rhenna to heedless action. A Sister of the Axe might defeat two or even three tribesmen, and her arrows would account for several more, but to attack this band openly was as good as a wish for death. She had not the luxury for revenge.

She had just begun to turn back for the horses when she saw the cage.

It had been placed well away from the picket lines and the fire, but in the moonlight Rhenna could see how the evil thing had been set on wheels to be drawn by men or horses. Its iron bars were serrated like the thorns of a spine-bush, and were rusted and bent, but intact.

Within the cage lay something man-sized and motionless. Rhenna curled her lip in disgust and pity. She couldn't tell if the prisoner was male or female, but she had never heard that even the foulest barbarians kept their captives in cages. Surely no ordinary woman of the Free People would warrant such particular torment.

There was no question now of skirting the camp to avoid a fight. Rhenna crept in the direction of the cage, angling for a better view.

The captive moved. It lifted its upper body on braced arms and raised its head. An abundance of dark hair shadowed the paler oval of its face. Black hair like the sheen of an Ailu's pelt. Eyes that mirrored the ambient light like golden coins.

Golden eyes.

Rhenna fell onto her back and stared up at the stars, her belly hollow with shock. Dangerous beasts were kept in cages. The most dangerous—and the most valuable.

The captive was Ailu.

She rolled to her stomach again, estimating the hour and the state of the Neuri's drunkenness. Several of the tribesmen were already far gone, bellowing out harsh, unlovely songs in their rough language.

Rhenna retreated to the stand of dwarf trees where she'd left Chaimon and Dory. She strapped axe and gorytos to her back, where they wouldn't hinder her movements, and returned to the camp by a different route, moving more slowly with the encumbrance of her weapons.

But she was not the only visitor to the Neuri fire. Some trick of the light caught a flash of metal shapes approaching from the southwest, moving in time to the rhythmic tread of marching feet. Rhenna lay flat and held very still.

Sixteen warriors descended on the camp in a formation of four perfectly even rows, spears held in matchless symmetry above their heads. The company carried neither totems nor standards, but each man was clad in iron and bronze armor, from fitted greaves to the crests of their helmets.

As the newcomers entered the circle of firelight, Rhenna saw that the helmets completely covered their faces, leaving narrow horizontal and vertical slits for eyes, nose and mouth. The metal was unadorned save for a slash of red paint across the brow. The warriors wore plain iron cuirasses and kilts of leather strips over thigh-length tunics. They carried short swords hung from straps across their chests and small shields on their backs.

Rhenna knew these men must be Hellenish soldiers from the South, but her knowledge came strictly from the tales of aged Sisters who had served Southern armies in the days before the empire. Hellenish infantry fought in formations they called phalanxes. Instead of individual skill and valor, Southerners relied upon sheer weight of arms and numbers. Even their mounted warriors attacked as a single unit.

This was no army, yet the drunken tribesmen came to hasty alert, reaching for abandoned weapons. The Neuri's leader stood before the Southerners, swaying in his broad boots. His hastily donned armor fit him like a second skin, leather and mail stretched over a belly swollen with drink. His wolf's-head cowl seemed to bare its yellow teeth.

One of the Hellenes stepped forward to meet him. The Southerner's arms between tunic sleeve and armband were well proportioned and muscular, as were his legs from mid-thigh to bronze greave. If he bore marks of rank to set him apart from the others, Rhenna couldn't see them. His expression was invisible behind the helmet.

"Well," the Neuri headman said, scratching the side of his bristling neck, "you've come quickly enough."

The Hellene barely moved his head. "You have the beast?" he asked in the Neuri tongue.

Several of the tribesmen laughed at the soldier's heavy accent. The headman smiled. "Not so fast," he said. "We Neuri don't trade unless we can see a man's face—and share a libation in friendship."

Rhenna knew mockery when she heard it. But the barbarians clearly intended to sell their unusual prisoner, doubtless at the most outrageous price they could negotiate.

The Hellenes wanted the Ailu. Why?

Evil from the South...

"The empire's offer has not changed," the Southerner said. "Do you wish to view the payment?"

"Maybe your offer hasn't changed, but our price has."

For a moment the Hellene was silent. "Show me the beast."

"Show me your face. Or are you afraid to, eh?" The headman rolled his eyes at his men, encouraging their laughter. "Are you a man at all? Is it true that Hellenes have so little beneath their skirts that they prefer to mount babes instead of full-grown wenches?"

Any ordinary band of warriors would have reacted violently to such blatant insults, but the Southerners didn't stir. Their leader put his hands to his helm and lifted it with a twist.

Rhenna caught her breath. The Neuri ceased their drone of taunt and ridicule, watching to see what disfigurement or blemish such a headpiece must conceal.

The Southerner removed his helmet and passed it to one of his men. The tribesmen stared, shocked into immobility.

The face was no monstrosity. Its owner was hardly more than a boy. His white skin might never have seen the sun, and his golden hair shone as if the moon had become entangled in its close-cropped locks. Every line of his features was perfectly formed. His mouth was so finely shaped that the blustering headman stared at it in abject worship.

Even Rhenna was not unmoved, though male comeliness had never been a matter of concern to her. Warriors given leave for mating and childbearing seldom considered mere physical beauty when they selected the fathers for their children.

She looked up to the Southerner's colorless eyes. If he felt pride in his beauty or anger at being so thoroughly examined, none of it showed in his gaze. But just above and between those indifferent eyes lay a single, stark defect on his otherwise flawless skin— a raised mark the very shape and color of a drop of blood.

It was not blood. The Southerner turned his head and the mark caught the firelight at a new and revealing angle.

It was a stone. A stone of fevered, hideous red.

Chapter Six

They carried the red stones.

Augwys's dying words trickled down Rhenna's spine like icy sweat. He had spoken of tribesmen, raiders, not Hellenes. Yet he had been deeply confused, almost incoherent in his distress.

Tahvo had said that the red stones were weapons....

The Neuri headman laughed. "A boy," he said scornfully, though his voice was strangely muted. He fumbled inside the neck of his scaled corselet and pulled out a length of braided horsehair cord. Tied to its end was a chip of red crystal, crude and irregular in shape. "Sit, and drink with us."

The Hellene commander gestured with one graceful hand. The man who held his helmet passed it back to him, and he slipped it on over his head. Four of his company stepped forward, producing small metal boxes from beneath their gray cloaks. They handled the boxes as if they contained items of both weight and value. The commander ordered them set before the fire.

"Count your payment," he said, "and deliver the beast."

The headman smiled uneasily. "I told you it wouldn't be enough. This is the last of the beast-men of the mountains. You'll get no others from us or anyone else."

The commander's featureless visage turned in the direction of the cage. "The beast must be alive, and in good condition. We will see it now." Before the headman could protest, the Hellene started around the fire. His men fell in behind him.

Rhenna flattened to the ground and followed. Unperturbed by the grumbling tribesmen, the Hellenes kept to their ranks. They enclosed the cage, interlocking shields and spears. Rhenna could see little of what passed within the human barrier. The commander spent several moments looking into the cage, then turned abruptly on his heel, coming face to face with the headman.

The tribesmen had formed an even broader circle about the Southerners, swords and axes at the ready. What the two leaders said was beyond the reach of Rhenna's hearing, but it was not a friendly exchange. Shortly afterward the Hellenes pushed through the loose wall of tribesmen and marched off the way they had come.

Angry mutters pursued them, but the Neuri did not. One by one they drifted back to the fire to growl at each other and continue their drinking with even more carelessness than before.

They were fools. Rhenna didn't believe that the Hellenes had come so far to retreat without their intended acquisition. Augwys had said that nothing could stop the men with the red stones. But which men?

For Rhenna, it didn't matter. She had a very small chance of freeing the Ailu before one or the other band claimed him. Her success depended on how rapidly the tribesmen drank themselves insensible, and how soon the Hellenes returned.

A few of the tribesmen were obliging enough to fall into a heavy sleep, but some, including the headman, only grew louder with each rooting at skin or flask. The headman lurched to his feet and turned his malignant gaze toward the cage. He pulled a branch from the fire and blew on the tip until it glowed white.

"Nothing but cursed trouble," he snarled, spittle flying from his lips. "Not worth the two men it killed. Maybe not worth Hellenish gold."

His men raised a chorus of agreement. They snatched up whatever weapons came to hand and staggered after their leader.

Rhenna pulled her bow from the gorytos and considered skewering the leader's head. That would certainly cause confusion among his men, but it would also expose her too soon. She released her bow and wiped her sweating palms on the grass.

If they hurt the Ailu—if they so much as touched him—she would attack, and let the devas pay the price for their faithlessness.

He opened one eye, saw the men weaving their way toward his cage, and knew there would be no rest tonight.

There had been no rest since they had hunted him down and captured him in the mountains. No rest while he lay pressed between the bars of the cage, scarcely able to move, jolted along on a scaffolding hung between two terrified horses. No rest when the tribesmen stopped for the night, because then the torment started all over again.

Time and again he had yearned to take panther form, well knowing the barbarians were not quite so brave when they faced a mouthful of fangs and wickedly curved claws. Time and again he had resisted the temptation. He could still taste human blood.

And he knew how easy it was to lose himself. Often he woke in darkness, struggling to remember his name. He couldn't remember it now, dazed as he was by the barbarians' torches and the thick stench of their bodies.

Remember. He closed his eyes and tried to shift position, easing the pressure on the sores that had formed where bars rubbed skin. He remembered a time when he had not been afraid—the days of running wild in the mountains before maturity, and bitter knowledge, had come upon him.

He remembered the day the women had brought him to the Shield. He had wept, like many of the other boys, and clung to his nurse's legs. She had kissed his brow and left him standing on a wide, smooth rock, where the Ailuri could come for him.

Cian. That was the name they had given him.

For years he had longed for the lost happiness of the women's village. But then he had learned, with the other cubs, how to change shape from man to cat and back again, how to stalk and hunt and kill, how to listen to the mountains. The Old Ones encouraged the competitions and rough games that built up muscle and speed and skill, for it was the strongest Ailuri who were called to mate most often.

Cian cared nothing for mating. He looked down on the steppe to the south and the valleys to the north and longed for what he could never have.

We were chosen to be guardians of the Shield, the Old Ones said. *We are far above ordinary men, for we are the children of the devas. They gave us the gift of changing. We honor them by preserving our race from all mortal taint and by mating only with those females proven worthy of our blood. This is a pact that may never be broken.*

The tales and sacred traditions were never enough for Cian. As he grew older, he spent his hours envisioning all the lands and people beyond the mountains: wide plains made for running, hills plentiful with game, rivers tumbling toward great seas bearing human vessels that carried rich cargo from port to port. And cities built of stone, filled with people of every color.

In the end, he had seen those things, and more. He had lived in freedom such as no Ailu could imagine, while his brothers had vanished, one by one....

The scent of burning skin wrenched Cian from the past. Smoldering wood scorched his shoulder, and he flinched away as far as the cage would permit. It made no difference.

The big-bellied headman laughed, displaying several rotted teeth. "It is awake after all. Well, beast? Haven't you got a snarl for us today?"

Cian shook his mind clear and slowly made sense of the Wolfskin's words. They wanted him to struggle—to prove again how dangerous he was, and how daring and courageous they'd been in capturing a demon who must be starved and beaten into submission. They'd learned that he healed quickly and had taken full advantage of that convenient fact.

Cian had learned that the children of devas bled as freely as any mortal.

The headmen poked Cian again. "You still haven't paid for the lives of my brothers," he said, leaning so close that Cian inhaled the foulness of his breath. "I expected the Southerners to make up for it, but if they don't—"

Perhaps this time they would end it. The headman had taken much satisfaction in telling Cian how he would be sold to the Hellenes and sent down to the very heart of the empire. But the barbarians would or could not reveal what had become of the Ailuri, or why the empire wanted them.

Cian remembered the Hellene who'd come to inspect him, staring through the narrow eye-slits of his red-streaked helmet. He had drawn and repelled Cian at the same time, exuding menace without lifting a finger to goad or punish.

But he was gone now, and the tribesmen were angry. Perhaps the Hellenes had failed to offer a high enough price for a cringing Ailu with jutting ribs and battered flesh. The Neuri only wanted an excuse to pounce.

Cian gave it to them. His stomach growled.

"Hungry, are you?" the headman taunted. "How long since his last meal, Uros? Three days?"

A tribesman held up a scrawny rabbit by its limp hind legs. "I must have forgotten."

"A pity." The headman snatched the rabbit from his underling's hand and dangled it before the bars. "Do you want to eat, beast? You'll have to earn it." He grinned broadly at the others. "We lack amusement, now that the Southern boys have run off, pissing down their hind legs. We want to see if you still have a man's parts—if you haven't gnawed them off yet."

Harsh laughter. Cian's mouth filled at the thought of the rabbit's flesh, but he knew the Wolfskins wouldn't keep their promises. Even now, there were some humiliations to which he would not submit. If they truly had decided to kill him, they would do so very slowly and with deliberate pleasure.

He had to make them do it quickly.

The headman jabbed his brand through the bars. "Is it still there, demon? Come, show it to us."

Cian stared at the cage floor without speaking. The headman poked him a few more times and then snorted in disgust.

"Give him the carcass," he said. His underling pushed the scrawny rabbit through the bars.

Cian stared at the carcass. The animal was two days dead, hardly more than sinew. In cat form he would eat animal flesh raw, but human shape gave him human tastes. He would gag with every bite.

It was that, or starve. But he had a third choice.

He raised his head. He smiled. He took the carcass between his hands, peeled back the skin where it was most loosely attached, and forced himself to take a bite. His throat sealed in protest. The mindless hunger of his body urged him to swallow, desperate for sustenance.

Cian looked directly at the headman and spat the chunk of flesh between the bars and into the barbarian's face.

Stunned silence lasted only heartbeats, and then the headman yelled. His men converged on the cage with their cudgels, pummelling Cian on every part of him that they could reach.

He drew himself into a ball and endured until the headman screamed for a halt. "Take the demon out," he snarled.

The Ailuri made no prayers such as ordinary men did, but Cian's heart swelled with gratitude. Once he was out of the cage, he could compel them to kill him. The headman needed only a little further provocation.

One of the Wolfskins hastily moved to unlock the cage door. Cian gathered his aching muscles, setting off a cascade of fiery pain. The tribesmen's cruel, eager voices became a dull drone in Cian's ears. He closed his eyes and thought again of his childhood, the gentle touch of a woman, his first run as a cat. The cage door swung open.

Someone yelled. Cian waited for a blow that didn't come. The gate clanged shut again.

Cian opened his eyes. The Wolfskins had deserted him, everyone running toward the center of camp and the blaze that roared up from the place where their fire had been.

The fire had escaped its boundaries and now burned a large swath of grass where the men had made their beds, taking much of the Wolfskins' gear with it. The horses had escaped their tethers; some of the tribesmen chased after them, while others dashed back and forth before the wall of flame, shouting and vainly searching for a way to extinguish it.

Cian leaned against the cage door. It rattled but refused to give. Some Wolfskin had kept his head and refastened the lock.

A croak of laughter scraped Cian's throat. Perhaps if he struck his head against the bars with enough force, his mind would be damaged, as men's sometimes were in bad falls. Then he would feel nothing, care for nothing. He would be as good as dead.

"No."

The command came in a language he had learned as a babe in the women's village. He scraped bloodied hair from his forehead and looked up in bewilderment.

The figure rose from the grass like a deva in human shape. At first it seemed almost invisible to Cian's senses, as if it were only an illusion of his fevered mind. The smell of burning all but eliminated the stranger's scent. It had blackened its face and hair with ashes, yet Cian's sharp sight detected enough of its form to reveal the clothing and gear of a steppe horseman.

But it wore no wolfskin, and after a startled moment Cian recognized what had so befuddled his senses.

The figure was female. A woman, well past her first blood, tall and broad-shouldered. The Wolfskins never carried females on their raids, save for prisoners; Cian had not seen a single one in their many days of travel from the Shield.

He glanced toward the fire, listening for the alarm. But the men continued to run about like insects disturbed in their nest, struggling with their panicked mounts.

The woman approached the cage on silent feet. Her carriage named her as no words could.

Free People. He had never expected to see a face like hers in what remained of his life. So far out of her territory, pursuing the Wolfskins…he could think of but one reason she was here.

She had come for *him.*

Cian shrank into the corner, sick with rage and shame. This was his fate—to meet such a woman not in a mating bower but as a broken animal with nothing left save a wish for death.

"Ailu," she said, her voice rough with urgency. "Prepare yourself. I've come to set you free."

He hated her in that moment, but he could not look away from the determination in her gaze. "The fire," he said, finding the words from a darkened corner of his memory. "It was you."

"There isn't much time. Can you run?"

He tried to laugh. "Go, before they see you."

"Not without you."

He knotted his fists and willed her to despise him. "You should have let me die."

The woman cast him a glance of amazement, as if he had spouted nonsense. "If you die, I die."

"No." He bared his teeth in a snarl, pitiful remnant of defiance though it was. "I will not have your blood on my hands."

"You've enough of your own to worry about." She moved closer to the cage, and he could smell the richness of her skin, her perspiration, the undercurrents of horseflesh, steppe grasses and herbs. She curled a long-fingered, capable hand around one of the bars. "Stay back, and I'll break the lock."

If he had retained his full strength he could have forced her away with real threats instead of bluffs. "Tell whoever sent you that I am not worth saving."

She ignored him and began to pick and hammer at the lock with her knife. Out of the corner of his eye Cian could see that the fire was gradually coming under the Wolfskins' control. He had to make her listen. He reached through the bars to grasp her wrist, and it was as if a wind had risen out of nothing to sweep over and through him, scouring his coward's soul.

The woman stopped. She raised her head to stare at him, meeting his gaze with incredulity and confusion.

Cian lost all sense of time and place. The cage was no more. He and the woman stood on a hillside in the shadow of a mating bower. She wore a thin linen shift, though the morning was cool, and the wind molded the cloth to the body naked beneath it. A body strong and beautiful, and enticing beyond his wildest imaginings.

"*I have come,*" he said to the woman, and lifted his hands to touch her breasts.

"*I have waited,*" she answered. She placed her hands over his and pressed his fingers against the frantic beat of her heart.

At last Cian understood the call that his brothers had followed with such eagerness. At last he would know what it was to lie down with a female—a female as magnificent as this—and get her with a child of his seed. A child half of the Ailuri, half of the Free People, offspring of the devas themselves...

His knuckles banged against the bars. The woman had broken free, and her eyes held only anger. Wind loosened her hair into a halo of black-streaked bronze.

Cian found his voice again. "Let me go," he begged.

She resumed her work with sharp, almost violent movements. "I'm taking you back."

But her promise was premature. Cian heard a change in the Wolfskins' voices and forced his attention from the ache in his loins. The tribesmen were clustered amid the scorched ruin of their camp, still facing away from the cage. Cian quickly discovered the reason.

The Hellenes had come back. He knew it not only from the metal on their bodies or the rhythmic *thump* of their marching steps, but also from the sick yearning that twisted in his gut, as if they called to him with a silent command.

"They return," he whispered.

The woman banged at the lock with even greater fury. Cian watched the tribesmen consult with the Hellenes, saw the two leaders touch hands in agreement. The deal had been struck.

"They are coming."

With a soft curse, the woman pulled at the lock with all her weight. Cian pushed from the other side, finding the strength he had thought lost to him. Metal grated and gave way.

The warrior hauled open the cage door and grabbed at Cian with both hands. Her touch seared his bruised flesh.

A shout rose from the Wolfskins. Dawn's light had begun to paint the eastern horizon. The woman had been seen.

"Go!" Cian gasped.

The woman yanked at Cian, scraping him against the sides of the door. She had set her mind on saving him, even if she must die in the act. The Wolfskins were halfway to the cage, and the Hellenish company had broken into a well-ordered trot behind them. The woman pulled Cian from the cage like a stopper from a flask.

He tumbled to the ground, rolling as he hit the trampled grass. Stars danced behind his eyelids. The thunder of footfalls shook the soil under his hands and knees.

Too late to run. Too late. He opened his eyes and raised his head. The woman stood over him, long knife in one hand and double-bladed axe in the other.

A naked man was of no use to her. He tried to shift to cat, and his bones began to melt. He screamed and tried again.

The first of the Wolfskins charged up to the woman, his sword raised for the downstroke that would cleave her from shoulder to hip. With only the tiniest shift of her body, the woman swung her axe to counter his blow.

That was the very moment the ground turned to ice.

Chapter Seven

The shock of the impact bent Rhenna's knees, but she sprang up again in time to meet the next attack.

It never came. The man who had been so eager to kill her skidded and fell, a look of shock on his face. Ice crystals formed in his beard, spiking the hair about his mouth. The tribesmen behind him were slipping and sliding and crashing into one another, dropping weapons as they lost their footing. Rhenna felt her face tingle with the frigid breath of winter.

"Magic!" a male voice cried.

Rhenna looked down at her former opponent. He was struggling to regain his footing, but the ground was slick and pale with a coating of ice so thick that the grass could be seen only as a darker smudge beneath. His breath rose in white clouds of exertion. His fellow tribesmen shouted in amazement and fear.

Ice. The very air sang with it. Bitter cold congealed in Rhenna's lungs and made her joints ache. To the east, the sun rose as always, prismed through a many-faceted lattice of snowflakes.

Rhenna dismissed her own astonishment. She clutched her axe handle with stiffening fingers, sheathed her knife and reached for the Ailu.

"Run!" she commanded. "Horses—northeast. Go!"

He scrambled up, managing far better on the ice than his captors. Rhenna prepared to follow, but her attacker suddenly found his balance and renewed his assault.

Rhenna braced her feet as best she could and swung her axe two-handed. The tribesman lunged too widely, his thrust missing Rhenna's middle by a finger's width. He continued to slide past her, exposed, and she buried her blade in the base of his spine. As she yanked the axe from his back, she looked in the direction the Ailu had gone.

He stood only a few paces distant, wreathed in mist, trembling and completely vulnerable. Rhenna averted her gaze just in time to ward off a second attack. The tribesmen were recovering, spurred on by shame and the Southerners behind them; the headman raised his sword above his head and howled a war-cry.

"Run!" Rhenna yelled. "Run for the horses!"

She had no time to confirm the Ailu's obedience. Three Neuri were upon her in seconds, more cautious than their companion, but every bit as hungry for her blood.

If the cursed shapechanger would only cooperate...

She snatched her knife free again and fought with both hands, as all Sisters of the Axe were taught to do. She didn't strike with the brutal strength of the tribesmen, but moved in the precise, almost dance-like steps young warriors learned before they ever held a weapon.

The tribesmen's anger was their one great disadvantage. Rhenna buried the knife hilt-deep in an overhasty barbarian's chest, angling up to reach the heart. The man's flailing death throes carried the blade beyond recovery. The axe made its own magic, finding flesh more often than not.

Yet she couldn't win. The ice and increasingly heavy snowfall continued to hinder the barbarians' attack, but they had grown correspondingly more determined to cut her down. Three Neuri fell, and there were still many left to take their places.

Rhenna dodged a sword strike, hissed as the glancing blade bit through the leather of her trousers, and risked a precarious dive as another barbarian came at her. She cut into his leg as she fell and rolled. And she glanced again toward the Ailu.

He was no longer there.

The momentary distraction cost her dear. The warrior whose leg she'd wounded was not wholly disabled. He rose again, stabbing downward with his short, curved sword.

He never completed the motion. Dagger teeth in black jaws closed on his wrist, crushing bone with a sound like thrown pebbles. A sinuous tail lashed Rhenna's face.

The Ailu. Rhenna sucked in a breath and clambered up, grabbing the cage for support. A huge black cat crouched before her. His dark fur was almost wholly obscured by a white coating of snow, but he was no less terrifying for his mottled appearance. Even the memory of Augwys didn't prepare Rhenna for the full effect of an Ailu on his feet and ready to fight.

The Neuri fared no better. They backed directly into the Hellenes, who had come at last to join the fight. The Southern leader had drawn his sword, and his men advanced with spears arrayed to mow down anything that stood in their path.

The Neuri scattered with cries of rage and fear. The Ailu, who had confronted the barbarians with a lashing tail and bone-chilling snarls, flattened his belly to the ground. His golden eyes stared coldly up and up at the approaching Southerners, as if the ice had worked all the way through to his heart.

Rhenna straddled him and held her axe before her. "Get up!"

she yelled. "We can't fight them." Blindly she reached for any part of the cat she could find and grabbed a handful of fur and loose skin.

He was too big, too heavy for her to lift. The whirling snow thickened between her and the Hellenes, but it was not enough. All they need do was continue forward at that same relentless pace. If the tribesmen attacked from the side and rear...

A streak of silver light whooshed past Rhenna's shoulder, glittering shards of ice that coalesced before her eyes into a creature as weightless as the snow. Fur of blue and white rippled over a body almost as large as the Ailu's. The creature touched ground, leaving no mark.

It was Tahvo's beast, the deva-wolf. The animal swung about to meet Rhenna's gaze with startling intelligence. It looked at the Ailu, and then turned gracefully as the Southern leader's sword arced down to lop off its head.

Teeth snapped at metal. Rhenna braced for a yelp of pain and a fountain of blood. But the wolf tossed its muzzle, and the ice-rimed blade snapped in two.

Long Hellenish spears descended as one to skewer the beast. Another blur skimmed past Rhenna's arm. The arrow caught a forward soldier in the narrow line of exposed flesh between helmet and shoulder guard. He clawed at his throat in utter silence and began to fall. The others simply filled in his place.

A second arrow found a Southerner's thigh above his greave. He stumbled and continued to march with the shaft protruding from his leg.

They were not human, these Hellenes. Rhenna licked her lips and shifted her weight until she was certain of her footing. She might account for two of them before she fell.

A human shape appeared at Rhenna's elbow. She struck backward with her arm. The figure gave a muffled cry and doubled over as the air left its lungs.

"No," it gasped in Tahvo's voice. "I am here to help you."

Disbelief was too great an indulgence. "You shoot well," Rhenna said. "Kill as many as you can."

"Slahtti will aid us," Tahvo said, still choking. "Come toward me."

"I can't move the Ailu."

The Northwoman straightened. A sheet of ice descended in the narrowing gap between the Southerners and the wolf. The sound of feet crunching on snow abruptly stopped. Shadows pressed against the glassy wall.

The wolf spun on its haunches and crouched in front of the Ailu. Feral eyes locked. To Rhenna's amazement, the Ailu pushed to all four legs. He shook his great head, casting away the mantle of snow, and looked up at Rhenna.

"Go," she commanded, and this time he obeyed. When she would have lingered to watch for pursuit, he bounded back to her and seized her hand in his jaws. The teeth barely pressed her skin. She glanced back at the wolf and the wall of ice. The wall held, but the enemy was attacking it from the other side—not with swords or shields but some magic of their own. The wolf retreated, hackles raised, as the ice began to glow a sickly red.

Tahvo had already started in the direction of the horses as if she knew where they were hidden. Her short legs pumped with surprising proficiency. Rhenna ran with her axe in hand, making certain that the Ailu stayed beside her. As they reached the point halfway between the Neuri camp and the horses, the snow and mist vanished. They broke into clean dawn air and sunlight.

The sudden warmth reminded Rhenna of the blood welling in her boot. Chaimon and Dory shied at the smell and the sight of the Ailu. Rhenna stopped and seized a handful of black fur, dragging the shapechanger to a halt.

"You'll have to change into a man," she said, breathless with pain. "The horses will be too frightened."

Yet even as she spoke, she wondered how two mounts could

carry three at the swift pace they must take. She looked back toward the camp, still encased in a bubble of ice and snow. The wolf had not emerged.

Tahvo ran to join her. Her round, upturned face was pale with fear and resolve. "Slahtti will keep them away until we can reach the forest."

"Can you ride?"

The Northwoman glanced at the horses with wide eyes. "I will try."

Asteria's blood. Rhenna felt fur between her fingers and realized the Ailu had not changed. She debated drawing her knife and holding it at his throat.

"I know little of horses," Tahvo said, "but would it not be easier if the Blessed One carried himself?"

Rhenna almost laughed at the bizarre image the words evoked. Tahvo had no idea if the Ailu was hurt, but neither did she.

She knelt to hold the shapechanger's golden gaze. "We must get to the forest. Dory can carry us both for a while, but if you can run—"

The Ailu snarled. Rhenna flinched in spite of herself.

"He will run," Tahvo said.

Rhenna got to her feet. "It's fortunate that one of us understands him."

The Northwoman ducked her head. "What of your injury?"

"It can wait." Rhenna untied Chaimon's lead. "Chaimon is gentlest, and tolerant of mistakes. Climb up."

Tahvo removed her gloves and edged close to the gelding. She began to speak, chant-wise, bowing at Chaimon all the while.

"You're wasting time," Rhenna said. "Do you need my help to mount?"

"I was but asking him to carry me," Tahvo said humbly.

Rhenna cursed and limped to the Northwoman's side, bending to cup her boot. She flung Tahvo up, pack and all. "I hope your deva is still protecting us," she said, pushing the reins into Tahvo's clumsy fingers. "Grip with your thighs and knees."

She left Tahvo to adjust and considered her own predicament. From Dory's saddlepack she drew out a length of binding cloth and wound it from her thigh to just below the top of her boot at mid-calf, trapping the blood beneath. The cloth would rapidly soak through, but if it prevented her from leaving a blood trail it would serve its purpose.

She mounted, agony ripping from ankle to hip, and looked for the Ailu. He sat on his haunches, mouth open in exhaustion and tail limp on the grass, no more dangerous than old Augwys just before he died.

Rhenna's heart sank into her belly. Augwys had been ancient, but this Ailu was young and free of crippling injuries. He had been prepared to die rather than make the effort to escape. How could she expect him to help her fight for his life?

She remembered how it had felt when he touched her. For a moment she had lost all sense of herself, as if she stood in another place and time, facing the man this Ailu might have been.

With alarm, she recognized that pain had clouded her judgment. She didn't even know the Ailu's name, and yet nothing was more important than that he survive to reach Heart of Oaks.

"We ride," she said. The horses sprang into motion.

Tahvo clung to Chaimon's back with fists knotted in the gelding's mane. The Ailu kept pace, though Rhenna noticed when his steady lope faltered or he stumbled on a hillock.

Devas save him, she prayed, *even if you will not aid me.*

The white wolf didn't reappear. Tahvo glanced back many times, her face crumpled in concern. Rhenna focused on the line of trees to the north and the necessity of reaching them before the Neuri organized pursuit. That they would pursue was never in question; blood debt must be paid, and the savages wouldn't hesitate to kill their mounts to reach the forest's shelter right behind their prey.

The Neuri had not caught up by the time they reached the outlying trees. This was strange country to Rhenna, but not so different from the forest of the Shield's Shadow. She sought rocky formations that indicated the likely presence of caves, where all five of them could hide for the remainder of the day—hide, rest and lick their wounds. Only then would she be able to consider the situation with a clear head.

Surefooted, Dory and Chaimon scrambled up among boulders flung from the ramparts of cliffs high above. The Ailu picked his way even more carefully, favoring one of his hind legs. He left bloody paw prints behind.

Rhenna reined Dory to a halt, took her waterskin and dismounted on her uninjured leg. The Ailu immediately stopped as well, twisting his body to nose at the injured foot.

"How long have you been bleeding?" Rhenna demanded.

The Ailu bared his teeth. Rhenna offered him water in her cupped hands, but he turned away. She looked for Chaimon and the Northwoman on the ledge above. "Healer. Can you bind his paw?"

Tahvo nodded and slid awkwardly from Chaimon's back, keeping a death-hold on the gelding's mane until her feet touched the ground. She skidded down from the ledge and approached at a stiff hobble.

Rhenna followed the Ailu's back trail, searching for the place where the bleeding had begun. A hundred paces down the slope she discovered the cluster of sharp rocks where the shapechanger had cut his pads. She gathered pine needles and last season's leaves from the forest floor and used them and the water to scrub the stains from the rocks. Then she scattered the stained leaves and needles under the trees some distance away, where they would be lost among countless others.

She returned to find Tahvo completing her binding of the Ailu's paw. Every outward hurt Rhenna hadn't noticed in the half light of dawn became cruelly obvious: fur falling out in tufts, one eye swollen half-shut, a torn ear. It might be worse under the skin. Neither he nor the horses could run much longer.

"Tahvo," she said, "we must find a safe place to rest. There are caves in these hills."

The Northwoman set the Ailu's paw gently back on the ground. "Your leg still bleeds," she said.

"We can't stay here. You continue on with the Ailu and find a place to shelter."

The Ailu growled. Tahvo set her hand on the panther's head. "We will not leave you," she said mildly. "Please wait." She and the shapechanger communed silently, as she had done with Augwys and her wolf.

Rhenna suffered a strange envy at the sight of it, almost as painful as her wound.

Forbidden . . .

"We can find one of these caves," Tahvo said.

"Then go, both of you. Take the horses."

The shapechanger pushed to his feet, holding his left rear paw above the ground, and lashed his tail in an answer even Rhenna could not mistake. Tahvo pulled her drum from her pack, hitched its strap over her shoulder and clambered onto Chaimon's back. She began to drum and chant very softly while Chaimon resumed his climb up the boulder-strewn hill toward the cliffs. Dory snorted and tossed her head.

"Go," Rhenna told the Ailu.

The beast chuffed under his breath, a panther's laugh, and refused to budge. Rhenna shook her head and braced her wounded leg with one hand as if sheer will could keep the cloth from giving way and releasing its burden of blood. She mounted with care. Dory walked with ears pricked and nostrils flared, as if she sensed their journey's end. The tapping of Tahvo's drum blended with the natural sounds of wind in tree branches and the clopping of horses' hooves.

Rhenna lost sight of Chaimon and slumped in the saddle, letting Dory find their companions. The cave was well hidden, tucked among a maze of rocks and bushes. Tahvo had dismounted and was pushing branches aside. The cave mouth was just high enough to permit the horses to enter.

The ground appeared much farther away from Dory's back than it had an hour before. Rhenna dismounted, looped her arm around the mare's withers and pulled Dory's head down. Tahvo followed with Chaimon. The horses were not pleased to enter so confined a space, but they did so without balking. Tahvo went back outside.

The angle of the cave's opening kept sunlight from penetrating more than a few paces within. Rhenna secured the horses as close to the light as possible and removed their packs and saddles.

The Ailu dropped to the ground well away from the horses and heaved a shuddering sigh. His coat all but disappeared against the cave wall, but his eyes burned with their own radiance. He closed them and rested his head on outstretched paws.

Tahvo was gone long enough that Rhenna had just begun to worry, when the Northwoman returned with an armful of small tree branches and kindling. She dropped the pile on the ground, rearranged the concealing bushes over the cave mouth and came to Rhenna.

"We will be safe here," she said. "Please sit. I will make a fire."

"That is not wise—"

"The smoke will not be seen. Your wound requires tending."

"The Ailu first."

Tahvo cocked her head, the ends of her blunt-cut silver hair brushing the curve of her jaw. "Yours is the greater injury. If you fall, how will you be sure your Ailu reaches safety? I do not know these lands."

Rhenna laughed. "You and your deva just saved our lives, and you worry about becoming lost?"

"You must stay with him. Your leg should heal if I begin at once, and if the spirits give their blessing."

All the arguments in the world would not change the truth. Rhenna worked her way to the floor, holding her leg out stiff before her. Tahvo produced flints and efficiently started a small fire. She fetched Rhenna's waterskin, delved in her pack for two small bronze bowls, and opened a pouch that Rhenna assumed must contain herbs such as the Free People used in treating injuries. She filled the bowls with water and shook brown and green flakes over one. She sprinkled another herbal mixture into the second bowl. When the water began to heat, she stirred the concoctions with a flat-tipped bone utensil.

Rhenna remained motionless as Tahvo used her short knife to slice the soaked bandage from the maimed leg. She looked over the Northwoman's bent head to the Ailu, whom she hoped would already be asleep.

He was not. He lay sprawled where he had fallen, but dark fur had given way to pale skin…pale where it was not covered in the black, blue and green of bruises. A bloodstained cloth hung half unraveled about the lower part of his left foot.

Rhenna examined him with a warrior's dispassionate eye. She could see no serious injuries, other than those she had noted outside. He had carried them from one shape into the other, though they seemed more stark without fur to conceal them. One shoulder bore the angry welt of a recent burn, the other arm a shallow laceration.

Could such a creature suffer like ordinary mortals? She would not have believed it of any Ailu until she had found Augwys. She still did not want to believe.

She tried to glimpse his face under the ragged hair, caught a flash of red-rimmed eyes under long lashes. Except for the swelling beneath one dark brow, his face was unmarked. It was well-shaped, with a firm chin, bold cheekbones and line of jaw that belied the very possibility of weakness. He was...

Handsome. Not like the Hellene, with his perfect features, but attractive in the way one of the Chosen might wish.

Rhenna grimaced, appalled at her thoughts. There could be nothing personal in what she did or felt for the Ailu. Devas knew she had little cause to love the Ailuri, and this one had not changed her mind. He'd been ready to surrender his life for no comprehensible reason. A Sister never did so until she was beaten to the ground with every bone shattered, unable to wield even hands and feet as weapons.

She did not understand him, or herself. She didn't know why she hated and pitied him at the same time, why she suffered this troublesome, heightened awareness of her own body that pricked at her nerves with every glance in his direction.

He had *touched* her. And she had dreamed...forbidden, dishonorable, impossible dreams.

Tahvo peeled the slashed leather of Rhenna's trousers away from her wound. Rhenna hissed and stared at the Ailu so fiercely that he lifted his head and met her gaze.

Golden eyes. They were little different from the ones he had worn as a panther, and she couldn't doubt what she saw in them. Pain, muted by the remnants of pride. Despair.

And shame.

Shame because he had not resisted his captors to the last particle of his strength? Shame for the weakness he displayed before one not of his kind, one not even Chosen?

Or shame to have been saved by a warrior so baldly marked by Ailuri disfavor, a misfit old Augwys had been too ill to recognize for what she was?

"I have prepared this drink for you," Tahvo said, interrupting Rhenna's grim speculation. The healer lifted the first bowl and held it close to Rhenna's lips. "It will ease the discomfort."

Rhenna's tongue was clumsy with thirst, and perspiration poured in rivulets over her face. "Will it cloud my mind?"

Tahvo's hesitation was answer enough. "Give me plain water," Rhenna said. "I can bear whatever you do."

With a sigh Tahvo set the bowl aside and gave Rhenna a waterskin. Rhenna gulped down half its contents and dampened one of Tahvo's rags to wipe the ashes from her face.

The Ailu was still watching her, curled in upon himself to conceal his male organ. Rhenna's silent laugh was cut short as Tahvo cleaned the gash with the blend from the second bowl.

Your modesty is misplaced, she thought through a gray haze of pain. *You are safe from me.*

She only realized she'd spoken aloud when Tahvo's sure and gentle hands stopped their work and the Ailu blinked in dismay.

"I must stitch the wound," Tahvo said. "You do not wish the drink?"

Rhenna shook her head savagely. After a moment the pain reached new planes of agony. The Ailu's pale face swam before her eyes.

"Why did you want to die?" she demanded.

Chapter Eight

Cian heard the woman's question without surprise and wondered yet again why he had stayed with her. Ever since they had arrived at the cave, he'd been painfully conscious of her pitiless stare, examining him with cold calculation, very much as the Southern commander had done.

She, like his erstwhile buyer, wanted him alive. He had wearily accepted her warrior's disdain as his just due. But he hadn't recognized her until she had washed the ashes from her face, exposing the scar to the firelight.

His memory flew back to the events that had turned him away from duty and Ailuri honor—that day nine years ago when she had suffered the punishment he evaded. He should never have forgotten those eyes, so filled with courage and hope and accusation....

But he *had* forgotten, even when he touched her through the bars of his cage, hopeless with self-loathing. *You are safe from me,* she said, mocking him. He knew that somehow she had sensed his thoughts when they touched, his fantasies of eager welcome and physical release. His body still tightened with the need to touch her again.

She would be the last female in the world to welcome his irrational desire. But he had been granted one small, undeserved bit of good fortune: she did not know him.

Why did you want to die?

He gathered his courage. "My name," he said, "is Cian. It seems you saved my life, warrior of the Free People."

Her eyes, the mingled hues of oak leaves and honey, regarded him steadily over the healer's head. "I am Rhenna," she said. Her voice was like her eyes, rich with all the hues of the forest.

He tore his gaze away from her face and looked pointedly at the healer. "I also owe you my thanks. . . ."

"Tahvo of the Samah," Rhenna said. "Will you answer my—"

She gasped as Tahvo tied off the sutures and severed the ends with her knife. Rhenna grabbed her waterskin and drank deeply.

You do feel pain, Cian thought, but kept the observation behind his teeth. The healer looked over her shoulder and bobbed her silver head.

Cian returned the nod. She was as unlike Rhenna as any woman could be, and not only in appearance; he hadn't even realized she was female until she had touched his panther's soul in the speechless communication his people used in that form. He didn't remember what she had said to him then, but he had accepted her without hesitation. For once he found it easy to trust his instincts.

"You are from the far North," he said.

She paused in surprise. "You know my people?"

"I have heard the name." He pieced together the confusing jumble of images that had passed through his mind during the escape. "You speak the language of the Free People very well."

"She says the devas taught her when we met in the Shield," Rhenna said.

"You are a wise-woman, Tahvo of the Samah?" he asked.

"I am noaidi."

"You brought the snow that stopped the Wolfskins."

"It was Slahtti's doing."

"The deva-wolf," Rhenna put in.

Cian remembered slanted blue eyes and a sleek, white-furred body almost as large as his own. "A deva?"

"Tahvo summoned it," Rhenna said.

Cian heard her grudging respect and knew such approval had not been easily won. "You're a long way from your home," he said to Tahvo. "What brought you to the Shield?"

"That is a complicated tale," Rhenna said. "Perhaps she can tell it once we're safe from our enemies."

"Your meeting must be an interesting tale in itself."

"We met when we found Augwys," Tahvo said softly.

Unbidden joy surged in Cian's heart. "He still lives?"

"He is gone," Rhenna said. "I'm sorry."

Cian bent double, pressing his face into his knees. *Gone.* But he had known. He had seen it coming.

I am the last.

A soothing hand touched his shoulder. "You, too, are injured," Tahvo said. "Will you take the drink?"

Something to ease the hurt and cloud the mind. Cian felt Rhenna's stare and shook his head. But Tahvo pressed the waterskin to his lips and wouldn't take it away until he had drained it dry.

"You are not fevered," she said. She bent close to his lacerated foot with a frown. "May I examine it?"

"I'm here only because of you," Cian said, swallowing the taste of bile.

"You are blessed by the spirits," she said with great seriousness.

Cian didn't dare to laugh. "Do what you will."

Tahvo inclined her head and waited for Cian to unfold himself. Heat raced down his spine. The healer's gaze did not disturb him, but Rhenna's was like a brand on his flesh.

He stretched out on his belly. Tahvo's fingers brushed so lightly that he scarcely perceived them. He had almost forgotten what gentleness was. Or how it felt to be free of pain.

Unwillingly he looked up at Rhenna. The rigid line of her mouth had eased a little, perhaps because Tahvo's work with her was finished. Once more he admired the stark beauty of her face, the straight yet surprisingly expressive brows, steadfast nose, firm lips…and the four-striped scar that marked her right cheek.

Cian stiffened, but a pass of the healer's hand loosened his muscles. She retrieved one of her bowls and mashed the thick grayish contents into a paste. After a time he risked speech again. "Tell me of Augwys."

"He was near death when we found him," Tahvo said, spreading the paste on Cian's bruises. "I tried to ease his passing."

"He told us how the Ailuri were taken," Rhenna said, "but he spoke only of the Neuri." She braced her arms and slid closer to Tahvo and Cian, clenching her teeth when her leg shifted. "What do the Hellenes want with your people?"

"The empire." Cian buried his face in his arms. "It is the Arrhidaean Empire that has put a price on our heads."

"Why?"

"The Wolfskins didn't tell me."

"How did they come to capture you?"

The only answer was a deluge of memories he couldn't put into words, especially not for her. Instead he asked, "Did you go into the Shield to look for my people?"

"My Elders sent me."

"Alone?"

She frowned. "The Elders said the Ailuri had vanished without explanation. Were there no others—"

"South," Tahvo said abruptly. "Your people are in the South."

Cian rolled on his side, dislodging the healer's dressings. "How do you know this?"

Tahvo rocked back on her heels, the heavy coat gaping open revealing all the fine stitching that bound one pelt to another. "South," she repeated. She turned to tear a fresh strip of bandage.

Cian gripped Tahvo's arm, fingers sinking into fur. "Do you know why they were taken? If you know anything that will help me find my brothers—"

"We owe much to Tahvo's deva," Rhenna interrupted, "and to Tahvo herself. But your questions are pointless. The fate of the Ailuri is no longer your concern. We are going home."

Cian let his hand fall from Tahvo's arm, fingers gone numb. The healer's eyes showed a flinty light he hadn't seen before. She fastened the bandage about Cian's upper arm with a decisive tug.

"The Stone God has taken your people," she said.

"The Stone God." The words chilled him. "What is it?"

"A matter for Earthspeakers and Elders," Rhenna said. She got to her feet, balancing against the cave wall. "My task is to return you to my people, where you'll be safe."

"There is no safety," Tahvo said, gazing into the fire. "The village burns...."

Rhenna swung on Tahvo as if to silence her, but Cian saw the pain in the warrior's eyes. "What has happened among the Free People?" he asked.

"Is the disappearance of the Ailuri not enough?"

The numbness in Cian's hands spread to his chest. "Who has attacked you? The Wolfskins? The Skudat?"

"We will drive them out. My people will care for you, Cian of the Ailuri."

He knew what her promise truly implied. The Free People

could be as hard and cold as granite when they perceived a threat to their way of life. They would guard the last Ailu as a precious object—a prisoner—expecting him to mate with one female and then another until he grew as old as Augwys.

He was struggling to find a response when Tahvo set herself firmly between him and Rhenna. "I have another broth—for healing," she said. "It will not cloud your thoughts. I will prepare it, and make a splint for your leg."

"I must be able to move freely." Rhenna jerked her chin at Cian. "Is he fit to travel?"

Cian's chest ached as if all the numbness had been scoured away by a great, hot wind that must either escape or smother him. "Look to your own fitness, Rhenna of the Free People."

Her brows rose in surprise, and he thought he detected a flash of respect in her eyes. Surely that was an illusion.

"Your gratitude warms my heart," she said.

"I did not ask for your help."

Tahvo clashed the bowls together with a sound like a smith's hammer. Liquid sloshed over the rims. She thrust one vessel at each of her patients, brooking no argument. Even Rhenna drank. Without another word, Tahvo gathered up a few stray branches at the edge of the fire, slung her pack over her shoulder and set off for the rear of the cave, disappearing through a narrow passageway.

Cian moved to follow, but Rhenna blocked his path. She stood very close. He was acutely aware of his nakedness. The silence stretched taut like swollen skin over a festering wound. Then the drumming began, a faint echo from another chamber.

"She summons her devas," Rhenna said with unexpected diffidence. "It was how she spoke to Augwys, before he died."

Was that sympathy, even pity, he saw in her face? He deserved neither. A woman like Rhenna would not forgive.

But she might let him go.

"You asked why I wished to die," he said, wrapping his arms

about his chest. "I was gone from the Shield when the barbarians came for my brothers. I was not there to share their fate."

"Gone?"

Cowardice extended clawed fingers to clutch at Cian's heart. "I fled the Shield to escape the fate decreed for the Ailuri by our ancient pact with your people."

She stared at him. He tried to move and lost his balance, wobbling like a newborn colt. Rhenna flushed a deep red beneath her tan and shrugged out of her blood-flecked cloak, thrusting it out before her. Cian hastily flung the fur-lined wool about his shoulders. Her scent overwhelmed him.

"You should rest," Rhenna said, a catch in her throat. She dropped a pouch into his hand.

His mouth watered at the smell of salted meat.

"Eat," she said. "You'll need your strength for the journey to Heart of Oaks."

"Did you not hear me? I traveled unknown lands and lived among strange peoples for nine years because I wanted no part of my obligation to your Chosen."

The flush returned to her cheek, outlining each ridge of the scar. "You mean...you wouldn't—"

"I didn't wait for my first summons to the mating grounds."

Comprehension lit her eyes, first with disbelief and then, inevitably, contempt. "You abandoned your people?"

He held his neck stiff, forbidding himself the relief of looking away. "I broke all the laws by which my people lived. I was the only one who did not pay."

"You didn't know the Ailuri would be attacked."

It would be so easy to take the escape she offered, embellish it until it would seem he bore no blame at all. "I returned to the Shield when it was already too late."

Private grief clouded her gaze. "Mistakes...are made. There is always a price."

She spoke not of him, but of herself. "You paid such a price," he said softly. "I saw it happen on the day a young warrior defied an Ailu."

Rhenna's eyes widened. *"You."*

So much conveyed in so small a word. Shock, realization, acceptance. Anger.

"I was never like the others," he said thickly. "I dreamed of a world and a life forbidden to Ailuri. I was too young to mate, but I was impatient to learn why the Elders claimed this act was so much more important than the freedom I imagined." He swallowed. "I tracked one of my brothers to the Chosen one's bower. I witnessed the forbidden rite, but there was no honor in it, no beauty. Only cruelty and ugliness—the work of a mindless beast."

"So...you ran."

"They would have punished me if they could, but they never caught me." He stared helplessly at Rhenna's mouth. "You suffered for us both."

She turned her back on him. Her shoulders rose and fell. "What happened then doesn't matter. I am a Sister of the Free People. I still have my duty."

Duty. Nine years ago Cian had seen rebellious spirit, wonder and passion in the eyes of a girl just come to womanhood. That girl was no more. Yet Rhenna had risked her life to save him, borne severe pain without flinching, held steadfast in the face of overwhelming odds. How terrible had been the lessons that made her speak of duty as if it were more important than life itself?

"You must let me go," he said.

She laughed. "You are mad."

"The Hellenes want me badly, and they'll follow even to your Heart of Oaks to take me back."

"You believe I would allow the Southerners to get so far?"

"The Wolfskins are familiar with this land."

"We will evade the barbarians and work our way to the northeast," she said. "Once we reach the Shield, we'll find my people. The Neuri party will not risk a direct confrontation with the Sisterhood, and the Hellenes have no horses."

"Do you think that will stop them?" he asked bitterly.

"Are they not men?"

"I don't know. It may be they are not."

"Neither are we."

Her dry humor astounded him more than anything he had seen or heard since first beholding her beside his cage. He saw the futility of trying to make her acknowledge her danger or the risk to her people. How could he explain what he didn't understand?

He had to find another way.

"You would take me back…" He cleared his throat, dizzy with foreboding. "You would take me back to perform a function that an entire race has carried out since our peoples first joined. One Ailu to fill a hundred empty wombs."

She turned to face him. "Do not speak of this."

"Do you find me worthy of such a task?" he demanded. The muscles in her jaw flexed, giving him his answer. "On the day I discovered the Ailuri gone from the Shield, I swore to find them. The Wolfskins took me instead. If any Ailuri still live—"

"—*you* cannot save them."

She is right. You're a coward, weak, alone….

"Will your Old Ones send warriors into the empire to search them out?" he asked.

"That is for the Elders to decide. We return to Heart of Oaks. If you do not come willingly, I'll do whatever is necessary to compel you—" Her voice cracked. "Now rest. Eat and sleep. I'll stand watch until it's time to go."

"*You* need rest. How will you compel anything if you—"

But she had already limped around the bend in the cave toward the entrance, out of sight. All the pain and weariness Cian had forced aside crashed over him, sapping the last strength from his muscles.

There was no arguing with her. She was a true warrior, stubborn and sworn to the commands of her Elders. Yet if their positions had been reversed...

You would go after them, Rhenna of the Free People. If they were your sisters, you would single-handedly drag them from the very pit of the Hellenes' underworld.

But they are Ailuri.

He laughed bitterly and made his way toward the echo of drumming.

Chapter Nine

Tahvo heard the shapechanger enter the chamber but did not cease her drumming.

The Ailu bent to avoid striking his head against the low cave ceiling and crouched against the wall, huddled within Rhenna's cloak. He was deeply troubled. Tahvo altered the rhythm of her chant to extend a healing prayer. If only the peace that had escaped her would flow forth and ease the Ailu's discomfort, of soul and of body.

She knew it would never be so simple. She could not even ease her own boundless grief.

The spirits were here. She felt them, as she had in the valley and the mountains and on the steppe. But their presence was fragmented, chaotic, refusing to settle no matter how determinedly she drummed.

Was it any wonder that they evaded the call of a healer who

had taken lives? She had made herself unfit, unclean for a noaidi's work. Even Slahtti did not return. Somehow she had failed him.

It was easier to believe such a ready explanation than to consider the other: that the spirits were afraid.

Tahvo's concentration broke like a rotten bowstring. The absolution she sought was as unreachable as the spirits themselves. Perhaps if she had used the dreambark...

But that would not change the past. It would not take away the stain of blood on her hands.

She let her fingers rest quietly on the rim of the drum and opened her eyes.

"Did I disturb you?" Cian asked.

"You did not." She wrapped the drum and returned it to her pack. "You are in pain?"

"No. I couldn't sleep. Rhenna...went to stand watch."

Tahvo heard the Ailu's disquiet as he spoke the warrior's name. Rhenna and Cian struck sparks off one another like a pair of flints, but Tahvo did not yet know if that fire might spread.

"Rhenna says that you drum to speak to your devas," Cian said. "Or is that a forbidden subject among your people?"

"Not forbidden." Tahvo crossed her legs and rested her palms on her knees. "You have come with questions."

He half smiled. "Many. Why did you drum? What did you ask your devas?"

Tahvo knew the shapechanger did not ask lightly, for she saw in his eyes a deep sadness and a longing stronger than hunger or thirst or physical pain. "I asked for the swift passage of the dead," Tahvo said. Her throat closed up, making words difficult. "I prayed for the peaceful guidance of their spirits beyond the Sky Veil."

"You mean the Wolfskins who died when you helped me escape?"

Among the Samah, it was said that tears were the melting of old ice trapped within the soul. Tahvo had not wept in a very long time. "The men I helped…to kill," she said. She lifted her hands, remembering how they had held the bow, fitted the shafts to the string, loosed the bone arrowheads to pierce bodies with terrible precision. "I am…I was a healer."

Cian pushed himself away from the wall and moved into the light of her small fire. "You are still a healer, Tahvo. I am sorry you were driven to kill for my sake."

"I have begun to learn that the ways of the Samah are not the ways of this world."

"I have learned that there are as many ways as there are people."

"You have traveled far," she said, meeting his gaze.

"Perhaps not as far as you."

He did not speak of distance measured in hours or days of walking. "You are wiser than I."

Cian turned his head so that Tahvo glimpsed only his sharp, troubled profile. "What did you see when you…spoke to me in my other shape?"

He pulled the cloak tighter and tighter until Tahvo was sure it must tear in two pieces.

"I don't always remember what happens. Not in the way a man would. Did I…fight?"

All at once she began to understand. "You stood with Rhenna. You would not leave her. But you did not kill."

He released a long breath and bowed his head. He dreaded the prospect of taking lives as much as she, but she felt there was much more he did not say.

"You call me blessed and give me the benefit of wisdom," he said. "But I was not wise enough to free myself from the Wolf-skins' cage. *I* did not summon the snow and ice."

"That was Slahtti. He came with me from the North. When I saw that Rhenna had found another Ailu and faced so many warriors, I drummed to ask for his help."

He frowned. "You and Rhenna were not traveling together."

"She told me not to follow her from the mountains, but Slahtti showed me the way. He awakened the spirits of this land who brought the cold—water spirits who dwell in the earth and the sky and know the ways of winter."

"But the wolf obeyed your summoning." Cian leaned forward, suddenly intent. "I have met men and women who claimed power from the devas, but it was never as great as they believed. You're not like them. You know more about my people than you learned from Rhenna in some chance meeting. Who are you, Tahvo of the Samah?"

She hesitated. "The spirits grant me visions."

"Visions?"

"Of other places and peoples. Of what will…what may come to pass." She pushed the terrible images out of her mind. "The visions sent me from my own lands. I knew that I must go south, but there was much I did not see. Then I met Rhenna. And Augwys."

"You said my people are in the South."

"With the Stone God."

"Some deva of the Arrhidaean Empire?"

Some deva…as if any natural spirit could intend the destruction of all that lived. "I do not know this 'empire.' Does the word not mean one land ruling over others?"

"Many others. Many lands. All ruled by one man."

"We do not have such men in my country. But the metal warriors—the Hellenes—belong to the empire? They also serve the Stone God?"

Drops of sweat stood out on Cian's forehead beneath the fringe of black hair. "The empire is over two hundred leagues from here. I am the only Ailu who ever willingly left the Shield, and I've never been south of the foothills. How does the empire know of us? What does a foreign deva want with my people?"

"I do not know." She had so pitifully little to offer after all that had happened. "But in the Stone God resides evil that threatens every creature of the earth. Those blessed of the spirits must see most clearly. The Ailuri have a purpose. Do you not feel this?"

His eyes turned flat and cold. "I'm neither deva nor seer, but if this Stone God took my people, I will find it."

"You will not be alone. We will go together."

He shuddered so violently that the cloak almost flew from his naked shoulders. "*She* will never permit it." He turned toward the cave's mouth.

Soon Tahvo heard the footsteps.

"Cian. Tahvo." Flickering light preceded Rhenna into the chamber. Her small torch picked out the lines and planes of her face as if they had been chipped from bone. "I've seen the enemy. It seems the Neuri have deserted their allies." Her mouth twisted in a humorless smile. "Tahvo's deva-wolf did his work well, at least in slowing them down."

"The Hellenes are still afoot?" Cian asked.

She looked at the Ailu without seeing him. "Yes. The Southerners' armor makes their movements easy to track as long as they remain on the steppe, but they're advancing steadily. We'll have to risk traveling by day—stay among the trees and wrap any metal so reflections won't betray us."

"It will make no difference," Cian said. "They won't stop."

Rhenna swung on him. "You have suffered at their hands. Are you still so ready to let them take you without a fight?" She bit hard on her lower lip. "We know too little of their ways. I will not underestimate them." She dismissed Cian with a lift of her shoulder and turned to Tahvo. "Will your deva help us again?"

"I do not know." Tahvo thought of the spirits' bewildering fear. Rhenna honored her by accepting her as part of the company, but the warrior asked more than Tahvo dared promise.

"You've already done the Free People a great service," Rhenna said. "You are welcome to come with us to Heart of Oaks." She glanced at Cian's borrowed cloak. "You'll travel as a man from now on. I have spare clothing that should cover you."

"Your leg—" Cian began.

"It doesn't trouble me." As if to prove her claim, Rhenna put her weight on the injured limb and marched from the chamber.

Cian watched her go. "She is a hard woman," he said in a voice stripped of feeling. "Her only purpose is to take me back. But there is no safety in the Shield's Shadow. Not for me."

"Not for anyone," Tahvo whispered.

"What will you do?"

He asked as if she had a choice. "I will go with you and Rhenna."

"Then stay close. And tell me, not Rhenna, if you have any more visions."

He left the chamber. Tahvo collected her belongings, lit a small branch to guide her way and put out the tiny fire.

Rhenna and Cian waited outside the cave, gazing down onto the steppe. The Ailu wore trousers and a shirt borrowed from the warrior. They were too tight through the shoulders and chest, but they were better protection than the cloak. His feet were bare. Rhenna had covered or removed the metal pieces on her armor and weapons, and dulled the horses' tack with dust.

Tahvo turned her coat inside out to hide the small bronze, bone and silver tokens that hung amidst the fur. The late afternoon sun filtered softly through the leaves of the trees on the hillsides, but it glared without mercy upon the plain below, reflecting the armor of the Southern warriors.

"We go east and north, higher into the hills, and double back when we can," Rhenna said. She took the gelding's lead rope and, leading him behind her, clambered up and away from the cave. Tahvo noticed that she was careful not to let her companions see any effect of her injury. She would pretend it did not exist.

Spirits lend her strength.

Cian took the second horse, but he didn't move to follow. He gazed, transfixed, at the drifting light on the steppe.

Tahvo tugged at his shirt. He blinked and stared at her face without recognition. Tremors racked his body.

"My brothers," he said.

"You will find them."

The Ailu bent his head, but the muscles in his jaw jumped and tightened. He pulled his horse's rope and began to climb.

Rhenna was not surprised when Tahvo chose to remain with her and Cian, nor did she waste time speculating on the healer's incomprehensible bond with the devas. That was the province of Earthspeakers; let them deal with her at Heart of Oaks.

Rhenna's business was keeping all three of them alive.

They traveled quickly on foot for the first few hours, leading the horses higher into the hills. Rhenna searched for paths that would leave the least trace of their passage, seeking forest cover whenever possible. At every stop for rest or water she examined the horses' hooves and legs for strain or lameness. Both animals must be prepared to run at a moment's notice.

She kept the waterskins filled and divided her limited supply of salted meat, cheese and dried fruit between Cian and Tahvo, leaving her own portion untouched. She listened for the echoes of falling stones that might warn of their pursuers' movements, since the rocky hills and deep, clefted valleys hid even the bold Hellenes from sight. Occasionally she caught glimpses of flashing metal and knew that the Southerners were gaining ground.

When she could spare a moment from the work of survival, Rhenna watched Cian.

She didn't dare trust him. Though he gave the appearance of resigned obedience and did not attempt to return to panther shape, she was certain of only two things: he'd abandoned both his duty and his people, and he was still too ready to throw his life away.

He was a coward.

He was a boy. A boy whose golden eyes had looked out from a face filled with fear and confusion. A boy who'd broken his own people's taboos, just as she had. A boy all bone and sinew, growing too fast for his body.

The boy who had witnessed Rhenna's shame.

But he was a child no longer. The thinness Rhenna had taken for frailty was lean, taut muscle, flexing and pulling against the snug wool of his borrowed shirt. His bare feet found purchase on the most difficult slopes. He never asked to stop. He kept pace or ranged ahead, turning back only when Tahvo stumbled under the weight of her coat and pack. He moved with natural grace in spite of the abuse he had received at the Neuri's hands.

But he was also human. He perspired as she and Tahvo did. His black hair hung in his face no matter how many times he tossed it behind his shoulders, and he wouldn't bind it up. He favored the foot he had cut in panther form, though he refused Tahvo's offer of bandages.

And his wary gaze met Rhenna's again and again, as if he expected her to seek some personal revenge for the past. Every time she saw him, her heart beat fast and her flesh tightened. Every time he looked at her, he saw the scar—and remembered.

The scar burned, but Rhenna didn't touch it. Far worse was the leg. Though Tahvo had treated the wound with expertise equal to that of any Healer of the Free People, Rhenna knew that only time and rest would complete the cure. She was keenly aware that it would hinder her in a fight.

And a fight must come. Rhenna had pledged not to underestimate the Hellenes' skill and determination, but she'd expected their heavier armor and accoutrements to put them at a disadvantage in the hills. She hadn't believed they would make such rapid and unrelenting progress. Her best efforts had neither slowed nor thrown off their pursuit.

By the time night fell, Rhenna was compelled to call a halt. She picketed the horses at the edge of a small meadow, close to the shelter of trees. The moonlit clearing gave her an unobstructed view of the country they had left behind.

To the west, the meadow ended in a steep slope of talus and hardy shrubs. At the bottom, a perennial stream cut a deep, narrow valley from north to south, and beyond that, the ground rose again in a series of steplike hills.

The Hellenes made camp on one of those hills, vaunting their position with the red glow of firelight. Cian, Tahvo and Rhenna did without a fire, settling within a small circle of pines. Tahvo insisted on checking Rhenna's dressings. The wound was clean, with only the expected drainage, but Tahvo could do little without the means to brew her potions. After much muttering in her native tongue, Tahvo left the circle, doubtless to address her spirits.

"How is your leg?"

Cian's low voice should not have startled Rhenna. She always knew exactly where he was, what he did, how he looked, even in darkness. His eyes held their own lambent glow. She found herself searching for the cat within the human frame, contours like flowing water, sinuous tail, mask of slitted eyes and gleaming teeth....

"It pains you," he said.

"It does not."

"I never heard that the Free People were good liars. Now I know why."

"If you left the Shield as a boy," she said, "you could never have known us."

He flinched. "Even Ailuri live among your people as young children. They are not given a choice to stay or go."

"I never heard that Ailuri yearned to return to their mothers' breasts."

His face receded into shadow. "We are what we are made to be," he said, his voice a rumble in his chest. "Your Elders shaped you into a warrior. Is that not all you ever wanted?"

He needed no claws to slash and tear. White anger washed the gnawing pain from Rhenna's leg.

"I know what I am," she said. "You named yourself a coward before you came to manhood. But it is not my place to judge your worthiness."

His sigh ruffled the short hairs on her arms like the winds she hadn't felt for so many days. "There was a time when you doubted your place and your destiny. Do you think you earned Ailuri violence all those years ago?"

Every word he spoke made a perversion of the world. Rhenna felt for the nearest tree, pulling herself to her feet. "Tahvo thinks the devas sent me to find you," she said. "If that's so, they have no love for either of us."

"Tahvo would say they have some greater purpose."

Rhenna's fingers bit into bark. "Do you believe that?"

"I don't know."

His humble admission drained her anger, leaving only pain to fill the hollows it left behind. "You swore to find your people," she said. "Such oaths are sacred. I can promise nothing, but…" She closed her eyes and continued before she could change her mind. "When you are safe with the Earthspeakers, I will petition to speak before the Council. If the Elders send warriors to search for the Ailuri, I'll ask to accompany them. I will search in your place."

He looked up, eyes glittering through the heavy tangle of his hair. "You would do this, even though you hate us?"

Hate? Rhenna stepped away from the tree, rejecting the desire to cling like an unweaned babe. Was it hatred that had sustained her through the years of shunning and loneliness? When Cian had told her who he was, how he had witnessed the inception of her punishment, had she hated then?

Your anger is not for me, Rhenna of the Free People. Tahvo's words. Tahvo, who saw too much with her silver eyes.

"A warrior saves hatred for her enemies," she said, hardly knowing whom she answered.

"I am not your enemy, Rhenna."

She met his hooded gaze, and once again she was beside the mating bower on the hillside, looking into the golden eyes of her lover, hungry for his touch, his weight upon her body....

Cian leaped to his feet. Rhenna lost her balance, jarred her injured leg and swayed with waves of fresh agony.

"You are not my friend," she snarled. "Remember that, Ailu."

"Rhenna."

She warded him off with outstretched arms and turned from the unquiet pools of his eyes, all her concentration focused on putting one foot in front of the other. By the time she reached the horses, she was able to walk instead of hobble.

The meadow collected the light of moon and stars, bright enough for Rhenna to find her way. Cool wind curled under her chin and tickled her cheek. She brushed it aside as if it were a troublesome insect, bent low and started across the grass.

She found Tahvo sprawled prone in the center of the meadow, her drum flung beyond her reach.

"Tahvo!" Rhenna knelt beside the healer's body and carefully turned her onto her back. Tahvo's eyes were open, staring up at the moon like yearning earthbound sisters.

"Tahvo," she repeated. "Do you hear me?" She put her ear to Tahvo's chest and heard the breath move normally, the heartbeat slow but steady. Her illness was not of the body.

Rhenna had seen such a look in young warriors suffering from battle-shock. The malady could strike long after the fighting was finished, but Rhenna had never considered the healer susceptible. Tahvo had fought the Neuri with the same unshakable calm and fortitude she had shown since their first meeting in the Shield.

Fool, Rhenna thought, unsure whether she meant Tahvo or herself. The only cure for battle-shock was time. If it was battle-shock at all.

Tahvo claimed to have visions. She'd spoken of evil and destruction as if they touched her only at a great distance. Her stubborn, pestiferous serenity had broken but once—when she had performed Augwys's death rites.

She had screamed. She'd screamed as if something worse than death waited on the other side.

Asteria's blood. The cause of the fit was of no importance. Perhaps Cian could reach her, as she had reached him when he walked as a cat.

Rhenna crouched to lift Tahvo in her arms. She remembered the drum at the last moment and balanced it on the healer's chest. Tahvo stirred, and Rhenna eased her back to the ground.

The Northwoman flailed out with her fists. Rhenna grabbed her wrists to keep her still.

"I did not know," Tahvo whispered. "I did not understand."

"Know what?" Rhenna asked. "Tahvo, look at me!"

"I should have seen. Why did I not see?"

"You can tell me everything when we return to camp."

Tahvo sat up. "Where is Cian?"

"Cian is safe. I'll take you to him."

Without warning Tahvo sprang to her feet and began to run—not toward the circle of trees but in the opposite direction. Rhenna leaped after her. She caught up with Tahvo at the steep edge of the riverbank.

Cian was already there, perched on the rim as if he could cross the valley in an easy jump. Fingers clawed at empty air above the sheer drop. He laughed.

"I am coming, my brothers!"

Chapter Ten

Rhenna grabbed Cian's shirt and tried to pull him away. He flung himself forward, nearly hurling them both into the chasm.

"Let me go!" he cried hoarsely.

In but a single day, Rhenna had become familiar with the many tones of Cian's voice, from chastened whisper to rebellious growl. This note was new, and it was not sane.

"Release me," he begged.

"Never."

Lips curled back in an unreasoning snarl, Cian lurched. Rock crumbled under his feet and rattled into darkness, striking water with a muffled splash.

"Do not let him go," Tahvo said behind Rhenna. "It is the stones."

"It calls me," Cian said, panting through clenched teeth. "Can't you see, bitch of a female? The light—"

The light.

Rhenna balanced to stand with Cian on the lip of the drop, twisting her fingers in his shirt. His eyes were no longer lit by moon and stars. They gathered the fevered luminescence of the Hellenish camp and turned the same infernal red.

Not a fire. *Red stones.*

Just as Cian swayed forward again, she felt a surprisingly strong grip seize her belt and pull her back from the brink. She, Cian and Tahvo tumbled into the grass.

Tahvo rolled to her knees. "We must leave this place."

Rhenna wasted no time wondering at the healer's swift recovery. Together, she and Tahvo dragged Cian away from the chasm and back across the meadow. He resisted, never turning from the light that so enraptured him, but he made no effort to hurt his captors. Rhenna was well acquainted with his passive strength by the time they had wrestled him to the ground beneath the trees.

"Bind him," Tahvo said between gasps for breath.

"Can you speak to him? Bring him out of this madness?"

Tahvo bit her lip and shook her head. While she pinned Cian's legs with the weight of her body, Rhenna secured his hands with spare rope from her saddlepacks. Touching him was difficult. Every contact drove tiny arrows of sensation from her fingers and hands into the core of her chest and belly.

"You will not hurt him," Tahvo said. "You could not."

Trust the healer to speak when words were most unwelcome. "He's always wanted to give himself up," Rhenna said, tightening the knots at Cian's back. "What's different now?"

Tahvo tried to force a small bowl of water between Cian's lips. "This is not his choice."

"These stones have so much power?"

"You saw how the metal warriors fought the spirits' wall of ice. We must go on."

"We'll be risking the horses. Can you do anything?"

The Northwoman's eyes took on the haunted stare of battle-shock, and Rhenna knew she was not as well as she appeared. "Help me get Cian on Dory's back," Rhenna said.

They struggled to lift Cian up and over the mare's saddle. Rhenna improvised a harness out of the remaining rope and hoped it would hold him.

Tahvo took Chaimon's lead. Rhenna led Dory out of the trees and up the next slope. The glow of the Southerners' camp remained on the other side of the chasm.

Every step had to be placed with care because of Dory's burden. Only moonlight kept them from disaster. For a time Cian was blessedly still, and then he began to struggle with silent ferocity. He twisted about in the saddle, upsetting Dory's balance. Rhenna took hold of the mare's bridle and murmured words of praise and comfort.

"It is not far enough," Tahvo said.

"You'll have to walk beside him while I lead the horses," Rhenna said. "Keep him quiet. You must—"

Cian shuddered, flung back his head and began to change shape on Dory's back. Black fur sprouted from his bound fists. The snarling mask of a panther contorted his features, glinting pale at the tips of bared fangs. The ropes stretched thin.

Dory half reared, showing the whites of her eyes. Rhenna pulled the mare's head down and pinched her nostrils to muffle her cries. Chaimon struck rock with his hooves.

Tahvo laid her hand on Cian's knee. "Peace," she said.

Cian ceased his struggles. Fur receded. The ravaged lines of his face became human again.

Tahvo set off again in the direction they had been traveling. Time moved as slowly as the moon in its arc. Rhenna took Tahvo's place in the lead, seeking a safe descent across the next ravine. She saw no sign of the crimson light. As long as they followed a southwesterly course, the way seemed almost too easy.

But once they turned east, Cian began to fight. He pulled on his ropes and wrenched his body to face the way they had come. The only sounds he made were grunts and growls, but his demeanor was eloquent enough. He was incapable of human understanding.

Dory stopped and would not be moved. A sharp, cool northern wind poured over the hillside and splashed at Rhenna's feet. The ache in her leg flared and as quickly subsided.

Tahvo placed her hand on Dory's neck and turned the mare's head south. Dory took one willing step and then another. Cian was quiet. Tahvo angled east again. Dory balked; Cian tugged against his bonds. North, and both horse and rider quivered. South once more with no trouble at all.

Rhenna had seen such magic after she had found Pantaris and sought to pursue the raiders, but this time Cian himself was the barrier.

"The Hellenes follow from the west," Tahvo said. "Cian resists when we turn east toward your country, or even to the north. But if we turn south—"

"Toward the empire," Rhenna said grimly.

"Toward Cian's people."

"Into a trap." Rhenna seized Dory's lead and pulled, compelling the mare to move east. Cian jerked back and forth, bucking in the saddle. Dory lashed the air with her hind legs.

No living creature within five leagues could have failed to hear Cian's bellow. Rhenna imagined that even the earth shook under her feet, and then she realized it was no illusion. A crack split the ground less than a hand's-width from Dory's prancing hooves. It cleft rock and dirt alike, racing south like a bolt of black lightning. Pebbles bounced and rolled.

Rhenna had heard that such earth trembling was known in the eastern tribal lands, but never in the Shield. She caught and held Dory's bridle, praying that Tahvo had done the same with Chaimon. Cian was rigid, face lifted toward the sky.

The ground heaved once more and lay quiet. Then the wind

came. It made hardly a sound as it bore down on horses and women alike. Tahvo's short body kept precarious balance in the gale, but Chaimon strained on his lead. Small branches and twigs snapped from protesting trees, slapping Rhenna's cheek. Driving in one inevitable direction.

"Spirit-winds," Tahvo shouted over the storm.

Rhenna spat debris from her mouth. "I've heard them before."

Tahvo gave her a startled look. Rhenna knew without asking that the healer had no power to halt the gale, just as she'd been unable to summon her wolf to stop the Hellenes a second time. They must go south. For the moment.

They walked alongside the crack in the earth, which stretched in a jagged line for half a league, following the contours of the land. Tahvo stopped once to examine the cleft. Exhaustion had carved new lines in the healer's face. Cian was eerily silent.

Their way gradually descended toward the steppe. The wind lent human and equine feet uncanny speed, but the moon was finally setting. It lingered just long enough to reveal the first unbroken stretch of grassland.

But the steppe was no sanctuary. Both moon and stars told Rhenna that her people's borders were still well to the east. She faced into the wind, narrowing her eyes against the stinging cold. A muddy red glow hung as if suspended on the face of the hill they had just left behind. Not even the shaking of the earth had stopped the Hellenes.

And still the wind blew.

Rhenna glimpsed the faint outline of a clump of shrub-sized oaks just to the west and led the horses to shelter. Chaimon and Dory crowded into the small space, protected from the wind. Rhenna made sure that Cian was still secure, hunkered down at the horses' feet and beckoned Tahvo to join her.

The healer leaned close, cupping her hands around her mouth. "You understand these spirit-winds?"

If ever there had been a time for plain speaking, it was now. Tahvo's knowledge might still save them. "In my own country," Rhenna said, "spirit-winds like these sent me from my post with the herds to the village of Sun's Rest, where I found the people slaughtered by invaders."

A swift succession of emotions crossed Tahvo's face, horror, then sympathy she had the wisdom not to speak aloud. "The spirits *sent* you," she said at last.

"I didn't ask to hear them. They led me to a place of death, where I could do nothing to help."

"They speak to you again."

Rhenna looked toward the south, and Tahvo followed her bleak stare. "When I saw what had happened at Sun's Rest," Rhenna said, "I pursued the barbarians into the west. The devas stopped me." She poked viciously at a tuft of grass. "I can neither call nor command them. They've given me no aid since I left Heart of Oaks."

"Even when they led you to Cian?"

Rhenna uprooted the tuft and let the pieces fly away on the wind. "Our devas don't venture beyond the Shield's Shadow."

"Slahtti showed himself to me only when I left the land of the Samah. This is not his working."

"Nothing is as it should be," Rhenna said. "I feel——" She caught her errant braid and twisted it between her hands. "There were no devas to protect the people of Sun's Rest or the Ailuri when the raiders attacked. Now these winds push us south when our only hope lies in the Shield. Do they wish our destruction?"

"The spirits do not destroy," Tahvo said with all her former certainty. "They sent you to witness the evil that comes to your land. They chose you."

"If you have no practical means to stop the Hellenes or these blighted winds, be quiet and let me think."

Tahvo glanced up at Cian, bent low and motionless over Dory's withers. "What lies just south of this place?"

Rhenna was absurdly relieved to hear a sensible question. "These are the northern lands of the Skudat, a man-tribe that controls hundreds of leagues in the steppe."

"Like the Neuri?"

"Far more numerous."

"Do you fight them?"

"They have been allies." A few words would never suffice to explain the complexity of that relationship. "They usually——" She broke off, alert to the subtle change in Tahvo's expression. "Do you suggest that we go to the Skudat for help?"

Tahvo ducked her head. "I do not know them," she said, her voice muffled by her fur hood, "but they are in the spirit-wind's path."

Rhenna snorted and tried to ignore the furious itching in her leg. The thought had not occurred to her, and with reason. The northeastern Skudat, unlike their more sedentary cousins in the south and west, followed their herds of cattle and sheep across the steppe. The nearest band might be anywhere within fifty leagues of this little patch of grass.

And the Skudat were ruled by men, even if their women were less subdued than those of other man-tribes. Men in any numbers were untrustworthy, capricious and cruel.

Still, Tahvo's idea had merit. The northern tribes wouldn't welcome the Hellenes. Even a small band could stop the soldiers.

Rhenna grabbed a handful of Chaimon's coarse tail and stood. "Are you satisfied?" she shouted into the gale.

Tahvo touched her arm and pointed at Cian. The Ailu sat erect, glaring down at them with the kind of indignant puzzlement that could only come with sanity.

"What have you done?" he demanded.

His question wiped the ridiculous smile from Rhenna's face. Cian was sane enough, and genuinely angry. The Hellenes and

their red stones had well and truly stolen his mind. He didn't remember what had happened in the meadow, or in all the time
since. He had awakened a bound prisoner with no explanation but
Rhenna's final words to him. *You are not my friend. Remember that,
Ailu.*

If she were in his place, she would judge herself betrayed—
somehow rendered unconscious and slung onto a horse like a
bundle of furs. But if he knew the truth, that he had turned into
a mindless beast at but a glimpse of the Hellenes' unnatural
light...

Cian flexed his shoulders, testing the ropes. "Untie me."

"I can't," Rhenna said. She glanced at Tahvo. "We've delayed
too long."

"Tahvo," Cian said. "Rhenna, this is not necessary."

The rough panic in his voice shriveled Rhenna's resolve. *No better than the Neuri with their cage...*

She gathered the horses' reins and turned away.

"Rhenna!"

She sealed her ears to his pleading. Tahvo trotted up beside her.
"Cian...he does not remember."

"If he knows how easily the Hellenes controlled him, he'll lose
what courage he has. Tell him I decided I couldn't risk trusting
him when I'm not at my full strength. Tell him you argued, and
I wouldn't listen. If he's angry, he won't have time to be afraid."

"I cannot lie."

"Then tell him nothing. When we reach the Skudat..." *If.* If
they could be found. If the Hellenes remained far enough behind.
"I'll let him go when we're either safe or have no hope left."

Tahvo fell back. Rhenna set a swift pace, striving in vain to out-
run her own petty fears.

Dawn came, and with it, the open steppe. Ahead lay rolling
grasslands and an immensity of sky, occasionally broken by the

moving shadows of small antelope herds or diving raptors. Dust and blowing vegetation raised a constant haze in the horses' wake. When the sun cleared the horizon, Rhenna mounted Chaimon and rode north as far as the wind would allow.

Sun glinted on iron and bronze. She turned back.

"We ride," she told Tahvo. She pulled the healer up behind her. Tahvo wrapped her arms around Rhenna's waist and muttered what might have been a prayer.

Rhenna clucked Chaimon into a lope. Dory followed without urging. Cian couldn't have stopped the mare even if his hands were free.

Rhenna observed the lay of the land and gradually worked toward a riverbed contoured by the darker greens of small trees and shrubs. She didn't know the river's name or course, but it tended south and slightly west, directly into the heart of Skudat country and the best grazing lands.

Chaimon and Dory splashed eagerly in the ankle-deep water. Rhenna dismounted, made the ritual invocation out of habit, and let the horses drink. She filled the waterskins upstream and held one to Cian's mouth. He turned his head aside, jaw set. The wind made dark, tilted slits of his eyes.

They rode along the river for another fifteen leagues, stopping frequently to rest. The journey was all too familiar in its flavor of helpless urgency. Rhenna cursed when the river curved east, intersecting the wind's relentless path.

She reined Chaimon to face the receding watercourse. Tahvo loosened her death grip around Rhenna's waist.

"The horses can't continue much farther at this pace," Rhenna said. "This would be a good time to call your wolf."

Tahvo's warm breath puffed in a sigh. "I am sorry."

"Never apologize for the whims of devas. They—"

Her words fell into silence. The winds had ceased. Cian stared to the south, his face flushed and taut.

"What do the devas say now?" Rhenna asked the air.

"They say," Cian growled, "that we are not alone."

Chapter Eleven

"Skudat," Rhenna said. "We've found them."

The horsemen appeared as only a smudge on the horizon, but Cian knew they were already riding to meet the intruders. He pulled on the ropes and considered, not for the first time, the risks of changing shape and slicing the ropes with his teeth.

Surely Rhenna would have accounted for that. She would be prepared to strike him down if he attempted to escape. And where could he run, except into the arms of strangers?

Rhenna turned Chaimon and rode up beside Dory, drawing her knife. "Hold still," she commanded.

She grabbed Cian's shoulder to steady him and deftly cut the ropes. They fell from his body in several long pieces. Dory side-stepped, and Cian grabbed instinctively for her mane.

His numb fingers missed their hold, but Rhenna caught Dory's reins and held the mare until sensation returned to Cian's limbs. Tahvo peered at Cian from her perch on Chaimon's rump, her ex-

pression grave and sad, as it had been since he had awakened on
the steppe with no memory of the journey. He had sensed many
times that she wished to speak, but Rhenna made that impossible.

Rhenna was unfathomable. If he concentrated, he could remember the last thing he'd seen before the dark: Rhenna's face
twisted in agony and loathing, her arms thrust out to push him
away lest he touch her before she fell. And just before that, a denial of hatred he had dared to believe for the span of a heartbeat.
Until…

You are not my friend. He remembered those words, as well, and
her command for him to remain at the camp. There had been a
light, and a sensation of falling. Fighting…something.

Rhenna must have drugged him, though he didn't know how
or when she had done it. Tahvo would not have helped without a
compelling reason. Rhenna must have convinced her that Cian was
a danger to himself, if not to them.

But what had provoked Rhenna to take such drastic action? He
had told her he was not her enemy. He had looked into her
eyes…and, just as before, when she had found him huddled mis-
erably in the Neuri's cage, he had *seen* himself with her on a hillside lush with spring—wanting and being wanted, starving for this
woman's embrace, one step away from completion….

"Listen to me," Rhenna said, shattering the dream. "We go to
the Skudat because they have long been allies of the Free People,
and the Hellenes will be forced to abandon their pursuit if they're
confronted by the tribes in open country."

Cian massaged his wrists. "Have you untied me because you no
longer fear I'll try to escape, or because you want me able to
fight?"

"The Skudat are not Neuri. They respect courage, and they
have laws to bind them. There will be no need to fight as long as
we behave as honorable guests in their land. You'll ride free with

your head up, Ailu, because that is what the Skudat expect of a warrior."

Cian laughed through his teeth. "Is that what I am? A warrior? A trusted companion, worthy of respect?" He glanced at Tahvo. "No one would mistake our healer for one of yours, but at least she's a woman. When did a lone Sister ever ride so far from the Shield's Shadow with a grown male at her side? Or do these tribesmen know how to recognize an Ailu?"

"My people never speak of the Ailuri to foreigners."

"The Ailuri never came out of their mountains," he said. "Except for me. Yet the Hellenes and their empire knew of us. The Neuri knew where to hunt for us. Why not these Skudat?"

"Because our warriors and Seekers deal with the Skudat every year. Our Earthspeakers would know if they had betrayed us."

"As they knew why the Ailuri vanished?"

He was savagely, detestably pleased at her momentary confusion, but he knew it wouldn't last. Rhenna was too practiced at seeing only what a warrior should see, knowing only what a warrior should know.

"The northern Skudat despise the Southerners with their walled towns and foreign ways," she said stiffly. "They would sooner die as a race than become hunting dogs for another people."

"Yet the empire's soldiers must have crossed Skudat land to reach the Neuri."

"Skudat lands are wide, and the Hellenes have proven themselves cunning. That's all the more reason why the Skudat chiefs will welcome warning of these intruders."

"The spirit-winds led us to this place," Tahvo said softly. "Did you feel them, Cian?"

Even in a gray haze of oblivion, he had sensed that constant pressure at his back. "Where did they come from?"

"Perhaps the Shield's devas finally took an interest in your fate,"

Rhenna said. "It doesn't matter. The Skudat have no need to know what *you* are, Cian of the Ailuri."

Cian was close to hating that deliberately blind conviction. "These tribes may not know the Ailuri," he said, "but *we* know that the Skudat sire many of the Free People's children."

Her face flushed from neck to hairline. Tahvo gazed at Rhenna and then Cian with curious, knowing eyes.

"It's true," he said to the healer. "The Free People keep no men, so they seek them out when they want offspring to train as warriors and craftswomen and farmers." He stared at Rhenna's mouth, sickened by the things he imagined. "Have you been among these Skudat before, Rhenna? Is that why you're so sure of them?"

Rhenna met his stare. "I entered a Skudat camp only once, when I was a new-made warrior on my first expedition beyond our borders. I was not left ignorant."

Cian dropped his gaze from the burning mockery in hers. Once he had fled the violence of an Ailu in rut, appalled at the prospect of facing the same beast within himself. Yet here it was, raging and clawing because it sensed a threat to its desires.

Was that the beast Rhenna had felt compelled to bind and carry like the hapless victim of a mad dog's bite?

He could have begged pardon and assuaged Rhenna's anger, but the humiliation of captivity was still too fresh. "I'll concede your superior knowledge," he said, "if you'll trust me not to run."

A fool might have mistaken the look in her eyes for remorse.

"You would not risk Tahvo's life by giving the Skudat cause to doubt the story I tell them." The corner of her mouth twitched. "You might even hesitate to risk mine."

Remorse, and now humor at her own expense. A strange, pained acknowledgment of bonds she found difficult to accept—bonds woven not of Sisterhood or kinship but of necessity, shared adversity and attraction that defied all sense and understanding.

And what did *he* know of such bonds, he who had left all bonds behind nine years ago?

Cian looked away. "Tell me what to do."

So she told him, sketching a hasty plan she must have devised while he raged against her in futile silence. Tahvo listened, as well, nodding to show that she understood her part.

By the time Rhenna finished, the Skudat horseman had taken the shape of seven ominous, sword-wielding creatures, half man and half beast. Their cries of challenge rang back and forth in the pall of dust surrounding them.

Rhenna gave Cian a final stern look and turned Chaimon to face the tribesmen. The Skudat charged at a full gallop, swinging iron swords over their heads. Vivid colors and patterns bordered the hems and seams of coats and trousers, which were cut and designed much like Rhenna's. Bow and arrow cases elaborately worked in leather and gold bounced against the tribesmen's left hips.

"If they meant to kill us," Rhenna said, "we would be full of arrows. They but test our courage."

Cian imitated Rhenna's pose of easy assurance, letting the reins hang loose in his hands. Tahvo straightened at Rhenna's back. Cian nodded to the healer with a smile he hardly felt.

Then the horsemen were upon them. At the last possible moment the horde broke apart like a river against a great stone, some riding to the left and others to the right. Blades sliced air in extravagant arcs. Hoarse voices competed to produce the most deafening yells.

"Irpata!" they cried. *"Irpata!"*

Rhenna cocked her head slightly, as if amused by the tribesmen's antics.

One of the Skudat reined his horse directly before Cian. His hair and beard were dark and matted, his eyes warrior-mad under his metal-studded cap. He addressed Cian in a guttural voice, while his companions closed up the circle.

"I do not understand you," Cian said honestly. He held up both hands to show them empty of weapons.

Rhenna spoke, her voice ringing and bright as the clash of new swords. The tongue she used was the Skudat's own, phrases couched in the rhythms of ritual. She made a sweeping gesture toward the north.

The Skudat looked at one another with scowls and mutters. The leader raised his hand. Suddenly he wheeled his horse about and returned the way he had come. Chaimon followed. Cian touched his heels to Dory's barrel and kept close to Rhenna, careful not to let any of the Skudat escort come between them.

Everything must have gone as Rhenna had hoped. She rode erect, grace and strength in the deceptively relaxed contours of her body. No fear could touch such a woman, nor any harm come to those who rode with her. The Skudat couldn't fail to believe whatever she chose to tell them. And if they were men, as they obviously intended to prove with their whoops and flourishes, they must be aware of her beauty.

I was not left ignorant. Did she see these barbarians as potential mates, or merely as means to an end?

Cian realized he was staring only when Rhenna looked at him with raised brows and lips pressed in disapproval. He gathered up his slack reins and gave his attention to the increasing commotion. Other horsemen had ridden up to join the original seven, many of them boys with skinny legs dangling over their mounts' bare backs. One or two of the riders proved, on closer inspection, to be girls. They chattered all at once, steadfastly ignored by their elders.

An impressive herd of longhorn cattle grazed by the river, an ever-shifting pattern of brown hide broken every so often by the gray, red or black of a horse's coat. Oxen raised broad heads dripping mouthfuls of grass.

The river took another sharp bend, and suddenly the Skudat camp came into view. Color splashed the trampled grass; everywhere rode horsemen with their gaudily decorated garments, but even more striking were the heavy wagons and scattered tents, felt and leather stretched over skeletons of precious wood. The Skudat had covered nearly every surface with depictions of fantastic beasts, lions and horses. Golden armbands, belts and necklaces flashed among the long-gowned women tending fires or watching children. Meat roasted on spits, reminding Cian how long he and the women had gone without fresh food.

The escort wound its way between midden heaps and plunged into the swarm of activity that marked the center of camp. The leader of the Skudat company spoke to Rhenna and pointed to a small tent pitched near a wagon painted with geometric designs and animal shapes. Rhenna took her time dismounting. She untied the saddlepacks and helped Tahvo down, putting as much weight on her healing leg as she did on the other.

Two boys came to take the horses. Rhenna let them walk away without a flicker of concern. Throwing the most casual of glances in Cian's direction, she took Tahvo's elbow and walked toward the open flap of the small tent.

Cian felt the warriors behind him, leaving no space for retreat. He bent almost double and followed Rhenna into the tent. It had been made to hold only a few occupants; a single ragged fur served as both seat and blanket. The sloping walls were too close and too low. Tahvo doffed her pack and held it tightly.

Rhenna unfastened the unwieldy gorytos from her belt, unbelted her axe, and laid bow and arrows within easy reach. "Are we being watched?" she asked Cian in a whisper.

Cian eyed the tent flap and listened to the noise outside. "No one stands close enough to hear. Is this to be our cage?"

Rhenna shook her head. "We are not prisoners. I invoked the hearth right due any woman of the Free People. The warriors accepted what little I told them—they know the Hellenes are on their land."

"What is this *Irpata*?" Cian asked. "Is it a curse?"

"It means 'man slayer,'" she said blandly.

"They think highly of your people."

She ignored his barb. "I was told that the chief of this clan, one Orod, is too busy to see me. His son Farkas will soon be returning from a hunt. I'll give him the same story in greater detail—how my band of Sisters found the Hellenes treating with the Neuri near our borders and engaged them in battle. You two—" she glanced at Tahvo "—were captives from Northern lands who broke free and helped in the fight. Two Sisters survived. One has gone to inform the Free People of the Hellene incursion, while I've come to the Skudat. Because of the aid you rendered us, I permitted you to accompany me."

"They won't be angry that you led the Hellenes to their camp?" Cian asked.

"The Hellenes are trespassers and greatly outnumbered. I doubt they'll linger to face Orod's eager young men." She stared into Cian's eyes. "You feel...well?"

"Shouldn't I?" He gestured at her leg. "What of you?"

"It's healing. This is not the time to reveal disadvantage."

Cian was distracted from his reply by the rich, overwhelming scent of spit-roasted meat. The delightful smell accompanied the gold-bedecked young woman who appeared at the tent flap, carrying before her an intricately worked platter piled with steaming chunks of meat.

The woman half crouched just inside the tent's entrance and spoke to Rhenna in her language. Rhenna bowed her head and took the platter from the Skudat woman's hands. Cian's stomach loudly protested its emptiness. The young woman hid a smile and ducked back out of the tent. She briefly returned with a clay vessel of water and three small gold cups.

Rhenna set the tray down and gazed at the meat as if it were an enemy to be defeated.

"Is it tainted?" Cian asked, dizzy with the taste already in his mouth. "I smell nothing wrong."

"It's part of the guest-right. Eat." Rhenna leaned back and folded her arms across her chest. She glared at Tahvo. "Eat!"

Tahvo reached for the smallest piece. Cian was not so delicate. He quickly disposed of a third of the meat and politely withdrew to allow the women their shares.

Rhenna started on hers only after Tahvo indicated she was finished. The warrior dined neatly and deliberately, too practical to forgo the chance to eat as much as she could hold. Even so, several slices remained. Rhenna pushed the platter toward Cian. He finished the last pieces and was rinsing his hands with water from the jug when some new tumult started outside the tent.

"Horses," he said, sniffing the air. "Prey freshly killed."

Rhenna poked her head out the flap. "Farkas has returned. Be ready." She took the water vessel and dampened a scrap of cloth from the saddlepacks, bathing her hands and face. Her skin shone once the patina of dust was gone. She tidied the braids pinned at the crown of her head.

Cian's mouth went dry. There was nothing intimate about what she did, nothing but the pragmatic desire to be at her best when she faced a foreign chief. He had seen many women in his aimless wandering, but, except for Tahvo, had never met one so devoid of vanity as Rhenna of the Free People.

Devoid of vanity, to be sure, and also of mercy. She disregarded his rightful anger as if it were of no consequence. He wasn't yet so weak that he couldn't leave whenever he chose.

Leave her and Tahvo here alone…

Shouts of greeting and raucous laughter shook the thin walls of the tent. "Someone comes," he warned Rhenna. She adjusted her belt knife and faced the tent flap. Another young woman leaned inside and addressed Rhenna, waving toward Cian and Tahvo.

"Farkas has summoned us," Rhenna translated. "Remember. Keep silent."

Tahvo glanced anxiously at her pack and left it where it lay. Cian ran his fingers through his hair and followed the women from the tent. Twilight had descended on the steppe, but fires around the wagon circle picked out the sparkle of golden ornaments and iron blades. A score of young and brawny Skudat warriors gathered about one man who outshone the rest in the sheer abundance of his finery. Two bejeweled women hung adoringly on his arms.

The dandy paused in mid-laugh to glance toward his guests. He appeared to be younger than Rhenna, but he carried himself like one accustomed to being obeyed. His gold collar reflected the firelight and highlighted full, curved lips, arched nose and broad cheekbones. He reeked of some flowery scent, sweat and newly shed blood.

Cian hated him instantly.

"Farkas," Rhenna murmured. She advanced toward the chief's son, spoke some ritual greeting and clasped the Skudat's gold-banded wrist. Farkas was very slow about releasing her.

Rhenna inclined her head and beckoned Tahvo and Cian forward. Cian obeyed, aware of his ill-fitting, borrowed clothing and bootless feet. Tahvo bobbed a bow. Farkas dismissed her after a glance, but his dark eyes raked Cian with obvious contempt.

"I greet you, Farkas-son-of-Orod," Cian said in the tongue of a race the Skudat would likely never meet. "May your women be barren and your cattle fall to disease."

Farkas stared at him. Rhenna's shoulders twitched. The Skudat leader tilted back his head and laughed, returning his attention to Rhenna. He waved his hand at one of the women standing at his side. She produced a large bowl, partially covered in leather and wide enough to fill both her small hands. Farkas took it from her, swallowed a mouthful of its contents, and offered it to Rhenna.

The bowl was the upper half of a human skull.

Rhenna barely hesitated. She extended her hands to accept the grotesque thing from Farkas. Their fingers touched. A growl started in the pit of Cian's belly. Tahvo staggered against him like a drunkard just as Rhenna sipped from the bowl. Farkas's woman took it away, and the ceremony was finished.

Rhenna stood in the midst of the glittering males like a sparrow hawk among eagles. She had never looked so vulnerable. She spoke briefly to one of the warriors attending Farkas, strode across the wagon circle and nudged Cian toward the tent. Tahvo already waited by the entrance; she glanced at Rhenna's face and hurried inside.

What had felt like a trap now seemed a refuge. Cian crouched beside the tent wall, balancing on the balls of his feet. Tahvo took up her pack again.

"There is no cause for worry," Rhenna said. She smiled at Tahvo, but Cian received a glower. "I don't know what you said to Farkas, but you came very near provoking him. You will not do that again." She gripped the hilt of her knife. "Farkas wishes to speak to me at greater length about the Hellenes. I'll learn what he knows of them and what goes on among his Southern kin. You'll remain here and behave like a grateful guest. Get some sleep. Tahvo, is there anything you need?"

Tahvo shook her head, but her round face was solemn. "You will be safe?"

Rhenna grimaced. "Farkas offered me his skull-cup. I've heard that this is a sign of honor and great favor."

"I judged the Wolfskins too harshly," Cian muttered. He reached toward Rhenna and clenched his fist. "Don't trust him."

"I agree," Tahvo said. "Can we not go with you?"

Rhenna stood, her hair brushing the roof of the tent. "Farkas has treated us as allies and guests. I stand in the place of my people. I will not insult him by refusing." She turned to the tent flap. "Be patient."

Cian jumped up to follow her. Tahvo laid a gentle hand on his. He spun and paced from one side of the tent to the other. The need to change, to become a beast with few constraints and the freedom to act, sapped his wits.

And if he changed, what then? Whom would he serve by acting without thought or reason? What would he prove, save how little control he had over his own most savage nature?

Rhenna was a woman who worshiped discipline as others venerated their devas and gods. Blasphemy to her was choosing personal desires over the demands of duty. She was neither weak nor, as she had made so clear, ignorant.

But even she could make mistakes.

The soft, hollow tapping of Tahvo's fingers on the rim of her drum reminded Cian that he was not alone in his doubts. He dropped to his haunches beside her.

"Something is wrong," he said, half-afraid to interrupt. If Rhenna is in danger—"

She shook her head and looked at him with a helplessness he had never seen in her before. She was truly afraid, but not of the commonplace peril these Skudat might offer.

Something had happened during Cian's period of unconsciousness, something that had affected the healer deeply.

"Tell me," he urged. He poured the last of the water into one of the golden cups and pressed it into her hands. "Why did Rhenna drug and bind me? I know it was not your doing."

She took the cup, gazing blindly over the rim. "I was not to tell you."

"Because Rhenna commanded your silence? You must believe she had good reason. Did I drive her to it?"

"It was the red stones," Tahvo said quietly. "The Hellenes used them to call you. You would have gone to them if she had not stopped you."

The ground gave way beneath Cian's feet. Tahvo's words resounded with the truth of rejected memory, and forgotten details slashed at his mind like swords: the Wolfskins luring him into a trap, his attempts to free himself, the killing—and then the red light, devouring rationality and the will to fight his captors.

The Wolfskin headman had carried the stone about his neck. And the Hellene commander...

The stone had been part of him, a third, red eye in the center of his forehead.

Cian retreated as far as the tent would allow. "Did I become..." *The taste of human blood, the lust to kill.* He pressed his hands to his face.

"You did not hurt us," Tahvo said. "It was not your doing, Cian."

So even in human shape, he had lost control. What had Rhenna not told him?

"There is more," he said. "Do you believe the Skudat can stop the Hellenes?"

"These, perhaps."

Despair. Resignation. This was not the Tahvo he had begun to know. "What do you see, Tahvo?"

She closed her eyes. "Men fight men to rule each other. Spirits fight spirits...." She rocked back and forth, back and forth. "I did not understand. They were already weak."

"Who?"

"The spirits who saved us from the Neuri." A sole tear squeezed from beneath her lashes.

Cian crossed the tent and touched her damp cheek. "What happened to the devas, Tahvo?"

"Grandfather said they could leave our world whenever they chose. They remained out of love for the Samah, as long as we lived in harmony with their ways. They did not know fear. Or death." She opened her eyes and gazed at Cian with the pleading of a child. "How could they die?"

He acted on instinct, pulling her into his arms to counter his own shock. Devas were as eternal as sunrise and the coming of spring, an unquestioned part of nature. Their powers were limited, usually to the places they chose to inhabit. Some were benevolent and some remote; rarely were they hostile. They could ignore their worshipers, or—as Cian had learned most painfully—even desert those they had protected for millennia.

But they did not *die*.

"The spirits who helped us went away, but not to their own world," Tahvo whispered. "They were destroyed by the Stone God's servants."

Cian's guts churned at the memory of red light sucking, pulling mind apart from body. *It is possible,* some inner sense insisted. *It can be done.*

"If I had known…" Tahvo said, shaking enough for both of them. "If I had not called Slahtti…"

"In all my travels," Cian said, "I have heard the names of a hundred gods, but never of one whose influence reached so far. Yet the Stone God's followers have used its tokens to kill what should not die. Do you think you could have stopped something powerful enough to destroy a deva?"

"The spirits chose me, but I no longer hear them." She wriggled from his arms and sank to the furs, curling about her pack. Soon she slept, exhausted by her confession. Cian was not so fortunate. He resumed his pacing, contemplating the murder of devas and waiting for Rhenna's return.

She entered the tent some endless time later, pausing just inside the flap. Her eyes seemed unfocused, and she avoided Cain's gaze.

Tahvo sat up as if someone had shaken her. "You are well?" she asked Rhenna.

The question drove all other thoughts from Cian's mind. Rhenna appeared unhurt. But her hair was different, as if her braids had come undone and been hastily pinned back in place.

She smelled of kumys, damp skin and Farkas. The scents prod-
ded Cian like the Wolfskins' burning brands. He stepped over
Tahvo and peered into Rhenna's face.

"The Skudat," he said. "He touched you."

She looked through him. "I was in his tent."

"No." He seized her upper arms. "If he—"

One short, efficient thrust of Rhenna's shoulders knocked his
hands away. "Take care, Ailu," she said. "I am not one of these
bound women." She turned to Tahvo, shutting Cian out. "I have
done you a disservice, Tahvo," she said. "I allowed the Skudat to
know that you were the healer who mended my leg."

"You do me too much honor," Tahvo said faintly.

"Not unless you're eager to practice your skills in this camp.
The chief's son asks you to attend his father, Orod, who has been
suffering some ailment of the stomach. He says the clan's own
soothsayers have been unable to help him."

Tahvo picked up her drum. "I will try."

"*No.* No. We should stay here, together, until morning. The
Hellenes have left this region. Nothing prevents us from going to
my people. Farkas is obliged to return our horses well-fed and
rested, and provide us with the supplies we require to travel."
Rhenna's voice was hoarse, the words coming much too fast.

Cian moved closer to Tahvo, so that Rhenna could not evade
him. "You're afraid for Tahvo," he said, "just as she feared for you.
What harm can come to her among allies?" He hunched forward,
compelling her to meet his eyes. "What did Farkas do to you?"

Chapter Twelve

Cian shook with such force that Tahvo could feel the ground quiver. Her body remembered his gentle touch, but she sensed the coiled power lying in wait under his deceptively mortal skin.

"Rhenna?" Cian said sharply.

"I am a Sister of the Free People," Rhenna snapped. "If you mean to insult me with your questions, you are beginning to succeed." Her eyes held Tahvo's in unmistakable plea. "Farkas is sending his men to escort you to Orod. When they come, you must refuse."

Tahvo bent her head. "Will the Skudat not be angry?"

"You shouldn't waste your strength tending some old man's aches."

Tahvo knew that there were things Rhenna did not say and that Tahvo herself was too dull to hear. She had walked through a tormenting dream since that horrible moment in the meadow, when she had finally understood what had happened in the battle with the Neuri—how the gentle spirits of air and water had sacrificed themselves to defend Cian from the metal warriors and their god.

Now she was deaf to the spirits and their messages. But they had spoken to Rhenna, who was so much more than Tahvo had first suspected. They had shown the way to refuge. The Southerners had been checked, at least for a time. And since Tahvo had lost the gift of learning foreign tongues, she had no good reason to doubt Rhenna's claims that all was well.

Then she had seen Farkas, soul brother to the cruel Neuri and the men in the wooden town. His smile had been false, his welcome without sincerity. She feared him, and she feared for Rhenna.

But she had no support for her feelings, no word from the spirits, no visions. She had let Rhenna go, and the warrior had suffered some hurt she refused to admit. Tahvo sensed a taint in the air about Rhenna, more than the smell of strong drink, and Tahvo did not know how to help her.

"Tahvo, did you hear me? They may come at any moment."

"I hear." Tahvo stroked the sacred symbols on the head of her drum, her fingertips feeling only lifeless skin. *The flaw is in me.* She was a cracked bowl, a broken arrow, a barren field, useless to anyone. Unless she could buy Cian and Rhenna a chance to escape.

"I will go to the chief," she said. "Tell his son that I will remain to heal him while you and Cian return to the North."

"You're as mad as he is," Rhenna said. "We will not—"

Her argument was drowned in the clank of metal and rough speech. The tent flap quivered. A male voice grunted a command.

Tahvo stood up. Rhenna blocked her way; she opened the flap and leaned out to argue with the Skudat warriors.

"Rhenna is right," Cian said. "You can't stay here."

"I have *seen* that I must do this," Tahvo said, speaking the deception as though it were truth. "There is danger in this place. You must make ready to depart."

The Ailu was about to argue again when Rhenna stepped out

of the tent. Tahvo moved quickly to follow, walking right into the midst of Farkas's warriors. Their breathing was heavy with the smell of their intoxicating drink.

Rhenna whirled about. "Go back, Tahvo!"

"No," Tahvo said in Rhenna's tongue. "Stay." She clutched her pack and retreated to stand among the warriors. Rhenna lunged. One of the men drew his long knife and waved it at her chest. Two Skudat held Rhenna, while the rest carried Tahvo off like a pod of hungry sea hunters.

She saw little of the camp. Men and women still moved about the fires, sparkling shadows in darkness. The Skudat warriors escorted Tahvo past many dwellings and between painted wagons, stopping before a tent twice as big as any of the others.

The tent flap was closed, but light shone through the thick felt walls. Men with long knives and spears stood watch nearby, and a group of women clustered beside the entrance. They whispered as Tahvo drew near.

Tahvo bowed to them, hoping they would see that she meant no harm. But one of the women moved closer with a scowl, and Tahvo realized she was not a woman at all.

Unlike most of the Skudat warriors, he had no trace of beard, and his hair was concealed by a tall cap and veil. He was dressed in a long skirt, soft boots and dangling gold earrings. At his belt hung a bronze mirror instead of a knife.

Tahvo met the hostile eyes with a shiver of recognition. This man assumed the part of a woman as Tahvo had assumed the part of a man to accept a noaidi's attributes. He must be a sort of noaidi. But Rhenna had said the chief's own soothsayers had been unable to cure him.

"I would not intrude," Tahvo said in the Samah tongue. "If your spirits permit—"

"*Enaree,*" one of her warrior escorts said with a laugh. He shoved the man-woman away and gave Tahvo a little push toward the tent.

She took a step and froze. The watchers near the tent had been joined by another. Filtered light silhouetted the shape of a cloaked and hooded man who seemed to repel the Skudat like an untended corpse. His cloak was the color of dried blood.

Like the mage, the hooded one from the walled town, who had worked magic that stank of evil...

The man-woman and his companions shrank against the tent walls. Tahvo's guard muttered a string of harsh words. Large hands tugged Tahvo's coat and lifted the embroidered felt hanging over the tent's entrance. She had no choice but to go inside.

The interior was large enough for a score of men to gather in comfort. A small fire burned near the center of the tent, illuminating chests of carved wood and large gold vessels worked with animal patterns in bold relief. The glitter of precious metals hurt the eye. Heated water and cloths stood ready beside the fire. On a raised pallet lay a man whose hoarse breathing robbed the tent of any other sound.

Tahvo put her hand over her mouth. The air was turbid with smoke that rose sluggishly toward the hole in the top of the tent, but even the scents of herbs and medicines could not hide the stench of sickness.

She approached the pallet cautiously. The man—the chief, Orod—should have been as imposing as his dwelling, for his legs and arms were sturdy and his shoulders broad. He had perhaps fifty years, but his long hair was not yet white. A thick brown beard covered the collar of his gold-plated tunic. The bones of his face thrust beneath his transparent skin like rocky crags.

His attendants had left Tahvo alone, for which she had much cause to be grateful. She set down her pack and leaned close to Orod. He had the look and smell of one unable to hold down food or drink, and the contents of a nearby bronze bowl confirmed her guess. She put her ear to his chest and heard the rattling of his lungs and the popping inside his belly. His skin was hotter than the fire. The beat of blood in his wrist was weak.

This was no mere ailment of the stomach. Tahvo's fear came back in a rush. In her own siida she had sometimes helped the sick without the spirits' aid, as she had treated Rhenna's wound. But she had never seen an affliction of this kind. A hideous miasma rose from the chief's whole body. It felt like...

It felt like the Stone God.

She lurched away from the pallet. Someone walked into the tent—the man-woman, who barely concealed his contempt with a short bow.

"I speak *Irpata,*" he said. "You save Orod?"

"I try," Tahvo answered. "You let the others go?"

"When you finish."

"Now. I stay."

The man-woman sneered. "They go when Orod is well." He backed out of the tent, leaving the felt door swinging behind him.

The soothsayer's warning was plain. She was expected to heal the chief in exchange for Cian and Rhenna's release. Tahvo doubted the Skudat had told Rhenna the same tale.

Her devas sent us here.

Tahvo sank to the furs at the pallet's foot. She must have the spirits' aid for such healing. What if they no longer came to her drumming? And if they did, could they help when the Skudat's own noaiddit were unable to cure their chief?

The Ailuri's guardians in the Shield had been incapable of defending their children. The winter spirits had died, too weak to stand long against the Stone God's warriors. Slahtti had seemed strong and unafraid, but he had not come back. If this, too, was the work of evil more powerful than the spirits themselves...

She would know, once and for all, whether she still had some purpose, if only to save Cian and Rhenna.

Tahvo crossed her legs and opened her pack. She took out

the drum and her bowls and the pouch of dreambark. There seemed so little of it, and nowhere in this land where she might go to replenish her supply. Yet now more than ever she needed its ability to heighten the senses and release the bonds of fear.

If she burned the dreambark, as was customary, she might use up too much. But there was another way. She had heard it said that even a few grains of the crushed bark were many times more potent than the smoke.

Tahvo untied the drawstring of the pouch, chanting prayers she was not sure the spirits would hear. She pinched a minute dusting of powder between her thumb and forefinger. Once she had begun this journey, there would be no going back, save by the paths the spirits decreed.

Carefully she laid the grains on her tongue. Her mouth snapped shut on the bitter taste. She placed the drum on her lap and tapped out the rhythms of summoning. A peculiar tingling started in her palate, trickled down her throat and spilled into her belly.

For what seemed like many moons she drummed and prayed. The tingling spread to her legs and arms. Her head grew very large and floated up from her body, higher and higher, until she looked down upon Orod from the top of the tent.

That was when the spirits arrived. She felt herself floating among them, crowded into the space beside the hole left for the smoke to escape. At first she couldn't tell them apart: five, ten, twenty or more hovered at the very edge of awareness. Some were almost too small to be perceived. But she felt them.

And then she knew them, each one separate from the next. Names came to Tahvo, and she repeated them in time to the chant: *Tabiti, Api, Argimpasa*... Skudat names for Skudat gods. Many spirits answered to each name, for the lands of the Skudat were wide and no one being could respond to every prayer.

Yet though the names held power, the spirits did not. They

were drawn to her call and at the same time recoiled from it, like moths dancing about the light of a deadly flame.

Afraid.

Tahvo was not afraid. She looked down at the chief again. His skin had stretched so thin that she could see the tiny streams that carried blood throughout his body, stagnant and clotted with debris. The air shimmered above him in a roiling shroud of nauseating red. His distended belly glowed from within, as if a second fire consumed gut and bone.

In memories not her own Tahvo saw people entering and leaving the tent in rapid succession, darting like gnats. Orod was there, as well, first hale and on his feet and then lying on the pallet. The fire waxed and waned and waxed bright again. Men in women's clothing brought steaming drinks for their leader and entreated the spirits in high, wailing voices. The chief sank deeper into illness.

Farkas visited many times. His movements slowed so that Tahvo could see his face, the way he smiled at his ailing father when the old man closed his eyes to sleep.

Then the red-cloaked man walked in at Farkas's side. From the mage's hands issued sorcery that enveloped Orod in a shell of fire. He left, and the healers came again, never recognizing the thing that besieged their chief.

The spirits circled Tahvo's head in silent distress, almost visible as motes of dust and light. They could not reach the healers who invoked them.

Tahvo returned to the present. She held out her hands, palms cupped, as if offering seeds to starving birds in the darkest days of winter. *Come with me,* she said. She drifted down, light as a snowflake. The spirits trailed behind, accepting her body as a shield. Her feet touched the coruscating shroud.

Tahvo watched with mild curiosity as her boots caught fire. She smelled scalding flesh. The spirits bumped against her like particles of ice, gathered at her feet.

She plummeted. Her body found substance once more. Her mortal eyes saw the hooded man across the chief's pallet just as the pain began.

"Who are you?" he cried.

She could not scream, though her feet were wreathed in agony. "Tabiti," she whispered. "Api, Argimpasa…"

"Whom do you serve?"

The man extended his bloodred sleeves. Tahvo knew what he held before his swollen fingers opened.

A red stone.

"Slahtti!"

The cowled head lifted. Roaring filled Tahvo's ears. Silver flashed and mingled with the ugly tones of rust, swirling around and around with dizzying speed. Suddenly the hooded man vanished with a cry, and a wolf's blue eyes peered into Tahvo's.

"Slahtti." She reached past her pain to touch the gleaming fur. He bent his head and brushed his muzzle against her feet. Pain and wolf disappeared in the same instant.

Tahvo felt down her legs to the tops of her boots. They were whole. No fire had singed the cloth and flesh beneath. She looked up to the top of the tent. The spirits had also fled.

"Farkas."

The grating whisper emerged from the pallet above. Tahvo scrambled to her feet. Orod's eyes were open, deep brown and bloodshot. His pulse pounded at the base of his throat. His skin was flushed with emotion, not illness.

"Farkas!" he repeated, and swung his legs over the side of the pallet. He tilted precariously. Tahvo went to help him, and he looked at her as if she were an irritating fly buzzing at his ear. "Where is my son?"

Tahvo understood his words and knew that the spirits had restored her gift of translation. Better Orod did not suspect. She bowed, mute, and he pushed her aside, staggering for the entrance. Skudat voices were already responding to his roar.

Tahvo retrieved drum and pack, searching for another exit. She discovered a large tear in the felt near the back, hidden behind a massive iron cauldron. The hole gave just enough to let her squeeze through.

None of the Skudat had attention to spare for her small and insignificant figure. They jostled each other for the places nearest their chief, who had emerged from the tent. He called again for his son. Farkas appeared at the edge of the crowd and froze, as if Orod were the last person he had expected to see. That was no less than the truth.

Tahvo scurried past the throng, retracing the path by which the warriors had brought her. The taste of dreambark still lingered on her tongue.

The dreambark had given her something remarkable. It had renewed her courage and bestowed a vision more complete than any that had come before. Above all, it had restored her faith.

Slahtti had returned to stop the Stone God's servant, but she had called the spirits without his help. They still lived. All the other riddles could wait until she, Rhenna and Cian had left the Skudat camp far behind.

Farkas's men didn't allow Rhenna to follow Tahvo, but they made no attempt to stop her from exploring the area surrounding the guest tent. She wasn't deceived. Skudat warriors watched the tent and stalked her from a discreet distance, ready to report any untoward movement to their master.

Cian remained in the tent. Rhenna waited outside for a while, prepared to reason, argue or bully him out of any stupidity. He had the sense to stay inside and leave the current problem in her hands.

He could only guess what that problem was, but he'd seen too much. She'd made poor work of hiding her worry from him and Tahvo. And poorer work of lying.

Asteria's blood. She needed a clear head, and so did they. Especially Tahvo. Mother-of-All grant that her spirits would stand beside her in her time of need.

Devas knew Rhenna had failed the healer. She had failed all of them with her pride and her stubborn refusal to recognize the danger. A warrior's instinct should have told her that Farkas was not to be trusted.

He had revealed too much, and he knew it. But his father was still chief. If Rhenna made herself visible in camp, avowed guest that she was, the older warriors were more likely to defend Skudat honor, even if Farkas and his contingent chose to break it. All she could do now was seek any small advantage that might serve as a chance for escape.

Rhenna moved quietly around the perimeter of the firelit circle. Children had long since gone to bed. Shouts and laughter and the clank of pots gave way to the trill of crickets and a mother humming lullabies.

Rhenna bumped her hip against a tall wagon wheel, wincing at the stab of pain in her leg. A young woman's head popped out of an opening in the felt-and-wood frame of the wagon's canopy. Her brown hair was mussed and loose, her skin flushed. She made a face at Rhenna. *"Irpata,"* she scolded.

The rumble of a male voice summoned her back into the wagon. Rhenna heard a giggle, and then the wagon began to rock and sway.

Rhenna's belly cramped, doubling her over with the need to expel the foul brew Farkas had poured down her throat. The crippling effects of the drink had worn off, but not the shame. Never that.

She ducked into the shadow of an unoccupied wagon. They would come looking for her if she stayed hidden, but for now her own body was enemy enough.

The sound of footfalls drew Rhenna from her misery. She spun about on her knees, hand on the hilt of her knife.

"Rhenna? Rhenna of the Free People?"

The words were Skudat and male, but they held no hostility. The man who stepped cautiously into her view was unremarkable for a tribesman, his brown hair and beard heavily streaked with the gray of an elder warrior. Rhenna straightened, casting a glance over her shoulder to check for Farkas's men.

"We are alone," the stranger whispered. He gazed into her eyes with searching intensity.

Rhenna half drew the knife.

"Peace," the man said. "I am Javed, and I come with warning for you and your companions."

Rhenna moved away from the stench of her illness and deeper into the shadows. Javed squatted on his heels, and she did the same.

"Speak," she said. "I listen."

He was silent too long, never taking his gaze from her face. She weighed the blade in her hand.

"There is no need for that," he said. "I am not Farkas."

So he knew, as all the camp must. Rhenna slammed the knife into its sheathe. "That is fortunate."

"I tell you what you already know, that Farkas is not to be trusted. He has gathered certain reckless young men around him who obey him without question, but others have long suspected that he intends to kill Orod and take his father's place. This is not the Skudat way." Javed looked out into the darkness. "Orod led us north so that we would not be further corrupted by the Hellenish taint that has weakened so many of our people. We were to return to the old life of following the herds. Farkas pretended to agree. We believe he lied."

"We?"

"We who follow Orod as the true chief," Javed said. "Farkas still has dealings with the Hellenes against his father's commands.

Orod's illness is the work of some Southern magic. Your coming
gave Farkas a means to blame our chief's death on outlanders."

Tahvo. Rhenna jumped up. Javed seized her boot.

"Hear me. You can do nothing alone. Tonight we who uphold
Skudat honor will take you beyond Farkas's reach. Be ready to
leave as soon as we come."

"Tahvo is already with Orod," Rhenna said.

"We know. Men watch, and will do what they can when the
moment strikes. You must return to the tent and wait."

"Farkas's young men also watch."

Javed snorted. "They have little respect for their elders, and that
is their mistake."

"You risk much for Skudat honor."

"As you would for your people." His mouth tightened. "If Orod
dies this night—"

He did not need to finish.

"My thanks," Rhenna said. "I will tell my people what you have
done."

"The old alliances must stand, now more than ever." He grasped
her wrist firmly. "May Tabiti favor you."

He retreated into the shadows. Rhenna left the wagon's shelter, wiping her mouth as if she had just been sick. She almost
walked into one of Farkas's warriors. He grinned knowingly.

"Too much kumys?" he asked.

Rhenna brushed past him and strode for the guest tent. Watchers stepped quickly out of her path. She lifted the flap.

"Cian," she said.

He was gone.

Chapter Thirteen

Rhenna pushed into the tent and knelt to examine the ground. There were no signs of struggle. Her gorytos and axe were where she had left them, but in the felt wall she found a man-sized tear that hadn't been there earlier.

She pounded her fists on her thighs. Devas forgive her for trusting Cian, even for a moment. She had known better. She should have bound him again when Tahvo threw herself at Farkas's men. She should have stayed by his side, though his stare had stripped her of all dignity.

He touched you, he had accused. She'd denied it, denied the rage in Cian's eyes. To do otherwise was to acknowledge the impossible, admit that Cian had some right or reason to hate another male on her behalf.

Pride. Pride and misplaced ideals would see them all dead. It didn't matter now whether Cian had gone after her or Tahvo. She had to find him, and quickly.

Rhenna fastened the gorytos to her belt and picked up the axe. She was almost ready to leave when Tahvo's breathless face poked through the tent flap.

"Tahvo!" Rhenna pulled the healer inside and cupped Tahvo's cheeks in her hands. "Farkas let you go?"

"Orod...Orod is healed." She gulped air and swallowed. "Farkas meant to kill his father with sorcery."

"So I was told. We do have allies among the Skudat—"

"The Stone God is here, Rhenna."

"The Hellenes are in camp?"

"Another who wields the red stones." Her eyes widened. "Where is Cian?"

"Gone. I was going to look for him, but if the stones—"

Distant screams interrupted her. Shouts and cries of alarm followed, growing ever nearer.

"Run for the edge of camp," Rhenna said, pushing Tahvo toward the entrance. "I'll find Cian."

Tahvo shook her head. "We must—"

The tent walls shook with some outward blow that nearly ripped the felt from its frame. Hands reached in to grab Tahvo, and Rhenna raised her axe.

"Javed!" a male voice cried. "We come from Javed!"

Rhenna lowered the axe and thrust Tahvo behind her. A bundle of fur and leather fell through the tent flap.

"It is time," Javed's man whispered hoarsely. "Some great beast has attacked Farkas in the chief's tent. Come!"

Some great beast. Rhenna's thoughts ran as clear as springwater. She sheathed her axe, took the bundle in one hand and Tahvo's arm in the other. She dragged Tahvo outside and faced the two Skudat who waited there, nervous as antelope downwind of a longtooth. Both were older warriors, like Javed, and bore some resemblance to him. The entire area was deserted, but Rhenna could see a swarm of activity across the camp.

"They have all gone to hunt the beast," one of Javed's men said. "Where is the other traveler?"

"I don't know."

The man shrugged. "We have your horses. Come quickly."

Rhenna hurried Tahvo along after the Skudat. Dory, Chaimon and a red mare stood saddled and ready just beyond the outermost wagons, their packs bulging with provisions. Three Skudat riders waited with them. Javed's men ran to consult with the mounted ones, gesturing toward Rhenna and Tahvo.

Chaimon whinnied softly, and the nearest rider leaned over to cup his muzzle. The rider was Javed. "Our chance came sooner than we had expected," he said. "These are my brothers, Borzin and Mithrayar." He bowed to Tahvo. "You healed our chief."

Rhenna was not surprised at his knowledge. Such news raced through any camp like wildfire, but it could burn both ways.

"This beast," she said. "What was it?"

"A great cat, black as pitch."

"Is Farkas dead?"

"His men drove it away, but I hear Farkas was wounded." Javed grimaced. "Orod will not be so quick to question him now."

"His father suspects him of treachery?"

"He will." Javed glanced at the extra mount. "We cannot wait for your other companion. I'm sorry."

He couldn't guess how much there was to be sorry for.

Rhenna helped Tahvo mount Chaimon, and then climbed onto Dory's back. Javed wheeled his stallion toward the north. Rhenna and Tahvo followed, flanked by Javed's brothers and the spare horse. The beat of hooves drowned out the din from camp. Rhenna urged Dory to a gallop until she and Javed rode neck and neck.

He dropped to a lope. Tahvo and his men fell back.

"I must return for Cian," Rhenna said.

He glanced at her, his expression blurred by motion and dark-

ness. "He is not just some outland captive who fought the Hellenes at your side."

"No."

"Is he the beast that attacked Farkas?"

She sucked in a breath. Dory broke stride, responding to her
dismay.

"I have heard tales," Javed said. "I keep them to myself."

Dory's rhythm eased. "I want Tahvo safe. Will you take her?"

Chaimon's muzzle appeared beside Dory's, nostrils flared with
effort. Tahvo clung to the gelding's back like a sparrow to a gale-
tossed branch.

"Do not go back," she said distinctly in the Skudat tongue. "You
will not help Cian."

"Listen to your healer," Javed said. "You'll do him no good as a
prisoner, or dead. Farkas is too clever to let Orod's recovery stop
his scheming. My brothers will take you both to safety. I'll return
to camp and mislead any who pursue."

"No," Rhenna said. "Javed——"

"I'll return in a few days to tell you what I've learned." Abruptly
he reined his stallion back toward his men and fell in alongside
them. The Skudat's voices were snatched away by a rising wind.
A short while later Javed's companions spurred their mounts to
join Dory and Chaimon, while Javed rode at a full gallop toward
camp.

"Do not fear," said the one named Mithrayar. "There is a place
where two rivers meet, and there we will wait for Javed."

Rhenna clenched Dory's reins. Tahvo's dogged presence held
her bound as if she were a prisoner indeed.

They rode slowly through the night and into the dawn. Another
half day's moderate ride brought them to the river joining, marked
by a small stand of trees. Rhenna dismounted and cared for Dory,
Chaimon and the red mare, tending to necessity with numb fingers and a heart sapped of emotion. Javed's brothers settled in
with their own mounts.

Tahvo started a small fire and cooked up her herbs, subjecting Rhenna's leg to a cleaning and re-bandaging. Then she went off alone and sat with her drum on a low hillock. Rhenna saw her withdraw a pinch of powder from a small leather pouch and place it in her mouth. The tapping of her drum made a sound like small rodents rustling in the grass.

Tahvo could certainly do no worse on Cian's behalf than Rhenna had done. She left the healer to her mysterious work and sorted through the bundle and packs Javed had made for them. The packs contained dried meat, cheese and other food-stuffs, as well as blankets and very welcome shirts, boots and trousers. The bundle proved to be several garments that tumbled from Rhenna's hands in long flows of fine wool—Skudat women's gowns, fixed around the waist with woven and embroidered belts.

Wrapped in one of the gowns was a round, flat metal object with a projecting handle, encased in stamped leather. Rhenna pulled it from its sheathe. Sunlight caught bronze polished to a high gloss that reflected Rhenna's face like still water.

A mirror. Skudat women were never without them, bearing the useless things at their waists like swords. Rhenna shoved the mirror back in its case and tossed it among the bound-women's garments. She could think of no good reason why Javed had included them among his gifts.

She retied the bundle and took a fresh shirt and trousers down to the riverbed. There she bathed thoroughly—one eye always on the Skudat, who wisely kept their distance—and rinsed out her worn garments. The warrior's clothing Javed had provided was made for men, but he had judged their fit well.

As the afternoon waned, she sat on the bank and watched Tahvo. The healer had hardly moved, and Rhenna knew she must soon interrupt and see that the Northwoman had food and a chance to wash her own clothing.

An hour before sunset, Rhenna approached Tahvo, taking care not to startle her. Tahvo neither saw nor heard. Her eyes were silver disks, black pupils shrunk to specks in their centers.

Rhenna groaned and fell to her knees. "Tahvo of the Samah, if you desert me again—"

Ice-laden air trickled down the back of Rhenna's collar. Slahtti materialized in the space between her and Tahvo, brushing Rhenna's chin with his silver tail. The wolf glanced once over his shoulder in eloquent warning and turned to the healer.

Rhenna withdrew to the bottom of the hillock. She breathed a sigh of relief when Tahvo acknowledged Slahtti with a smile. Wolf and woman gazed at each other, neither making a sound, until the sun touched the horizon.

Suddenly, as if at some undetectable signal, the wolf lunged. He knocked Tahvo to her back before Rhenna could climb more than a few steps up the hillock.

Rhenna's feet froze to the ground. Crystals of ice enveloped Tahvo and Slahtti, forming a wall like the one that had briefly stopped Cian's captors. Two shapes became a single dark blur behind it. Rhenna drew her knife and pried at the earth where it gripped her boots. Grass crackled but would not break.

The ice wall shimmered. Tiny drops of water formed on its opaque surface. In moments it was melting from within, sending rivulets down the hillock like miniature cascades. Water touched the toes of Rhenna's boots and dissolved the invisible bonds that held her. By the time she reached the top of the hillock, only one figure remained.

Tahvo sat up, knuckling her face like a child awakened from deep sleep. The pupils of her eyes were normal, black in balance with silver again. Her coat and the grass under her were as dry as year-old bones. She noticed Rhenna and nodded slowly, as if the two of them shared some new and profound understanding.

"You saw Slahtti?" she asked.

"I saw him attack you."

Tahvo laughed—a soft, incredulous sound of wonder. "Oh, no. He was only saying goodbye."

"I don't care for your deva's kind of farewell."

"He must go away for a while, so that he does not become too weak. He is stronger than the other spirits, but even he——" She looked at Rhenna more closely. "You were afraid for me? There was no need."

"You set my heart at ease."

Tahvo touched her hand. "I have *seen* Cian," she said.

"Is he alive——" Rhenna's voice cracked on the last word. She looked toward the stand of trees where Javed's men must surely be searching for their wayward charges. "Tell me," she said.

"He is well."

"Where is he?"

"He goes south, into the lands of the empire."

"Of his own free will?"

"The Stone God does not have him," she said, "but I do not believe he has any choice."

Rhenna closed her eyes. "Was it his choice to attack Farkas?"

Tahvo shifted in the darkness, rattling the small tokens on her coat. "I do not——"

"He knew better than to reveal his nature to the Skudat. I wouldn't have let harm come to you, no matter what Farkas planned. Cian had only to be patient, to wait——"

"He knew why we bound him," Tahvo whispered. "I told him that the Hellenish warriors called him with the red stones."

"He would have learned sooner or later."

"He did not know that Farkas had dealings with the Stone God's servants."

"Maybe he sensed it. He disliked Farkas on sight."

But Rhenna knew that was not the reason. Cian had not gone after Farkas because of the red stones...or even his fears for Tahvo's safety.

He did it because of me.

She stood and worked the knots from her neck and shoulders. "We've both had too little rest. Tonight we must sleep."

"Will you wait for Javed?"

"There is nothing more we can do now."

Tahvo nodded and hugged her drum. Rhenna helped her up. They narrowly avoided bumping into Mithrayar, who looked them over hastily, as if he feared they had suffered some mishap.

"We saw a wolf," he said. "Javed would not be pleased if you died under our protection."

"A wolf?" Rhenna repeated. She glanced at Tahvo. "We didn't see it."

She walked ahead of the Skudat and ignored the curious stare of the second brother, Borzin, who had laid out blankets under the small trees. She checked on the horses, made a separate place for herself and Tahvo, and divided the blankets between them. Tahvo ate with much better appetite than she had shown in the Skudat camp.

Rhenna forced the food down. She offered to stand first watch while Tahvo and the Skudat slept, though her eyes were gritty and her limbs weighted with exhaustion. She gazed up at the stars until their patterns seemed permanently burned into her sight. When Mithrayar came to relieve her, she stretched out on the blankets and tried to let her thoughts be soothed by the gentle, even rhythm of Tahvo's breathing.

At last she slipped into a restless twilight, where Skudat fires burned innumerable as the stars. She entered a tent resplendent with golden ornaments and Hellenish amphorae decorated in scenes of naked men and women. Farkas reclined on a pallet heaped with blankets and furs. He smiled at Rhenna and held out his hand.

"Come closer," he urged. "Are you afraid, man slayer?"

She approached, watching his eyes. "The Hellenes—"

"Drink with me." He held out the skull-cup, and suddenly she was choking on the bitter liquid, tasting blood. A tiny red crystal rolled at the bottom of the vessel. She knocked the cup from his hands. The tent walls reeled and spun.

"Ugly bitch," Farkas said pleasantly. "How much longer do you think your kind will remain free?" He lunged up from the pallet, tearing at Rhenna's shirt with fingernails grown long and arched like claws. His hot tongue pushed at her mouth. She flailed with arms and legs that belonged to someone else, heard laughter that stabbed and churned in her belly like some unnatural offspring frantic to be born.

Cian.

Farkas's twisted features wavered. She pulled free and staggered for the tent entrance. Hands caught in her braids and yanked her back.

"Your friends are not what they seem," Farkas hissed in her ear. "Would you watch them die?"

Rhenna's legs gave way. She fell, and Farkas fell with her.

She bolted from sleep with her knife in her fist. In two pounding heartbeats she remembered where she was. Only two Skudat shared this camp, and they had no fire. Borzin slept, and Mithrayar stood plainly silhouetted in moonlight, speaking foolish endearments to the horses.

Tahvo lay wrapped in her coat and blankets like a chubby worm in its cocoon. Perspiration tarnished the brightness of her hair. Her lips moved.

"Sleep," Rhenna murmured. "Sleep." She sheathed the knife and sat with her arms locked around her knees, listening to Mithrayar's surprisingly agreeable voice. Later she dozed, but never deeply enough to dream.

Dawn came as a gift. Tahvo appeared well-rested in spite of her spell of restlessness. She didn't mention dreams.

Rhenna stood guard while Tahvo made use of the river. Tahvo

carefully spread her coat over a broad bush before she undressed. Her body was not nearly so shapeless underneath as it had seemed. A fine deerskin shirt and trousers, embellished with intricate beadwork, fit snugly over generous breasts and hips. She moved almost lightly without the burden of the heavy furs. Once she had shed her clothes and stepped into the water, no one could have mistaken her for a man.

Yet she was content to conceal her sex. Women who lived outside the Shield's Shadow must take such precautions—even an Earthspeaker.

Or a warrior…

Rhenna turned away, itching with the desire to plunge into the water and wash again and again, strip her skin of even the memory of a man's touch.

Cian.

She fixed her gaze on the southern horizon. Tahvo climbed out of the river, squeezing water from her hair, and disappeared behind the shrubs where Rhenna had left Javed's gifts of clothing. She emerged in a linen shirt that hung past her knees, and trousers bunched in sagging folds over the tops of her boots.

Rhenna laughed. Her chest ached with the release of so much unfitting emotion, but there was no calling it back.

Tahvo smiled, shook out her overlong sleeves and flapped them like wings. "Should I not save these to make a tent?"

Rhenna pressed her hands to her face and sat down hard. She felt the beat of galloping hooves before she heard them—one horse, approaching from the southeast.

"Javed has come," she said.

Tahvo quickly shrugged into her coat. By the time they reached the Skudat, Javed was already sliding from the back of his sweating mount. He gave the reins to Borzin and drew Rhenna aside. Tahvo joined them.

"I have word from the camp," he said. "Farkas is alive. The beast that attacked him escaped. The soothsayers claim that you and your companions set the creature on him after you failed to kill Orod, but the chief held Farkas from pursuit. You are safe."

"Did you see a stranger, a Southerner carrying a red stone?"

"No strangers. You saw this man?"

"Tahvo did."

He looked at Tahvo. "I know you speak our tongue, Healer. What can you tell us?"

"The Stone God's servants bear red stones and work unnatural magic. One of them helped Farkas to harm your chief."

Javed frowned. "Before we left the Southlands many months ago, there was talk of such a god."

"Then you know as much as we," Rhenna said. "Evil stalks your people, Javed."

"As it does yours." He held up his hands. "You didn't come with such strange companions only to alert the Skudat. If the empire has sent warriors as far as the Shield's Shadow, none of the tribes is secure."

Tahvo glanced away so that he wouldn't see how close he had struck to the truth. "If Farkas knows what you've done—"

"—he will not look kindly on me and my brothers. That is why we'll wait to return until Orod has dealt with him."

Rhenna hoped that his faith in his chief was justified. "Skudat honor is safe in your hands. I will not forget."

"Nor will I. As I have never forgotten your mother."

Her heart stopped as his words sank into her mind. "Klyemne?"

"You are much like her," Javed said, his brown eyes tender with memory. "But of course she has never spoken of me…."

Rhenna backed away as if he had spat in her face. "It is forbidden."

"Yes," he said sadly. "No daughter of the Free People ever knows the man who gave her life."

"Klyemne gave me life."

"And her beauty."

Rhenna remembered her reflection in the Skudat mirror and touched her scar. She was nothing like Klyemne. Javed should not know her. She had no father.

"Speak no more of this," she said hoarsely.

He stared at the earth between his boots. "The eagle can never return to the egg. But you are kin, and I am proud."

The pain in Rhenna's chest made her gasp. Tahvo curled her fingers around Rhenna's arm and held fast.

Javed watched Borzin lead his horse along the riverbank. "You will not return to your people."

At first Rhenna did not understand him. All the muscles in her body twisted into a single knot of dread.

"Cian goes to the South," Tahvo said. "We follow."

Rhenna squeezed Tahvo's hand and faced Javed with dignity, as a free warrior should. "We follow," she said.

"Yet not, I think, for the sake of one man, nor even one people.... I would go with you."

"You have a different path," Tahvo said. Her face shone with its own inner light. "You have faith in your gods, Javed of the Skudat. They will have need of your devotion."

Javed laughed uneasily. "I didn't know that the gods need men." He sobered and met Rhenna's gaze. "There is much I do not know. How far will you travel?"

Cian had answered that question for her. "Perhaps as far as the empire itself."

"Then you will come to the river called Borysthenes, which leads to the shores of the Dark Sea and the free port city of Hypanis. There Skudat and Hellenes live side by side. Its citizens do not know the Free People save what Skudat have told them. Your garments and weapons will attract much attention."

"So Tahvo and I must cover ourselves in the long robes of your women," she said. "You were wise in your gifts to us, Javed."

"Not so wise."

Rhenna turned to go.

"Rhenna."

She stopped, shoulders stiff.

"Does Klyemne live?"

"When I left the Shield's Shadow. She would not recognize you, even if she remembers."

"I understand."

She didn't believe him. If she had escaped the Skudat camp without meeting Javed and his brothers, she might have spent the rest of her life detesting all his race and her sire's blood flowing in her veins. But Javed was not Farkas. She couldn't despise the improper feelings he still held for Klyemne.

Or for Klyemne's child.

She left Javed with Tahvo and gathered up the blankets and provisions, rolling them into bundles that could be stuffed into the horses' packs or tied to the saddles. She returned the red mare to Javed's brothers. Chaimon and Dory whinnied in protest.

"You will not take her?" Javed asked.

Rhenna finished adjusting Chaimon's saddle. "I wouldn't deprive you of such a fine animal."

"You may need her when you find your Cian."

"He is not my—" She swallowed and tightened Chaimon's belly strap.

"If you won't take Sarosh, at least accept this." He grasped Rhenna's hand and curled her fingers around a heavy pouch of coins.

She tried to return it. "My Elders provided me with Southern money."

"There is no telling how long you may sojourn in Hellenish

lands, and the townsfolk are greedy." He smiled. "Always give them less than they ask."

She tucked the pouch under her belt. "I cannot repay you."

"You have paid me in full. I have seen my daughter's face."

"And now you must forget it."

"My memory is long, warrior."

He walked away before she could speak. He and his brothers mounted their horses, raised arms in farewell, and reined toward the southwest.

"Do not grieve," Tahvo said to her. "You will meet again."

Rhenna passed Chaimon's reins to the healer. "Do you have more useful advice, such as where in the south Cian is headed?"

"I will find him."

"You spoke with such certainty when we first met, and I didn't believe you. You proved yourself against the Neuri and many times since. But twice you've changed—once in the meadow where the red stones took Cian, and again after you returned from Orod's tent." She held Tahvo's gaze, giving her no chance to escape with a duck of the head or a humble disavowal. "From now on we travel as Sisters. There can be no secrets between us."

Tahvo nodded, unperturbed. "We will teach each other," she said, clambering onto Chaimon's back.

But as Rhenna mounted Dory and turned the horses to the westering sun, she realized just what she had promised.

Chapter Fourteen

The lessons began quickly, but not with anything so simple as words.

As Tahvo and Rhenna traveled across the steppe, more vast than the frozen sea Tahvo had glimpsed in childhood, Tahvo learned just how great a gift Slahtti and the spirits had given her.

Everywhere she perceived life. Rhenna knew the birds and beasts—antelope, lynx and hare; marmot and vole; eagle, crow and hawk—but Tahvo felt the spirits. Sometimes she almost saw them as indefinable shapes on the edge of her sight. More often she merely sensed their presence: dancing in the air, imbuing the rich soil, flowing through the water deep underground, and in the many streams and rivers.

The Skudat spirits had been weakened by the evil work of the Stone God's servant. Tahvo knew she had not witnessed the last of such manifestations or their terrible consequences, but these spirits of the plains were as yet untouched. They rejoiced in their freedom.

All she need do was call, and they would hear. Tahvo was content to watch, listen and follow the faint but unmistakable trace of Cian's passage, lapping among the feathered grasses like waves rippling in a pool.

Rhenna beat the only false note in a world of harmonious rhythm. The spirits quivered as she passed among them, and a persistent gust of wind flattened the grass behind her. She did not notice it. Her thoughts were turned inward, circling round and round the pain she refused to share.

They made the first night's camp beside a small stream. There was no wood for a fire, so they shared a small supper of Javed's cheese and salted meat. Tahvo filled the waterskins, with proper thanks to the spirits, while Rhenna tended the horses.

Long after sunset, Rhenna stretched out on her blankets and pretended to sleep. Finally she dreamed, while Tahvo still lay awake. Rhenna rose with deep hollows under her eyes. They broke camp just before dawn. By midday they reached another river, much larger than any Tahvo had seen. Its course wound south, marked here and there with stands of trees.

"I think this is Javed's Borysthenes," Rhenna said. "It turns west some twenty-five leagues from here, and drains into the Dark Sea." She looked expectantly at Tahvo. "Do we follow?"

Tahvo climbed from Chaimon's back, removed her boots and waded into the current. Water spirits slapped playfully at her ankles. "Cian has passed this way," she said. "Will the river take us to the empire?"

"It leads to the free trade city of Hypanis."

"Hypanis." Tahvo tasted the tiny droplets of water that hung in the air and clung to her skin. "This place has boats that cross the dark water?"

"So I have heard."

"Then let us go there."

Rhenna let the horses drink and divided the last of the cheese. "Have you ever seen a city, Tahvo?"

"I saw a village in the North, surrounded by walls made of trees. People traded and lived inside the walls." She shivered. "I did not understand then, but one of the Stone God's servants was there. He wore the same red cloak as the man in Orod's tent."

"North of the Shield," Rhenna said softly.

"His power was no match for Slahtti's, but I think he was…scouting, as hunters wander apart from the siida to search out the reindeer herds."

Rhenna mounted and waited for Tahvo to do the same, her mouth drawn into a thin, rigid line. She urged the horses into a faster pace, and for a while they loped along the riverbank, avoiding boggy places where the tall reeds grew. At last they reined to a walk, side by side. Rhenna stared straight ahead.

"What happened the night I found you lying in the meadow?" she asked abruptly.

Tahvo let her hands rest on Chaimon's neck and watched the ground pass under his hooves. "I had killed men of the Neuri," she said. "I thought I had angered the spirits by taking lives, and that was why Slahtti did not return after we escaped. But I thought too much of my own importance. I did not see the truth laid out before me."

She spoke then of the shattering revelation that had come upon her in the meadow: that the spirits could die. Everything she had believed, the very foundation of the world itself, had ceased to exist.

"I was afraid," she whispered. "I could not summon the spirits. I could not even feel them. When the red stones called Cian, I could do nothing to help. But then your winds came—"

"They were never mine."

"The spirits spoke."

Susan Krinard

"They sent us into greater danger."

Tahvo sighed. "In the Skudat camp, I did not know if even the skill of healing remained to me. But the spirits gave me a new vision. Farkas had asked the Stone God's servant to bring an evil sickness upon his father. He made a shield of fire to keep the Skudat spirits from helping Orod. That was when I——" She paused, caught up in a swell of joy and awe. "I saw the spirits. I joined with them, and together we broke the evil magic."

The words sounded not only arrogant but preposterous. She waited for Rhenna to laugh or make her snorting sound of disbelief. She did not.

"You told Javed that the devas need men," Rhenna said. It was an accusation, and a challenge.

Once the question itself would have frightened Tahvo. "I believed that the spirits would not willingly remain in this world if the Stone God's evil continued to grow. I did not hear their message clearly. They have no other world but this. Once they are gone, they cannot return. The Stone God is their enemy, as it is the enemy of all people."

"Devas killing each other. Gods with red stones." Rhenna tossed her braid over her shoulder with a snap. "These Earthspeaker matters are beyond my ken. But if all devas are threatened, why don't they stand together to fight this enemy?"

Tahvo closed her eyes, seeking in her heart for the answer. "They do not know how."

The expected laugh finally came. "So. Now I see why they deserted the Ailuri and my people. Everything the Earthspeakers taught us in childhood—all false. Lies."

Tahvo pulled sharply on the reins. "Not lies. Spirits and humans are...part of the same life. We need each other."

Dory sidestepped, sensing Rhenna's agitation. "Perhaps the world will continue to exist without the devas."

"Not as we know it. Not long."

Dory surged ahead in a burst of speed, but Tahvo knew the conversation was not finished.

Several hours later they stopped to let the horses rest and graze. Rhenna sat beside Tahvo at the river's edge.

"You never said what the Stone God wants with the Ailuri."

"I think it is afraid of them."

"Afraid?" Rhenna hurled a stone into the water. "Cian couldn't escape the Neuri, let alone harm a god."

"Your people call the Ailuri children of devas. What are they?"

"Legends," Rhenna said. She rested her chin in her palm, weariness etched in every line of her face. "I'll tell you the story all girls hear when their first blood comes upon them, and you may judge for yourself.

"The Mother of my people was named Asteria. She fled to the Shield's Shadow in a time before memory, driven from her home by males who would punish her for daring to learn the secret ways of battle. Some say she came from the West, others from the East. But she fled for her life, because she refused to bear the yoke of men.

"At the foot of the mountains she found forests and plains abundant with game and rich soil for the growing of crops. She prayed that the devas might send other women to live there in peace and freedom. But the men of her tribe followed her trail and drove her high into the Shield of the Sky. They abandoned their pursuit only when they were certain she would die of cold and starvation.

"She did not die. The devas took pity and sent to her a great cat, black as night, who took her to his cave and brought her offerings of furs and meat."

"An Ailu," Tahvo whispered.

"The great cat taught Asteria the ways of the mountains, and she learned to understand his silent speech. She grew strong and agile as any beast of the mountains. But she yearned for the company of her own kind. One day, after many sad farewells, she left the mountains. She ventured boldly into the tribal lands to seek women with courage enough to live with her in the Shield's Shadow. The devas blessed her with many followers. She taught her people how to fight—so well that even the males were forced to retreat when the Free People rode to battle.

"In time Asteria saw that the Free People must have children of their own, so she made a pact with the man-tribes to meet for the purpose of mating. But the men were consumed with lust. They schemed to take the Shield's Shadow from the Free People. Asteria returned to the mountains to pray for the devas' help and protection.

"The great cat came to her. He had grieved in her absence, shrunk to skin and bone. Yet he spoke to her with the voice of a deva: if she would take him as her mate, the Free People need never fear their enemies again.

"Asteria was afraid, but she agreed in order to save her people. When she descended from the mountains her belly was already swelling with new life. She soon bore six children, three girls and three boys. These children grew more swiftly than any mortal creature. The males ran wild and fled to the Shield, but the girls had the gifts of the devas and used their powers to protect the Free People. They were the first of the Earthspeakers, Healers and Seekers.

"Asteria vanished, and her daughters said she had gone to live with her mate and bear him more Ailuri sons. The People grieved, but the devas kept their promises."

"You did not have to fight the man-tribes?" Tahvo asked.

"Some we fought, and others became our allies. But none ever defeated us." Rhenna gathered a handful of small pebbles and rattled them in her fist. "While most of the Free People continued to mate with men of the tribes, Asteria's daughters chose three women above the rest and sent them into the mountains. Asteria's sons gave them children—sons who returned to the Ailuri, and daughters who bore the Earthspeakers' gifts."

"The ones you call 'Chosen.'"

Rhenna shrugged. "So it has always been. We were taught to revere the Ailuri, forbidden to enter the mountains or question the old ways."

"But you questioned them."

Rhenna opened her hand and the pebbles spilled to the ground.

Tahvo knew she must tread carefully. "Augwys was not the first Ailu you saw."

Rhenna met her gaze. "The scar I bear was an Ailu's gift, and my just punishment for seeking what was forbidden. But I have seen an Ailu die and watched Cian driven mad. The Ailuri are no better than the Free People."

"Your people could survive without them."

"Not in the judgment of our leaders. The Ailuri disappeared. The Chosen returned from the Shield with empty wombs—" She broke off, flushing deeply. "They sent me. Of all the warriors in the Shield's Shadow... *I* was to find the Ailuri and restore them to our people."

"There was purpose in your noaiddit's choice."

"Then even the Earthspeakers are mad. Where is Cian now?"

It was not a question she expected to have answered. They rode south until dark. At noon on the following day the Borysthenes cut west as Rhenna had predicted. Toward sunset the land changed. A low line of forested hills crept down from the northwest. Tahvo sensed the woodland spirits before she saw the trees themselves.

That evening Rhenna went hunting and returned with a pair of small hares. Tahvo made a brief prayer to the guardian spirits and to the animals, thanking them for their sacrifice. She and Rhenna ate heartily for the first time in days.

Rhenna bade Tahvo a brusque good-night. Tiny air spirits buzzed about Rhenna's head like bees disturbed in their hive. Exhaustion finally claimed her, and she closed her eyes.

And dreamed.

She couldn't breathe.

The air in the tent was stifling, but she knew as soon as she took the offered drink that it was poison. It would not kill her. His laughter told her that he had something else in mind.

His words beat upon her ears—mad ravings about the empire and a power that could not be resisted. But behind the talk was hatred. Hatred of any who would dream of remaining free.

Never in her life had she been helpless as she was now. She felt him pulling at her clothing, pawing at her skin. She did not cry out, even when he pinned her to the furs.

This was what it was to bear a man's touch, the loathsome invasion of alien flesh, the grunting of a beast in rut. Pain was nothing. Shame was the world.

Shame.

Stop.

Never.

Cian—

Tahvo shot up, flinging the blankets aside. Sweat ran into her eyes.

She crawled on her knees to Rhenna's side, gripped the warrior's rigid shoulder and fell back into the vision.

Bitter. Darkness. Climbing out, crawling, feeling with numb fingers to close wool and leather over skin. Finding the knife he had kicked aside, knowing she must not kill.

Dishonor. Humiliation. Degradation.

"Tahvo."

Something stung her cheek. She raised a fist to strike back. Iron bands gripped her wrists. Hatred gave her strength. She lashed out with her feet, but a hot weight pinned her to the ground.

Never. Never again.

"Tahvo!"

A face swam in her vision. Darkness receded.

"Rhenna!" Tahvo gasped.

"Asteria's mercy!" Rhenna let go of Tahvo's arms and sat back. "What ails you? I thought you would try to kill me."

Tahvo pushed up on her elbows and stared into the fire's cooling ashes until she was certain the dream was gone. "You did not hurt Farkas," she said, "because you feared for me and Cian."

Rhenna snatched up one of her blankets and draped it around her shoulders. "I don't know what you mean."

"Farkas hurt you," Tahvo said. She wrapped her arms around her stomach as if she could squeeze the memories out of her body. "I dreamed your dream."

"My—" Rhenna hunched under the blanket. "You saw it."

It. Tahvo's mouth filled with a sour taste, and she thought of the dreambark. It would make this feeling go away. Then she could help Rhenna to…to…

"I couldn't tell you," Rhenna said, her voice hoarse and brittle. "You have never known a man's touch, not like—"

Not like that. Not in violence, but also not in tenderness. She had no experience to compare. Neither had Rhenna.

"Is there pain?" Tahvo asked softly.

"No."

She lied, of course. The pain was not of the body. Tahvo felt how easy it would be to let Rhenna withdraw, let them both forget the dream as such things were usually forgotten. But Tahvo did not forget her visions, and Rhenna could not forget Farkas.

Violation.

"This is a sickness inside you," Tahvo said. "A wound that closes on the top but rots under the skin. The spirits feel it."

She knew at once that it was the wrong thing to say.

Rhenna's head snapped back like that of a serpent about to strike. "The devas who don't know how to fight? Will they punish me for my impurity?"

"They do not punish. You must believe——"

Rhenna laughed, and some trick of moonlight gave her eyes a liquid sheen. She tossed the blanket from her shoulders and walked away. The air spirits grew calm again, as if nothing had happened.

Tahvo took out her drum and traced the painted symbols. The spirits did not punish. Rhenna's suffering came out of the Stone God's evil. If the spirits needed humans to fight the Stone God, the Stone God also used men for its own vile purposes. Farkas had been a willing tool. There were many like him—like the Neuri, and the folk of the Northern town—who had already turned away from the spirits. They were like dry streambeds eager to be filled, but not with water, with blood.

In Rhenna, Farkas had seen something that could not be corrupted, and so he had tried to defile her as he had let himself be defiled.

Rhenna did not understand that he lacked such power. She was a thousand times stronger than he would ever comprehend. The spirits needed her strength. Her time of choosing had not yet come.

But Cian…

Tahvo put the drum away and opened the pouch of dreambark. She pinched a few grains and dropped them into her mouth.

Cian had known that Rhenna lied about her injury at Farkas's hands. He had meant to punish Farkas, but more than anger had spurred him to such a reckless act. The very thought that any other male should touch Rhenna—that was the animal instinct working in the blood of the Ailu. Rhenna was not of the Chosen, but Cian had made his choice.

A choice he had forsaken when he fled the Skudat camp.

Tahvo trembled as the dreambark worked its blessing. She had seen none of these things when her knowledge might have made a difference. But the dreambark had more yet to tell her.

Let me help Rhenna. Let me ease her pain.

Sudden nausea seized her throat. She braced for the sweeping visions that often came with sickness, but the fire and red stones stayed away. It was life, not death, that spoke to her now. Life springing from despair.

Tahvo spread her hands over her belly and felt it swell, growing with the new soul inside. She lay back on the blankets and raised her knees. She had no healer to bring the babe forth, but the spirits stroked invisible hands over her body and took away the pain.

She sat up to take the child in her arms. He waved tiny fists and peered through a chubby, wrinkled face. The eyes were not blue but golden-green. The hair was a feathery fringe of black. Tahvo laughed with joy.

My son.

Her breasts ached with need, but the boy did not cry. His gaze held hers with a grandfather's wisdom and infinite sadness. He became heavier and heavier. Tahvo bent to the earth as an ancient tale raced through her memory.

"These children grew more swiftly than any mortal creature."

The boy touched Tahvo's cheek and slipped from her arms. He floated for a moment, carried by the spirits of the air, and then disappeared.

Dizziness forced Tahvo onto her back again. The stars spun and danced. Rhenna woke her when the brightest had given way to the sun's first light.

Tahvo searched the warrior's face for some new awareness, but Rhenna's eyes were surprisingly at peace.

A funnel of wind stirred cold ashes in the firepit. Rhenna knelt to sift the charred dust through her fingers. "When we find Cian…say nothing, Tahvo. What happened in the Skudat camp is no longer of any importance."

Tahvo opened her mouth, and closed it without speaking her thoughts. Rhenna knew why Cian had attacked Farkas. She would never mention it again. But a seed had been planted, and one day Rhenna must harvest the fruit of its secret heart.

When Tahvo and Rhenna made camp that night after a long, quiet ride, there were no more dreams.

Chapter Fifteen

The river grew wider with every day's travel, and the forested hills rose higher in the west. Tahvo recognized cultivated fields at the base of the hills, squares cut out of the trees like a patchwork of neatly sewn skins.

"The soil is rich where the trees grow," Rhenna explained. "The farmer Skudat and their kin raise crops of grain, and trade them for gold and other goods in the South."

Though Rhenna kept to the east bank of the river, the west revealed more and more evidence of human activity. Herds of cattle grazed on the wild grasses close to the water. Wagon paths, worn by oxen hooves and heavy wheels, crisscrossed the steppe. A well-worn path sprang out of the grass to parallel the river. Riders very like the Skudat rode past the farmers in their fields.

Few of the farmers or horsemen noticed the pair across the river, but Rhenna kept their evening fires small and veered away when men came near. She led Tahvo and the horses in a wide arc to skirt a village of squat buildings and brick walls. It was the first of many such villages on the west bank.

Cian had not stopped in any of them.

Tahvo listened for the spirits of this strange new land, remembering the plowed fields she had seen in the North. The farmers had not forgotten to offer thanks to the river for its nourishment, or to the spirits of the soil for making their crops grow strong and tall.

Once Rhenna pointed out a small figure carved of pale rock, set on a low pedestal.

"They make statues to hold their devas," she said, twisting her lips in disapproval.

Tahvo almost laughed at the notion, but she felt a presence lingering near the carved figure and knew the spirits were not displeased.

Six days into the journey, Rhenna began to share the bits and pieces of information about the South that she had heard from the elder warriors of her tribe. She spoke of the conqueror Alexandros, who was said to have founded the Arrhidaean Empire and subjected many peoples to the yoke of Hellas.

"That was over forty years ago," Rhenna said. "Before then, the Free People had traded with the Southerners, but our Elders chose to withdraw from the Hellenes' aggression. We did not need anything they had to offer."

"The Skudat continued to trade with them?"

"Those tribesmen who found it more profitable to raise crops than follow the ancient traditions. The blood of many races mingle in the folk of this country. Hypanis was always a free city, if any such place can be called free, but it is Hellenish in custom."

Rhenna straightened in the saddle, stretching the muscles in her thighs, and Tahvo was gratified to see that she no longer favored the injured leg.

"Southern women are said to spend all their lives inside stone houses, dominated by their men," said the warrior. "You and I do not look like Hellenish females," said Rhenna.

Tahvo stroked the sleeve of her coat, remembering how her twin brother's stillbirth had set the path of her life. *You are not like other girls,* Grandfather had told her. *Yours is the calling of the spirits. You will remain apart.* The spirits had blessed her with gifts that might have gone to another more worthy.

If her brother had lived.

She circled her palm over her belly. "What will we do?" she asked Rhenna.

"You can pray to your devas that we find Cian before we reach the city."

So Tahvo prayed, though she left the drum in her pack. She chanted the songs under her breath, general entreaties addressed to all the spirits of earth, sky, water and fire. They clustered thick where Tahvo passed, but they had little to tell.

The first premonition of change came the next morning. Tahvo started her prayers as soon as she and Rhenna left their camp, but the spirits were slow in answering. They came with reluctance, and Tahvo felt the heaviness of fear. She watched the plowed clearings and roads with greater alertness.

For many leagues the fields appeared much like those to the north. The transformation was subtle. Rhenna did not notice the brown and withered patches scattered amidst the fertile green, but Tahvo sensed dark gaps where spirits had once resided.

Hour by hour the number of tainted fields increased. Cattle alternated between sleek and scrawny. Riders traveled alone, heads lowered as if in the face of a blinding storm.

But there was no wind. The sun's heat beat on the earth's surface like a brutal fist. The small animals Tahvo had grown so used to glimpsing in Chaimon's shadow—mice and moles, serpents and insects—were nowhere to be seen.

At day's end they made the usual camp. Chaimon and Dory bobbed their heads nervously, lipping the grass but refusing to eat. Rhenna left to hunt. Tahvo drummed softly. A few timid spirits flickered in and out of her awareness. Rhenna returned empty-handed.

She and Tahvo lay staring at the night sky, hearing only the gurgle of their hollow bellies. By moonfall, Tahvo was certain that her terrible suspicions were correct.

The spirits were deserting the land.

They were not dead, gone forever like Slahtti's snow spirits in the Neuri lands. They had simply fled. Those that remained were like lost children darting to and fro, unable to find comfort.

"What is it?" Rhenna asked as she saddled the horses in the light of a sickly sunrise.

Tahvo didn't answer at once but went down to the river and dipped her hands in the water. The current was stagnant, catching around her fingers as if choked with mud. She scooped a palmful of water and tasted it. The liquid was cool. It would quench thirst. But it was empty.

Rhenna's footsteps rustled in the grass behind her. "What's wrong?"

"The spirits are leaving," Tahvo said.

"Leaving?"

She followed Rhenna to the horses. "There are very few here now. They are afraid."

Rhenna stroked Dory's withers. "I couldn't find any game last night. Nothing stirred." She stared toward the south. "We are less than forty leagues from Hypanis."

"Watch the fields," Tahvo said. "Watch for—"

"I always watch."

The river angled west again. Villages huddled closer together, and many had small docks crowded with flat boats. None of the crafts was in use.

Rhenna's face tightened as she noted the wasting crops and skinny livestock. She studied every person who passed on the road across the river. Tahvo looked for the one thing she most dreaded—the man with the red cloak—but he did not appear. Instead, the fields took on yet another strange pattern—ordinary plots squeezed between tracts of shriveled brown and those whose grain was thick and high as if its growth had advanced weeks beyond the season. Each head of wheat stood straight and motionless and level with its neighbors, flawlessly formed.

The spirits were as surely gone from the perfect fields as they were from the dying ones.

"Cian?" Rhenna asked.

Tahvo shook her head. They traveled steadily until dusk, then rode to the top of a low rise set well back from the bank. From that slight vantage they could see the Borysthenes opening onto a wide inlet that gave off a smell of salt. Some twenty leagues to the west a second river flowed into the estuary, which in turn broadened into a gray plain of water stretching to the southern horizon.

"The Dark Sea," Rhenna said. "And Hypanis."

At the mouth of the second river stood a city. Its pale buildings, huddled behind high stone ramparts, gleamed pink in a wash of late afternoon sunlight. Shapes Tahvo recognized as boats—ships—rested on the flat surface of the water. The fields, and the ever-widening road, continued all the way to the walls.

Tahvo leaned her head over Chaimon's neck, uncertain of her balance. The nameless settlement in the North was tiny compared to Hypanis, but both exuded the same sense of wrongness. If the spirits had deserted this land, she would not find them in Hypanis.

"Is he there?" Rhenna asked.

Tahvo nodded. "But I do not want to enter that place."

"I'll go alone. You wait here with the horses."

Tahvo raised her head carefully. Rhenna's face floated in a haze of red. "Together," she said.

"You'll have to take off your coat."

Tahvo had known that such a time must come. "I will carry it."

Rhenna dismounted, led the horses to the other side of the hill and opened one of the bulging saddlepacks. "I won't leave the horses here," she said. "Hypanis must be able to accommodate Skudat riders." She shook out a wrinkled length of green cloth. "These gowns are loose enough to fit over our own clothes. We'll attract less attention dressed as Skudat females."

"What of your weapons?"

"Some Skudat women carry gorytoi, and I can hide my knives." She shrugged. "I'll be ready to fight."

Rhenna produced another gown, this one blue, embroidered at the hems and long sleeves with circles and squares of green and ocher. She tossed the garment to Tahvo. A leather belt, studded with gold and bronze ornaments, fell out of the cloth.

Tahvo dismounted, knelt and slowly unfastened her coat, pulling it from her shoulders. The tokens clinked and rattled. She laid the coat across her knees and touched each charm one by one. Then she rolled the garment snugly with the skin-side out, tying it with a length of braided cord.

Rhenna removed her axe with the same reluctance. She held it before her and touched her brow to the joining of the double blades. After a moment she walked away, the axe cradled in her arms.

Tahvo tied her coat to Chaimon's pack and examined the cut of the blue gown. She struggled to tug its gathered neckline over her head, forced her arms through the sleeves and wriggled until the skirt covered her trousers. The hem pooled at her feet.

With a sigh she hitched up the top of the gown and cinched the loose cloth with the belt. Her waist vanished among the folds sagging down to her hips. She took a few steps and found that she could walk.

"Asteria's blood!" Rhenna exclaimed. She had returned without the axe. She gazed at Tahvo, hands on hips and eyebrows raised. "It will have to do," she said. She withdrew several more objects from the saddlepacks. "These bracelets will keep your sleeves above your hands. Cover your hair with the cap, and let the veil fall at your back." She turned to regard her own gown as if it might leap up and assault her.

Tahvo adjusted the cap, veil and silver armbands as Rhenna had instructed. She practiced walking again, giving Rhenna a few moments to herself. Rhenna's fierce muttering accompanied Tahvo around the base of the hill and back to where she had started.

Rhenna had pulled the green garment over her own clothing and fastened a belt made of linked golden plaques. To the belt she had attached her sheathed knife and a disk-shaped object in its own tooled leather case. Her gorytos hung from a separate strap slung over her shoulder. A cap and veil similar to Tahvo's covered her hair; the hem of the gown brushed the tops of her boots. She strode back and forth, testing the sweep of the skirt.

Her expression was enough to reveal her disgust. She approached Dory and attempted to mount. The gown stretched and began to tear. Rhenna snatched her knife and slit both sides of the skirt from hem to knee. She knelt and did the same for Tahvo.

"If we ride quickly," she said, "we can reach Hypanis by sunset. These people will understand the Skudat tongue and speak another the Hellenes call 'koine,' which I know. Let me do the talking. You look for Cian."

She did not suggest the possibility that Cian might not be found, nor did Tahvo. Neither of them was willing to believe that the spirits would have guided them so far only to forsake them now.

Riding in a gown proved awkward but not impossible, thanks to Rhenna's adjustments. Rhenna searched for a likely place to ford the river. Tahvo prayed for assistance and was answered by the handful of spirits who still inhabited the water. The spirits slowed the currents, and Tahvo led Rhenna and the horses across.

The road had changed from a rutted path to a broad stretch of beaten earth on the northern shore of the estuary, and soon Tahvo and Rhenna found themselves in the midst of a silent flood of men and women headed for the city. Most, dressed in rough and drab clothing, carried packs and walked; some rode, and fewer still drove small carts or perched atop ox-drawn wagons. Small children toddled alongside their parents or dangled from weary arms. No one spoke or looked long at their fellow travelers.

Fear. But these folk did not flee like the spirits. They went toward the source of the spirits' distress. As Cian had.

Tahvo remembered approaching the walls of the Northern town, awed and astounded that such places existed. Hypanis left no room in her heart for wonder.

She prayed for herself, for Rhenna, for Cian and the horses. She prayed for the strangers who passed into the shadows of Hypanis's massive walls.

And when at last they came to the square-towered northern gates and Tahvo saw the glint of torchlight on Hellenish armor, slitted helmets hiding the faces beneath, she prayed for all the world.

Rhenna signaled for Tahvo to dismount, tucked her skirts about her legs, and let the horses blend into the crowd of beasts and men gathered at the open gates.

She keenly missed the heft of her axe at her shoulder and hated the gown that restricted her movements. But such small inconveniences slipped from her mind as she recognized the dozen men presiding over the constant stream of visitors.

The Hellenish soldiers at first appeared identical to those who'd tried to buy Cian—rigid metal statues armed with long spears that dipped to bar a Skudat horseman or gestured a docile family through the gates. Unlike the other warriors, however, the gate-keepers bore symbols instead of red bands painted on the brow-pieces of their helmets. Rhenna recognized a character from Hellenish writing—*alpha,* the first letter of the name Alexandros. And Arrhidaeos.

The empire had come to Hypanis. If these men also carried the red stones, then Cian was surely lost.

Rhenna tried to catch Tahvo's gaze amid the jumble of shift-ing bodies and flickering light. The healer was too conspicuous in the sack-like dress, her silver eyes too bright beneath the tilted headdress. Yet none of the people shuffling toward the gates no-ticed Tahvo. Oxen hooves as big as plates nearly trampled an inat-tentive child, but her mother gathered her up without a harsh word or a glance at the wagon's driver. The woman's eyes were fixed on the soldiers ahead.

The crowd swayed forward. Dory nuzzled Rhenna's shoulder, and the other two horses pushed close. Tahvo kept her head low.

The man directly in front of them was a Skudat horseman, cer-tain of his right to go anywhere he chose. He attempted to ride through the gates. Two of the Hellenes barred his way and ad-dressed him in low voices. After an angry silence, the Skudat dis-mounted and removed his sword and gorytos. One of the soldiers took the weapons and handed them off to another, who deposited them in an open wagon. The Skudat cursed and led his horse be-tween the guards, turning sharply to the right just inside the gate.

"Your tribe?"

Rhenna jerked her attention back to the faceless soldier. He spoke in accented Skudat, flat and emotionless. She tugged her veil forward to conceal her scar.

"I am Parmis," she said with proper female humility, "and this is my cousin, Tandor, of the Paralati Skudat."

"What is your business in Hypanis?"

"We come to visit my husband and his brothers, who journeyed to the great city in the month of New Grass. They—"

The Hellene raised his hand and turned to Tahvo. "You are not of the Skudat."

Tahvo made herself very small. "My father——"

"Her father was of a Northern tribe," Rhenna said. "She is simpleminded. We cannot get her a husband. Perhaps here…"

The soldier beckoned Tahvo closer. Rhenna held her breath.

"You must surrender your weapons," the Hellene said at last. "Beasts must be stabled. You will find accommodations to the north at the inner wall."

Rhenna gave him her gorytos and untied Tahvo's bow-case from Chaimon's saddle. She left her knife on her belt, but the Hellene ignored it. He gestured them through the gate. Rhenna turned north as the guard directed, leading the horses into a passage between the inner and outer walls of the city. She noted that the high outer wall had been recently built. Warriors on either wall could easily trap an enemy in the middle.

Soon she and Tahvo caught up with the Skudat horseman and several ox- and horse-drawn wagons. Men were unharnessing the beasts and leading them through an entrance in the low wall, while the animals' owners argued with another Hypanian over the price of their care. Rhenna felt in her pouch for Javed's coins. Tahvo hastily untied her rolled coat and pack from Chaimon's saddle, rewrapping her drum and pouches inside the fur.

"Two horses," the Hypanian said in a bored voice. He was short and stout, dressed in what Rhenna guessed to be a Hellenish tunic over Skudat trousers. "Two oboloi each per day. If you cannot pay, the beasts are forfeit."

Rhenna straightened and gazed down at the man's balding head. "This is theft," she said. "One obolos each."

The man arched his brows as if he had not expected her to dispute him. "Two oboloi, woman, or I call the soldiers."

Tahvo touched Rhenna's arm. "Two days," Rhenna said. She

counted the coins into the man's outstretched palm. One rolled out of his grasp and plopped in the mud.

Tahvo bent to retrieve it before the Hypanian could open his mouth. She bobbed to him, smiling foolishly. "My lord, how do we enter the city?"

"Back to the main gate," he said, dismissing her as the stable-men led Chaimon and Dory through the opening in the inner wall.

Rhenna smiled around clenched teeth. "You will take excellent care of our horses," she said pleasantly.

The man held her stare, then suddenly looked away. "Return in two days, or forfeit." He shouldered Rhenna aside and summoned the oxcart behind her.

"Come, cousin," Tahvo said, pulling Rhenna with the full force of her low-set weight. Rhenna went.

"*'My lord?'*" she repeated incredulously.

"Is this not an address of respect?"

Rhenna snorted, well aware that Tahvo had shown far more sense than she. "If he harms our horses—"

"He will not. They are protected."

"I thought you said the devas—" She was unable to finish her question, for they had reached the main gate.

Though Rhenna had heard the Elder Sisters' stories, she was not prepared for the crush of people and buildings. One main road and any number of narrower side streets and alleys branched out from the inner gate, cutting like canyons between structures made of mud-brick and roofed with curved tiles. Some of the houses, if houses they were, towered the height of several women. Most had small windows like square, unblinking eyes, and wooden doors opening onto the street. To the south, even taller buildings, white stone turned pink by the sunset, rose above the humbler dwellings.

Residents and visitors of Hypanis crowded the streets and

lanes, moving quickly, as if they expected to be accosted at any moment. Many wore the same odd assortment of clothing as the stablemaster, a mixture of colorful Skudat apparel and the more restrained linen garments typical of Hellenish civilians. Rhenna noted large numbers of slaves of both sexes, marked out by the simplicity of their dress and their even more submissive manner.

Someone bumped hard into Rhenna from behind and cursed in Hellenish koine. Rhenna pulled Tahvo out of the stream of pedestrians coming through the gate.

"Cian?" she asked.

Tahvo's eyes were wide and slightly dazed. "Where do we find the boats?"

"In the harbor, at the south end of the city. We should pass through the marketplace on our way. The Hellenes call it the agora, where they conduct their trade. If there's any talk of Cian or the red stones, we'll hear it there. And keep quiet, Tahvo."

The healer nodded. She and Rhenna rejoined the crowd, letting themselves be carried along the main street. Mud and dirt gave way to paving stones underfoot. Houses and small shops passed by in a blur. Rhenna's skin twitched at every unwanted brush of some male's sleeve, the stench of enveloping bodies, the din of rumbling voices. Her belt knife and the small daggers hidden in her boots gave her very little peace of mind—especially when the imperial soldiers arrived.

A full score of them bore down the center of the road, marching in lockstep, spears ready to impale any stragglers in their path. The crowd parted like fish avoiding a net. Rhenna didn't need Tahvo's gifts to smell fear—not the resigned wariness of a subdued people but the vivid terror of immediate personal harm.

The sight of Hellenish soldiers soon became all too familiar. Their numbers seemed to double every few hundred paces, slowing traffic to a crawl. Darkness fell before Rhenna and Tahvo could reach the marketplace. The street was emptying as people returned to their homes or sought shelter for the night.

Rhenna knew that Hellenish cities had guest houses for those who could pay, but she didn't trust either the worth of her coins or the men who would accept them. Dodging the telltale gleam of armor, she located an alley reasonably clean and free of vermin. She and Tahvo found an alcove formed by the lopsided juncture of two houses, keeping well away from the nearest doors.

"We'll stay here until sunrise," Rhenna said.

Tahvo slumped against a lime-coated wall, misery in her eyes. "I did not foresee the metal warriors."

"Hypanis is a free city no longer." Rhenna sat down beside her. "What of the Stone God?"

"The spirits that remain in this place are very weak. I sense them under the earth and in the water, but..." She shivered in spite of the evening's warmth. "Cian has passed this way. That is all I know."

"Then we'll find him."

No further conversation was necessary. Tahvo struggled to stay awake, but soon she sagged sideways and laid her cheek on Rhenna's shoulder. Rhenna dozed in the warrior's way, lightly and without dreams. She woke to the occasional sound of boots tramping along the main street, but the footsteps never ventured into the alley.

Dawn arrived, more felt than seen, painting the sky and the alley walls the same torpid gray. Rhenna listened for the crowing of cocks and the snuffling of scavengers—rats and dogs and pigs—in search of men's discarded rubbish. All she heard were human voices and the resumption of regular movement on the paved road.

She woke Tahvo gently, and they crept out of the alley. The street was already crowded with people swarming toward the marketplace. Soldiers watched from every corner. Rhenna walked as fast as she dared, eager to reach a more open space. At last the road poured its human cargo into a triangular stone-paved sea: the agora, filled with the carts, stalls and awnings of vendors, the smell of fish, and the first reassuringly normal activity Rhenna had seen since their entrance to the city.

Imperial guards were numerous, but the vast expanse of the marketplace seemed to diminish their menace. Grand structures rose on the borders of the agora, halls and temples built of huge marble blocks in the formal Hellenish style. High, evenly spaced columns, designed to dwarf any person who walked between them, supported triangular roofs paneled with friezes of fighting men and elegant horses. Grand pedestals bore the shattered remnants of enormous feet and limbs—Hellenish gods, struck down from their divine eminence. Why, or by whom, Rhenna couldn't guess.

In the agora itself, traders hawked their wares, singing, chanting or shouting to extol the freshness of their bread or the fine workmanship of their pottery. A woman in Skudat dress sold golden trinkets from a run-down wagon. Farmers offered vegetables, cheeses and grain heaped in wide-mouthed bronze cauldrons.

But the prosperous tumult was not all it appeared to be. Rhenna, though she knew little of cities, could see that some of the shops were deserted and much empty space separated the merchants' stalls. Females were almost as rare as trees on the steppe, and males wandered about with an air of ease and confidence that didn't match the furtive expressions in their eyes. A few of the food vendors attracted flocks of wistful observers, but more customers looked than bought.

Even so, the vapor of fear was much less oppressive here than in the streets near the gate. Wherever people gathered they also gossiped, and much could be learned from idle chatter.

A handful of women clustered about a large fountain near the center of the agora, filling pots and talking softly among themselves. Since Hellenish females lived as captives in their own cities, Rhenna doubted they would know anything of use. She left Tahvo by the fountain and stalked a trio of males whose clothing was more Skudat than Hellenish.

For a time Rhenna listened to dull conversation of food and weather and family life that anyone might overhear without particular interest. Occasionally the men glanced toward the nearest soldiers, but Rhenna might as well have been invisible.

She pricked up her ears as the tone of their conversation changed.

"...and then there is the new wall." The tallest of the three men addressed his companions. "You were not here when they began, Giyos, but I have never seen any structure raised so quickly."

"On the backs of your slaves, Hector," the second, heavily bearded man said. "Conscripted by our new 'masters.'"

"A small enough price—"

"Quiet," snapped the third man, drawing his gold-embellished cap low over his brow.

"These soldiers are as deaf and dumb as stones," Giyos said. "There is no law against talking in the agora."

"Not yet." The man with the cap dropped his voice. "You have been home only two weeks, Giyos. You will learn to watch your tongue, as others have before you."

"As you do now?" Giyos snorted. "It is always the same. The emperor's minions will take their tribute and leave us alone again. They need us, and I for one will not be silent—"

"Have you not heard how crops belonging to certain imprudent citizens have withered and died, no matter how well they are watered, and how the finest ships have been wrecked by storms on the way to Hellas—all because their masters spoke too freely?"

"I do not believe it." Giyos scratched his beard nervously, belying his words. "I have been as far as the lands of the Taprobane, and I tell you that no man or god has such power."

"Have you ridden out in the chora? Have you visited the villages? Look around you. See how the farmers come to our city, abandoning their fields. Why?"

"Because the sorcerer priests from Karchedon already move among them," Hector said, "promising fortune beyond measure to those who make obeisance to the new god."

"The emperor uses these priests to frighten foolish and superstitious peasants."

"You have been in the East too long, my friend," the tall man said. "It's said that all other gods have been cast out of Hellas, and the——" He flinched as a quartet of soldiers marched by, looking neither to the left nor to the right. "Protogenes made sacrifice to Zeus Hypanis. His daughter disappeared the next day. I have heard that the old temples are to be razed——"

"I tell you, the empire will do nothing to threaten the supply of grain."

"Where is the threat?" the capped man said. "The Assembly chose not to resist the empire's terms. Half the tribes have given up their fields and gone north rather than fight or submit. Heroson himself welcomed the head priest and made an offering of land for the new god's altar. Now his grain grows more swiftly than that of any other man in the city, and his cattle..." He cast another glance around, hunching his shoulders.

"Those who bow their heads are rewarded," Hector said. "And those who do not——"

Suddenly he turned and stared at Rhenna. She assumed he and his friends had finally become aware of her observation, but she was not the cause of their alarm. A procession had emerged into the marketplace from the north road, a half-dozen imperial soldiers followed by three hooded men clad in cloaks the hue of dried blood. The garments concealed even their hands and faces, leaching the light and color from everything around them. Each man wore on his chest a pendant of faceted red stone at the end of a heavy golden chain.

Red stones. Red cloaks. *Sorcerer priests…*

Rhenna and Tahvo had found the Stone God.

Chapter Sixteen

The hooded priests walked at a measured pace across the center of the agora, and as they came nearer, Rhenna saw that other cloaked figures walked behind them, perhaps ten men or women dressed in dull gray and carrying platters heaped with statuary, jewelry and gold. Four soldiers brought up the rear. The entourage soon collected a throng of spectators who abandoned any pretense of interest in the market vendors' wares and followed the priests' wake.

Rhenna looked toward the fountain where she'd left Tahvo. The women with the amphorae had gone, but Tahvo stood directly in the marching column's path. The crowd swept her along in their midst, and Rhenna lost sight of her small form. The agora quickly emptied of shoppers and soldiers alike.

Rhenna hurried to join the last stragglers, catching up at the southern perimeter of the marketplace. The main road grew wider and busier as it approached the southern end of the city.

Large residences built of dressed stone gave way to warehouses, granaries and factories for the making of pottery and curing of fish. Wealthy merchants shouted at bare-chested laborers stacking amphorae or fitting bricks for some new construction. Foreigners in bizarre costume chattered in outlandish tongues. Slaves, branded by the ragged scraps of their loincloths and the scars on their backs, struggled under heavy loads that would better have been carried by the markedly absent beasts of burden.

Every face turned to watch the procession pass, and many laid down their work to join in the retinue. The acrid odors of marsh and seawater overwhelmed scents of sweat, baking bread and human waste.

Soon the harbor itself came into view, a forest of masts rising where seagoing vessels of all sizes and shapes had been anchored or drawn up on shore. Rhenna had never see their like: elegant ships with curious eyes painted on their prows; deep-hulled cargo haulers; triremes with rows of oars like whiskers on some enormous beast; tiny fishing craft with nets neatly stowed for the next day's work. But even the most impressive was dwarfed in the shadow of the monster anchored far out in the estuary.

The greatest ship had not eyes nor oars nor visible sails. It rode high, black from stem to stern, its deck partly covered with roofed platforms. Figures scurried over it like ants, and the air above and around the hull shimmered and rippled.

Such a wonder should have drawn Tahvo's attention, Rhenna thought, but she was not among those who gaped from the pier. The soldiers and the hooded men had turned west at the docks, pacing solemnly beside the water. The crowd, nearly doubled in size, spread to fill every available space between the water and the closely packed wharfside buildings. A roiling mass of smoke rose above them, tainted with the stench of scorched offal, burning flesh and rot.

The smoke came from a place that might once have been the

foundation of a warehouse but had been razed to make room for a single enormous slab of red-laced gray stone. Its base was hidden by the people massed ten deep around it, but the top of the block stood higher than the tallest spectator.

The stone had been cut into the shape of a giant chair, with one edge raised as a back and the opposite side deeply notched. Its sides were slick and smooth, naked of carvings or inscriptions, but the russet veins in its surface made disturbing patterns, like symbols of an unknown language. Darker stains streaked the top of the slab. The smoke—now black, now green or brown— seemed to burn the stone itself.

One of the three red-cloaked priests stood on a raised platform near the base of the stone, speaking the Hellenish koine in a sonorous voice that never rose to a shout and yet carried like rolling thunder. Nothing could be seen of his face or even the tips of his fingers in their long belled sleeves, yet such was the power of his presence that the crowd hung on his every word with parted lips and fervent stares. Rhenna used her elbows and shoulders to push through the audience, seeking a glimpse of blue gown or silver hair.

She was three rows away from the stone when the priest lifted his arm and the fire surged up in a glare of brilliant purple. Two people stepped up onto the platform—a man in a finely made Hellenish robe and a thin, nearly naked boy who limped on a twisted leg. The Hellene bowed to the priest. The boy shrank away.

The priest placed his hand under the boy's chin. The red sleeve fell back to reveal long, pale fingers that stroked the crippled child's face with utmost tenderness. The boy swayed and closed his eyes.

From within his robe the wealthy Hellene drew an intricately sculpted figurine of a full-breasted woman draped in a clinging gown, her folded hands clasping sheaves of ripe wheat. The Hel-

lene's arms trembled as he lifted the figurine in a gesture of sup-
plication, first toward the priest and then to the fire on the vast
stone block. The Hellene stepped up to the notch in the front of
the stone.

No.

The Hellene tossed the figurine onto the fire. Immediately the
blaze erupted in a conflagration of green and gold. Pain that was
not pain throbbed between Rhenna's brows. The crowd moaned
with one voice, fear and dread and awe intermingled.

The priest turned from the fire. He raised his hands to his hood
and pushed it away from his face. Lean and beautiful features fell
out of shadow, illuminated by the radiance of the flames. He
smiled upon the crowd and cupped his faceted pendant in his
palm. Crimson light shone through his fingers. He drew the red
stone to the end of its golden chain and touched it to the crippled boy's forehead.

The child's head snapped back and his limbs went rigid. The
Hellene who had made the offering rushed forward to support
him. The boy convulsed twice as the light from the stone washed
through him, pulsing under his sallow skin.

Silence.

The boy opened his eyes. He straightened, putting his full
weight on both his legs. Two strong, completely normal legs.

The murmurs were hesitant at first—single words and brief
phrases that rose into cries of approval. The boy grinned and
shook his newly whole leg, bouncing up and down with bone-jar-
ring enthusiasm. The Hellene bowed deeply to the priest.

"Healed!" a Skudat voice cried. "He is healed!"

The people near Rhenna pressed forward, then retreated again
as soldiers closed about the platform and crossed their spears to
hold the mob at bay. The flame on the altar lost its golden glow,
casting off a nauseating stink that no one but Rhenna seemed to
notice.

Rhenna angled toward the platform, still searching for Tahvo while she kept one eye on the guards and priest. Men trampled the hem of her robe and kicked her legs, but she succeeded in reaching the front of the pack just as the soldiers began to clear a path to the base of the altar.

The first priest had been joined by a second, whose cowl remained firmly over his face. He gestured to the soldiers maintaining the open path through the crowd. A gray-cloaked figure, one of those from the original procession, stepped into the clearing. He carried a tray stacked with the golden ornaments and costly trinkets favored by Hellenes and Skudat alike. He marched up to the platform, bowed to the priests and passed the tray to an attendant in servant's garb.

The second priest selected an object from the tray, a silver bracelet molded in the shape of interlaced vines thick with fruit. He placed it in the gray-cloaked man's outstretched hand. The man stepped between the priests onto the platform and dropped the bracelet into the fire. Flames the color of Hellenish wine shot skyward, showering sparks that sizzled and died on the soldiers' armor.

No.

Rhenna winced as the pain struck inside her head a second time. The agony lingered for several heartbeats, blurring her vision. She forced it clear with a swipe of her hand.

The gray-cloaked man turned to the people and removed his hood. Golden hair framed a pretty boy's face, unlined by suffering or experience. A sigh of recognition swept through the crowd.

"Gordias!" they cried. "Gordias!"

He smiled as the priest had smiled, benevolently and tenderly. "People of Hypanis," he said, "I come today to give myself in joy to the one true god. He is called the Stone God, because he needs no other name. He wears no face, because he is seen in all things. He promises wealth beyond measure to those who serve him willingly, and endless life beyond death." He beckoned to the servant with the tray. "I reject the old gods who offer nothing but misery and sacrifice. I embrace the perfection of eternal fire."

All at once the path through the crowd filled with the other gray-cloaked figures—radiant young men and women in the first blush of their youth, each attended by a servant bearing a fortune in jewels and precious metals. Gordias descended from the platform to join them.

"Soon we go to Karchedon!" he cried. "To you, my friends, we bequeath small gifts of farewell, for the Stone God will requite us a thousandfold." He nodded to his companions. The young men and women shook back their sleeves. Delicate, graceful fingers dipped into the treasure and flung it by open handfuls into the audience.

Chaos erupted. Rhenna locked her knees as people scrambled to collect coins and rings, plaques and pendants, fighting each other for the choicest prizes. Men grunted and snuffled and squabbled like swine over slops. Blows and curses fell amid the rain of silver and gold. Rhenna looked over heaving backs and plunging shoulders to the sole point of stillness.

The first priest waited on the platform, observing the tumult with expressionless eyes. Tahvo stood at the foot of the platform, her gown torn and stained, her silver head bare. She looked up at the priest, and Rhenna understood exactly what she was about to do.

The smoke of desolation choked Tahvo's lungs, and the cries still rang in her ears—cries of the spirits given up to the Stone God's fire.

She had felt them die, the small and courageous beings who clung to scraps of rock and metal fashioned by human hands. They bore names shared with countless others like them, shaped in a thousand different forms: Demeter of the bountiful harvest, Dionysos who brought the grape. Not so long ago they had been summoned with love and gratitude, crafted with reverence, bound so thoroughly into the substance of carving and ornament that they knew no other existence.

Now they were gone, melted into the stone, tormented by the betrayal of those who had revered them, devoured alive as spirit-bones shattered and spirit-blood bathed the evil one's altar. No trace of them endured, not even ash.

The Stone God's servant stood at the center of the holocaust. He smiled, assuming a mask as false as the hopes of his gray-clad followers, and for the first time in her life Tahvo knew what it was to hate. Hate as Rhenna hated Farkas and the enemies of her people. Hate like jagged teeth ripping breasts and belly. Hate beyond the greatest horrors of her visions.

The priest stroked the red stone hung over his heart. Fire gathered in the faceted crystal and pulsed in the altar, invisible to mortal senses. No one but Tahvo saw how the flames spread until they engulfed the very air, burning that which should not burn, obliterating, everlasting. Her blood boiled, and her skin blackened to shriveled scraps. Her lungs turned to powder. Only her rage was not consumed. It had its own indestructible body, infinite, eternal....

Tahvo stepped forward. A grip like iron tongs seized her wrist and yanked her back and down among scrambling bodies. The prickle of a beard scratched her cheek.

"Quickly," the man whispered in her ear. "Come with—"

"Let her go."

Rhenna blocked the man's way, the tip of her knife blade pressed to the base of his throat. He released Tahvo, who slipped free and peered up into her captor's face.

"Mithrayar?"

"Healer." The Skudat cautiously raised his hands. "Rhenna of the Free People. Praise Tabiti that I have found you."

Rhenna lowered her knife and tucked it out of sight. "What are you doing in Hypanis?"

"We cannot speak here," he said, indicating with his eyes. All around them people were rising, cradling their prizes of gold and jewels, and darting suspicious glances at each other as if they expected to be robbed by their neighbors. The gray-robed acolytes walked among them, and the priest on his dais smiled and smiled.

Tahvo reeled. The rage had receded, and with it the madness that had nearly exposed her to the Stone God's servant. If she had confronted him…if he had seen her for what she was, she would have died like the spirits, and not alone. Rhenna would have tried to interfere, losing her own life on the spears of the soldiers. And now Mithrayar…

"Tahvo is ill," Rhenna said, her voice very far away.

"I know a safe place," Mithrayar said. "Come."

The two warriors enfolded Tahvo like a shaman's robe, half carrying her between them. She closed her eyes. The terrible anger had numbed her to any sense of the spirits. She welcomed the emptiness.

She did not open her eyes again until she tasted air free of foul smoke and the stench of human treachery. Rhenna and Mithrayar set her on her feet. They stood in an open space surrounded by collapsing houses that must once have been like those near the harbor. Tree stumps thrust out of the ground in rows like rotting teeth. A low hill rose from the silent grove, flanked by a broken wall. Patches of green struggled to survive in the cracks between crumbling bricks set into the hillside.

In the hill was a spring. A narrow band of water trickled from the smashed stone visage of a serene and beautiful woman. Her eyes had been put out and her lips crushed, but she still shared what she had.

Tahvo ran to kneel beside the shallow basin once intended to collect the water. The scanty flow was barely enough to wet her fingertips, but she knew the spring was alive in this city of death. She chanted a prayer of thanksgiving.

Susan Krinard

Rhenna glanced at Tahvo with a faint frown and turned on Mithrayar. "Now you can speak freely. Why are you in Hypanis?"

The Skudat folded his hands behind his back. "Javed set me to follow you, and so I have done since we left him."

"We don't need your help."

"Peace. Your courage and skill were never in question, my brother's daughter. Javed knew you might come to Hypanis in search of your companion, and that the city would be strange to one of the Free People. I was not to interfere unless I judged your life in danger." His eyes darkened. "It is much worse now than when Orod led us to the North. He expected the empire's coming, but we didn't know that Hypanis had been taken. We would have warned you—"

"It would have made no difference."

"I know." He nodded to Tahvo. "I did not mean to hurt you, Healer, but when you went so near the red priest—"

"You did well to stop her," Rhenna said. She gave Tahvo another long, worried look. "What possessed you, Tahvo?"

Possessed. A strange word to describe what Tahvo had felt, but it had the ring of truth. "Spirits died in the Stone's fire," she said, trying to make the warriors understand. "They were…taken. Consumed. And the boy was not cured. It was only a semblance of healing."

"That I believe," Rhenna said, her mouth twisting in disgust. "Will he die?"

"I do not know. I was…very angry."

Rhenna rubbed her forehead, knocking her hat and veil to the ground. She nudged the tangled mass with the toe of her boot. "You didn't sense Cian."

Tahvo shook her head. She cupped her hand under the trickle of pure water, opening her heart to the spirit's gentle presence. "Did you know of the spring when you brought us to this place?" she asked Mithrayar.

He raised a brow at her change of subject. "I know it was here even before the founding of the city."

"She is very old," Tahvo said. Very rich in the life that had given so much to the people of Hypanis. Men and women had created a face for her, but no sculpture or working of metal could contain her. She was a mother of spirits, so ancient that she had forgotten her own name.

She had stayed to keep watch when lesser spirits of field, rock and tree had fled the Stone God's domination. The red priests had toppled statues and burned sacred tokens; they persuaded the people to abjure their gods because they understood, as Tahvo had most painfully learned, that spirits bound to men grew weak without reverence. Weak enough to die.

The Stone God's servants could not destroy the spring so easily. Her slender fingers stretched far under the ground, nourishing the last fragile web that bound water to earth, earth to sky, sky to natural fire. She was hope, and as long as she survived, some part of the city lived.

"I will ask *her* to look for Cian," Tahvo said. "She will know."

Rhenna and Mithrayar exchanged glances. "I have little understanding of god magic," the Skudat said, "but I know this city as you do not. I'll return to the harbor and ask for word of your friend."

He strode away. Rhenna muttered under her breath and crouched by the basin opposite Tahvo. She tore her gown, already split at the sides from hem to mid-thigh, neatly up to her belt.

Rhenna shoved the cloth free of her trousers and rested her palm against the spirit's cracked stone forehead. An expression of surprise crossed her face.

"You feel her," Tahvo said.

Rhenna quickly withdrew her hand. "It will help us?"

"Listen." Tahvo closed her eyes and rested her fingertips on the spirit's smiling, shattered lips. Sweet water spilled over her skin.

Follow.

The voice spoke only in her mind, but it was more beautiful than any music. Tahvo glided along the melody of a thousand tiny droplets. She seeped into the carved stone and the earth beneath, raced joyously along the hidden paths that no man or woman had ever traveled. For there was joy even in the midst of sorrow, tenderness stronger than cruelty.

Follow.

Tahvo felt the press of dirt and rock over her head, the intricate pattern of roots reaching for nourishment, the burrowing of animals and insects that remained safe where the perverted fire could not touch them. Above, in the city, sickness robbed the soil of vitality and left a distorted reflection of life in its wake. But the spring flowed on, sending tiny fragments of herself to brave the tainted ground.

She did not find Cian.

Tahvo felt the first stirrings of fear. The spring cast runners under the parts of the city she had abandoned. She struck great, serrated pillars of red stone growing down from the surface, razor edges that severed her delicate fingers.

Still she pushed on, into the harbor and toward the salty, alien waters of the estuary. She flinched from the brackish liquid, but not because she trespassed in the realm of other spirits. Here there were none. They had gone like so many, gone or been devoured, and red currents spiraled among the ships' keels like the ichor of some dying sea beast.

The black ship rode there, rudderless and oarless, and not even the smallest fish swam within a hundred body-lengths of its monstrous hull. The spring recoiled, but as she fled she caught the trace of remembered motion, a vestige of light in darkness.

Tahvo came back to herself like a wave slapping the shore. Her cheek was pressed into the basin, cool and damp. Instinctively she felt for the spirit's gently curving lips.

They were dry. The spring had no more to give. She had spread too far and lost too much; now she did what she could to preserve her life, withdrawing even beyond the reach of a noaidi's prayers. This water would never flow again.

Tahvo pressed her hands to her face. Rhenna pried her fingers away and clasped Tahvo's hands in her own rough palms.

"Cian—" Tahvo began, her throat thick with grief. "Cian has left Hypanis. He has gone across the dark water."

Rhenna's skin leached white. She sprang up and began to pace furiously, six long strides to the right and then a violent spin to the left. Tahvo crouched against the wall beside the dry spring, remembering all she had promised.

She had promised Cian that he would find his brothers, and he had believed her. She had promised Rhenna that she would find Cian, and he had escaped them both.

But he still lived. The Stone God had not taken him.

After a while, when the shadows of the ruined buildings stretched long over the felled grove and the sad little hill, Rhenna sat down beside Tahvo and folded her arms around her knees. Tahvo knew she would speak when she was ready, and not before. But Mithrayar returned by starlight, a bundle in his arms and an expression of foreboding on his good-natured face.

"We know," Rhenna said, rising to meet him. "I have no plans to kill the one who brings bad tidings."

The lines in Mithrayar's brow relaxed. He set the bundle down on top of the wall and placed a second, smaller packet beside it.

"Food," he said. "And garments you'll need across the Dark Sea."

Rhenna met his gaze. "How much did Javed tell you?"

"That you would never cease until you brought your friend back. And that he is no ordinary man. But Borzin and I also have eyes. I see the evil that will take the Skudat as surely as it has taken the Hellenes. The gods have some purpose in all this." He glanced down at Tahvo with curiosity and respect. "Is this not so, Healer?"

Tahvo felt the slow return of the peace she had lost. "It is so, Mithrayar of the loyal heart."

"How did Cian go?" Rhenna asked.

"Many folk in the harbor remembered him because of his golden eyes and his strange accent," Mithrayar said. "He joined the pilgrims on the black ship that left Hypanis two days ago."

"A black ship like the one now in the harbor?"

"The same. They belong to a special fleet the empire built to transport priests, pilgrims and tribute between the provinces and Karchedon."

"The chief city of the empire."

"Cian goes to Karchedon," Tahvo said, "where the gray-robed ones seek the Stone God."

Mithrayar shuddered. "It lies on the other side of the great water the Hellenes call the Aigaion. There is no swifter means to reach Karchedon than by the black ships, for common vessels seldom venture into the open sea. Some of the black ships stop at ports between here and Hellas, but all dock in the Hellenish port of Piraeos before crossing the Aigaion."

"Then we may find Cian there."

"Only if you take the black ship." He picked up the larger bundle and untied the cord. He unrolled two gray hooded cloaks and pale linen squares sewn together at the sides to form a simple, robe-like garment similar to those worn by the women Tahvo had seen by the fountain. Another cord held bronze pins meant to fasten the garment along the tops of the shoulders and arms.

"The chiton," Mithrayar said. "All Hellenes wear some version of this tunic. It's not much good for riding or fighting, but it is cooler than skins or furs, and you'll find the South very warm. These may also be of some use—" He gave Rhenna one of the long, needle-sharp pins. "None but soldiers bear weapons in the empire."

Rhenna thrust the pin into one of the linen squares. "And the cloaks? You would have us join these mad acolytes?"

"The priests of the black ships accept all who would make the pilgrimage to Karchedon, rich or poor, even women. Gordias is popular and very wealthy. He'll draw many new followers among whom you may hide." His eyes glinted. "You must be very humble, brother's daughter. Do not let the little healer go near the priests."

"I won't." Rhenna gave Tahvo a fierce look for good measure. "I wouldn't take her at all if I thought I could make her stay."

Tahvo bowed her head. "I know I am very much trouble," she said. "But the spirits have said——"

"I know." Rhenna sighed deeply. "When does this black ship depart?"

"Tomorrow," Mithrayar said. "You'll be safe here—the priests and soldiers never visit the old quarter. I will take you to the docks when the time comes."

Rhenna turned away, seeking the privacy of her thoughts. Mithrayar unwrapped the packet of food and gave Tahvo a slab of boiled fish and a chunk of crusty bread.

"Is this man Cian worth your life, Healer?" he asked softly.

"Much more," she said. "And Rhenna——" She brushed her hand across her belly, remembering the child in the vision. Rhenna's battle lay ahead, hers and Cian's and Tahvo's, as well. Three against the Stone God—three humans and the spirits who would come, like the spirit of the spring, when they were most needed.

Tahvo leaned her head back against the wall, fish and bread forgotten. She *saw* the black ship, gliding through black water without the aid of wind or human strength to impel it. She saw a city, like and unlike Hypanis.

And she saw a man, dark haired and gray eyed, striding boldly among the blank-faced throngs of the empire's minions. He was nothing like Cian in nature or appearance, but the Stone God had reason to fear him.

There will be others. Other allies Tahvo could not foresee, as there would be great sacrifices made by men and spirits alike. Sacrifice, surrender, renunciation. Death.

"And Rhenna?" Mithrayar repeated.

Tahvo shivered and found the bread crumbled in her hands. "Rhenna will return," she whispered. *But I—*

She felt for the roll of her shaman's coat and drum. She could touch the coat, run her fingers through the thick furs, set the bone and metal tokens swinging. But the precious garment seemed to fade before her eyes, losing substance like ice melting in the sun.

Sacrifice.

She gathered the bundle in her arms and rocked, humming a song of mourning and sorrow. With trembling fingers she loosened the binding cords and unrolled the coat, exposing the drum and bowls and pouches nestled within. She took the pouch of dreambark and tucked it into her belt, then rewrapped the bundle and thrust it at Mithrayar before she could lose her courage.

Mithrayar stared at the coat. "I do not understand."

"Take it," she gasped.

Rhenna joined them. "Tahvo?"

"By these things they will know me," she said. "The priests will know what I am."

Mithrayar flushed and held the coat awkwardly, as if it might come alive and try to escape. "You would trust me.... Are these not—"

"She is an Earthspeaker," Rhenna said. "These things are sacred to her. Guard them with care."

The Skudat muttered a prayer. Tahvo turned and walked to the ruined grove. She knelt among the stumps, opened the pouch of dreambark and laid a single grain on her tongue.

No visions came. She did not ask to see more than the spirits had already shown her. She simply let the dreambark work through her body, raising her above the constraints of human weakness, replacing anguish with rapture.

She laughed until the tears spilled down her face.

The crowd at the harbor was quiet, almost solemn, as the Stone God's priests and their gray-clad acolytes waited beside the boat that would carry them to the black ship. There were no soldiers. Some of the bystanders were kin to the pilgrims, taking their leave; the rest were merely curious, perhaps hoping for one last dispensation of treasure from Gordias and his generous companions.

Rhenna, Tahvo and Mithrayar stood apart from the other travelers, feigning an emotional farewell. The gray cloak lay heavy as a yoke on Rhenna's shoulders. Her flimsy sandals—another of Mithrayar's gifts—were too tight, but the chiton allowed some freedom of movement, and she had bundled up her shirt, trousers and boots into a small pack like those carried by the other pilgrims. Mithrayar had advised her to leave her knives behind.

Tahvo had very few belongings left to surrender. She hadn't been herself since giving up her coat and drum. On several occasions Rhenna had seen the healer eat something from the pouch she had saved, concealing her movements behind her cloak. Each time Tahvo's moods swung from grief to elation to unearthly calm over the course of hours. Rhenna worried but didn't interfere.

Tahvo was calm now that they were finally done with the intolerable waiting. Rhenna kept her very close.

She clasped Mithrayar's hand in the warrior's way, wrist to wrist. "You know where we left the horses?"

He returned her grip firmly. "With that dog of a stableman, where I left mine."

"I give Dory and Chaimon to you, to care for as your children."

"I'll keep your horses for you—until you return."

Rhenna shook her head. "I owe you more than I can repay."

"I would not walk in your boots for all the great king's finest stallions." He placed his hand on his chest and bowed to Tahvo. "May Tabiti and all the gods go with you."

Tahvo reached up to touch Mithrayar's woolly cheek. "Look after your people. Tell them…" Her eyes clouded. "Tell them that they, too, will be called."

His reply was lost in the cry of the priests at the dock, calling the pilgrims to their holy journey. Rhenna nodded to Mithrayar. He thought better of attempting to embrace her.

She took Tahvo's elbow and guided her toward the gathering. Tahvo walked stiffly, knees locked. Her terror made it easier for Rhenna to bear the fear in her own heart.

"You can still stay behind," she whispered. "I'll claim you're ill."

"No." Tahvo stared at the priests. One of the red-cloaked ones greeted each pilgrim as he or she stepped into the boat, offering a gem-encrusted golden goblet. The pilgrims drank readily.

"Do not let it pass your lips," Tahvo said, as if Rhenna needed such a warning. The last few gray-clad bodies shuffled up to the priest with the cup. Tahvo pushed ahead of Rhenna and stopped before him, slowly raising her eyes.

The priest smiled. "Drink," he said in koine. "Drink to the one true god."

Tahvo took the goblet from his hands. She pressed the rim to her lips. Rhenna clenched her fists beneath her cloak.

Tahvo lowered the cup and smiled, her mouth stretching into an expression anyone but Rhenna might have mistaken for joy.

"To the Stone God," she said, and returned the cup. She stepped into the gently rocking boat.

There was no one left to drink save Rhenna. She smelled the noxious stuff before the smooth gold rim touched her skin.

"Drink," the priest urged.

Rhenna tilted the cup and let the bitter liquid wash over her closed teeth. Red crystal glinted at the bottom of the goblet. Rhenna stilled the trembling in her hands and gave the vile thing back to the priest. She followed Tahvo into the boat, and the priest stepped in behind her.

A score of acolytes and two priests stood on the swaying deck while the rowers took up their places at the oars. The craft threaded its way between the other ordinary ships, setting course for the hulking black vessel. The painted eyes of the boats they passed seemed to blink and roll in warning.

Save yourselves, the eyes pleaded. *Save us.*

Rhenna's stomach heaved. She walked unsteadily to the side of the boat and stared into the oily water. Hardly a ripple touched its surface. The oars dipped and swung. The air hung motionless and stifling.

Air. Asteria's blood, if only the wind would blow…

A breeze stirred the tendrils of hair at her temples. It circled her face, fresh and pungent with salt. Rhenna glanced toward the priests, but they and the other acolytes were intent on the black ship. No draft disturbed red robes or gray cloaks.

Tahvo came to stand beside her. "We are not alone," she whispered.

Rhenna gripped the side of the boat until her knuckles stood white against the brown of her skin.

Wind of the devas, she prayed, *tell Cian we are coming.*

Part II

Shadow of the Stone

Chapter Seventeen

The wide, even streets of Piraeos swarmed with slaves, citizens and barbarians, fishmongers and merchants, men of the Two Lands with painted eyes and Keltoi in bright-colored trousers. The native Hellenes, Athinaians once justly proud of their great cities, paid no particular attention to the foreigners, however exotic their appearance; their eyes were empty of the curiosity and ambition that had driven their ancestors in days of legend.

Quintus remembered the legends, the tales of Odysseos and Herakles, of Troy and the mighty soldiers of Sparta. In his childhood, before the coming of the empire, he had absorbed the stories as greedily as bread soaks up wine. He had dreamed of the day he might walk the same narrow paths and rocky shores that those heroes had trod.

But that Hellas was no more.

Quintus leaned against a fluted marble column and watched a dealer in spices bargain with some wealthy citizen's servant. Despite the wide difference in their stations, the two men had one unmistakable quality in common: the vague, untroubled expressions of sheep. Even their arguments rang hollow, as if they carried out the negotiations merely because it was expected.

The empire claimed peace for all who yielded their freedom. Men unsusceptible to the red stone's influence kept themselves well hidden, or they died. And as for the rest...

Quintus pulled his hood farther over his face and adjusted the left side of his cloak. He knew what the priests would do to him if they saw the disfigurement he concealed. No beggars or cripples lingered in the Piraean marketplace or on the steps of the grand municipal buildings. They had all been given to the god.

Quintus took care not to stand out from the crowd. He spoke the language of Hellas as well as he did his own. To the fine, fat, prosperous citizens of Piraeos, he was an ignorant sheepherder out of the northeastern hinterlands, not a rebel from the mutinous province of Tiberia.

But he, like all visitors, would be required to present himself at the Stone God's temple and submit to the priests' examination. He had a few days at most to find the Tiberians' sole rebel contact in Attika and arrange transport to Karchedon.

He moved away from the column and wandered under the long roof of a stoa, sometimes pausing at a stall to gawk with rustic awe at delicate papyrus from Aigyptos, ivory from Libya and costly spices from the Far East. He bought dried figs to fill his belly and well-watered wine to quench his thirst, though he drank slowly. He noted the positions of the Arrhidaean soldiers who kept perpetual watch over the city. They seldom stirred, responding only to the infrequent disturbance or the summons of a priest.

Until he had killed his first soldier in the hills outside Ambrakia, Quintus hadn't been sure they were mortal. Not all of them were human.

Two women in slave-borne litters stopped the traffic around them to converse through the sheer curtains of their canopies, gossiping like women everywhere. They didn't notice the priests and soldiers escorting a line of children across the agora, bound for the harbor and the black ships. Children were taken every day. It was the price of peace, just tribute to the everlasting glory of the one true god.

Quintus reached for the sword he had abandoned many milliaria outside the city and shook his head at his own foolishness. A weapon would expose him as surely as his disfigurement—and the sorcerer priests of Piraeos must not know who walked among them.

He cut across the agora toward the eastern wall of the city, avoiding priests and the favored citizens who carried red stones. He had just successfully negotiated the hazardous course when he saw the boy steal the melon from the vendor's cart.

He stopped between two stalls bordering the marketplace and watched in amazement as the ragged child shoved the undersized fruit down the neck of his tunic and darted away from the stall. The thief dodged the unexpected obstacle of a lady's litter, slammed headlong into a fat Persian merchant and whirled in the opposite direction, straight toward Quintus.

The victim of the theft raised a wordless cry. The boy doubled his speed, striking bystanders right and left. Other cries followed the first, wailing like the howls of wolves. Contorted faces turned along the boy's path. Hands shot out to grab and hold. The howling rose to a brutal pitch.

Two imperial soldiers stepped out from the keening mob. The little thief charged at Quintus, sidestepped at the last minute, and lost his balance. Quintus caught him by the elbow.

The boy struggled fiercely, but his eyes pleaded without hope or expectation of mercy. A crowd formed about Quintus and his captive, pressing in from every side. Quintus maneuvered the boy behind him as the soldiers approached.

"Be still," he commanded. The boy ceased his struggles and went limp, a passive weight in Quintus's grip.

The soldiers came to a perfectly coordinated halt, grounding their spears with a thump. The mob fell silent. A thin man with lank hair—the melon seller—dashed up to the soldiers and quickly retreated several paces beyond the reach of their spears.

"This is the boy?" one of the soldiers asked, his voice flat and metallic behind his slitted helmet.

The melon seller's narrow eyes lit with avid pleasure. "That's him."

The onlookers rumbled. The soldier tilted his spear toward Quintus.

"Give us the child," he said in the same indifferent tone.

The thief whimpered. Quintus met the soldier's hidden gaze and estimated his chances of escaping this encounter. Soldiers were not priests, but if these bore the red stones...

"Give us the boy," the second soldier said. "He is for the god."

Quintus forgot he was a shepherd, forgot his mission and his most sacred oaths. "Why?" he asked softly.

"He's a thief!" the melon seller cried.

The first soldier turned his head the merest fraction, and the merchant closed his mouth.

"I saw the whole thing," a new voice said.

Quintus glanced toward the man who had come to stand beside him. The newcomer wore a Hellenish chiton over barbarian trousers and boots, the tunic relatively new, but dusty and stained. His feet were bare. He was tall and well built, with strong and even features, but most striking were his golden eyes; they shone through the shaggy fringe of long black hair with a peculiar intensity that drew all attention to him.

"I saw no theft," the man continued. His koine was thickly accented but soft, its timbre very like a purr. People shuffled closer to hear him more clearly. "The child knocked a melon from the stand. I picked it up." He held out his hand. The melon, much the worse for wear, lay cupped in his long fingers. He tossed the fruit at the vendor, who barely caught it.

"I will pay for the damage," Quintus said. He was compelled to release the boy in order to open his purse, but the child huddled close between him and the barbarian stranger. Quintus picked out an obolos. "Will this be enough?"

Someone snickered at the rustic's ignorance. No one else made a sound or offered to contradict the stranger's story. All the faces and eyes looked the same, regardless of shape, age or color: aroused and yet passive, hungry and hollow, awaiting some signal to act.

The soldiers tilted their helmets as if deep in thought. "The boy must be questioned," one said. They took a step forward, and staggered as the ground heaved under their boots. Earth shuddered. Loaves of bread tumbled from a peddler's cart. The high screams of women rose above the startled grunts of men. People fell to their knees.

The barbarian closed his eyes, legs braced against the rolling tremors. "Does the earth often shake in Hellas?" he asked.

"It is the god!" someone cried.

"He is angry!"

He is a fool, Quintus thought. He glanced behind him and saw that the boy had escaped. The ground gave one final, violent spasm, and then the golden-eyed stranger was gone as mysteriously as he had arrived.

Quintus took advantage of the momentary confusion, slipping between a pair of gape-mouthed laborers. He hopped the low border stones that marked the edge of the agora and turned into an alley beside a row of shops. Once he was well away from the marketplace and any chance of pursuit, he paused to catch his breath and his bearings.

If the soldiers raised an alarm, they were unlikely to be able to identify yet another visitor in a hooded cloak. The same could not be said for the boy or the barbarian. Their behavior had proven that neither was bound by the Stone, and so both would be marked for death. Few witnesses could forget those almost bestial golden eyes.

Quintus must. The barbarian might still be lucky enough to get away. And however courageous he had been, his life was as nothing, hung in the balance against the fate of the world.

At least the child lives. And if he survives to become a man, let him never forget what it is to be free.

Cian crouched behind a low brick wall and watched the young man pause to study the city's eastern gate. Soldiers patrolled the ramparts, but the youth showed no sign of fear. His instinct for survival was as evident as his courage; he'd proven his mettle by helping the little thief and escaping the soldiers afterward. He couldn't be blamed for failing to realize that he'd been followed across Piraeos by a creature more beast than human.

Animal instinct had kept Cian alive during the weeks since he'd left the Skudat camp. Instinct had carried him a hundred leagues across the steppe, south and west to the very shores of the Dark Sea. He had run in panther shape, pausing to hunt and sleep but never to think. It was easy to avoid thought when one became a beast, and the beast's bloody memories were more welcome than the human reason he'd left behind.

As he had left Rhenna.

He remembered his last sight of her face in the Skudat tent— the pain she refused to show, her stubborn courage—and his own mindless rage.

How Farkas had screamed...

The rattle of a passing cart pulled Cian back to the darkening streets of Piraeos. Late afternoon brought a deeper gloom to this accursed city, a few more forgotten corners in which to hide. But even the blackest crevice gave Cian no shelter from the call that drummed in his head. The red stones beat at him from the altars that stood on every corner, from every hooded priest and privileged convert who proudly bore a stone in ring or amulet.

Farkas still lived because he wore such a stone. Tahvo had tried to warn Cian of their power over him, but the cat knew no fear. Not until his jaws had begun to close around Farkas's neck and the stone touched his tongue.

He'd escaped and regained human form just long enough to recognize what he had done and where he must go. South, ever south, to the port city of Hypanis, where the red stones were waiting. As a man he had entered the empire's high new walls, bent only on reaching the harbor. He'd fought the stones to board a black ship bound for Byzantios, on the far shore of the Dark Sea.

Other ports had followed, every one riddled with the priests and their stones. Cian's sole advantage was his knowledge of the universal koine, taught to him by a Hellenish exile who'd been his traveling companion for a few months during his years away from the Shield. The old man's schooling had prepared Cian for Hellenish customs as well as speech.

But he hadn't expected the utter torment of traveling on the black ships. They had borne him across the Propontis, through the straits, into the island-rich Aigaion and finally to Piraeos. And he realized that as long as he searched for his brothers, as long as he remained within the borders of the empire, each moment of his existence would be a struggle for freedom and sanity.

The Stone God wanted him. Its priests didn't know what he was, but the stones were merciless. To surrender would be comfort, peace, bliss. No warrior or shaman stood in his way.

Come to me. Come. . . .

He had wandered this strange new city, dazed, clinging to the rationality his very nature wished to deny him. He knew the Ailuri were not in Piraeos, that he must get to the empire's capital of Karchedon, but he feared returning to the docks and the black ships. He remembered the sweet taste of blood and considered the easiest way of joining his brothers, in life or death.

Come to me. Surrender.

Then he had seen the young man save the child in the agora, an act of astonishing defiance among people who had forsaken their souls to an evil god. The youth's bravery had reminded Cian that he was no longer the Neuri's caged, cringing prisoner. He had intervened, recognizing the sheer madness of the attempt…and suddenly the incessant din of the red stones had ceased.

He saw with unclouded vision for the first time in days. The youth stood at the center of a profound stillness, the calm at the heart of the storm, and Cian knew that the red stones had no power where the young man walked.

He is the Stone God's enemy.

That was all he had time to grasp before the earth began to shake. A man might attribute such good fortune to the intervention of Tahvo's spirits, but a beast was driven only by the need to survive. It tracked its prey while the man inside clung to unfounded, irrational hope.

The youth was no fool. He was as much a stranger to this land as Cian, an eagle among starlings, and he had some purpose of his own. He'd chosen a convoluted route across the city that would have confounded an ordinary pursuer. Now he walked through the eastern gate as boldly as any priest, and the soldiers barely turned their heads to watch him pass.

Cian released his breath and weighed his own options. Instinct chose for him. He found a portion of the wall where the guards were farthest apart and scaled it easily, leaping to the other side.

He landed on hands and feet like the cat he was and ran half-crouched to the nearest sizable shrub.

Cian had seen nothing of the Attik countryside from the port, but his old traveling companion had described his former home in loving detail. The chora of Piraeos was unlike the level steppe or the fertile farmland surrounding Hypanis. Here the hills were dry and rocky, dotted with hardy shrubs and trees adapted to hot summers and mild winters. The farmers of Hellas had cultivated crops suited to poor soil and drought, scratching life out of the ground wherever they could. They sought tranquillity in sanctuaries protected from the encroachment of man. They honored the gods of mountain, spring and forest, as well as the deities of vine and harvest.

The old Hellene's nostalgic tales had depicted a time and place that no longer existed. Once Cian reached the road he saw that the fields and farm plots seemed of a different world than the wilderness that bordered them. There were few walls, yet land not covered in crops or groves was nearly barren, desiccated and withered, as if the scanty rain had been directed to fall in one place and not another.

Cian had glimpsed unusual conditions in the fields outside Hypanis: shriveled plots beside healthy ones, fat cattle and skeletal beasts in adjoining pastures. But he had been too consumed by his battle with the stones to understand what such signs portended.

Now he began to see. Groves of olive trees grew in rigid, symmetrical rows too perfect for even the most fastidious husbandman to devise. Grapevines marching up the hillsides made tight, interlocking patterns, one shrub exactly like the next. On some the grapes were already ripening, weeks before the traditional harvest. The bunches hung in triangular, evenly spaced tiers.

As in Hypanis, even the smallest wild animals were entirely absent. No birds sang, and no wildflowers intruded in field, grove or vineyard. Cattle and oxen, extraordinarily fat and glossy, wandered in unfenced pastures dense with grass as level as still water. No flies tormented them. They moved only to eat, these creatures made of animated stone rather then flesh.

The few people on the road or working the fields ignored Cian, dull-eyed as their livestock. The modest farmhouses seemed built as if by a single hand. There were no crumbling walls or little gardens bright with flowers tended by women with babes riding on their hips. The small yards were barren of laughing children, honking geese or hounds lazing in the sun.

But there were empty spaces where shrines had stood, miniature temples once dedicated to benevolent devas of nature who had been condemned in the name of the one true god.

Cian found himself standing beside the remnants of one such shrine, Piraeos a half league behind him and his young quarry almost out of sight around the next hill. A few fragile flower vines wound among the rubble left by the shrine's despoiler.

Cian knelt in the dirt and stroked a wilting leaf. The beast's rage and the red stones had stripped him of all emotion, but suddenly his heart opened to unbearable grief. The flower stem pulsed in his hand. An unfamiliar sensation crawled up from his feet, and his legs went numb.

Touch me.

Dizziness made him reach for the earth. His fingers splayed to take his weight.

Touch me.

The man in Cian was lost, but the beast heard.

You are the Earth.

Cian scooped up a handful of soil. The stuff sifted dry and dead through his fingers.

The blood and bones of Earth.

He closed his eyes. The red stones were all around him, yet his mind was clear. He pressed his palm to the ground. Stabbing pain struck his hand like the bite of some titanic serpent, and its venom throbbed in his veins. Poison saturated the soil and every growing thing. It drove bees from the hive and mice from their nests. It shaped each tree, each vine, each blade of grass, and made them thrive with perfect, soulless, unnatural life.

Seek. Seek and find.

Cian pushed toward the agony, unaware of what he sought. His fingers sank into the soil. It gave like shifting sand, swallowing his hand and then his wrist. His arm moved as freely in the earth as it did through air.

In amazement he flexed his fingers, and his skin hummed and tingled. Particles of dirt flowed like currents around his arm—currents of untainted life, struggling to survive. He felt layers of coolness and warmth, minute alterations of moisture and texture, the weight of every pebble.

And the poison collected on his flesh to suck and burn like hundreds of ravenous maggots on a corpse.

He snatched his arm free and shook it violently, expecting blackened skin and weeping sores. His arm and hand were reddened but whole. His fingers still functioned. The soil lay smooth and undisturbed where he had pierced it.

He had moved inside the earth. For a moment he'd *become*...

Cian sprang to his feet and held his head between his hands. *I am no deva.* The Ailuri were not divine, no matter what they or the Free People had chosen to believe. They had no magic save the change itself. The red stone's madness had claimed him again.

A man stared at Cian from the nearest field, his spade poised in midair. The call of the red stones grew stronger, tolling out from the city.

Cian set off at a fast walk, driving all thoughts of the earth from his mind. The farmer went back to his digging. A woman threw grain to a silent flock of chickens. Cian rounded the bend in the road and picked up the young man's trail. He had turned on a side path between two low hills, descending to another farmhouse set in an arid hollow. Cian circled the hill and settled to watch behind a jumble of rocks at its base.

The house was completely unlike the identical farmsteads along the road. The haphazard mud-mortared brick construction tilted drunkenly toward the north. A wall with many wide gaps and a crooked gate surrounded the main building, yellow wildflowers ablaze between the breaks. Outside the wall scraggly vines contended with one another, ancient wrestlers with rope-muscled arms. A goat tore at weeds among discarded bricks and clay potsherds. Two olive trees embraced across the wall, thick-rooted and uncontrolled.

The young man approached the gate. He hesitated for several moments, studying his surroundings with a warrior's caution, and began a wide circuit of the house.

Just as he rounded the corner, an old man darted out of the structure. He was the first truly old person Cian had seen since landing in Piraeos, and he was well suited to his tumbledown hovel. The hem of his long chiton dragged on the ground. He wore only one sandal. A white mane of hair stood up from his high forehead, matched by an untidy beard. He shouted at the goat, shaking his fist, and then wandered along the wall as if he had forgotten why he had come outside.

The youth remained hidden until the old man limped back into the house. Again he stopped at the gate. He extended his hand to open the latch.

The old man burst out the door. He and the intruder stared at each other. Suddenly the old man grinned and flung his arms up in an unmistakable gesture of welcome.

Shock showed in every line of the younger man's body. He stopped sharply just within the gate, as if he had stepped on a thorn. His voice rose in question. The old man waved him on, and after a moment the two went inside the house.

Cian opened his senses to the world. He felt safe here; the red stone's clamor seemed far away. A bird called hesitantly from one of the old man's olive trees, and a mouse pattered in the tall, brown grass poking through the contorted grapevines. The air was clean, and the earth...

He dared to touch the ground and felt how easily he could slip inside it again. The earth welcomed him as a lover, accepting his penetration as if he had the power to heal it, draw the poison from soil and stone.

I am no deva.

The blade nearly sliced his throat before he realized it was there.

"Don't move," the voice said at his ear. "I will kill you."

Cian locked his muscles. The knife's edge bit into his skin. "May I speak?"

"You've been following me since the agora," the young man said. "Why?"

"I helped you...save the child."

"That isn't what I asked."

Cian reckoned that he'd grossly underestimated the youth's skill and intentions. "You're a stranger to this country," Cian said. "As I am. You oppose the empire and its god. So do I."

The blade's pressure remained steady. "Why should I believe you?"

"Because you have the ability to mute the red stone's power, which the priests would have found most interesting—"

The youth shifted his weight to strike. Cian summoned the change without thought. Iron slipped on black fur. Cian leaped straight up, throwing the young man from his back, and spun in midair. His opponent rolled to the ground and scrambled to his feet with a fighter's skill, but his face was pale with astonishment. He would be easy to kill.

Cian crouched to spring.

"Stop!" The old man ran between boy and beast, the grimy folds of his chiton fluttering behind him. "We are not your enemies, Watcher of the Stone!"

Chapter Eighteen

The huge black beast drew back on its haunches. Its long tail slashed back and forth in banked rage, scattering scraps of clothing with each wide sweep. It glared at Philokrates from slitted yellow eyes. Quintus shoved the old man aside.

"No." Philokrates patted Quintus's arm as if they were teacher and pupil again. "Put the knife away, my boy. It is quite unnecessary." He bent his skinny frame and addressed the cat in a voice that too readily betrayed his excitement.

"You *are* a Watcher," he said. "You must be. I was not sure your kind still existed, or if I had correctly interpreted the prophecies, but now I see——" He rubbed his hands and grinned. "You do understand me? You must become a man again. There is so much to discuss...."

The cat blinked, arrested by the storm of words. Suddenly it cringed, flattened to the ground with its tail curled tight to its flank, and changed.

A naked man lay where the cat had been. He snapped into a defensive crouch. Quintus did likewise.

Philokrates wrung his hands. "We mean you no harm, Watcher. Surely we must be allies."

The man arched a black brow so high that it vanished beneath the unruly tangle of his hair. "What did you call me?"

"Watcher of the... You do not know? Fascinating." He mumbled to himself.

Quintus rested a firm hand on his shoulder. "Yes, yes," the old man said. Philokrates bowed. "I am Philokrates, and this is my...this young man is Quintus Horatius Corvinus, of—"

"Quintus. Only Quintus."

"Of course, of course." He leaned forward, almost losing his balance. Quintus held him steady. "Do your kind have names, Watcher?"

The man-beast got to his feet, seemingly untroubled by his nudity. "I am Cian," he said. "I thank you for your welcome." He met Quintus's gaze. "And yours."

Quintus thrust his knife into its hidden sheathe. "I don't know what you are," he said, "or how you managed such a trick. But I see no reason to trust a foreigner who threatens me with exposure to the priests."

"Threaten you?" He laughed. The sound was edged with self-mockery, but it was very human. "You would have killed me before you knew what I was or why I am here."

Philokrates shushed through pursed lips and shook his head. "Peace, my young hotheads. There will be no more talk of killing." He clapped dusty hands. "Clearly you are both here for a purpose, and such things are not discovered with threats. We will go inside. No one will bother us. They don't watch me carefully anymore, as your presence here proves. Your arm, young Quintus."

"You make a serious mistake, Philokrates. Only the sorcerer priests have such magic. What if they sent him?"

"According to the writings—" he squinted at Cian from curious brown eyes "—we will know as soon as he passes the gate. You'll see."

Quintus lent Philokrates his right arm, but his eyes never left the creature Cian. The foreigner had caught him off guard, forcing him to defend his secret with violence. And now Philokrates expected him to trust without proof save for vague assurances and mad talk of ancient prophecies.

He knew better than to drop his defenses so easily. He'd trusted the Tiberian rebels to let him fight for his people and his family, and they'd imprisoned him instead. His trust in Philokrates might be equally foolish. But if his old tutor was capable of treachery, the world itself wasn't worth saving.

"Go ahead," he told Cian in a voice that brooked no argument.

The man-beast preceded them across the weedy lot to the gate, where he paused as Quintus had done the first time he approached.

"Ah. You sense it, do you?" Philokrates said with satisfaction. "Just what I would expect. Please continue. It will let you pass as long as you carry no taint of the Stone."

Cian shivered, and Quintus felt for his knife. But the man-beast pushed through the gate, hunching his shoulders as he crossed the yard. He waited for them by the door, wary and self-contained. Intelligent. Dangerous.

"You see," Philokrates said. "He cannot be of the Stone. My pneumata would have warned me."

Quintus sighed. "I know nothing of this device of yours, Philokrates, but—"

"You were always impatient, my son. All will be explained." He blithely strolled into his home.

Quintus gestured to Cian. Both had to step over a long metal rod that lay across the threshold.

The main room was filled with worktables, every surface littered with scrolls, papyri and shards of pottery covered with dense writing. A wooden sleeping couch with a woven reed mattress had been shoved into a corner between cupboards and amphorae of all sizes and shapes. Quintus could see a smaller room in the rear of the house, where the back door stood open to catch the sluggish breeze.

But one astounding object dominated the scholarly chaos. Just inside the front door stood a peculiar amalgamation of interconnected metal tubes, boxes and jars, many objects fused together into fantastical shapes, some glowing with mysterious inner light. Cian stared at the device with obvious interest. His nostrils flared as if he smelled an odor he couldn't define.

"My sentinels," Philokrates said, beaming like a king in his palace. "My pneumata are far better guardians than any goose or watchdog. Of course, they have no minds as we know them, but they are naturally antithetic to the Stone and all its works. They become quite agitated in the presence of the enemy." He nodded to Cian. "You do feel them, don't you?"

"Pneumata," Cian said. "Breaths?"

"My own terminology. Your language must have other words…" He ran his hands through his white hair, sending it straight up from his head. "What is your language? You speak koine well."

Cian stepped away from the device. "I learned it from one of your own people, a traveler in the North."

"Ah, the North. Where is your homeland? Do many of you survive? The texts say so little."

"Philokrates," Quintus warned.

The old man swung toward him. "And you, my boy…you had quite a different effect on my pneumata. I have so many questions." He embraced Quintus warmly, tears in his eyes. "It is good to see you. So much has changed."

Everything has changed. Six years ago Quintus had been a child who spent more time in study than with the boys who taunted his deformity. Philokrates, like Quintus's mother and his brothers, had tried to protect him from the harsh realities of life. Surely he would never be able to protect himself.

None of them had foreseen what he would become, or how he alone would be left to avenge them.

Quintus patted Philokrates's shoulder and set the old man behind him. Cian wandered among the tables, studying the writings as if he were capable of reading their spidery scrawls. Quintus wasn't deceived by his casualness. The cool, yellow, beast's eyes were constantly in motion, aware of everything in the room.

"Ancient texts," Cian said. "Are these not written in your own language?"

Philokrates jumped like a little white mouse, and Quintus had to hold him back from rushing to the table. "They are copies, of course," the old man said. "Translations. The originals are...elsewhere."

"And they tell of my people?"

"They are prophecies and histories passed through many generations of priests and scholars, all the way back to the time of—" He stopped abruptly. "But where are my manners?" He gestured to another table, where scrolls had been shoved aside to make room for a platter of cheese, clay cups and a jug of wine. "You have both come a very long way."

Cian met Quintus's gaze. Neither moved.

Philokrates sighed. "Suspicion is a luxury we can ill afford," he said. The flighty bounce in his step was gone, and his eyes were sober. All at once he was the man Quintus remembered. The man he had never expected to meet again.

"I know you worry for my sanity as well as my safety, Quintus," he said, "but you need not. At least let me provide our guest with the necessities." He opened one of the cupboards, pulled out a folded length of brown linen and tossed it to Cian. "It is not your accustomed garment, no doubt, but it is quite acceptable in any part of Hellas or the empire."

Cian pulled the chiton over his head and adjusted the left shoulder, leaving his right arm bare. The drape fell to his knees. Philokrates gave him a cloth belt to bind the tunic around his waist, raising the hem to mid-thigh.

The old man clucked in approval. Quintus understood his admiration. The Hellenes had always been known for their love of beauty, and the barbarian's lean, muscular build might have inspired the finest sculptor.

Quintus flexed his twisted left hand. The inefficient muscles of his forearm spasmed painfully.

"As for your hair," Philokrates continued, "it is as long as a Lakedaimonian's, but I am no barber." He glanced down at his own mismatched feet. "I think I have another pair of sandals...."

"This is more than sufficient," Cian said. "My thanks."

"You are most welcome." Philokrates poured a cup of well-watered wine. "And now we must start from the beginning." He whistled. A boy of about ten years poked his head through the back door, grinning from ear to ear.

"You may remember Timon," Philokrates said, beckoning the child into the room. "He is unlikely to forget either of you."

The little thief. Quintus almost smiled in his surprise and relief. "You keep unusual company these days, Philokrates."

"Any man who walks freely through that door is my friend." He put his arm around the child. "Timon is very observant. He serves as my eyes in the city. He came straight to me after you helped him escape the soldiers, and described you both in detail." His eyes warmed with memory. "You have become a man, Quintus. You are your father's son."

Only since the invasion put a sword in my hand.

Quintus avoided the old man's affectionate gaze and gave the boy a stern look. "If your Timon continues as he is," he said, "he won't live to reach manhood."

The child made a rude face, and Philokrates cuffed him lightly across the ear. "He is right, and so I've told you, Timon. You can live here with me—"

The boy wriggled out of his grasp and ran across the room, stopping before Cian. "You took my melon."

"Yes. I lied to the soldiers, as well."

Timon grinned. "You're good. Did *you* make the earth shake?"

The question startled Cian as much as it did Quintus. The man-beast opened his mouth and closed it again, bereft of speech.

"Why do you ask such a thing, Timon?" Philokrates said.

"Because I saw him turn into a panther," Timon said. "It's all magic, isn't it?"

"You aren't afraid of him?"

Timon wrinkled his grimy nose. "Of course not."

Philokrates chuckled. "I know no better judge of character than Timon. He had to learn to quickly, since his parents…"

"The priests took them," Timon said, staring up at Cian as if it were important for the barbarian to understand. "They take every-one who doesn't—" He glanced at Philokrates for help.

"They take anyone not susceptible to the Stone's power," the old man finished. "Like both of you."

"Not susceptible?" Cian asked, leaning forward on the table. "But I hear—"

"Hear what?" Quintus demanded.

Cian took a deep breath. "You asked why I followed you. My people, the Ailuri, come from the mountains we call the Shield of the Sky, where even your empire is all but unknown."

"So far," Philokrates murmured.

"I was away from the mountains when my people disappeared.

I went in search of them and was taken prisoner by tribesmen who sold me to imperial soldiers for reasons they refused to explain. With the help of...unexpected allies, I escaped. From other tribes I heard stories of your Stone God and its power. I came south to learn more, but the red stones..." He looked directly at Quintus, and Quintus saw fear in the golden eyes. "They call to me. It's like a madness, clouding the mind—" He shook his head sharply. "When I met you in the agora, you silenced them."

Quintus took great care to show no reaction. "I did nothing. Why do the stones call you if you're not part of them?" He turned to Philokrates. "You called him 'Watcher of the Stone.'"

"It is not what you think," the old man said. He peered at Cian. "Men must touch the stones to be affected by them. Most simply become...biddable—"

"Slaves," Quintus said.

"—and are easily ruled by the priests. Some are unaffected, like Timon and his parents, and they are taken away if they are caught. Some go mad. Some keep their will but give themselves freely to the Stone God's service. You say the stones *call* you, but you are no ordinary man. Surely this proves—"

"I knew nothing of the Stone God until the soldiers bought me from the Neuri," Cian said.

Philokrates clasped his hands in agitation. "The sorcerer priests have the secret texts. They must know that you have power that makes you their enemy.... What became of your people?"

"The empire took them. I was the last who remained free. I've come to find them, if they live. If you have knowledge—" he spread his hands on the table, scattering the stacked papyri "—tell me."

Philokrates rubbed his hand through his hair. "Karchedon," he said. "That must be where the priests have taken them. Quintus is bound there, as well."

"Say nothing, old man," Quintus snapped.

"Your friends in Tiberia sent warning that you might come." Philokrates smiled sadly. "You've become hard, my son, as a soldier must."

Quintus felt heat gather beneath his skin. *Soldier? I was never anything but a tool. They would have used me when they were ready and put me away again like some legendary sword, keeping me safe while others died for freedom. I couldn't bear it, Magister. Not another day.*

But Philokrates must know these things, and he clearly intended to share his knowledge with Cian. The Tiberians had lost control of their precious secret. All Quintus could do was keep tenacious hold of his own destiny.

"I will always respect what you taught me, Philokrates," he said. "I haven't forgotten. Now I ask for your help and advice."

"To get to Karchedon, where you will most certainly die in some rash attempt to defeat the empire single-handed? I do not remember teaching you such wisdom." He glanced at Cian. "Yet there is purpose in these events, in our coming together at this time." He bent his chin to his chest. "So many pieces. If only I could find the rest…"

"I do not know this Tiberia," Cian said to Quintus. "Your people fight the empire?"

"It has been six years since the conquest began," Philokrates said, "and many of the empire's resources are still absorbed in dealing with Tiberia's rebellious population. They are an excessively stubborn people." He snapped his fingers and rushed to one of his cupboards, withdrawing a roll of papyrus. "I have drawn a map based upon my own travels and the works of the great Herodotus. Perhaps it will serve to illustrate." He unrolled the papyrus and weighed down the edges with stones.

Quintus studied the map with real interest. Philokrates had drawn in not only Hellas, Italia and the Mediterranean—called by the Hellenes Ta Thalassa—but the irregular oval of the entire known world. The dominant mass of Europa extended off the upper edge of the sheet, bordered on the left by the Tin Islands and the lower right by India. Many rivers flowed from the unexplored Northern lands into the Euxeinos Pontos, which was in turn connected by narrow waterways to the Propontis and Aigaion Sea. Libya was a smaller shape below Ta Thalassa, marked by the curving course of the Neilos River and ending with the country of the Aithiopians. Around the whole to east, south and west was Okeanos, the world sea.

"Italia," Philokrates said, pointing to the forked peninsula of Quintus's homeland. "And here is Hellas, and Athinai. You see that the two lands are very close in distance, and there have been Hellenic colonies in southern Italia for many years. But neither Alexandros nor his brother approached Tiberia."

"They left that to Nikodemos," Quintus said.

Philokrates indicated a broken line drawn over a wide portion of the map from Iberia to Persis, from Libya and Aigyptos to the northern shore of the Euxeinos. "This is the extent of the Arrhidaean Empire as I know it. And this—" he traced his finger south across Ta Thalassa "—is Karchedon." He pressed his thumb over the black mark as if it were a blemish he could eradicate with a touch. "Cian, can you show me the location of your homeland?"

Cian hesitated, frowning over the map, and Quintus wondered if he had any comprehension of what he was seeing. After a long moment the barbarian pointed to the empty, unnamed space far north and east of the Euxeinos.

"The Shield of the Sky," he said.

Philokrates hissed through his teeth. "Even beyond Skythike." He measured the empty space with his wrinkled hand. "Your land seems very far away," he said, "but the empire will find it, as the soldiers found your people."

"Destroy the Stone God," Quintus said, "and the empire follows."

Philokrates rolled up the map and held it tightly in both hands. "You will not achieve this alone, my son."

"You know the rebel contacts in Karchedon. All I ask is to share in that knowledge, so that I can seek their help."

Cian looked from Quintus to Philokrates, his eyes mere slivers of gold. "There are others who resist?"

"In every land where the empire rules," Philokrates said. "All our hidden allies are in constant danger, for few possess magic equal to that of the sorcerer priests and their stones. There are so many...."

"Why does the empire fear my people?" Cian asked.

"I can tell you only what I have learned from the writings." He closed his eyes, and his voice rang with the assurance of a sacred oracle. "They who are the chosen children of the good gods, they who are both and neither man nor beast are the Watchers of the Stone. Only they may keep the crystal cage. Beware, beware if ever they should fail...." He stopped and opened his eyes. "If I'd had more time..."

Cian paced away, and Quintus imagined a lashing black tail.

"It means nothing to me. Crystal cages..." He spun on his heel. "There must be more."

"Much I have not interpreted," Philokrates said, deep creases buckling his brow. "Timon?"

The boy, who had been watching his elders with surprising patience, hopped to the alert. "Grandfather?"

"Do you remember where I keep the crystal?"

"Of course."

"Please fetch it for me."

The boy nodded and ran off through the back door. Philokrates shuffled his papyri and scrolls about, searching for something he couldn't find. Timon returned, carrying a fleece-wrapped object in both hands. He set it down on the table.

"Excellent," Philokrates said. "You run along now, before the gates close for the night...unless you would rather remain here?"

"I have important things to do," the boy said, puffing out his thin chest. "How can you know what happens in the city without me?"

Philokrates sighed. "In that case—"

"I know. Be careful." Timon pulled a face and sprinted out the front door, leaving a swirl of dust in his wake.

"I tell him not to take foolish chances," Philokrates muttered. "But as you see—"

"He's a boy," Cian said, his voice weighted with sadness. He noticed Quintus's stare and looked away, touching the sheepskin-covered object. Instantly he recoiled and stepped back from the table.

Philokrates unwrapped the object, laying the fleece aside. Clear crystal deflected the light from the complex pattern of its faceted surface. Inside the crystal was a fleck of red, no larger than a drop of blood.

Quintus glanced at the door, half expecting an invasion of imperial soldiers. "Are you mad, Philokrates?" he asked softly.

"Just mad enough." He cocked his head at Cian. "Do you hear the stone now?"

"No." Cian drew closer, muscles tensed to spring away again. "Crystal. The crystal cage…"

"Indeed." The old man touched it gingerly. "The stone has no power as long as it is contained within. I have found no means to break or even chip it. Does it seem familiar to you?"

Cian shook his head. Quintus held his right hand above the crystal. The red stone pulsed like a frantic heartbeat.

"Ah," Philokrates breathed. "It feels *you,* my young friend. But I do not think you can affect it, either."

Quintus let his arm fall. "Where did you get this, Philokrates?"

"I have…traveled widely in my day. I was young when Alexandros was crowned pharaoh of Aigyptos. I purchased this from a man in Thebes many years ago, not knowing then what I had obtained. I have kept it hidden ever since."

"It is evil," Cian whispered.

"Yes," Philokrates said. "But it is only a fragment, like my pneumata. A small piece of the whole. It must be studied and understood."

Quintus swept the crystal aside. "So you examine it here, openly, with texts that tell of Watchers and cages?" His gesture took in the room and all its contents. "You have a device that warns you of the Stone's servants, yet they leave you alone to plot against them?"

"They leave me alone because they, like you, think me mad."

"The mad are not spared." Quintus gripped the old man's arm, sick with rage at his own gullibility. "How did you come to be my people's contact in Hellas, an enemy of the Stone God and yet ignored by its priests?"

Cian moved to interfere, but Philokrates waved him back. "You have reason for your doubts, my son. You wonder why I left Tiberia during the first attack, abandoning your family, who gave me shelter and accepted me as one of them." He met Quintus's gaze. "Before I came to your family, I had been...sought by the empire."

"As a rebel?"

"In a manner of speaking, yes."

Quintus clenched his fist. *You lied to me.* "You lied to my father."

"I was afraid, and I thought Tiberia would be a safe haven for many years. Arrhidaeos had grown complacent with his empire. He knew the Tiberians would be no easy conquest. But his son..." He clasped his hands. "I knew your father would get you and your people safely to the hills. I could do nothing but slow your escape, and I could not let myself be discovered."

Quintus laughed, bitter with disbelief. "So you returned to Hellas?"

"I was caught, you see. But Nikodemos had not been long on

the throne, and he found it expedient to pardon a few minor transgressors as a gesture of the new emperor's beneficence." Philokrates bent his head. "I was old, and so they let me live—as long as I remained where I could be watched. In six years I have convinced the authorities that I am quite harmless, and I have my sentinel to warn me should they ever approach. But the priests have never come, and my neighbors leave me quite alone."

"The empire was never so merciful."

"I am proof that they can allow a known rebel to live in their midst, yet still they need fear nothing."

"If they had followed me from Piraeos…"

"I would not have offered myself as your people's contact in Attika if my doing so put others in danger. But no one has been caught. Were you stopped at the gate? Were you followed by anyone save Cian?"

Quintus felt the fragility of the bony arm in his grasp and let Philokrates go. He didn't trust himself to speak.

"You saw the people of Piraeos," Philokrates said. "It is the same in every polis, every deme. After forty years of occupation, the empire is too sure of Hellas to waste attention here, when the priests and soldiers are fighting rebels in Tiberia and conquering new lands. Even they are not all-powerful. If they were, there would be no hope. But I have hope, young Quintus."

"As I do," Cian said. He walked past Quintus to examine Philokrates's strange apparatus. "Pneumata," he murmured. "Fragments of a greater whole, you said."

"Yes." Philokrates spoke to the foreigner, but his gaze was fixed on Quintus, begging for his belief. "All matter is composed of the four elements—earth, air, fire, water—and indivisible parts called atomoi. But pneumata are imbued with distinct natural powers. Many joined together become far more powerful than one alone. Each of us, with our human hearts and minds, is part of something greater than we understand. It is the choice of men to decide what to make of the world."

"Men and women," Cian said. "And devas." He knelt and touched the hard-packed earth of the farmhouse floor. His hand disappeared up to the elbow.

"By Zeus's hairy thighs," Philokrates whispered.

"The poison does not enter here," Cian said. "It can be stopped." He closed his eyes. "Do you honor your gods, Philokrates?"

"I honor knowledge. I honor truth, and what is right."

"I have met men who doubt the devas' very existence. My people lived with them every day. We shared the guardianship of our sacred mountains. The Ailuri were the children of gods, better and greater than men, blessed above all mortal creatures. But I have learned that just as gods are said to have shaped men, so men shape the devas."

"The gods of Tiberia abandoned her," Quintus said. "And the gods of Hellas left these lands long ago."

"Yet something of them remains." Cian withdrew his hand. Not so much as a grain of soil clung to his skin, and the ground was firm and unbroken. "Once I swore that I would find my lost people. I make that oath again. I swear on this good earth that I will make any sacrifice to find them and set them free."

Quintus felt the power of the barbarian's words as a physical sensation in his legs and chest, reminding him of the oaths he had given and broken and made anew. Then the earth began to tremble, showering loose plaster from the walls and shifting Philokrates's papyri like windblown leaves. Quintus braced his feet and caught Philokrates to steady him. He followed the old man's stare to the pipe that ran across the front door's threshold. With every rattle the tube gave off a burst of amber-green radiance.

Cian stretched to touch the pipe. Streaks of spectral light raced up his arm and set his golden eyes aflame. He groaned from the bottom of his chest.

The tremors ceased. The glow faded from Cian's skin, and the pipe grew dark and cold. Cian stood, holding his hands out from his sides as if he feared the ground might swallow him whole.

"I believe——" Philokrates coughed gently. "I believe your oath has been witnessed."

Chapter Nineteen

"Timon was right," Quintus said, fighting his astonishment. "The earthquake in the agora...it was your doing."

Cian seemed not to hear. He folded his arms tightly across his chest, trembling though the ground was still.

"These pneumata," he said. "Once they were something else."

"All substance is eternal," Philokrates replied. "Nothing dies, my young friend. It only changes. Everything must change."

Everything.

Quintus stepped around Cian and walked out into the courtyard. Full dark had fallen, giving him the privacy he craved. This was a country without the ordinary little sounds of evenings—crickets and owls, weasels on the prowl and dogs barking at the least disturbance. Yet Philokrates's house was an island of life, like the mountain strongholds where Tiberian rebels clung so tenaciously to freedom.

Freedom for every man but one. The rebels had accepted a

boy's oath and twisted it into something he couldn't keep, forbidding him to take up a sword in defense and vengeance.

He'd given his first and only promise on the day Corvinium fell. He'd been hunting high in the mountains when he saw the smoke, heard screams like the calls of birds across the valley. The Stone God's priests had done their work by the time he scrambled down to the village, legs and arms scored with cuts and bruises in a mockery of battle wounds honorably won.

His father and brothers had died defending Corvinium, his mother dragged weeping from her hearth. Quintus had been left with the ashes. He'd sworn to fight until the empire and its god were nothing but bones and rubble.

And he must do it alone. Even Philokrates had proven unreliable. The only heart Quintus knew was his own.

A footstep sounded behind him, deliberately loud. Cian leaned against the courtyard wall and gazed into the night, his eyes black pools rimmed with gold.

"You will go to Karchedon," he said, "no matter what your friend advises. How do you expect to destroy the Stone God?"

"In any way I can."

"Yet Philokrates warns you not to act alone. Is your power so great?"

Quintus stiffened, then relaxed his muscles, working to match the barbarian's composure. *Tell him nothing.* That was the voice of his elders in Tiberia, who had always been afraid—afraid the empire would discover his existence.

He would not live in fear, no matter what marvels and terrors he witnessed.

Inside the house, Philokrates lit a lamp. Warm light poured from the small, high windows, glinting on Cian's sharp white teeth. "We all have our secrets," Cian said. "I know that you have the courage to face a phalanx of imperial soldiers, and abilities I don't understand." He laughed. "I am not particularly courageous. Nor am I certain…of anything."

"You admit your weaknesses."

"You wouldn't trust me more if I concealed them. I, too, go to Karchedon. We can be of service to each other."

You mean you would find me useful as a tool, just as the others did. "You wish me to protect you from the stones while you search for your lost people?"

Cian heard the Tiberian's mockery and remembered what it was to be so young, so convinced of one's good judgment. By the devas' blood, how well he remembered. "I have some skill in fighting," he said dryly. "You'll need someone to watch your back until you find these Karchedonian rebels, and it seems that even I may be of some use in this war of men and gods."

"To make the earth shake is a useful skill," Quintus admitted. "But the priests hunt your kind. I cannot allow you to compromise my mission or my contacts."

Cian sighed. "I knew another very much like you. She refused to listen to anything but her own stubborn—"

"She?"

"Most definitely 'she,'" Cian said. His body ached with the need that never left him. "A warrior from a race of warriors. They call themselves the Free People in their tongue, and they suffer no men to live among them."

"Women who fight? Women without men? No such creatures exist."

Cian grinned, imagining a meeting between Rhenna and the young Tiberian. But that would never happen.

"You had never seen my like before," he said soberly. "Would you have believed such a creature could exist?"

Quintus opened his mouth to answer, but he was interrupted by Philokrates's sudden appearance in the courtyard.

"I have found it!" the old man said, waving a scroll in one hand, while balancing a lamp in the other. He set the lamp on top of the wall and unrolled the papyrus. "This is the prophecy of which I spoke." He squinted at the crabbed writing. "'As it has been foretold since the beginning— No, no." He brought the papyrus closer to his eyes. "Here. 'If the Watchers fail, the Exalted will rise again. They will come in fire and flood, in miasma and drought, to claim the Earth anew.'"

"What are these Exalted?" Cian asked.

Philokrates lowered the papyrus. "The Hellenes have legends of the birth of the first gods, the Titanes, from the mating of Ouranos the Sky and Gaia the Earth. The Titanes overthrew their father and ruled the Earth until the younger gods of Olympos, led by Zeus, overthrew them in turn. The Olympians gave rise to the daimones, spirits of air, earth, sea and underworld."

"Such tales exist in many lands, though the gods have different names."

"Yes. But I believe these Exalted are beings even more ancient than the Titanes—so ancient that men have forgotten their names. I also believe the Exalted and the Stone God are the same, powerful deities imprisoned for some great evil in a time before the first pharaohs ruled Aigyptos."

"If the Exalted were so powerful, what could imprison them?"

"Others of equal power who chose not to join in their evil works. The Watchers—"

"My people can't be the Watchers you seek," Cian said. "The Ailuri have no memories, not even legends, of such events."

"Even the children of gods may forget," Philokrates said.

"If these Exalted escaped, it was not of our doing."

"*If* the Exalted and the Stone God are the same," Quintus said. "*If* these prophecies are anything but superstition or some madman's visions meant to frighten children."

Philokrates bent his head. "And if I have not misinterpreted out of my own ignorance. But I know the prophecy continues." His eyes caught the lamplight, shining with passion. "It may contain the secrets not only of the past, but of the future. The answers we all seek. The means to defeat the Stone." He shook the scroll and it went flying out of his hand.

Quintus moved to intercept it, tossing back the cloak that covered the left side of his body. Contorted fingers clawed the air. The Tiberian's twisted left hand struck the scroll, knocking it sideways, and he deftly caught it in his strong right hand. He returned the scroll to Philokrates without a word, but his defiant gaze sought Cian's. He made no attempt to cover the crippled limb.

The silence was stifling. Cian took a step toward Quintus.

The young man spun toward the gate and strode through it, his cloak swinging out behind him. Only one of his fists was clenched.

"Let him go," Philokrates said. "His family and countrymen never let him forget his infirmity."

"He was born that way?"

"So he was told. His mother protected him far beyond the age that any boy could tolerate. His father deemed him unfit to bear a sword, even after the Tiberians lost half their capable men to imperial troops during the conquest. They have become a hard people, and they suffer no weakness." He turned the scroll over and over in his hands. "Quintus taught himself to fight in secret. He was fifteen when the empire came."

"He's older than he looks."

"He has always been older." Philokrates tried again to smooth his flyaway hair. "After I left Italia, I received occasional word of him. His family was killed two years after the invasion, while hiding in the hills east of Tiberia. Quintus was the only survivor. He attempted to join one of the rebel bands. They would have rejected him, save that they discovered…his talent for quenching the red stones."

"He can destroy them?"

"I am told that he can drain or extinguish their power at a touch."

"Then what he seeks is not impossible."

"The Tiberians believed so. They kept him safe in isolation, waiting for the right opportunity to strike the priests and the empire. They knew they might have only one chance. But Quintus…he could not bear the confinement, the memory of his family's deaths unavenged."

Cian closed his eyes, beginning to understand. "He escaped."

"A few days ago I received a message that Quintus might come to find the rebels' contact in Attika. He did not know it would be me. I was told to detain him until the Tiberians could fetch him back."

"And will you?"

Philokrates laughed and broke into a cough. "With my great strength? Or my irresistible powers of persuasion? Once he might have listened. No more."

"He doesn't believe in your prophecy."

"Perhaps belief is not necessary." He looked past Cian toward the gate and the darkness beyond. "We'll find Quintus at the docks in the morning."

"We?"

"Of course. I am coming with you. I have some knowledge of Karchedon from my previous travels."

Cian stepped back. "I cannot help you, Philokrates. My first loyalty is to my own kind."

"Is it?" the old man asked gently. "I heard you tell Quintus that you might be of some use in this war of men and gods. Did you lie to him? Will you save your people, return to your land and wait for the empire to come? For come it will. The Stone and its priests will see to that—unless they are stopped."

Cian pounded his fist on the wall, nearly upsetting the lamp. "What would you have me do?"

"Open your mind to the possibility that you may be destined for a greater purpose than setting your people free."

Destiny—the very bondage he had always sought to evade. Cian shuddered. "We must take a black ship to Karchedon."

"There is no better method of travel as yet known to man."

"Is there not some danger to Quintus, being what he is?"

Philokrates picked up the lamp and beckoned Cian inside the house. "If Quintus's nature has not been discovered in his travels across Hellas from Italia, I can but speculate that his very power to destroy the stones shields him from their notice. As for me, I am but a harmless, foolish old man...."

Who lies now? Cian thought, but he joined Philokrates in a modest evening meal and answered his questions about the tribes of the North. He left the old man snoring over his papyrus a few hours later. Then he found his way back to the city gate and scaled the wall unseen.

Nothing could have prepared him for the stones' renewed onslaught. Half mad with the clatter in his head, he made slow and unsteady progress toward the city's western harbor. Piraeos came awake just before dawn, as merchants began to lay out their wares in the agora near the docks. Cian avoided soldiers and priests until full daylight brought out the morning shoppers and gray-robed pilgrims, who clustered near the foot of the harbor's enormous, bloodstained altar. A black ship squatted on the water like a fat carrion beetle.

Quintus was nearby. Cian knew he couldn't have fought the red stones' influence if not for the Tiberian's presence, nor could he have detected the sweet, compelling scent that made his heart swell near to bursting.

He forgot Quintus. He forgot the stones. He followed the scent until he found its source.

Her head rose above nearly all the others around her, but she had not yet seen him. He could escape again.

Nothing has changed. Nothing...

Another face turned in his direction. Tahvo tugged on her companion's arm. Cian felt Rhenna's gaze like a balm of ice and fire. He took a step toward her. A pair of brawny dockhands came between them. That brief moment of separation was more than Cian could bear.

Rhenna.

She smiled. Fleeting, uncertain, quickly gone, but a smile nonetheless. By the time he reached her side, her face was stern but her eyes shone like leaf-dappled sunlight.

"Cian," she said, husky and low.

"Rhenna." He looked down, not daring to hold her gaze too long. "Tahvo. You are well?"

"Yes." Tahvo extended her hands, and Cian took them. They were thinner and more rough than he remembered, and her silver eyes did not quite focus, as if a whole world of spirits lived within them.

"We knew we would find you," she said.

Rhenna shook her head, lips pressed thin. Cian despised himself. He couldn't bear that Rhenna should believe he'd abandoned them simply to escape her or her duty. He was afraid to search for the signs of her suffering, afraid of his shame and the rage that had no outlet save blood-lust or self-destruction.

"The beast took me," he said, leaning close so that only they could hear.

"We know," Rhenna said. "Farkas...survived."

"I can't always control that part of me, Rhenna. I wanted to spare you both...spare you more—"

She stopped him with a motion of her hand. Her fingers hovered near his face and slowly, hesitantly brushed at a strand of his hair.

"Spare us your foolishness," she said. She dropped her hand. "You haven't found your people."

"I know where to look for them." He almost touched her as she had touched him, but fear restrained him. Fear of this warrior and her relentless duty. Fear for her and for himself.

"You've come very far to take me back," he whispered.

She looked away. "Cian. I—"

Tahvo saved them both further awkwardness by choosing that moment to walk off into the crowd. Rhenna immediately followed, and Cian strode after them. When the stones' perpetual keening quieted to a distant hum, he knew that Tahvo had found Quintus.

Philokrates and the young Tiberian stood in the shadow of a warehouse near the dock, far from the altar. Quintus's face was obscured by his hood, but the old man's eyes lit with curiosity as he caught sight of Tahvo and Rhenna.

"Thank the Fates you are safe," he said to Cian.

"Philokrates...last night—"

"No matter. I am here, as I promised. And now I see why you were so eager to return to Piraeos. I did not realize that you knew anyone in Attika."

"Fellow travelers from an earlier part of my journey. We were...separated."

"He is one we seek," Tahvo said, gazing up at Quintus.

Quintus emerged from some grim meditation and looked at Tahvo without comprehension. Cian rested a hand on the healer's shoulder. "This is Tahvo. She comes from a land farther to the north than my own. She is also…" He hesitated, aware of possible eavesdroppers. "An ally."

Philokrates bowed. "Welcome to Piraeos." His gaze skipped to Rhenna, who regarded him warily.

"Cian?" she prompted.

"Rhenna, these are my new…associates, Quintus and Philokrates. And this is Rhenna of the Free People."

Quintus stared at Rhenna as if she might sprout a second head or fling poison darts from beneath her cloak. "This is the female who fights?"

"You have spoken of me?" Rhenna said in Cian's ear.

Cian warned Rhenna with a glance. "My companions have aided me in my search," he said to Philokrates. "Until we became—"

"Companions?" Quintus said, giving the word a dubious emphasis. "I had heard that some barbarians take several wives."

Cian winced. "They are not—"

"The Free People take no husbands," Rhenna said.

"Ah." Philokrates nodded, stroking his beard. "Are you of the tribe called Amazons?"

"I do not know that name. You are of this city?"

"Of Hellas, yes. Not of this—" His gesture encompassed the harbor and its human cattle. "Young Quintus is of another land, but I assure you that he is also a friend."

Rhenna pinned the Tiberian with her iron stare. "Do your people also keep their females in captivity?"

"Our women know their place," Quintus replied, holding her gaze.

Rhenna snorted. "And these are allies, Cian?"

Tahvo touched Quintus's cloak, unintimidated by his forbidding manner. "This meeting was not by chance," she said. "I *saw* him— in Hypanis."

"Look at her eyes, Quintus," Philokrates said. "I believe she is a seer of some kind."

"First prophecies, and now seers," Quintus said harshly. "You have acquired a strange kind of faith, Philokrates."

"Tahvo understands your words," Rhenna said. "As I do."

"You claim the ability to predict the future?" Philokrates asked Tahvo.

"Sometimes the spirits let me *see*." She gazed steadily at Quintus. "He is to come with us. Without him, we will fail."

Chapter Twenty

Asteria's blood. Rhenna looked at Quintus's stony, arrogant face. "Fail?" she repeated softly. "In what?"

But she was afraid she understood all too well.

Tahvo was more lucid now than she had been at any time since boarding the black ship. Deprived of her coat and drum, she had come to rely more and more on the mysterious contents of her pouch. The substance seemed to ease her sorrow and help her to sleep.

There was little else to do. Except when it stopped in imperial ports for pilgrims and tribute—grain and gold, fine cloth or wine—the black ship sailed both night and day. The priests kept to themselves under the hut-like platforms to the fore and aft of the ship, or disappeared beneath the deck for hours at a time. Rhenna had paced when she dared, worried about Tahvo, and dreamed of Cian.

The black ship's prolonged stop at Piraeos permitted the passengers to disembark. For Rhenna the chance to walk on firm, dry land—and search for Cian—seemed a blessing…until the city revealed its loathsome nature.

While Hypanis had but recently fallen under the empire's control, the mainland of Hellas had worn its chains for forty years. Its people were without spirit, and priests almost outnumbered soldiers. Altars were everywhere, perpetually ablaze with the sacrifice of beasts large and small, many burned alive.

The living offerings had disturbed Rhenna, but it was worse for Tahvo. The healer had trembled so violently that Rhenna feared even the dull-eyed natives would notice her strange behavior.

Then, wonder of wonders, Cian had found them. The hollowness in Rhenna's chest had filled with the absurd desire to take him in her arms and dance like a mead-struck girl at her first Winterfest.

She no longer felt like dancing.

Cian avoided Rhenna's eyes. "Quintus has certain…unusual talents," he said. His voice dropped to a whisper. "He weakens the stones' power. He may even be able to destroy them."

Rhenna laughed, but Cian wasn't smiling.

"It is true," he said. "Every moment since I entered Hypanis…the stones have called me. It's because of Quintus that I'm still alive."

His words confirmed what Rhenna had feared since Cian had run away from the Skudat camp. The stones had nearly taken him, in spite of Tahvo's reassurances. She studied Quintus with new interest. "If you've aided Cian, then I have cause to thank you."

"Save your thanks," Quintus said. "Any aid I rendered was unintentional."

Philokrates raised his hands. "It is not wise to quarrel too openly," he said. "Disputes of any kind are rare in Piraeos."

Rhenna carefully looked about them, but no stranger stood close enough to listen. "We should find shelter," she said.

"We are safe enough in this public place as long as we behave with discretion." Philokrates smiled like one half-witted. "I am told that Cian's purpose in Karchedon is to find and free his people."

Rhenna straightened. "What do you know of them?"

"Only what I have learned from my study of ancient prophecy—of the Watchers and the rise of the Stone God."

She searched out Cian's gaze, suddenly afraid. "His people and mine have been allies for centuries. I know of no prophecy regarding the Ailuri."

"Have you not come to help him in his quest?"

Cian's eyes posed the request she dread above all others: *Let me go.* She hesitated too long in her response.

Philokrates turned to Quintus. "It is obvious that we must accompany them."

"I go alone," Quintus said.

Philokrates addressed Rhenna as if his friend hadn't spoken. "You came to Piraeos on the black ship that arrived before dawn this morning? It continues on to Karchedon. Quintus and I will arrange for passage."

Abruptly Quintus strode away. Tahvo gathered her short legs and dashed off in pursuit. She tripped over her chiton's overlong hem and tumbled at the young man's feet.

Some vestige of courtesy obliged Quintus to help her up. He half crouched to listen as Tahvo spoke, unexpected gentleness in his expression.

"Tahvo wastes her time with that one," Rhenna said.

Cian cocked his head. "Perhaps not."

Tahvo took Quintus's hand, and for the first time Rhenna noticed that he wore his cloak placed to cover his left side from shoulder to fingertips. Tahvo touched the shape of his left hand through the cloak. Quintus flinched. Tahvo spoke again, and the young man's tense frame relaxed. He and Tahvo turned and walked back, side by side.

Quintus caught Rhenna's look, and his brief vulnerability evaporated. His gait took on the hint of a swagger.

"Since it seems that we are to be traveling companions after all," he said, "I trust that I will have the personal opportunity to learn more of your people's customs. Such freedom from male discipline and proper guidance must permit you to develop most unusual...talents."

Cian stiffened. Rhenna couldn't fail to take the boy's meaning. "You confuse me with some other female, perhaps," she said softly.

"The Hellenes have a name for women who walk freely among men and behave as their equals, and it is not sister, daughter, mother or wife. Since you are none of these..." He shrugged.

"I have been a daughter," Rhenna said, "and a Sister. My skills are reserved for my true friends."

"A pity. I would enjoy wielding my sword again."

"I'm surprised you're old enough to hold one, let alone fight. Or perhaps that's all you've done...hold it."

Quintus narrowed his gray eyes. "You are obviously unacquainted with Tiberians. I can remedy your ignorance."

Cian growled.

Philokrates insinuated himself between the two men and cast a pleading glance at Rhenna. "The black ship leaves in a few hours," he said. "We should not remain together once we board. Quintus, you will be most useful staying with Cian. You ladies—" he bowed to Rhenna and Tahvo "—should continue as before, though I do hope I may speak more with you about the Northern lands." He smiled at Quintus. "Don't worry, my boy. I'll arrange everything. Meet me at the pilgrims' landing in an hour."

He hurried off. Rhenna turned her back on Quintus, facing the smoking altar stone across the agora.

"He is not what he seems," Tahvo said beside her.

"He has much to learn."

"He has lost much."

"More than Cian? More than——" She quelled the memories. "You say he has some purpose. If he keeps the stones from hurting Cian…"

"He is more. He——"

Strident horns blared, drowning Tahvo's words. A half-dozen priests paced to the altar platform, followed by chanting pilgrims and a herd of young children ranging in age from toddlers to youths. They were bound together with lengths of rope harnessed about their waists. Some wept, but others stared with the same empty eyes as the men and women assembling to observe this new diversion.

Cian well remembered how the docile citizens of Piraeos had changed into a ravening mob after Timon's theft of the melon. Though he and his companions stood far from the crowd gathering about the alter, Cian heard the cry of the red stones like the clash of cymbals. He watched the children with growing dread. Tahvo clutched at the hem of Rhenna's tunic as if she feared the warrior would bolt.

One of the priests mounted the dais before the altar, his face hidden beneath his hood. The stone pendant on his chest was bigger than any Cian had seen, so deep a red that it seemed almost black. The ever-expanding congregation fell silent.

The priest spoke. Cian understood nothing. Two priests wearing smaller stones separated one child out from the rest and led him to the dais. They raised his limp form high to face the altar, and as they turned, Cian saw his face.

It was Timon.

He lunged, and Rhenna lunged with him. They were of one heart then, unhindered by sense or reason. But Rhenna was weaponless, defenseless.

Cian was not. He willed the change. His body flouted his command. Someone grabbed a fistful of his tunic and belt, braced against his struggles.

Change. Change, and no one can stop you....

But he couldn't. His limbs locked in mid-motion.

Rhenna froze, her lips parted in shock.

Magic held their bodies in bondage, magic that felt like the stones and yet was utterly different. No amount of exertion altered its disabling force.

Quintus stepped in front of them, unencumbered by their paralysis. He lifted his right arm as if he could reach out and touch the altar. His hood fell to his shoulders. Perspiration broke out on his upper lip and forehead.

Timon's body became stiff as the two priests laid him on the platform below the altar. Cian moaned, but no sound escaped his throat. The lesser clerics stepped back, and the head priest advanced with his stone cupped in his hands.

Some inexplicable compulsion drew Cian's gaze from the horror. He could just see Quintus's profile, the marks of strain on his young face, the tendons standing out on his neck.

Quintus can destroy the stones. He will save Timon.

Cian repeated the thought again and again as the priests bound Timon to the iron rings sunk into the altar's gray surface. The head priest raised his arms and shouted an invocation. Fire burst from the center of the altar behind Timon. The boy opened his eyes.

The priest angled his stone toward Timon. Light caught the stone's facets and directed a crimson beam into the center of the boy's chest. A wisp of smoke drifted up from Timon's chiton.

He screamed.

Rhenna keened through gritted teeth. Quintus tilted his head skyward. Runnels of sweat soaked the edge of his cloak. He slowly clenched his right hand.

The priest still held his stone aimed at Timon, but something had interrupted the ceremony. The beam thinned. The agony in Cian's head subsided.

Quintus was succeeding.

The priest cried out to his god. He hunched over Timon like a carrion bird and placed the stone directly on Timon's hollow chest. Fire surged, and Cian smelled burning flesh. Timon screamed again. Hot tears ran unchecked down Cian's face.

Quintus fell to his knees. The fire on the altar flared into a seething, bubbling sphere. It swallowed Timon little by little, searing his skin into blackened blisters, creeping like a thousand flesh-eating worms that burrowed down to the bone before moving on to the next sweet morsel.

Cian filled his mind with a single intent. His muscles convulsed. Budding fur prickled under his skin.

Rhenna took a wrenching step toward him, her mouth stretched in a grimace of supreme effort. Tahvo crawled to Quintus and supported him as best she could.

Suddenly there was a roar—of the crowd, of the fire, of the stones themselves—and the altar flames exploded. The priest flailed away. His underlings slapped at the sparks alighting on his robes.

When at last the fire shrank to a normal blaze, Timon was gone.

"Praised be the one true god!" cried the priest. "And blessed be his holy sacrifice."

"Praised be the Stone God!" the citizens of Piraeos answered in one hideous voice.

Cian's muscles loosened all at once. His body relinquished the change. He and Rhenna fell against each other, weak as infants. His tears mingled with hers.

"I couldn't move," she whispered. "The boy—"

"I saw Timon…only hours ago."

Grief and pity and hatred burned the tears from her eyes. "You knew him."

"I couldn't save him," he croaked.

"He was saved," Tahvo said. She led Quintus by the hand as she might a bewildered child. Her face was mottled with weeping. "Quintus weakened the stone's power. It did not take the child's soul."

Quintus jerked and quivered like a statue brought clumsily to life. Color rushed into his cheeks, and he blinked haunted eyes. "I failed," he said.

"No," Tahvo said. "You did all you could."

"It was not enough."

"He did not go into the stone like the animals and the spirits. Now he is free."

"He is dead."

"Only the body. You must believe."

Quintus averted his face. Cian had no comfort to offer. He tasted blood from his bitten lips, wishing it was the priest's, instead. He dimly noted that the crowd was dispersing. The children had been taken away, and the pilgrims had gone to gaze upon the black ship. The altar's fire smoldered.

"The priests," Rhenna said, her voice still unsteady. "Didn't they realize what happened?"

"They felt it," Tahvo said, "but they did not understand."

"It was you who stopped me and Cian," Rhenna said to Quintus. "Won't they search for one who has such power?"

"They have never known I existed," Quintus said. "But now—"

"You must go."

Quintas lifted his head, and a spark lit his eyes. "To Karchedon."

Cian met Rhenna's gaze. If they had rushed to Timon's aid, his quest would have come to a swift and fatal conclusion. But an innocent child had been murdered by unspeakable evil, and he wouldn't be the last. Tahvo's visions, Philokrates's prophecies, Cian's own pitiful hopes—all were as false as Ailuri dreams of divinity. The earth had not shaken to halt the sacrifice. The stone had not been destroyed.

"Will you save your people, return to your land and wait for the empire to come?" Philokrates had asked. Cian shuddered with silent laughter. The first was beyond his power, the last inevitable. Let Rhenna take him back to the Shield's Shadow. Let him service her people's Chosen until he died. It would not matter in the end.

Rhenna shoved at the hood half covering her head. Smoke-filtered sunlight transformed her hair from common brown to gold and set her eyes ablaze. She stared at the altar as if she could tear it down with her own two hands.

"You were right, Cian," she said. "I came a very long way to take you home. But there is no going back while *that* exists in the world. We will fight."

No going back. Cian had never thought to hear such words from Rhenna's lips. Her courage and determination blew through him like a fresh, invigorating wind out of the Shield.

If she could believe, then he must.

Tahvo enfolded Rhenna's fists in her hands. "We will fight," she said. "In Karchedon."

Rhenna sat on the black ship's deck and watched Cian leaning on the bulwark, staring out at the open sea. His body was concealed in the common gray cloak, but she would have recognized the angle of his head, his stance, his smallest gesture, from among any thousand males of similar height and build, anywhere in the world.

He spent most of his time close to Quintus, though the two men hardly acknowledged each other. It was better so. Rhenna knew Cian suffered because of the stones; she glimpsed the pain in his face when he passed by, feigning indifference like the other pilgrims. She could do nothing to help.

Yet the mere sight of him was a welcome distraction from the awful, incessant drone that issued from the vessel's deepest heart.

Though the vast Ta Thalassa was to the Dark Sea as the steppe to a meadow, the black ship glided over the water in a bubble of perfect calm. No harsh winds blew the ship off course, no storms lashed its hull. Its wake left an oily trail that absorbed all light, killing any unfortunate creature that passed through the low, greasy waves.

Tahvo never spoke of her devas. Occasionally she emerged from some deep inward reflection, lifting her head to the sky, and Rhenna guessed that she heard some water spirit's faraway voice. But she didn't try to call them, and she always returned to her silent contemplation. Waiting. Enduring.

"You are well?" Philokrates moved quietly for so elderly a male, but he didn't have Cian's skill.

Rhenna leaned back on her sleeping mat, keeping her face half covered. Tahvo slept.

"Well enough," she said. "And you?"

The old man squatted just near enough to hear and be heard. "Quite acceptable, but I fear it is not so for young Quintus."

Rhenna frowned. "He's ill?"

"He has the sea-sickness. It strikes some worse than others, and he was weakened by what he attempted in Piraeos. The black ships seldom provoke it so strongly."

"You've been on one of these ships before?"

"Once or twice." He glanced across the deck, and Rhenna followed his gaze to Quintus's noticeably greenish face. The young man hung his head over the bulwark, back heaving.

"I regret that he suffers," Rhenna said.

"Even though he has been far from cordial to you and your friends? Your people must not be accustomed to such arrogance from men."

"We are not generally accustomed to men at all."

"Ah. Then it is very much like the old stories. But you do not mutilate your bodies."

Rhenna raised a brow.

Philokrates shifted his position, bones creaking. "It is commonly said that Amazons remove their right breasts the better to pull a bow in battle."

"This is what your Hellenes have heard of us?"

"We've heard little and know less. It would be wise to conceal your origins in Karchedon."

"I have already learned a woman's place in your world," she said dryly. "But you speak to me as if I were a man."

"Several of my country's greatest philosophers were of the opinion that women ought to share many of the same rights as men. I also hold this opinion."

"Many rights, but not all?"

"The sexes are not identical, as I think even you must admit."

"Indeed."

He smiled. "Women are clearly superior?"

"I did not know that men could grow to be so wise."

He quickly sobered. "The Stone God encourages women to serve and join its cult equally with men, but do not be deceived."

"I am not. This place holds much evil."

"It was not always so," he said softly. "Once Hellas was a land of learning and beauty. Athinai was renowned throughout the world. We had a thing called demokratia, rule by the people, not by a privileged few."

"Then came this Alexandros."

"There are tales that he fought the Amazons."

"Our people never met his in battle," she said. "All we have are stories. Your empire..." She reconsidered her words. *Trust or don't trust. There is nothing between.* "Your empire keeps allies who are our enemies. Hellenish soldiers have been seen near our borders. My people do not recognize the monster that comes."

"And that is why you are here, Rhenna of the Free People? To learn how your race can defeat it?

"I came South for Cian's sake. But everything has changed." She glanced down at Tahvo's peaceful face. "She sees what we cannot. I have learned to follow her visions."

"You are not of the same people, you and the seer."

"No. But she taught me to recognize my enemy."

"And Cian? What is he to you?"

Once Rhenna would have taken offense, but she had seen too much horror to resent an old man's questions. "Cian's people and mine share...certain traditions."

"I understand that all Ailuri are male, yet you said you are not accustomed to men."

"They are not ordinary men."

"So I have seen."

"The Ailuri dwelt in the mountains north of our lands. When they disappeared, I was sent to learn what had become of them."

"Cian told us of his abduction by imperial soldiers, and how he is called by the red stones." He glanced toward Cian. "Do you know why they call him?"

Rhenna found it difficult to admit how little she knew. "You named Cian's people 'Watchers.'"

"Yes. The Watchers have some power that is greatly feared by the priests—"

"Because the Ailuri can help defeat them," Tahvo whispered. She sat up, all silver eyes and hair.

"Seer," Philokrates acknowledged. "You persuaded Quintus to join us. Do you see him destroying the Stone God?"

The silence was sudden and absolute. Rhenna stood up and pretended to stretch, her gaze sweeping from bow to stern. The pilgrims paid them no mind.

"As I said in Piraeos," Philokrates said, "*they* will not listen. As long as the priests remain below, there is no safer place to speak than on this deck."

Rhenna sat down again. "If they are such fools, how could they conquer anyone?"

"Not all priests are alike, and they did not begin the empire. Nor are there yet enough of them to hold it without the emperor's armies. They send their least skilled acolytes to shepherd pilgrims and guide the black ships."

"You say there are not yet enough of them," Rhenna said, "as if these priests are made."

"Yes." Philokrates arranged his long tunic around his knees. "You know that the Stone was first discovered by Alexandros."

"I do not even know what form this god takes, except for the altars and the red stones. It is not like our devas."

"It's said that only a few have looked upon the Stone itself...the highest priests, the emperor and those who preceded him, Arrhidaeos and Alexandros. It is not made in the image of man, like Zeus or Apollon. I believe—" He lowered his voice, in spite of his reassurances. "I believe it is literally a stone, a very great one. Alexandros is said to have found it in Libya, moved all or part of it to some unknown place, and appointed priests to attend it." He sighed. "They were nothing then. Alexandros was building his empire around Ta Thalassa and had little time for a new god's cult. Yet he always carried a piece of the stone in an amulet, believing it brought him victory."

"False victory," Tahvo said.

"I have translated age-old writings that predict the rise of the Stone God, also called the Exalted, and the reawakening of ancient evil. Perhaps Alexandros knew the stories. Perhaps he was warned, but he did not listen. He began to go mad soon after his conquest of Persis and return to Hellas. His brother Arrhidaeos inherited his new empire when he died. Arrhidaeos was a true votary of the new god's cult. Soon after his succession, he was given a great revelation—the Stone God was to rise above all others. The Stone God's blessing would expand the empire's borders beyond Alexandros's most ambitious dreams."

"This was many years ago," Rhenna said. "Why did my people hear nothing of this for so long?"

"There was much confusion after Alexandros's death—revolts, years of fighting between his satraps and generals who had claimed parts of the lands he had conquered. Arrhidaeos was not a great man like his brother, able to win the personal loyalty of his soldiers. But he had the Stone God, whose priests had learned to wield a potent sorcery with fragments of the god itself."

"The red stones are pieces of the god?" Rhenna asked, incredulous.

"As each drop of water is part of this sea we travel upon. Arrhidaeos chose a High Priest to advise him. He was told to move his capital from his homeland in Hellas to the formidable city of Karchedon, which he won after three years of warfare and siege.

"During these years of fighting, Arrhidaeos had three sons by three different women. The first son, Nikodemos, was the fruit of the emperor's union with Alexandros's widow. She died in childbirth. The second child was stillborn, and Arrhidaeos set aside the wife who bore it. The third child disappeared soon after its birth, and a rumor spread that the emperor had given the babe to the Stone God to assure his ultimate victory over his enemies and complete control of the empire. Whatever the truth of that rumor, it began a terrible new tradition of human sacrifice."

Tahvo shivered, and Rhenna put her arm around the healer's shoulders. "Like Timon," she said.

"Like Timon." Philokrates rubbed at his eyes. "The Stone God had always demanded the blood of beasts for its altars, but that was no longer enough. Arrhidaeos did as he was told, and soon Alexandros's empire was firmly under his heel. The Stone God's priesthood became a power unto itself. For seventeen years they had spread the cult of their god by persuasion, promising prosperity and peace for all—eternal bliss for those who gave themselves willingly to the Stone God's worship."

"As we saw in Hypanis," Rhenna said.

"But then the priests decreed that every land under the empire abandon its old gods and swear to the new. They destroyed the temples and altars, and apprehended those who defied them. When many refused to renounce their deities, the emperor passed a law that required every man, woman and child to be tested by the priests or face death by sacrifice. And that was the true end of hope, for a man's response to the stones determined his fate."

"The people in Piraeos," Rhenna said. "Their faces—"

"—are the faces of sheep. So Quintus calls them. Most men and women who touch the stone fall under its influence and become what you saw in Hellas…or they embrace the Stone God and serve as its true acolytes. At some time you and Tahvo must both have touched the Stone and resisted its effects."

Rhenna closed her eyes, remembering the stone in the cup Farkas had given her. How well had she resisted him? "What of the pilgrims?" she asked.

"They believe they will be granted good fortune by visiting Karchedon and the Stone temple."

"In Hypanis the priests made such promises."

"And the priests' lies will convince many before the empire must deal with the inevitable rebellion. Once that is crushed, Hypanis will be like every other imperial city."

"Why did the empire wait so long to enter the North? Was Hypanis not also part of Hellas?"

"It was a colony, shared with the Skythes—"

"The Skudat," Rhenna said.

"If you know them, you may also know that they resisted Alexandros's attempts to conquer them. They do not fight like Hellenes, and their homeland is vast. That may be why they were left alone so long.

"You see, after forty years of constant strife, Arrhidaeos was ready for peace. He declined the High Priests' suggestion to expand the Stone God's reign by conquering new territories such as Italia and the lands north of the Euxeinos. The priests warned him that the Stone God was angry at his lack of piety in spreading the true word. But in his old age he grew stubborn. He sat on his throne and refused to call up his armies. His son Nikodemos was not so complacent. He took the High Priests' part against his father. The old emperor died of some mysterious ailment soon after, and Nikodemos ascended the throne."

"He killed his own father?"

"No one dared to suggest it. But Nikodemos continued in his grandfather Alexandros's footsteps. He conquered Italia—Tiberia, Quintus's homeland—and began to push east over the deserts beyond Persis. The priests kept complete authority in all matters of religion. As long as Nikodemos holds secular control, he allows the priests to use their powers as they judge necessary."

"To kill," Tahvo said. "To destroy all the spirits."

Philokrates smoothed his hair. "To gather all the world's power—yes. The priests have even changed the empire's army. Once the soldiers were mercenaries or men personally devoted to the emperor. Now the army largely consists of young men from conquered lands trained to mindless obedience under the stones. And there is a new breed, an elite sent to patrol the newest provinces."

Rhenna thought of the Hellenish commander who had removed his helmet for the Neuri...his beautiful, perfect, expressionless face. "The stones grow out of their foreheads."

"The stones are part of them, yet they retain some measure of free will. I believe the Stone God creates them."

"The Stone God takes life—" Tahvo said.

She breathed in and out so quickly that Rhenna feared she would make herself ill.

"Fire goes to earth, earth to water, water to sky, sky to fire again," she continued. "But what the Stone God changes can never be restored. Its fire is everlasting."

She slumped in Rhenna's arms. Rhenna eased her down to her mat and stroked the fine hair from the healer's face. Tahvo's eyelids fluttered, and she sank into sleep.

"It's been too much for her to bear," Rhenna said, spreading Tahvo's cloak to cover her feet. "Her own world was nothing like this. She has felt devas die."

"Life does not end even in death." He looked at Tahvo with pity. "Do you know what propels this ship?"

"I do not wish to know."

"I call them pneumata," he said. "Fragments of life that can be used to create what you name magic. When daimones—your devas—expire in certain ways, they break up into these pneumata and can be captured by…one prepared to receive them."

Rhenna leaped to a terrible conclusion. "Then the devas in Hypanis…the ones sacrificed on the Stone God's altar…"

"I have come to believe that both men and daimones possess a psyche—an intelligence or life-essence—that survives beyond the body. The altars contain stones like those carried by the priests, but larger and more powerful. When the priests make a sacrifice, they steal the psyche, and it becomes—" He coughed behind his hand, and his eyes began to water.

Rhenna squeezed the old man's arm. "Tahvo said that Quintus set Timon free."

"The Stone God will never be satisfied. It grows more powerful every day, like the empire. We who resist are so few."

"Destroy the Stone God, and the empire follows." Quintus passed Philokrates without stopping, his face still very pale but no less determined. He leaned on the bulwark not far from Rhenna. "I must speak to you, Philokrates."

The old man worked to his feet, groaning softly, and nodded to Rhenna before wandering off in the Tiberian's direction.

Rhenna also rose, stretched, and strolled the deck until she was almost within Cian's reach. She didn't need to speak. He scarcely glanced at her. A wind, astonishingly fresh, swept past Rhenna's face and continued on to caress the obsidian strands of Cian's unbound hair. Rhenna felt as if she were touching it herself.

"The stones?" she asked.

"Quiet."

"Quintus?"

He cocked his head toward the two men, deep in their conversation. "Angry. Philokrates won't tell him where to find the Karchedonian rebels until we enter the city."

"Then he'll find it necessary to remain with us, since Philokrates is on our side."

"You like the old man."

"He has considerable knowledge, and his rebels may help us find your people."

"You have changed, Rhenna."

She hesitated, wondering how to regard his comment. "I hope you aren't suggesting I've gotten soft."

His smile was fleeting and sad. "You? Never."

"My duty hasn't changed, Cian. It has only...altered its form."

"To encompass the saving of the world?"

"Look to Tahvo for such grand visions."

"I understand them no better than you."

"When an Elder Sister teaches a novice to fight, she is very patient. She knows that each move, each shift of muscle, must be learned one step at a time. There is no other way."

He turned his head, and his hair whipped over his face. "I've never had a warrior's perseverance."

"Your heart holds everything you need."

"Not everything."

His voice, soft and low, was indescribable torment. She stepped back from the bulwark.

"I would have killed him," he said, "if not for the stone."

She had no need to ask who Cian meant. "It's over."

"Is it?"

She turned and walked away.

Chapter Twenty-One

From the small, high window in her sleeping chamber, Danae could see the boats and ships come and go in the harbor of Karchedon. She enjoyed watching the small fishing ships and merchant vessels that plied the north Libyan coast; they were the same boats she remembered from childhood, hardly changed for a hundred years.

Not so the black ships. She could not avoid observing them as they arrived daily from the far corners of the empire, almost as regular as Nikodemos's prized water clock. The clock was so precise because its inner workings were influenced by the priests' magic. So, too, were the black ships, sailless and soulless as they thrust their way among the humbler vessels.

Today's black ship was identical to all the others, down to the tiny figures of gray-cloaked pilgrims crowding its forward deck. They were so full of hope, those newcomers, certain that their salvation awaited them in the empire's capital city, home to the Stone God's first and greatest temple.

Danae found it difficult to pity them. She saved her pity for the children kept in the hold where the pilgrims would not see.

She turned from the window, sick at heart. Most of those children would live to become servants of the priests and temples, or—if male, and so inclined by temperament or natural talent—to be trained as priests or officers in the imperial army. The girls were less fortunate, for if they showed even a spark of aptitude they might serve as temple broodmares until they died in childbirth or wore out their bodies.

They were the forgotten children, the orphans, the unwanted, the offspring of parents too poor to pay temple or imperial taxes. Sometimes they were gifts of wealthy families seeking favor of the priests. None had any choice in his fate.

Danae always had choices. Her father might outwardly disapprove of her decisions, but he could not very well object. As long as she remained Nikodemos's favorite, the family of Kallimachos of the emperor's First Council would remain powerful, wealthy and free of the Stone.

Sometimes, on those rare occasions when she allowed herself to think, she came close to hating her father almost as much as she hated the priests. But hatred achieved little. It was far better to laugh and dance and sing to get what she wanted.

Danae glanced into her polished bronze mirror and adjusted the artful curl her hairdresser had allowed to escape the deceptively modest coiffure. Nikodemos was aroused by the prospect of taking out the pins and undoing the tightly bound loops one by one, for only he was permitted to see the golden spill of hair loose about her shoulders.

He would come soon, and she welcomed the distraction. She lifted her chin to admire the slender curve of her neck and upper shoulders, left bare by the cut of her chiton. If she lost her beauty or her power to please, the small good she did would be lost as well. She would become no better than her father—a sycophant, living in constant fear. That she would never allow.

She laughed and spun on her toes, setting the pleated folds of her chiton swirling around her ankles. The tiny golden bells in her ears chimed merrily.

I come and go as I please. How many others can say the same? Who else can whisper in the emperor's ear late at night and ask a favor, knowing it will be done?

She had asked a favor four nights ago. Perhaps, if she pleased Nikodemos well, she would ask again when the children from the latest black ship were tested and assigned their fates.

She smiled at her reflection. Perhaps the Stone God would go hungry one more night....

"My lady!"

Danae already knew what Nefer would say. Interpreting tone of voice was a useful skill among the best hetairai, and Danae did not object to being compared to those elegant and educated women who provided pleasure and companionship to the most distinguished men. Indeed, such talents were necessary for survival at the imperial court.

Nefer appeared in the doorway to Danae's outer rooms, her black eyes agleam with terror. "My lady...the...he is..."

"I know, Nefer. Bring wine and sweetmeats for our guest... though of course he won't touch them." She smiled to set the maid at ease. Nefer scurried off to do her mistress's bidding, and Danae skimmed lightly through the door.

Baalshillek stood in the antechamber like a man-sized smear of blood amid the gold, furs and tapestries Danae had so lovingly selected. His hood was drawn, though Danae knew he had no reason to hide his features; he'd never suffered either the wasting sickness or the weeping sores that so often afflicted his lesser brethren. Some might have called him handsome.

Danae suppressed a shudder and waited for him to turn. He did so, unhurried, disarmingly graceful, and the huge gold-mounted stone on his chest swung gently with his movement.

"My lord," she said, sweeping him a bow too low to be respectful. "It is, as always, an unexpected honor to find you at my door."

He didn't laugh. Baalshillek never laughed aloud, though she suspected he did so in that black pit that others might call a heart. He merely bowed in return and rested his long-fingered hand on his pendant.

Always the reminder.

"I rejoice in your welcome," he said in his pleasant, emotionless voice. "But you know why I have come, Danae."

She despised hearing her name on his lips, but she only smiled. "Will you not sit, Holy One? I have wine, and the ripest fruit...."

He lifted his hand. That was enough to silence most courtiers, officers, and even the emperor's Companions, the privileged Hetairoi. It was not enough for Danae. "If you will not have the usual refreshments, perhaps something more substantial? I hear that a fresh shipment of babes has just arrived in the harbor."

He stiffened, and she knew she had pressed to the very limits of his tolerance. She bowed again, most profoundly. "But of course you know this, my lord, as you know everything that passes in the empire. If only I knew how to please you."

The nape of her neck tingled in anticipation as she waited for his reply. It was a game between them, always the same, always dangerous. For her.

"You know what will please me," he said. He cast off his hood, exposing the clean, hairless lines of his jaw and lips and brow. His head—also hairless, though palace gossip claimed he was never shaved—had the appearance of painstakingly polished marble. A tracery of purple veins just under the skin only heightened the illusion.

Danae met his gaze and continued to smile. "I sorrow at having no better answer for you, Holy One. What Nikodemos commands, I will do."

"What Nikodemos commands," he repeated softly. He glided to a nearby table and picked up an intricately decorated golden cup, studded with gems. It was one of Nikodemos's most recent gifts. Danae knew she would never drink from it now. "He knows I only wish to bring you the peace of the one true god."

Thank the Goddess that Nikodemos would never force that upon her, or upon any member of her family. He kept his First Council free of the Stone God's power, a royal prerogative that created one of the greatest rifts between the emperor and the priesthood.

That didn't mean that Baalshillek wouldn't keep trying to suborn the Council members, their wives, concubines, sons and servants. And most especially the emperor's mistress…the one female capable of stirring Baalshillek's icy soul to something approaching desire.

It was a game, and Danae knew that someday she might lose.

"Even the Most Holy cannot always have his way," she said, playfully snatching the cup from Baalshillek's hand. She allowed her fingers to brush his. Her warm skin was cold against his burning heat, so contrary to his pale appearance.

The Stone God's fire. It consumed them all eventually…all save Baalshillek, the Most Holy, High Priest of the Nameless One True God.

Watch him, Nikodemos. Oh, watch him, most carefully.

Baalshillek turned his head to observe her as she replaced the goblet on its ivory-inlaid stand and flitted about the room, bending and twisting her body so that her breasts strained against the linen of her chiton and her hips swayed enticingly. *I'll die before you touch me,* she thought, shuddering with delicious fear. *I'll throw myself on your god's altar and sing sweet blessings to its name.*

"Take care," Baalshillek said, his voice rasping like snake scales on tile. "You tread very close to blasphemy."

She spun about, pressing her hands to her mouth. "Oh, no, my lord. Never that."

His mouth was a grim, flat line that never altered with joy or rage. "You have interfered with lawful sacrifice one time too many, Danae. If you meddle in such holy matters again, I will not be able to protect you."

"As greatly as I treasure your protection, my lord, I am but a woman. I must look to my master for guidance in all things."

"Then I will speak to your master," he said, as if he had not already done so many times. "He is the Stone God's chosen."

And will remain so only as long as the Most Holy deems expedient, she added for him. But he did not know Nikodemos, who was nothing like his father. Nikodemos was Alexandros reborn, Alexandros before his madness. Before the Stone God.

Nikodemos would end the sacrifices when the time was right. He would topple the priests from their pedestals and return the Stone God to what it had been before—a forgotten deity of the wastes, powerless without its constant feeding on human hope and human lives.

Nefer forestalled Danae's witty reply with her arrival at the outer doorway, bearing a plate of refreshments in her trembling hands. She tried to bow to the High Priest and nearly toppled the pitcher of wine. Danae walked between Nefer and the priest and took the plate.

"No wine, my lord? Then you must forgive me. I expect a guest of high estate within the next hour, and I wish to be ready to serve his pleasure."

Baalshillek blanched, though that should not have been possible, and caressed his stone. Danae felt the touch as if it stroked her own body, fondling her breasts and her belly and her thighs with a tongue of fire. Pain and pleasure, torment and ecstasy…

She overturned the tray, and the pitcher shattered on the mosaic floor. Nefer gasped and fell to her knees. Baalshillek released his pendant.

"How clumsy I am," Danae cried, shaking drops of wine from the hem of her chiton. "I did not soil your robes, Holy One? Nefer, clean this up at once." She gazed at Baalshillek through half-lidded eyes. "I regret our untimely parting, but we will surely meet again."

Baalshillek smiled. Only one who knew him well would call it a smile, for his lips merely twitched at the corners. No one who saw the expression could forget it.

"Most assuredly," he said. "May the blessings of the god be upon you."

She bowed, omitting the obligatory response. Baalshillek took a single step that carried him over the pool of wine and to the doorway. He paused to lift his hood over his head. Danae felt a tightness in her chest, as if the air in her lungs had been sucked out all at once. Then the High Priest vanished, theatrical to the end, and she could breathe again.

Nefer knelt amid the shards of pottery, weeping as she tried to gather them up in the skirts of her chiton. Danae pulled the maid to her feet.

"Enough," she chided. "This can wait. Go and compose yourself." She pushed Nefer gently toward the maid's room and closed the door between the hall and her apartments, leaving it unbarred. She could not keep Baalshillek out even if she wished, and she must be available to the emperor at all times of the day or night. No one else would dare intrude.

She entered her private chamber and went to her sleeping couch. Under the heaps of furs, fine linens and dyed fleece, the mattress lifted to reveal a hidden compartment filled with inlaid boxes of cedar and cypress. Any housebreaker in search of jewels would find them here—all of Nikodemos's gifts and the adornments she had brought with her when she left her father's house. But no common trespasser would bother to look under the boxes to discover the hollow just big enough for Danae's most precious treasure.

The figure of the goddess was hardly bigger than Danae's hand. She had come from Aigyptos, shaped in bronze by some skilled and reverent artisan who had sculpted her wise face in startling detail and inlaid her eyes with blue lapis. Her head was topped by the solar disk and horns of Hathor, and in one hand she grasped the ankh, symbol of eternal life.

Danae cradled the figurine in her cupped hands and carried it to the table she reserved as an altar. She placed the goddess in the center of the altar and lit the incense. As the sweet scent spiraled about her head, Danae crossed her arms over her chest and knelt in humility and devotion.

"Isis Myrionymos," she whispered, "Mistress of the House of Life, Beloved of Osiris, Mother of Horos, Queen of the Heavens, Great of Magic, hear your servant. Lift up thy hand to protect all those who stand against the Stone God, he who is Set and Apophis, the Evil One, Great Enemy, Seizer of Souls, Bringer of Darkness. Bend thine eyes upon the innocent so that they may live to serve thee. Send thy son to defeat the Eternal Fire."

She made an offering of fruit and bowed her head to the floor. The goddess had little attention to spare for one insignificant devotee, yet the prayers seldom failed to bring Danae comfort. *Some claimed Isis was dead. Danae did not believe such lies.* Isis heard, and one day she would answer.

Danae returned the goddess to her hiding place, snuffed the incense and bathed her hands in rose-scented water. She exchanged her soiled chiton for another of the sheerest linen, letting it fall loose and unbelted from her shoulders.

By the time she finished, Nefer had swept and cleared away the mess of wine and shattered pottery, and gone to fetch the vintage Nikodemos preferred. The maid was composed and smiling as she laid out Danae's best tableware and retreated to a position of watchful discretion.

Danae waited in the antechamber, prepared to match whatever mood the emperor might reveal. Nikodemos arrived within the hour. He pushed through the door like a blast of desert wind, and instantly she knew that this night would not be one for tenderness. He paused for a moment, majestic in his purple robes of state and the deceptively simple golden circlet that marked him Alexandros's heir and master of the Arrhidaean Empire.

Nikodemos was beautiful, as they said Alexandros had been, with his grandfather's light hair and eyes that could win men to his side with a single glance. Those eyes held but one thought as he gazed at Danae. He snatched off the circlet and dropped it into Nefer's ready hands. The maid received his outer robes and his heavy belt, the ceremonial sword and bejeweled dagger. She knelt to unlace his sandals, but he stepped away and advanced on Danae. His mouth seized hers, tongue thrusting deep with the unreasoning cruelty of overwhelming hunger. She was just able to wave Nefer from the room before he tore the delicate ties that bound Danae's chiton across her shoulders.

He yanked his chiton above his hips and bore her into the bedchamber, already prepared to mount as she fell back among the furs of her couch. She wrapped her thighs around his hips. He plunged inside and she closed her eyes, carried into oblivion by his desperate violence.

"Danae," he cried hoarsely in time to his thrusts. "Danae."

I am here, my lord. I will not leave you...oh, Isis.

He finished, heaving his seed into her body. Never had that seed taken root, and it never would. Not while newborn babes could be ripped from their mothers' arms and given to the Stone God's fire.

Nikodemos rolled off, groaning with satisfaction. Danae rose, made him comfortable upon the pallet, and walked naked across the room to fetch the wine. She knelt and served it to him as a slave might, but his eyes acknowledged her with affection no mere concubine could ever win.

He stroked her hair, pulling loose the strands he had left in their bindings. "Beautiful Danae of the golden tresses," he said. "You please me well."

"Then Danae is pleased," she said, dipping her head.

He lifted her chin. "Baalshillek came to you."

"Yes." She held his gaze. "It was…as always."

"He warns me of your insolence and impiety." Nikodemos wound a lock of her hair around his finger, slowly drawing her face closer to his. "Did you provoke him, my Danae?"

"As always," she repeated. She smiled and ran her tongue over his lower lip. "Would you have me do otherwise, my lord?"

"And if I said yes?" He sat up, tugging on her hair. "If I bade you share your bed with our High Priest?"

She shivered, caught in an instant of sheer terror. But this, too, was a game. She laughed. "Then I would win for you all his secrets and teach him—"

Suddenly Nikodemos dragged her head to the couch, pinning her hair in both his fists. He stretched atop her, bearing down with his full, muscular weight, and she felt his body stir anew. He nipped her arched neck and licked the hurt he had made.

"You are mine," he said gently. He drew his fingernails over her breasts and pinched her nipples. "These are mine. And this—" He pushed his finger inside her. "If any other touches you, I will burn you myself."

Danae closed her eyes, holding very still. "And what of Baalshillek? Would you kill him?"

He struck her. Her head snapped to the side, but she gave no resistance. Immediately he took her face between his hands and kissed her lips, her stinging cheek, her brow. He kissed her until she no longer felt the pain of his punishment, only the earnestness of his remorse.

"Never question me, my Danae," he whispered. "In these rooms there are no gods or priests or councillors, only love." Tenderly he spread her hair over the pillows. He kissed her again and left the bed, pausing to fill and drain another cup of wine.

Nefer appeared with his outer garments and accoutrements. He let the maid dress him and set the circlet upon his own fair curls.

"I will come again tonight," he told Danae. "Be ready."

She lay where she was until he was gone and Nefer had closed the door to the hall. The maid rushed to the bed and, fluttered in distress from one end to the other, deciding at last to bring Danae a plain house chiton and her most comfortable sandals. She poured Danae a fresh cup of wine.

"Will you take supper, my lady?" she asked anxiously.

"Later, perhaps. Go and seek your own meal."

"My lady—"

"I wish to be alone." Danae set down the wine half-finished and went to the window. The lowering sun cast patterns of red and gold on the bay, rippling fabric flecked with the darker nubs of ships dropping anchor for the night. But the celestial weaver had left a single great flaw in her work: the black ship, sapping all color wherever its shadow fell.

"My lady," Nefer whispered at her shoulder. "I will prepare a bath for you, scented with myrrh. If it pleases you, I will sing the old songs."

Danae spread her fingers to block the window's view. "I think that will please me very much." She laughed, the heedless note she had shaped and burnished to such a high sheen of joy. "Let us be merry, for tonight the emperor comes."

* * *

The harbor of Karchedon was not unlike that of Piraeos, save for its greater size, and its hordes of foreigners, merchants, laborers, citizens and slaves might have walked the streets of any imperial city. The same kinds of ships, manned by brown-backed sailors who knew every curse in the known world, cruised in and out of the long canal to the docks.

But this was Karchedon. Quintus felt the difference in his bones, even before his gut ceased churning and his legs grew accustomed to the blessed immobility of solid ground.

Karchedon, capital of the empire, sacred center of the Stone God's dominion. Once it had been the home of a mighty seafaring people, the Poeni, conquered and absorbed by Arrhidaeos to become only another race under the tyrant's heel. Even from the harbor one could see the fortified citadel of the upper town, where stood the temple and the emperor's palace, surrounded by the residences of the city's wealthiest and most privileged citizens.

Even in Karchedon there were rich and poor. Each face wore the same blank, pleasant stare Quintus had come to know so well in Hellas.

The shepherd priests of the black ship had released their charges at the dock and then hurried into the city on some urgent business, leaving the passengers to find their own way. This did not present a significant problem for the newcomers, for there were many signs advertising inns that catered specifically to pilgrims. All that concerned Quintus was that he would be free to go where he pleased.

"Will you tell me where to find our contacts?" he asked Philokrates once again.

"Patience, my dear boy." The old man turned to watch Cian and the two barbarian females approach, the little "seer" supported between the shapechanger and the so-called Amazon. Rhenna's cloak was drawn up over her head, giving her a false air of modesty, but she failed to conceal the pride in her walk and bearing. Tahvo slumped as if she could barely keep her feet.

Quintus frowned. Tahvo bore no resemblance to his lost sister, yet she awoke the same feelings in him: protectiveness, concern, an inexplicable desire to see her safe. Horatia had been too wise for her young age, almost otherworldly. The sorcerer priests had taken her on the first day of the invasion.

"Is she well?" he asked Cian.

"She needs a place to rest," Rhenna said, "away from the cursed priests."

Philokrates clucked his tongue. "Soon it will be dark, and it is not advisable for strangers to be out after nightfall. We will find an inn, and consider our plans in the morning."

Quintus knew that protest would be mere wasted breath. "Do you have a specific lodging in mind?"

Philokrates stroked his beard, perused the multitude of signs, and pointed toward a mud-brick building far down the wharf.

Quintus set off, not waiting to see if the others followed. The inn's narrow courtyard was already packed with new arrivals seeking shelter. Quintus pushed his way through and stopped at a cheap wooden table that served to separate the middle-aged female innkeeper from her restive customers.

"Yes?" she said without looking up from her ledgers.

"I require three rooms——"

"Three?" She arched a black-painted brow. "Impossible. I may find you a corner...."

"Three," he repeated firmly. "I have——"

"Husband." Iron fingers clutched Quintus's arm, and Rhenna's moss-green eyes contrived to gaze up at him from under her surprisingly long lashes. Her voice was soft and deferential. "Husband, I fear that my sister is very ill from the voyage. My brother and grandfather will gladly share our room." She looked straight at the innkeeper and held out a handful of coins. "We have come all the way from Arkadia, good lady, and..." She closed her eyes and swayed as if she might swoon.

Cian caught her, one arm still supporting Tahvo. Quintus was speechless.

The innkeeper scowled and glanced over their heads at the shuffling crowd. "One room," she said. "No cooking. Privies and water outside, public baths down the road." The coins quickly disappeared into the innkeeper's leathery hands. "Akil, show these people their room."

A boy near Timon's age scurried from behind the innkeeper and sketched a bow in Quintus's direction. Quintus seized Rhenna's arm and hauled her after the guide. Cian, Tahvo and Philokrates trailed at his heels. The boy led them up a narrow flight of stairs to a hall on the second story and a doorway hung with a half-rotten mat of leather in place of a door. The echo of voices from the other doorways gave ample evidence that every other room was occupied.

The boy stood aside to let Quintus and Rhenna enter. The stench was just bearable. The room's last residents had disobeyed the innkeeper's orders not to cook, and they had not bathed in some time. The walls were stained with smoke and nameless substances. But the three small pallets and blankets looked relatively clean, and the floor had been recently swept.

Quintus gave the boy the smallest coin he had and sent him off. Rhenna twitched her arm from Quintus's grip. Cian led Tahvo directly to one of the pallets and eased her down upon it. The seer never opened her eyes.

"Woman," Quintus said to Rhenna, "what possessed you?"

"Common sense." She flung back her hood. "Your frivolous male pride would have called too much attention to us."

"And you do not?" He looked her up and down. "I admit you played the part of a proper female remarkably well. A pity that a Thespian's skill is not enough. No Tiberian of good family would have you for a wife. Your complete lack of modesty... your feet, your hands..." His gaze drifted to her scarred face.

"You're right," Cian said, unexpectedly near. "Rhenna's beauty is not for one such as you."

Quintus met Cian's stare. "Nor, apparently, for you."

"Enough," Rhenna said quietly. "It's all right, Cian."

"I don't fear your protector, woman," Quintus said. "Do *you* protect *him?*"

"Children," Philokrates interrupted. "Quintus, you draw conclusions based on little fact. You may achieve knowledge more readily with diplomacy than insult." His gaze encompassed the others. "Remember where you are. These walls are thin. Make no attempt to approach the innkeeper. You will be safe here while I look for the ones we seek."

"I'm coming with you," Quintus said.

"They know me. They do not know you. Resolve your quarrels and lay down your swords. You may have cause to take them up again soon enough."

"You can find me weapons?" Rhenna asked.

"If necessary. In the meantime, continue to play your role as you have been." His eyes lost some of the sadness that had haunted him since Timon's death. "If I were younger, I might have courted you myself, Rhenna of the Free People."

"Perhaps I would have accepted you, Philokrates of Hellas."

They nodded to each other in mutual respect, and Philokrates slipped out the door.

Quintus folded his hands behind his back with feigned indifference. Let the wolf bitch glare. If Philokrates had not returned within the hour after nightfall...

Cian paced across the room, sidestepping Quintus so as to avoid any contact between them. Rhenna sat beside Tahvo, whose face, usually so obdurate, was wrinkled with worry.

"She needs fresh water," Rhenna said.

"I'll find a fountain," Cian offered.

"If the stones don't take you…" Quintus said. "I'll come along."

"Why do you continue to help us?" Rhenna asked gruffly.

"Because I honor Philokrates, as I do courage."

She tossed him the waterskin she had carried under her cloak. He caught it with his right hand. Cian left the leather door flap swinging behind him.

The hallway was quiet save for a baby's wail and a rattling snore from the next room. Cian had stopped at the foot of the stairs. As soon as Quintus reached the bottom, Cian slammed him against the wall.

"I owe you my life and my freedom," he whispered, "but I may forget my gratitude if you insult her again."

"Insult *her*—or your manhood?"

Cian showed his teeth. "You question my manhood, but it's the beast that will answer."

"I doubt your warrior maid will thank you for this gallant defense."

Cian released him and stepped back, his breath coming hard and fast. "If you knew her as she truly is, you'd run whimpering back to your—" He stopped, hunching his shoulders. "You're afraid of her, Tiberian, because you fear what you can't define."

Quintus went very cold. "I fear no man or woman alive."

"Except something in yourself." Cian glanced left and right, smelling the air. "Go your own way. Somehow we will contrive without your assistance." He snatched the waterskin from Quintus's hand and strode down the alley.

Quintus clenched his fist and waited until his heartbeat resumed its normal pace. The sky had grown dark, but lights had sprung up all over the harbor, lamps set in alcoves or on poles running alongside the docks, streets and narrow lanes. Quintus continued the way Cian had gone. When he reached the nearest lamp, set on a pedestal beside a wooden doorway, he examined the almost transparent vessel that contained the unwavering flame. It held neither oil nor wick. He touched the lamp, and the light went out.

He walked away quickly, covering his face, and soon located the public fountain. Cian stood beside it, unmoving, the waterskin at his feet. Women filled jugs and amphorae without seeming to notice the stranger.

Quintus hesitated, weighed pride against reason, and approached the fountain. The shapechanger continued to stare toward the hill of the upper town and the temple precincts. Beams of red light cut across the night sky.

They call you, Quintus thought. *I could so easily let you go.*

He picked up the waterskin, filled it, and held it up to Cian's face. Golden eyes blinked.

"We're finished," Quintus said. "Come."

Slowly Cian shook his head. "You go."

"And what of you?"

"I know my people are here. I must find them."

Quintus grasped Cian's arm. "If I leave you, Philokrates isn't likely to forgive me. And as for your woman..."

The beast crouched behind Cian's eyes, savage and unreasoning. "Release me."

"Are you and Rhenna not bound by promises and oaths?"

"My only bond is to my own."

Quintus barked a laugh. "You once said that you might be of

some use in this war of men and gods. Philokrates and your seer are wrong. You're of no use to anyone, even yourself."

Cian blinked again, some measure of sanity returning. "I—"

"I see now why you rely on the protection of a woman. Gods forbid she ever needs yours."

Quintus braced for a blow that never came. Between one moment and the next Cian had crossed half the distance back to the inn.

Chapter Twenty-Two

"They're here."

Cian paced the room, back and forth, back and forth, while Tahvo slept and Quintus observed from a corner, cool and expressionless.

Rhenna knew that something had happened between the men when they'd gone to fetch the water. She admitted complete ignorance about the peculiar convolutions of male thought, but this was more than some petty male quarrel or the head-butting of two young bucks testing each other's strength.

Quintus could look after himself, but she worried for Cian. The stones were driving him to madness. The glaze in his eyes reminded her of the time when she'd returned to their tent after her meeting with Farkas. Cian seemed just as ready now to jump out of his skin.

Or change it.

"I tell you, I feel them," Cian insisted, coming to a halt before her. "My brothers live, here in this city."

Rhenna adjusted the blankets around Tahvo's shoulders and rose to face him. "Do you know where?"

He grimaced, breaking into motion again. "I can track my own kind."

Rhenna felt Quintus's gaze. He shook his head ever so slightly, as if in warning.

She bit her lip hard enough to sting. "We can't leave until Philokrates returns," she said, keeping her voice low and steady. "He can help us."

Cian stopped with his face to the far wall, fists clenched. "I am Ailuri. All the years of denial…they have brought me to this. My true purpose." He swung about, tossing black hair from his eyes. "I must go to them before it's too late."

He started for the door. Quintus blocked his way. Rhenna pushed between them and grasped Cian's taut arms.

"I know what you are feeling," she whispered.

His eyes scalded her. *"You?"*

She couldn't let him see her falter, not for an instant. "I know what it is to be…to be unable to act. I was beside you in Piraeos. Do you think I've forgotten the boy? And before I found you, in the Shield's Shadow——" She paused to smooth the crack in her voice. "I saw my people slaughtered, Cian. The elderly, the children, all left dead by the barbarians…and I could do nothing. Nothing."

"I will not let that happen to mine."

"*We* won't let it happen. Tahvo said we should go on together——"

"We?" He wrenched from her hold. "Tahvo has no power here. Neither do you. You are both *human*."

Rhenna would have welcomed a blow from his fist far more

than such startling cruelty from his mouth. "The stones have you, Cian. You speak—"

"The truth? You want my people for your own sordid reasons. You have done nothing but try to stop me, as if you had the right—" He broke off, flushed and furious. Some vestige of the old Cian seized control, and then he turned on Quintus. "And what have you to do with the Ailuri? What do you care what becomes of them?"

Quintus stepped back. "Nothing," he said coldly. "I have no interest in you or your people. I thought you cared for the women."

Cian bared his teeth as if he would gladly lock them around the Tiberian's throat. "Keep your thoughts behind your tongue, or I'll—"

"Excellent advice," Philokrates said from the doorway. "Since your voices carry clearly into the street."

Rhenna's heart rattled like a handful of pebbles. Quintus's face betrayed a flash of relief. Cian lowered his head like a bull about to charge.

"I am pleased to find you all together," Philokrates said. He placed a basket on the floor. "I have news, if any here are interested."

Cian retreated and slumped in a corner, slit-eyed and hostile. "My people are here," he growled.

"I should not be at all surprised," the old man said calmly. He gestured at the basket. "Food, even if not particularly fresh at this hour of the night." He sat beside his offering, waiting for the others to join him.

"What did you learn?" Quintus demanded.

Philokrates delved in the basket to reveal the familiar loaf and fish, with the addition of fruit Rhenna didn't recognize. "I have been to the great temple," he said, tearing off a chunk of bread. "There I made my obeisance to the god and left a certain sign for those who know where to look."

"Did they answer?"

"It may take time," Philokrates said. He took a bite of bread and chewed it thoroughly. "They must be cautious. That is why we will become true pilgrims and visit the temple twice a day with appropriate offerings until we receive the sign of acknowledgment."

"Offerings," Rhenna said grimly. "What kind?"

"The priests seldom demand blood of newcomers. Gold will suffice."

"Then our contacts had better come quickly," Quintus said.

"I considered these things before we left Hellas." Philokrates patted his belt. "It is most important to present the correct appearance. As in Piraeos, we will be expected to submit to the priests within a certain span of time, but they will not anticipate deliberate deception."

"They must know of the Resistance," Quintus said.

"They judge it little threat," Philokrates said heavily, "and they are not wrong to think so. For now." He accepted the waterskin from Rhenna. "Still, we should avoid direct contact with the priests, the stones or the altar."

"And what of Cian?" Rhenna said quietly. "Quintus is no longer able to shield him."

Cian laughed. "You think the stones control me? I don't even feel them."

Quintus seemed about to speak, but Tahvo's voice broke the startled silence. "He is right," she said, letting her blankets fall. "Another call has become stronger." She looked at Rhenna through red-rimmed eyes. "You must leave me here when you go to the temple."

Rhenna started up, concern overwhelming relief. "You're ill, Tahvo. You do nothing but sleep, and when you wake..." She caught Tahvo's furtive gesture toward the pouch beneath her chiton. "What is that powder you take every day?"

Tahvo wrapped her arms around her chest. "It helps me." Her teeth chattered. "The spirits do not answer here. I must *see*."

"I think you should let me keep the pouch, Tahvo," Rhenna said. "Just for a while, until you recover from this illness."

The healer hesitated as if she would protest and slowly withdrew the pouch. Her hands trembled as she gave it to Rhenna. "I will be better," she whispered. "But I cannot go with you."

Rhenna shoved the pouch under her belt. "We can't leave you here alone."

Tahvo lay down again, rolling up in the blankets. "I will not suffer any harm in this place, but you must stay together."

Rhenna glanced at Quintus. He was staring at Tahvo, a deep crease between his brows. Cian brooded in his corner. Philokrates rubbed the bristle of white hair beneath his lower lip.

"I suggest we eat, then sleep as best we can," he said. "We cannot foresee what tomorrow will demand of us."

"I'll take first watch," Rhenna said. No one gainsaid her. Quintus stood second watch, but Rhenna didn't risk even a warrior's doze for fear that Cian would try another escape. His golden eyes shone like lamps through the night.

At dawn Philokrates went for fresh water, and each of them bathed hands and faces and as much of their bodies as they could safely expose. Cian poured the remaining water over his head and shook his long hair like a dog. His expression seemed more sober than threatening in the wan morning light.

Tahvo continued to insist that she would be safe in the room. Quintus agreed with Rhenna that the seer was in no condition to face evil priests or red stones. After final adjustments of pilgrims' robes and a shaking of dusty chitons, Rhenna and the others left the inn.

The oldest part of Karchedon lay near the harbor with its warehouses, workshops and trade district, leading to a market square similar to the agora in Piraeos. Streets were narrow and winding, and most of the houses, chiefly mud-brick and tile, had been patched and rebuilt many times over decades or perhaps even centuries.

As in the Hellenish city, men began their work early and moved quietly. Women were few, children entirely absent. Not even weeds grew in the narrow spaces between buildings. The lower town was nearly devoid of soldiers or priests, but their absence didn't lessen the miasma of sickness even Rhenna could feel.

The Stone God was here. Not mere pieces of it like the pendants, but the god itself. Its power was a heaviness in the air that settled in the lungs so that each breath became labor. It bled under the earth, sucking at every step. It drained all color from the eyes of the smiling citizens and placid slaves.

Cian also felt it. He stalked with lowered head like a hunting cat seeking a mortal adversary. Quintus marched straight ahead as if he could mow down any obstacle that stood in his path. Only Philokrates seemed unaware.

Tahvo could not have borne this. Yet Rhenna was worried when she should be most alert—worried for the healer alone at the inn, and for Cian, who had mocked her, and Tahvo for being human.

Cian claimed he was no longer under the influence of the stones, but this city had changed him almost beyond recognition. Rhenna accepted his capacity for violence, yet he had never before turned willingly against his companions. His *friends*.

She had relied too much on Cian's bond to her, the bond of Ailu to one of the Free People, on too many fragile and inconstant emotions. She had dared to believe that she understood him. How could she predict his feelings when her own were in turmoil?

He had found his brothers. If he appeared docile now, it was only because she, Philokrates and Quintus went where he wished to go. She herself was a warrior without weapons, useless to Cian or anyone else.

Oblivious to Rhenna's grim thoughts, Philokrates led them toward the hill that dominated Karchedon. The main street widened and began to climb. As the houses became larger and the road more steep, the number of gray-cloaked pilgrims increased, bound for the same destination: the Stone God's citadel.

Karchedon's temple and palace were enclosed in high stone walls patrolled by imperial soldiers, but the wide gates stood open to admit all who approached. Quintus drew his hood farther over his face. Cian strode toward the gate. Rhenna fell into step just behind him, despising her helplessness.

The upper city was as different from the lower as Heart of Oaks from Hypanis. Every building appeared new, a flawless stone and marble structure of Hellenish style. The roads were paved and even underfoot. Though there were neither trees nor statues representing men or gods, the very symmetry of the great open square had a cold and sterile beauty.

"The emperor's palace," Philokrates murmured, gesturing toward an immense, multistoried edifice noticeably more ornate than the surrounding buildings. It stood almost against the citadel wall on the side facing the harbor, its tiny upper-floor windows looking out on the water. Murals and mosaics depicting some great military engagement, teeming with men and horses, covered much of the palace's walls.

Even the palace shrank to nothing compared to the great temple across the square. It was completely unadorned save for the red-veined pattern of its gigantic stone sides, but from its flat roof sprang a triangular wedge of red crystal many times the height of a woman. The crystal cast off blinding shafts of red light that stabbed the sky as far as the eye could see. The temple's high, doorless entrances, one in each wall, reduced the stream of priests and visiting pilgrims to a trail of ants.

At the rear of the temple lay a walled enclosure, a second citadel, containing many smaller buildings and courtyards.

"What is that place?" Cian asked.

"The temple compound, or temenos. Priests' dormitories, training grounds, storage facilities for tribute and sacrificial offerings...and cells for temple prisoners."

"My people are there."

"Take care, my friends." Philokrates addressed all of them. "We will enter the temple with the other pilgrims. You will approach the first dais, where you will make an offering of one coin and accept the ritual cleansing. You need not fear touching the stones, nor will you be compelled to continue beyond. Mingle with the other pilgrims. Behave as you see them behave, no matter how repellent it seems to you. I will go to the appointed place and learn if my sign has been recognized."

Cian's eyes narrowed. "I have no need—"

"Patience," Rhenna said. She touched his arm and flinched at the jolt of physical awareness that crowded out every other sense. Cian stared at her hand and then at her face. He did not push her away.

Confused and shaken, Rhenna followed Philokrates and Quintus as they joined the pilgrims entering the temple. The portal delivered them into a cavernous space divided by a series of low-walled rooms, tables and altars. Bands of symbols marked the walls at regular intervals, but Rhenna didn't recognize the writing as anything she had seen in Hellas. Braziers belched nearly smokeless flame, illuminating even the farthest corners of the echoing chamber.

A great altar filled the center rear of the temple, a smaller but still massive copy of the building that housed it. It, too, had its own open doorways through which priests and pilgrims came and went.

Philokrates left Rhenna, Cian and Quintus at a table where a line of visitors made donations of coins and small gold or silver objects. A red-robed man, bare-headed and lacking the priests' usual red stone pendant, dropped the offerings into a bronze amphora behind the table. He directed each supplicant to remove his or her hood, dipped a cup of what appeared to be plain water out of a second vessel and spilled it over the pilgrim's head.

Some of the pilgrims proceeded to the next table, where a priest offered some drink in exchange for the requisite contribution. Enough visitors hung back that Rhenna, Quintus and Cian could lose themselves among the milling gray cloaks. Quintus gazed at the altar with an admirable imitation of slack-jawed devotion.

Rhenna couldn't bring herself to do the same. She hated this place. It drove her to thoughts of rash assaults and suicidal vengeance. She'd told Cian to be patient, but her words were sheer hypocrisy.

Philokrates did not return. The crowd near the table thinned. Rhenna looked for a less conspicuous place to wait, and found a mass of pilgrims facing the altar, rhythmically chanting praises to the Stone God. By unspoken agreement she, Cian and Quintus joined the celebrants. The words of the chant were simple enough, but they stuck in Rhenna's throat like broken bones.

The day passed. Light in the temple never changed, nor was there any other way of reckoning the time. Pilgrims melted away from the group, only to be replaced by other, nearly identical worshipers. Rhenna, who had endured far more severe discipline in her warrior's training, felt her eyelids grow heavy and her legs go numb. The chanting, the unity of the voices and the pilgrims' unquestioning devotion, worked an evil magic of its own, lulling her into a treacherous peace.

She reached for Cian's hand, and he clutched her fingers with desperate strength. The pupils of his eyes had shrunk to black specks.

Philokrates arrived just as Rhenna determined they could wait no longer. The old man pushed between Quintus and Rhenna, beaming impartially at all his fellow pilgrims.

"The one we seek is here," he whispered to Quintus. "Rhenna and Cian will wait outside the temple doors."

"If they know of my people——" Cian began.

"We will ask," Philokrates reassured him. "Do nothing until we return."

A deep rumble started in Cian's chest. Rhenna leaned into him, inadvertently brushing his cheek. His sharp scent of angry arousal set her hair on end.

"We will find them," she said. "Trust me a little longer, Cian. Please."

He looked into her eyes. "Yes," he said.

She took his arm and led him out of the temple before he could change his mind.

Quintus watched the Northerners leave and immediately put them from his thoughts. He could think of little but the altar and the evil within it. During the interminable hours of waiting he had observed the movements of pilgrims through the altar's black doorways. Of every four who entered, only three reemerged.

He was sure that those who did not were taken, like Timon. Quintus knew that if he entered the altar he could destroy its resident stone—and expose himself before his true work was done. He might save a few souls...and thereby lose the world.

"Come," Philokrates said. He turned and led Quintus along a convoluted, mazelike path among the tables and braziers to a roofless enclosure divided into many smaller chambers. Each chamber was large enough for two or three pilgrims, and all were occupied.

"Do as I do," Philokrates whispered. He chose one of the chambers, squeezed past the cloaked and kneeling figure within it, and made a place for himself on the other side. Quintus had no choice but to crouch just inside the chamber's entrance.

The original occupant turned slightly toward Quintus, staring at him from jet-black eyes in a brown and exotic face. She adjusted her hood to expose dark, tightly braided hair framing her forehead and full lips pursed in disapproval.

Without a word of acknowledgment she faced the stone platform before which she knelt. The platform bore a shallow groove that drained into a pipe set in the chamber wall. Beside the groove lay a small, red-hilted knife and long strips of cloth. The woman lifted the knife, bowed her head and cut a slit in the center of her right palm. She held her hand over the stone. Her blood flowed with unnatural swiftness into the pipe.

Quintus caught the woman's wrist, but it soon became clear that she did not intend to further harm herself. Philokrates took the knife and sliced his own flesh. Quintus's mouth flooded with revulsion, and he reached for the blade.

Philokrates withheld it. "Wait," he said. He addressed the dark-skinned woman. "Is it safe to speak?"

"It is never safe," she answered in a rich, husky voice. "Why have you summoned us?"

"I must find the Stone," Quintus said.

She glanced at him in amazement. "We have no time for madmen. I have only come to warn you that we cannot risk any further contact. One of our leaders and several others have been taken by the priests and are to be sacrificed tonight in celebration of the Festival."

"Festival?" Philokrates murmured. "I had not known—"

"If you wish to remain alive, return to the harbor before night falls." She shook the last blood from her palm, bound her head with a strip of linen and gathered her robes.

"Stop," Quintus said. "I have come from Tiberia itself to fight the Stone. You must tell me its true location."

She laughed soft and low. "Even if I knew, I would not send a novice to his death so readily." She nodded to Philokrates. "I must go. Do not seek us again."

Philokrates made as if to reply, but she slipped from the chamber with consummate grace. Quintus rose to follow.

"No," Philokrates said. "She said it is the day of Festival. We must do as she advised and return to the inn." He bound his hand with one of the cloths. "We will come another day."

"She was unwilling to help us," Quintus said. "That is not acceptable. If they knew——"

"If they knew what you could do, how would it be any different from Tiberia? They would not permit you to risk such a gift so recklessly. You may believe you can do this alone, but I tell you——" He stopped as a stranger's face peered in at them.

"The peace of the Stone God be upon you, brother," Philokrates intoned.

"And upon you," the stranger answered. But he continued to stare with a faint, unsettling smile on his lips.

Philokrates urged Quintus from the chamber, bowed to the stranger and left the enclosure at an unhurried pace.

Quintus palmed the ceremonial knife and hid it under his cloak, listening for footsteps behind them as they left the temple. There was no sign of pursuit. Dusk had begun to fall over Karchedon, but the stone-fed lamps had not yet been ignited.

Rhenna and Cian waited close to the entrance, hoods drawn over their faces.

"She told us nothing," Quintus said.

"Except that some of their own are to be sacrificed this very night," Philokrates said. He glanced about with obvious unease. "The Resistance may attempt to free the prisoners. We would be wise to return to the inn at once."

"If there's to be action," Quintus said, "then I stay."

"And I," Cian said.

"But it is Festival," Philokrates said. "You have no idea——"

"Look!" Rhenna said.

A thick column of smoke rose from the exterior temple compound. Flames poured over the walls and splashed onto the ground outside.

"That is no part of a sacrifice," Philokrates said. "We must go."

"This could be a diversion by the Resistance," Quintus said.

"It's succeeding," Rhenna said.

Already they could hear shouts and screams from the compound. Pilgrims rushed out of the temple doorways. Soldiers appeared, wielding spears and swords.

"If you attempt to interfere," Philokrates said, "you will be caught. You—"

Quintus didn't wait to hear the rest of the warning.

Chapter Twenty-Three

Cian lunged after the Tiberian. Rhenna grabbed his robes. He wrenched free and wheeled to face her, blind with rage.

She met his gaze, pity and sorrow in her eyes. "Philokrates is right," she said. "You'll be caught. I can't let you die."

He saw her through a haze of emotion that drove away all reason. *Human,* instinct snarled. *Forget her.*

But it was not merely anger and contempt that shaped his frenzied thoughts. He saw her as he remembered her from his very first dreams, welcoming him with a smile and open arms. Lying naked beneath him on a bed of moss and leaves and blossoms. Gasping and moaning as he spilled his seed inside her...

With a roar he cast off his robes and his chiton, standing naked, ravenous and blatantly aroused. He took a step toward Rhenna. She held her ground, unafraid. The beast knew it could not defeat her. Dizzy with the upheaval of his thoughts, Cian crouched at her feet and changed. An instant later he was hard on Quintus's scent trail, skimming past startled pilgrims as he dodged soldiers and priests.

Night fell swiftly. Cian ran low to the ground, keeping to the darkest margins of the square. The fire continued to grow inside the temenos, attracting more priests and soldiers. Cian circled the compound to the opposite side. The walls, though not formidably high, were topped with close-set iron spikes meant to impale any intruder.

Cian traced Quintus's path to a place in the wall that looked like every other, save for the almost invisible cracks running through the stone from top to bottom. The Tiberian's scent was heavy on the rough surface. Cian reared up on his hind legs and pressed his paws against the wall. It gave under his weight. A door swung inward. Set into the inner edge of the door and its frame were tiny chips of crystal that bore the unmistakable taint of evil magic. They were black and lifeless.

Cian slid through the opening and pushed the door closed from inside. Quintus's spoor was still strong, but another scent struck Cian with overwhelming intensity.

Ailu.

Cian swayed, whipping tail against flanks with punishing violence. He did not know why he chose to go after Quintus. The beast decided for him. He negotiated a maze of storage sheds, granaries, silent animal pens and windowless dwellings. Light from the fire reached only the southern quarter of the temenos, leaving the rest in darkness.

The stench of unwashed humans came to Cian before he found the cages. They stood in barred rows, each cell with several occupants crowded into a small and filthy space.

"Cian!"

He heard and understood his name just in time. Quintus crouched in a defensive posture, hand raised to ward off attack.

Behind him knelt a dark-skinned woman clutching a plaque of bronze set with red crystal.

The woman's black eyes widened, and she swore in a musical alien tongue.

"Do not fear him," Quintus said. "He's an ally."

"Watcher," the woman said in accented koine. "How did you escape?"

Cian changed. His mind awakened from the beast's ruthless hold. "Who are you?"

"No time," she said. She addressed Quintus. "If you would help us, Tiberian, watch for our enemies while I use the key."

Quintus nodded sharply and pulled Cian beside him. Smoke cast a pall in the air, and the occasional shouted order rang from the direction of the fire. The woman dashed to the row of cages. Hands and arms thrust through the bars.

The woman hesitated. Cian felt the thump of booted feet resound in the earth.

"Soldiers," he hissed.

Quintus leaped up, but it was too late. The soldiers had already seen the woman. They moved astonishingly fast in their heavy armor, boxing her in with their spears. Quintus froze.

The woman surrendered, throwing up her hands. She no longer held the bronze plaque she had called a key. Three of the soldiers set iron spear tips to her throat, while the fourth bound her arms behind her back. She never glanced in her allies' direction, and the soldiers were too intent upon her to look elsewhere. But when they led her away, two remained behind to guard the cages.

Quintus said nothing, but Cian knew what he was about to attempt. Cian still had a choice: to help the Tiberian or seek his brothers. Either way, he could let the beast take control. Rhenna was safe from him, and it wouldn't matter if he tasted the blood of a hundred priests....

He stopped in mid-change, muscles and bones protesting the

abuse. A red-robed figure was approaching the guards, speaking in a familiar voice. Cian moved, Quintus right behind him. The distracted guards swung about. Cian seized one spear just below its head and plucked the man from his feet. Quintus charged the other soldier, who struggled with the sham priest. Long brown hair escaped the red hood. Rhenna pinned the soldier, while Quintus drew a small knife and slit his throat.

Cian knocked off the second guard's helmet and snapped his neck. The pale, beautiful face gazed up at him; the red crystal lodged in the soldier's forehead dulled from red to black.

"Cian," Rhenna said, breathing hard.

"Did you kill a priest?" he asked, terrified and relieved.

"I hope so," she said. "But he didn't have a stone. I—"

"Nyx dropped the key," a masculine voice said from within one of the cages. "Find it. Quickly!"

Quintus knelt, sweeping the ground with his hands. He rose with the plaque pinched between his thumb and forefinger. He thrust it at Rhenna.

"Take it," he said. "I can't—"

Just as she accepted the key, its red crystal went black. Rhenna held it flat on her palm and glanced up at Quintus. He clenched his fist.

"What have you done?" the man in the cage cried. "Without the key—"

Quintus rounded on the cage and slammed his hand on the door. It rattled but did not unlatch.

"So you are the one," the man said. He pressed against the bars, and Cian glimpsed light brown skin, and eyes beneath dirty bronze hair. Several other prisoners crowded the space behind him. "Go, before more soldiers come."

"What of Nyx?" Quintus said.

"You can't help her, or us."

"The fire is almost out," Rhenna said.

Quintus looked suddenly at Cian. "You're more than a man," he said. "Prove it."

Cian closed his eyes, assaulted by too many sensations, sight and sound and smell vying for dominance. He had killed with his own hands. Rhenna was too close. Quintus asked too much. His brothers were nearly within reach.

Leave the humans to their fates. They do not matter....

He fell to his knees and splayed his fingers on the earth. It felt as dead as the red stones in the key and in the soldier's face. He pushed. His hand sank deep. No life stirred. Still Cian stretched until his bones cracked and his flesh began to melt into the soil.

He muffled a cry of pain. Thunder welled up from a place beyond the span of his touch. It came not from the sky but from the ground, rising and rising.

The wave engulfed him and broke upon the surface, opening a chasm from his buried hand to the cage. The fissure drove under the cell. The cage door tilted precariously and tore from its hinges, riven by the force of the earth's convulsions. Men burst through the door and scrambled for safety.

Cian remembered little after that. Friendly hands urged him away. He ran. There was much noise, and more than once he breathed in the acrid odor of blood. Then he was looking into Philokrates's worried brown eyes, and his friends were all around him, gathered in the doorway of a tightly closed shop.

Friends, and a stranger...the man from the cage. Somehow they had come to be outside the citadel gates, which were shut and manned by a company of soldiers. People in every state and style of dress rushed to and fro on the streets of the lower city. The hair on Cian's arms and legs stood erect, and he shivered in the cloak his companions had given him.

He knew a hunt when he smelled it, heard the pounding pulse of both pursuer and pursued. The air stank of aggression and terror. He found Rhenna beside him and seized her shoulder.

"It worked," he said hoarsely.

"Yes. We freed several of the prisoners—"

"Not all?"

"No time. It's all right, Cian."

"It is Festival," the stranger said. "We are in grave danger."

"We are also far from the inn, Geleon," Philokrates said. "What would you advise?"

"We can get to a safe house as long as we are not pursued."

"You take the others," Rhenna said. "I'll stay behind and watch."

"You wouldn't know who to watch for," Quintus said.

"I know red robes and armor when I see them."

"Not all the Stone's servants are so obvious," Geleon said. "And once the priests realize how we escaped..." He glanced from Rhenna to Philokrates. "You do not know me, yet you cheated the god at great peril to yourselves. All hands will be raised against you this night. The Watcher and Quintus must be protected."

"Listen to him, Quintus," Philokrates urged. "Rhenna and I will watch for pursuit and lead it astray, if need be."

"I'm not a child," Quintus snapped. "I will not be used, or cosseted like a woman—"

Cian struck him. Philokrates caught Quintus's arm before he could return the blow. Cian stared at his own stinging hand.

"We are none of us children," Geleon said harshly, "but there will be no children anywhere if the priests and their god—"

An inhuman wailing severed his words. Inhuman, though it came from a woman's throat—a cry so grotesque that the very earth held its breath. The people in the streets stopped in their tracks. The cry was taken up by a man in a stained leather apron and another whose hands bore the stains of Karchedon's famous purple dye. A young woman tore her chiton from neck to waist, baring her breasts. A boy hardly past adolescence snatched at her hair and threw her to the ground, grunting like a hog.

"We are too late. It has begun," Geleon whispered.

* * *

The unfortunate messenger was new-come to the priesthood, or he would not have been chosen to deliver the unpleasant tidings. He trembled on his knees at Baalshillek's feet, head bared—recently shaven, for his hair had not yet ceased to grow—and clutching at his tiny pendant as if it might save him from the High Priest's wrath.

Baalshillek might almost have mistaken the boy for one of the few who escaped the Stone's ravagement, but he was not so blessed. The first small weeping sore had begun to form on his cheek. It would remain small for months; perhaps there would be no others to trouble him for a year or more. He would still be of some use in spreading good tidings to recently conquered territories and cities such as Hypanis, where a handsome appearance lent sincerity to the one true god's revelations.

Fear was a necessary tool, but it lost its edge if used injudiciously. That was a lesson many in the priesthood had not learned.

"Rise," Baalshillek said. "You will instruct Zetes to summon the synod to meet in three hours. I will speak to the emperor myself. This blasphemy will not go unpunished."

"Yes, Most Holy."

Baalshillek dismissed the boy and paced across the anteroom of his chambers. Though he kept a residence here as well as in the temenos, the two suites were equally spare. He demanded no more of his underlings than he did of himself. The windowless walls and plain furnishings reflected function without waste, expedience without extravagance. Uniformity, symmetry, the harmony of perfect order.

Order disrupted by the work of infidels who had betrayed themselves with their rebellious acts.

"Orkos."

The soldier stepped out of the adjoining room. He made no genuflection; such gestures were unnecessary from the Stone's

Children, whose loyalty could not be questioned. Orkos and his breed were incapable of sedition.

Zetes' messenger had been late with his news. Orkos had interrupted Baalshillek in counsel with the emperor, a privilege only the Temple Guard and a few select Hetairoi were permitted. By the time Zetes had gathered the courage to inform his master of the outrage, Orkos had already sent men to guard the sacrificial cages.

Two of the Guard and an omega priest were dead, killed by the ones who had breached the temenos walls and freed several prisoners. Yet Orkos did not fear for himself as Zetes did; he lived only to serve the Stone. He had enough volition to act without direct orders and calculate the possible consequences, but no compulsion to mourn his failures. The Children who had died were imperfect; there must be another culling, and soon.

"Tell me what you have learned," Baalshillek commanded.

"An Ailu was observed outside the temenos," Orkos said. "The creature is not one of those previously collected. Apparently the Ailu and its companions entered Karchedon and the citadel as common pilgrims from Hellas."

He paused, as if he expected an exclamation of rage from his master. He should have known better. Like Orkos, Baalshillek didn't bewail what could not be undone. No one had anticipated that an Ailu, if any survived outside Karchedon, might come willingly to its enemy. Even Ag hadn't sensed an Annihilator's arrival. Only a testing at the docks could have exposed the incursion, and such testing had ceased years ago, upon the emperor's command.

"Continue," he instructed Orkos.

"The fire was set at the fifth granary, farthest from the cells. I dispatched four men to secure the offerings. Two guards took a female prisoner but failed to note the presence of her accomplices. One killed an omega priest and took his robes. Another is believed to be the Ailu. A third may have been responsible for the destruction of the locks."

Baalshillek stroked the hot, multifaceted surface of his stone, knowing that Ag would not be silent much longer. "A new Ailu," he said. "One who may have the power to shape Earth in the way of his ancestors. And with him one who annuls the stones."

Only small stones, to be sure. Strong enough to thwart any but priests and Children, but not indestructible.

A true Annihilator would have far more power. He would use it to greater purpose than the freeing of rebel prisoners. Either this one was not the Reborn...

Or he had laid the fires of his own destruction.

"The emperor has been informed of this incident," Baalshillek said. "He will send his own men in search of the rebels. You will select only Children of the highest rank to engage in the hunt. These three rebels must be taken alive."

"It is Festival," Orkos said.

"If these newcomers can invade the temenos, they will likely survive long enough to be captured. You will bring these and any other rebels directly to the temple. They are not to be given to the Palace Guard."

"I understand."

"Go."

Orkos turned smartly and exited by the hidden door. Sudden heat welled in Baalshillek's stone, a reminder that Ag must soon have his release. But Festival had begun, and that alone distracted the god. Lesser priests would be wandering the streets, collecting the psyches of the dying, souls infested with fear and hatred.

Hungry, Ag said.

Baalshillek stroked the stone. *Soon.*

His thoughts turned to other hungers. Danae had rejected him again, as he had foreseen, but he had enjoyed mild satisfaction in observing the special amusement Nikodemos had devised for his court. The emperor had forced his mistress to strip naked and ride on the back of a bull selected from the sacrificial lots, mocking the old Olympian gods by naming the pretty whore Pasiphae. In ancient legend, the wife of King Minos had mated with Poseidon's bull, producing the monstrous minotaur.

Unnatural union, unnatural offspring. Yet in those times the beings men called gods had mated freely with mortals. The descendants of such unions still walked the Earth. Some bore unearthly gifts, others the latent power of their mixed blood.

They were the only men and women who presented a challenge to the Stone. But the testing always exposed them; males who submitted became the Stone's most useful servants, alpha priests given the holy task of conquest and supervision of the colonies.

Those who did not submit...

Baalshillek licked his lips, remembering how Danae had walked so proudly in her nakedness, flaunting it, returning the emperor's mockery in full measure. But Nikodemos had watched the Stone God's High Priest, looking for evidence of unbridled lust.

Oh, no, My Lord Emperor. That is the least of your mistakes.

Disturbed by his emotions, Baalshillek left his chambers and took the most public way through the palace. It was good to let himself be seen, to reassure the faithless that one rebel attack meant nothing. Slaves and courtiers shrank from him like whipped curs. They knew better than to assume they would remain forever under the emperor's protection.

The Stone God would have its own.

In honor of Festival, no lamps had been lit in the citadel. The upper city's residents remained in their homes or ventured out with only torches to guide them. Baalshillek knew his path in dark or light. He crossed the square, listening for the cries in the city below. Many would suffer so that the unsusceptible and defective could be rooted out. That was law, and necessity.

He entered the temple from a small side door, bowed to the altar, and went in without acknowledging the greetings of the attendants. The pilgrims were gone, driven out of the citadel by the fire and resulting panic. They would take their chances with Festival.

The altar appeared deceptively smaller outside than within. It contained the testing rooms, stations for attendants and doors to the underground chambers. Baalshillek raised his pendant to one such door, which swung open silently. Stairs descended steeply beneath the temple. The hallway, burned out of the living earth, held a warmth belied by its slick, crystalline walls.

He went first to the brood chambers. Rows of pallets stretched into the gloom, each identical, each with its pregnant female awaiting the birth of an exceptional child. Gray-robed nurses tended the females with impersonal efficiency. They and their charges never saw daylight, nor yearned for it.

Baalshillek paused by the nearest pallet and stared at the female's tranquil face. She was not beautiful. Beauty was irrelevant, though it often accompanied the godborn. Her belly was swollen with impending delivery. A promising red light saturated the thin blanket stretched over her abdomen. Perhaps she would be honored to bear the perfect one, the first mortal body worthy to carry a god's soul.

Mine, Ag said.

Perhaps, Baalshillek answered. Or perhaps the Exalted must wait another month, or year, while the method was tested and refined. In the meantime, there would be many Stone's Children to serve as Orkos served, faultlessly loyal and all but invulnerable for the short duration of their lives.

Baalshillek touched the breeder's dull brown hair. Not like Danae's gold. He imagined Danae heavy with his child, seed of the High Priest himself. He saw the babe as a boy grown to manhood, bestriding the world with the true god's power.

Power to find and wield the Elemental Weapons…

He stopped the thought and the image, drowning them in chants of praise. Ag had not heard. Ag did not know how much of himself Baalshillek kept apart, how fiercely he had struggled to remain Baalshillek; without the High Priest to control the god's rage and greed, the Exalted would simply destroy the world and themselves along with it.

Baalshillek left the brood chambers and passed down the hall to the next doorway. It opened to a chamber of many small, curtained rooms. From one room issued the low moans of a woman and the grunts of a man in the throes of mating. Baalshillek's lips curled in contempt, but he waited until the noises had ceased and the priest emerged from his room, adjusting his robes over his skinny flanks. He saw Baalshillek as he moved to pull up his hood.

"Most Holy," he said, not quite able to extinguish the gleam of satiation from his eyes. He bowed, and Baalshillek examined his pocked and ravaged face, the scabrous flesh and open sores. This one had little time left before he must be culled. The fire ate him up from within, and he was in the last stages of his usefulness as a sire of the Stone's Children. It was a paradox that as the body failed, the Stone's power became most potent in the seed. Until the very end.

Baalshillek waved the man away and flipped open the curtain to the mating room. The woman lay sprawled nearly senseless on the furs, still under the influence of the pacifying drug. It was another paradox that those godborn females best suited to producing the Stone's Children were often the least pliable. They did not appreciate the honor in creating bodies worthy of the god—bodies that would survive long after these females were ash.

The woman on the pallet stirred and opened her eyes. She pathetically tried to cover her private parts, smeared with a virgin's blood. Baalshillek closed the curtain.

He almost smiled as he continued down the hall, anticipating his next stop. But a crowd of lesser priests blocked his way; they bowed and retreated as he approached, exposing the work in which they had been engaged.

A vast crack split the wall, extending halfway across the floor. Baalshillek walked to the edge of the crack and looked in. Nothing could be seen, but he knew it reached deep into the places where a few daimones of the earth might yet survive.

The strange Ailu had done this. He had rediscovered powers his brethren had forgotten and couldn't summon even under the most rigorous torture. But soon the Ailu, too, would be in the Stone's tender care. He would surrender his secrets, and the Watchers could be consigned to the holy flames.

"Repair this immediately," he told the leader of the crew. The priests hastened to continue their work. Baalshillek went on to the training grounds.

The space carved out of the rock was bigger than any other under the temenos, a suitable dimension for the education of hundreds of young Children. A score of boys trained on the field, sparring in pairs, their perfect bodies free of perspiration or any signs of weariness. Their movements were coordinated and yet never stiff, precise and yet possessed of their own peculiar grace. They appeared to range in age from ten to fifteen. In fact they were much younger by mortal count, and much older in their competence. By the end of their training they would go out into the world as adults, a few years old in literal age but fully developed as Children of the Stone.

One of the trainers saw Baalshillek and saluted with his bronze training sword. His youths came to instant attention. Baalshillek inspected them, studying the stone chip lodged in each boy's forehead—pieces of the Exalted, extensions of the Stone itself. That was why these beautiful bodies would burn out all too quickly, like the hottest of candles, and why they must continuously be replaced.

Baalshillek extended his hand. The trainer gave him the bronze sword, hilt first. Baalshillek tested its edge, chose one of the boys and neatly sliced the child's cheek. The boy hardly blinked. Blood welled in the cut and dripped down his chin. After a moment Baalshillek gestured, and an attendant slave arrived with cloths to bind the wound. The boy never moved. Baalshillek nodded approval and left the Children to their education.

There were other places he might have visited: the purifying and initiation chambers, the interrogation rooms, the library where scholar priests studied the ancient documents. But he chose instead to hear Ag's cries, and descended to the deepest level of the temenos.

The priests who tended the Stone did not look up as he entered. They were intent upon their god...or gods, because some part of all Eight were here in this piece, the largest in the world save for the True Stone itself. The souls and ultimate being of the Exalted lay in the True Stone, hidden where only the highest priesthood and the emperor could address them.

But the Eight, strengthened by sacrifice, could extend power even to the merest slivers of the crystal that contained them. By such means they took part in the conquest. It was not enough. Ag, his two sisters and five brothers remembered a time when they had ruled the Earth in shapes of their own choosing. They bided in the Stones, awaiting their freedom.

When the time was right, this piece would be reunited with the whole, and each of the Exalted would walk as a separate being with ultimate power over earth, water, air and fire.

Baalshillek knelt before the crimson dome of the Stone and touched his forehead to the ground.

Ag.

The spirit of the god filled him, lifting him to his feet. Ag's fire brought pain, always, but it was a strange ecstatic agony, emotion so engulfing that Baalshillek knew it as love and hatred, disgust and desire, joy and fear all at once.

He opened himself as Ag demanded, everything but the shrouded heart the god must never find.

An alpha priest crept to the Stone and laid a sacrificial vessel upon the marble platform that encircled it. The vessel was made of metal forged over stone-fed fires, created especially to contain and eventually release the captured psyches within it. These were only the spirits of beasts, since Festival had just begun, and they were swiftly absorbed into the Stone just as their blood had flowed into the altars.

Ag and his fellow Exalted gave cries of unsatisfied hunger. Baalshillek felt the god seize his body and move it across the sanctum, watching with detachment as his own hand clutched the robes of an unfortunate priest and dragged the man to the Stone.

Such was the power of the Stone that only the slightest contact of living flesh on crystal set skin and bone ablaze. The priest screamed as his body was consumed. Flesh blackened and peeled; bones cracked and split. His psyche was last to be devoured, so that he suffered every instant of torment and provided the Exalted with an even more savory feast.

Baalshillek-Ag released what remained of the sacrifice. Ash sizzled and smoked on the red crystal's surface. The other priests were utterly silent.

Have they been found? Ag asked.

The question was always the same, whether hours or days had passed. Not one question, but three: *Have the bodies been made? Have the weapons been found? Have the enemies been destroyed?*

Ag knew the answers. Scholar priests worked day and night to interpret the texts and find the locations of the four free Exalted, the Elemental Weapons and the Reborn.

Ag's frustration seethed in Baalshillek's veins. Ag was compelled to share his High Priest's body, the only one capable of holding the god's essence without being obliterated. But he was eager to have a physical form of his own, one without a mind or psyche that could hinder complete possession.

They must be found! Ag roared in Baalshillek's voice, magnified a hundred times. Priests fell on their faces and covered their ears. Baalshillek-Ag paced the sanctum, kicking men out of his path. He considered flinging more of the priests onto the Stone, and Ag's siblings clamored in agreement. But Baalshillek spoke silently, carefully: *They are needed. For now.*

Control. Order. This was the key to victory—an end to chaos, to the irregularity and randomness of nature and its daimones. No more would men sustain the spirits of turmoil and independence. The gods of Hellas and Karchedon were vanquished and absorbed, those of Aigyptos and Persis and Italia near total defeat. With every new conquest came more daimones, more errant souls to feed the Stone. And more servants who saw that the world was changing and would never return to what it had been.

The priests wielded the Stone's power, tending the population like cattle, feeding them, guiding them, culling out the sick or deviant, and selecting the finest stock for breeding. There was no war, no starvation, no lasting illness or the suffering of old age. Every imperial subject, from slave to aristocrat, knew his place and was content in it. And so there would be no struggle, no resistance to the Exalted's ultimate design.

Control, Baalshillek said. *That was what you lacked before. That is your servant's most humble offering.*

Ag roared again, burning several priests for the simple pleasure of it. And then he retreated, for he knew that if he spent too long in his borrowed body, strong though it was, it must putrefy like all the others.

He needed Baalshillek. And Baalshillek understood his Lord, his Master, his god.

Baalshillek opened his eyes. The Stone cast its roiling, ruddy light. The priests cowered. Baalshillek turned his back on them and returned to the surface, where the cries of the dying rose up from the lower city like dissonant music.

The Stone would feed well tonight. Ag's power still burned in Baalshillek's limbs. He strode briskly toward the palace, dreaming of a woman's white and languid arms.

Chapter Twenty-Four

The first attack was unexpected, yet Rhenna was ready. She turned her body just enough to twist the man over her shoulder, flinging him to the ground. She placed her foot on her assailant's throat as two other howling citizens rushed at Cian.

He crouched to meet them, teeth bared. Quintus punched one of them in the belly and stepped aside. Cian caught the other, knocking the man's head against the nearest wall. Geleon and Philokrates were already faced with opponents of their own.

These Karchedonians were not warriors; they bore only the slightest of weapons, and yet Rhenna could not mistake their intentions. She warded off a middle-aged woman with a bronze hairpin, grabbed one of the long pins that closed the shoulders of her chiton and wielded it like a knife. She worked her way past the ever-growing horde of wailing adversaries, slashing and stabbing.

Cian, whom she most wanted to protect, least needed her aid.

Philokrates was struggling, but Geleon was at his side. Quintus fought one-handed, fending off attackers with his cloaked left arm as he struck with his right.

The crowd pushed Rhenna toward Quintus. She fetched up at his back like a bit of flotsam on the sea, tossed among waves of adversaries. The Tiberian glanced at her over his shoulder. He had lost the small knife he'd used in the temple compound. Rhenna snatched another of her shoulder pins and passed it to him. Soon she would be as naked under her cloak as Cian was.

Asteria's blood. She looked for Cian and could no longer find him in the seething mass of bodies. "Do you see the others?" she shouted to Quintus.

He shook his head, intent on driving off a brick-wielding merchant.

Rhenna's latest opponent retreated from the savage thrusts of her pin, and space opened up before her. At first she thought that the mob had lost interest in baiting prey who fought back, and then she realized that a group of attackers—all male—had discovered a more promising victim.

The girl couldn't have been more than twelve, perhaps just entering her first blood. The men had driven her into a narrow alley, and one was already on top of her, tearing her chiton with vicious abandon. His accomplices urged him on with shouts, spittle dripping from their contorted lips.

For a heartbeat Rhenna froze, stricken with terror. Then she ran, her pin raised to strike.

The rapist received warning enough to roll to the side before she could deliver a fatal wound. He screamed as the pin pierced his arm. Two men sprang to his defense, but the others converged on the girl as if they could not conceive of any threat from a woman. Rhenna sliced the cheek of one enemy and deflected the attack of the second, dodging his charge and stabbing at his hamstrings. He fell to the ground, crippled. The rapist scrambled away, and several of his friends deserted the fight.

Rhenna turned to the men with the girl. The grunting pig taking his pleasure died before he could complete the next thrust. Three men rushed at Rhenna, one armed with a knife. He fell on his own blade, tripped by Quintus, who flashed Rhenna a startling grin.

He dispatched the second antagonist with a deft sideways twist of his body and a kick to the back of the falling man's skull. "See to the girl!" he shouted, facing off with the third.

Rhenna knelt by the child, whose weeping was all the more terrible in its silence. She closed the victim's chiton and removed her own cloak to cover blood and bruises.

She rose with the girl in her arms as Quintus won his battle. The crowd numbered among the hundreds, one shape merging into another until the streets flowed like rivers. Philokrates, Cian and Geleon had vanished. Men and women attacked each other without apparent purpose. Their hoarse cries and moans were those of animals.

Like beasts, they scented blood. A new band of Karchedonians discovered the outsiders and began to advance, each face as witlessly brutal as the next.

"How is the girl?" Quintus asked, wiping blood from his face.

"She'll survive," Rhenna said grimly. "If we do."

"We're trapped here. If we can get into the street…"

The foremost rank of the pack advanced, death in their eyes. Quintus stepped in front of Rhenna and the girl. A sinuous length of dark leather snapped out of the darkness, catching an enemy about the neck; he choked and stumbled. Whips cracked into the startled faces of the mob. A wall of men sprang up between the hunters and their quarry.

"Come with me," one of the new men said. His eyes were clear, his voice level.

Rhenna didn't hesitate. She and Quintus accompanied him as his companions thrashed the air and any man or woman imprudent enough to venture within range of their lashes.

The crowd split apart. In the center of a wide, pulsing ring of humanity was a sort of carrying couch such as Rhenna had seen in Piraeos, borne by servants in short chitons. The men with the whips wore identical tunics and leather cuirasses, and it soon became apparent that they answered to the occupant of the chair.

The curtains were drawn back just enough to give Rhenna an unobstructed view of the woman inside. Torches revealed the soft amber of her hair and the green of tilted eyes in a distinctively lovely face. Her lips curved up in a smile.

"You seem to be having some difficulty," she said. "I think you had best be my guests this night."

Quintus approached the chair and was firmly restrained by one of the guards. "Who are you?" he asked.

"I am Danae. But introductions can wait." She met Quintus's stare, and her smile widened. "Unless, of course, you would prefer to be torn limb from limb?"

"Why should we trust you?"

The woman's gaze moved past Quintus to Rhenna and her limp burden. "Perhaps because it is not your own life you wish to protect. And perhaps because I am not like them." She gestured eloquently toward the watching crowd and leaned out of the chair, one golden lock spilling over her bare shoulder.

Quintus gaped.

"We accept your offer," Rhenna said. "Will you take the child?"

"Give her to me."

Rhenna lifted the girl through the gap in the diaphanous curtains. Danae accepted the insignificant weight into her own arms and settled the child beside her, fussing with furs and pillows. She signaled with a flicker of beringed fingers. Her guards formed a cordon about the chair, whips at the ready, and the procession began to advance.

The mob groaned savage frustration. It gave way to snapping whips. The people behind followed as close as they dared.

For a while chair and retinue made progress up one of the streets leading to the higher ground near the citadel. But the Karchedonians seemed to gain more confidence with every step. The guards protecting the rear of the chair struck more furiously at the boldest pursuers. The men to the fore made little headway as the mob stood fast. Their mutterings rose in volume like a storm about to break.

The night was airless, sucked dry of movement save for that of the boiling populace. Rhenna glanced up at the cloudless sky. She imagined the sharp, fresh breezes of the steppe, longed for its scent of dried grasses and wildflowers and horse dung. She even missed the wind that had driven her north to that first terrible harbinger of the evil to come, and the gale that had pushed her, Tahvo and Cian into the Skudat camp. If some Earthspeaker could but call upon the wild vitality of the open plain…

Dust swirled up from cracks in the clean-wept pavement. The chair's curtains fluttered. Air with the taste of salt, and something else achingly familiar, tickled Rhenna's cheek.

Then the wind rose out of nothing and slammed into the human barrier blocking the chair's path. It drove each howling man apart from his neighbor. Danae's guards increased their pace. Their whips continued to strike true in spite of the gusts that staggered anyone outside the perimeter of their defense.

In a few moments they had broken through the barricade and trotted briskly up to high wooden gates not unlike those of the palace citadel. The gates swung open just enough to admit the chair and its guards. They slammed closed on the coughing, flailing mob.

Inside the gates, everything changed. The wind ceased, left behind with the enemy. The streets were quiet, and lights shone from a few high windows and doorways.

Danae slid back the curtains. "The girl sleeps," she said. "We are safe now."

"Why here and not there?" Quintus asked.

She smiled with an ease that made the expression seem a natural part of her features. "You are a very curious sort, young traveler. Suffice it to say that Festival does not enter where the emperor's Council holds sway."

Quintus stopped abruptly. "You are of the emperor's court?"

She sighed, and her long lashes dropped over her eyes. "You have nothing to fear from me or anyone in my household. I come and go as I please. And I don't share my secrets." She extended her hand—not to Quintus, but to Rhenna. "I have heard rumors of a fire at the temple and the escape of prisoners bound for sacrifice, but I am quite certain that the villains who committed such crimes have either fled or are safely in the hands of the priests."

Rhenna gingerly took the delicate, graceful hand in her own. Danae's skin was soft, unscarred. Each nail was shaped and painted. But her gaze was as direct as a warrior's.

"I think you're right," Rhenna said gravely.

Danae squeezed Rhenna's hand and released it. "We go to the house of my father, who is away on the emperor's business. My servants are loyal to my family. No one outside will know you are here."

Quintus wore a stubborn look that threatened impending argument, but he had the sense to realize that this was neither the time nor the place. He walked on ahead with the guards.

Danae arched a golden brow. "He is not of Hellas," she said. "And neither are you. I saw you fight the mob with the skill of a warrior. Saving the girl took great courage when your own lives were threatened."

Rhenna shook her head. "Why such madness? What is this Festival?"

"It is, as you said, madness. Calculated madness."

Rhenna gripped the edge of the chair. "I have a friend in an inn at the harbor. Will she be safe?"

"Such places are generally out of Festival bounds," Danae said. "Your friend should be safe from the mob as long as she remains near the harbor."

Rhenna thought of Cian and Philokrates, adrift in that tempest. "I have other friends still in the city. When does Festival end?"

"At dawn, usually with a grand sacrifice." Danae's gaze sharpened. "You think of returning to help your friends, but put such thoughts from your mind. You must wait."

They walked in silence, climbing up the hill among ever more luxurious dwellings. A few even possessed gardens of a sort, courtyards of small trees and trailing vines that defied the lifelessness of the lower city.

At last the chair turned on a side street and stopped at inlaid wooden doors set in a high stone wall. A few bold flowers crept over the top like escaping prisoners. The doors opened from within, and servants emerged to meet the new arrivals. They led their mistress and her guests into a large reception room furnished with tables, couches and sculptures of naked men and graceful women. Guards closed the doors and stood sentinel as the bearers laid down their burden and a young, dark-haired woman hastened to help Danae from the chair.

"Take the girl first," Danae instructed. "Give her the best room and summon the physician...discreetly."

The maid bowed. "Yes, my lady. At once." She instructed a male servant to lift the injured girl, but the child began to struggle as soon as he touched her.

"I'll take her," Rhenna offered. She cradled the girl in her arms and waited for the maidservant to show her the way.

The house was made up of a series of rooms built around a colonnaded central courtyard where trees grew and a fountain bubbled merrily. The floors were almost entirely surfaced with colorful mosaics, some flat and others intricately designed out of black and white pebbles. The smell of recent cooking lingered in the air, contending with the scent of flowers.

The courtyard was a tiny bit of paradise in the midst of desolation, and Rhenna breathed in the moist, sweet air with gratitude. Even the injured girl seemed to feel the garden's gentle protection.

The room chosen for her had been painted to represent an ocean scene in soothing blues and greens. The furnishings were simple but exquisitely made, from the carved three-legged chair to the storage chests. Rhenna laid the girl on the pillow-heaped couch and covered her with linen blankets. The maid brought a pitcher of water and a bronze cup. Rhenna supported the girl while she drank and then settled her as comfortably as might be.

Danae appeared in the doorway, Quintus at her shoulder. She smoothed her pale yellow chiton to best display the grace of her figure, a gesture that seemed less vain than habitual.

"You will have your own room, of course," she said to Rhenna. "Nefer will care for the girl until the physician arrives."

"I would remain close."

"You may have the adjoining chamber." She cocked her head. "I believe introductions are now in order. I am Danae, daughter of Kallimachos."

"I am Rhenna, of the Free People."

"How delightful that sounds." Danae glanced at Quintus, brow raised in invitation.

"Quintus," he said, lifting his chin. "Of Tiberia."

"Ah. Tiberia, which has given the emperor and the priests such great trouble." She smiled as she spoke, as if the matter were of no importance to her whatsoever. "Your room will be across the courtyard in the andron, the men's quarters. You'll find that we—my family—are not so formal as the Hellenes, who keep strict separation between men and women. We sometimes even dine together."

"As we do in Tiberia," Quintus said with surprising gracious-ness. He met Rhenna's dubious gaze over Danae's slender shoul-der. "We thank you for your hospitality."

"Then you do trust me, after all."

He responded to her flirtatious tone with a direct stare. "Are you of the Resistance?"

Her smile wavered. "Speak such words with care, my friend. I am merely...uncommitted."

"To the Stone."

"To anything but that which gives me pleasure. And tonight it pleased me to thwart the mob." She signaled to a stout and digni-fied male servant who stood some distance away. "Aqhat will pro-vide whatever you require. Everything in the house is yours. I would be most honored to learn more of your people, Rhenna, if you and Quintus will join me in a small supper. In the mean-time, you will wish to bathe." She nodded to both of them and swept across the courtyard.

Rhenna waited until their hostess had returned to the main salon, and joined Quintus. "You took a great chance speaking to her as you did," she said.

"No more than you in accepting her protection."

"You didn't protest too vigorously."

Quintus flushed, and Rhenna considered how Danae must ap-pear to a young man with typical male desires. She behaved as one who knew men intimately and enjoyed their company.

"There is much I might learn from one who is part of the em-peror's court," Quintus said gruffly. "But we must be on our guard until it's safe to leave."

Rhenna snorted. "Teach a mare to eat grass. I intend to accept the bath she offered us."

Quintus raked his hand through his dark hair. "I——" He paused as the portly servant Aqhat bowed and offered to lead him to his room. "I will speak to you later."

He walked away. Rhenna looked in on the girl and found the maid Nefer already at her bedside. Another maid waited for Rhenna in the adjoining chamber. She presented wine and a selection of fresh clothing much finer than anything Rhenna had ever worn against her skin.

"Your bath will be heated and ready within the hour," the young woman promised, and bowed her way out.

Rhenna paced the room for a time, gazed out into the courtyard, and finally sat on the couch. She closed her eyes.

Cian. Tahvo. Philokrates. They overflowed her thoughts as Danae's wine might spill from the untouched cup at Rhenna's bedside.

Devas, keep them safe, she prayed, pretending the gods would hear.

Danae knew they had not been followed. She'd sent her most trusted men to roam the streets and watch the gates. While Festival raged below, the upper city kept to itself, wrapped in false serenity.

Nevertheless, Danae felt compelled to visit the children. The private temple had been converted into a storage room when the priests passed their edicts forbidding the old gods, but its fluted marble columns still declared its original function. It was cool in summer and warm in winter, though the entryway appeared open to the elements and was partially blocked with the rubble of discarded statues.

Both openness and obstacles were illusory. Danae negotiated the seemingly random maze of crumbling stone and passed through the hidden entrance into the small but comfortable interior.

Naturally the children were asleep, though their nurse was vigilant enough to wake at Danae's approach. Sebethis was a stout, rough-skinned woman whose husband and daughters had been given to the altar last year, and her devotion to the children was as solid as her hatred of the Stone.

"My lady," Sebethis said softly. "They are all well."

"So I see." Danae sat on a stool beside one of the pallets and watched the little boy's chest rise and fall beneath the blanket. "We have other guests tonight, but they are friends. We need have no fear of them."

"I do not fear, my lady."

"We should be able to transport the children from Karchedon tomorrow or the next day. The priests will be well sated after Festival."

Sebethis nodded grimly. "These would have burned if not for you, my lady."

Danae waved her hand. "It is my pleasure to steal from Baalshillek whenever I—"

"So you lied."

She turned sharply. Quintus leaned against the wall just inside the hidden entrance. Sebethis surged to her feet.

"Hush, or you'll wake the children," Danae said. She gathered her skirts and faced Quintus calmly. "I did not invite you to follow me, let alone make such unpleasant accusations. But since you are here—"

"You lied when you said you were not part of the Resistance."

Danae moved closer to him, intensely aware of his musky male scent and his painfully honest face. Not so much younger than she, truly, but so earnest, so firm in his convictions.

"Are the men of Tiberia always so plainspoken?" she asked with a teasing smile.

"When we are permitted to be. When we're free."

"Of course." She drew closer still, and he shifted his weight ever so slightly, drawing away. Uneasy. Attracted to her and refusing to admit it.

That was no surprise. But why should *she* find a grubby, if handsome, stranger in the least bit interesting?

Because he is different, her heart whispered. *Because he is not of the court or of the Stone, and he looks upon you with more than lust.*

"Is she your lover?" Danae asked.

He jerked and flushed, such a charming and unworldly reaction. "Rhenna? No." He breathed deeply, and the muscles of his chest flexed under his tunic. "She is...she is my..."

"Friend? Perhaps you do not ordinarily apply that word to a woman, yet it is clear that you have shared much together." She glanced at a glowering Sebethis. "I have heard that the rebels accept women as equals because they cannot afford to reject the aid of any who would risk their lives for the cause."

"Your cause," he accused.

"I am not one of them, nor do I oppose them."

"And these children?"

"Saved from the altar," Sebethis said. "As she's saved so many others."

Quintus searched Danae's eyes, a scrutiny she found almost disconcerting.

"Yet you are a member of the emperor's court?" he asked.

She stepped back and traced a languorous circuit about the room. "What do you see when you look at me, Tiberian?"

He stared, tongue-tied. After a moment he remembered how to speak. "I see a woman of great beauty, courage...and mystery."

"I will take that as a true compliment from one who does not give praise lightly." She waved Sebethis back to her pallet and led Quintus from the old temple. "You still have many questions, Quintus of Tiberia. Where shall I begin?"

"What will you do with the children?"

"I have my own means of protecting them."

"And you helped them only to 'steal' from this Baalshillek?"

"I do not like the High Priest," she said. "I find him most unpleasant, and his god's habits even more so."

"The High Priest," Quintus repeated. "You choose your enemies well."

"I always choose well." She entered the courtyard. "How long have you been in Karchedon?"

"We arrived the day before yesterday."

"And you didn't know of Festival, or you would not have been caught out tonight." She paused to cup a flower in her palm and breathe in its fragrance. "Do you know why you were attacked?"

"It was violence without purpose, men striking each other—"

"And hurting children," she said. "But there is great purpose in the Stone God's Festival. It is a cleansing and purifying of the people and the city, the night—four times a year—when all restraint is abandoned and the peaceful citizens of Karchedon give themselves to madness. For them it is the only true freedom. But for anyone not bound by the Stone—" She hesitated, hating the necessity of putting the horror into words. "For them it is almost certain death."

"Not bound," Quintus said, snapping a flower from its stem. "The rebels?"

"Any man or woman who has not been fully tested or dedicated to the god—those who somehow escaped initiation or deceived the priests, invaders who must be removed lest they corrupt the blessed."

"Then the mob recognized us—"

"As outsiders apart from the Stone." She took the flower from Quintus's hand, and their fingers touched. "Festival is also the time when those who have become ill since their last testing...or too old to work, or weak of mind...are eliminated. At Festival, every citizen and slave becomes a hound of the priests. They sense those who do not belong. They hunt their prey and tear them apart, not always quickly. All who die are deemed proper sacrifice to the god."

"The girl was unaffected by the Stone?"

"Many children aren't tested until they reach her age. If her attackers let her live after they were finished with her, any child she bore would belong to the priests."

He paced across the courtyard, seizing the lower branch of a small olive tree. "You knew we opposed the Stone."

She brushed the flower's petals across the back of her hand. "A simple guess."

"The mob would have attacked you, as well."

"Oh, yes, if they had dared. You see, I have never been tested. The emperor chooses to keep his hetairoi and courtiers free of the Stone's influence and the priests' control. It greatly vexes Baalshillek, but after all——" His breath stirred her hair, and she tried to disregard the pleasant tingle at the back of her neck. "After all," she said lightly, "it would not do if the emperor's favorite hetairai should become mad, or dull as an unmounted ewe."

Her words had the desired effect. Quintus blanched.

"You are the emperor's mistress?" he stammered.

She dropped the flower into the fountain. It bobbed and danced on the rippling water. "Now perhaps you understand why I am not a rebel, in spite of my dislike of the priests and their spilling of innocent blood. I am loyal to my emperor."

Quintus was silent for a very long time. "I do not understand you."

"Understanding is not necessary. Once it's safe for you to leave, we are unlikely to meet again. But I will not betray you, and you will not betray me." She glanced toward the bathhouse. "Surely you wish to bathe. I would advise it. My servants will bring clothing that will not attract attention in the city, and we will dine before sleep."

He answered with a bow meant to cut like the stroke of a sword, turned on his heel and left her.

Danae scooped the flower from the fountain and tore the petals into tiny pieces.

Chapter Twenty-Five

Cian, Philokrates and the rebel leader Geleon reached the safe house just ahead of the mob. A sudden turn down an alley followed by two more in rapid succession led to a door painted so as to blend seamlessly with the wall in which it was set.

Geleon touched the door, and it opened almost magically. Philokrates paused to examine it, intense curiosity on his face, but Cian pulled him through and Geleon shut the door firmly behind them.

The walls of the house did not keep out the roars and screams, but Cian felt that at last he could breathe again. His hair was tangled from the clutch of vicious hands, and his arms were streaked with blood, not all of it his own.

He hadn't been compelled to change, and for that he was grateful. But Rhenna and Quintus were not here. He had never intended to leave Rhenna's side.

And when did she ever require your protection?

Cian leaned against the wall and slid to the floor. The room was dark, lit by a single lamp on a rickety table. Geleon had gone through another doorway within the house, leaving Cian and Philokrates to recover from the ordeal.

"You are all right?" Cian asked the old man.

"Bruised and abraded, most painfully in my dignity." Philokrates regarded his bony hands with a rueful smile. "It has been a very long time since I was required to engage in a brawl."

Cian rubbed his face. "What was all that?"

"Festival," Geleon said, returning through the door with a clay pitcher and cups. Three men and a woman entered the room behind him. They took up positions around the room as Geleon passed the water to Cian and Philokrates.

"These are my associates," Geleon said, indicating the newcomers. "You do not need to know their names, but they will remember you and what you've done this night." He glanced at his friends. "This man," he said, pointing to Cian, "is a Watcher, recently arrived in the city."

"Some Watchers remain free?" the woman asked.

Cian stood. "I am the last. I came to seek my brothers."

"Cian traveled to Karchedon with others who share our cause," Geleon said. "He, a Tiberian named Quintus and a woman of the far North, set me and several other prisoners free. The mob separated us."

"May Melquart preserve them," one of the men said.

Geleon briefly bowed his head. "Nyx was taken."

A sigh passed among the rebels. "When do we go?" asked a brown-skinned man with tightly curled black hair.

"It may not be possible to save her. The priests will be crawling over the city like flies on a carcass."

"All the more reason they won't expect us to attempt a rescue."

"We'll speak of that later, in full assembly. A far more pressing matter requires our attention." He looked from face to face. "The Tiberian Quintus has the power to silence the stones."

A thin man with dark, tilted eyes hissed through his teeth. "The one who was foretold?"

"If you believe the scribblings of ancient madmen," said his neighbor, a red-haired giant with a twist of metal about his neck. "I believe in what I can touch. Or kill."

"I saw the Watcher change shape with my own eyes," Geleon said. "I saw him split the earth. We know the priests fear his kind. They believe the writings. Even if only some are true——"

"They are," Philokrates interrupted, stepping into the light. "I have studied them…fragments, but enough that I believe if we can only locate the missing texts——"

"*You.*"

Everyone turned as a fifth man walked through the door. "It isn't possible," he said, staring at Philokrates. "You? Here?"

"Shahriar," Geleon said. "I thought——"

"Yes." Shahriar picked up the lamp and thrust it in Philokrates's face. "I have not forgotten you, Talos." He slammed the lamp on the table and reached for the curved knife at his belt.

Geleon caught his arm. "You make no sense, my friend."

"No sense?" He advanced on Philokrates, and Cian stepped between them. Shahriar's sharp-nosed face twisted into a mask of hatred. "Thirty years ago I was a child, fascinated by his evil devices even as they smashed the walls of our city. Until all I knew was gone."

"Stand back," Cian warned. "Philokrates——"

"Is that what he calls himself?" Shahriar asked. "He had another name then."

"Talos." Geleon spoke the word in a tone devoid of feeling. "He vanished twenty-six years ago."

"He has changed, but not beyond recognition." Shahriar attempted to pass Cian and failed. "Where did you go for so many years, Talos? How do you dare to show your face among us?"

Philokrates rested his hand on Cian's shoulder. "Enough," he said softly. "I am Talos."

Cian shook his head. "I don't understand."

"Talos," Geleon said, "was Arrhidaeos's great builder of war machines, a genius who constructed weapons and siege engines that could be neither defeated nor destroyed. With these machines Arrhidaeos's army laid waste to half of Persis and put down a dozen smaller revolts in the tenth year of his reign." He stared at Philokrates. "You admit you are Talos. You are as much our enemy as Nikodemos himself."

"He is an old man," Cian said.

Shahriar laughed. "Evil does not weaken with age. It only alters its form."

"Why are you here, Talos?" Geleon demanded. "Why do you travel with a Watcher? Do you intend to betray us to the priests or the emperor?"

Philokrates moved to stand at Cian's side. "I was Talos," he said. "I did the things you claim. I made these machines for the emperor when I was still young and arrogant. I did not think of the lives my creations would destroy."

"You did not *think*?" Shahriar spat.

Philokrates bowed his head. "I remained with the emperor for four years after the events of which you speak, and then I contrived to escape. I hid in Tiberia for nearly twenty years, until it, too, was taken—"

"With your machines," Geleon said.

"In the hands of those who did not understand them. Do any of them still function?"

The rebels exchanged glances. "We heard that Nikodemos retired them as unreliable."

"Ah." Philokrates sighed. "When I left Tiberia, Nikodemos's men found me. They hoped to...persuade me to aid the new emperor as I had his father. I declined."

"You declined the emperor?" Shahriar cried.

"I...convinced him that I had gone mad. Nikodemos permitted me to live in Hellas, near Athinai, where I remained alone but within the emperor's reach. He did not know that I became the Tiberian rebels' contact."

"He came with us to Karchedon," Cian said, troubled by what he had heard, yet not quite able to believe it. "He knows what Quintus can do, and he recognized my nature from the beginning. He could have betrayed us the moment we arrived. Instead, he made contact with your Nyx, and so we were able to help—"

"How do we know he didn't arrange for Nyx's capture?" said the dark-skinned man.

"And yet allow Geleon and the others to escape?" Cian bared his teeth. "We risked our lives to save yours, and *my* people are still captive. Our companions may be taken. Whatever your ancient grudges, they are meaningless now."

"Meaningless?" Shahriar raised his knife. "I'll—"

Cian batted the blade aside. "I don't know Talos. Philokrates is my friend, and the friend of Quintus. If you have some use for us, do not threaten our friends."

Geleon met Cian's gaze. "Your loyalty does you honor, and I am grateful for what you've done. But Talos has admitted his crimes. His attempts to atone do not revoke his evil acts. At the very least, he is a danger to all we have worked to achieve. I have no choice but to keep him here for judgment."

"And then? Will you kill him as the priests would kill you?"

"There are others who will remember him," Shahriar said. "He can't be allowed to leave this room."

"And I," Philokrates said, "cannot permit you to hold me." He drew a small object from among his robes. The metal tube was no longer or thicker than a finger. Multihued light glittered through the clear crystal stopper at one end. "I had hoped never to use this," he said, "but it seems I, too, have no choice." He smiled sadly at Cian. "This will summon the emperor's men within a league's radius. If you allow me to leave, I won't use the device until I am well away from your sanctuary."

"He bluffs," Shahriar snarled.

"You doubt his abilities now?" Geleon murmured. "I believe him. No matter what happens, this place will be useless to us after tonight."

"Then let us dispose of him."

"We are not murderers," said the red-haired giant. "It is for Geleon to decide."

The rebel leader hesitated, looking from Philokrates to Cian. "You will defend him, Watcher? In spite of what you've heard?"

Cian knew the answer, yet doubt choked him. What if Philokrates had done what they claimed? The rebels had no reason to lie. Cian had seen the strange contraption in the old man's house, and Philokrates had possessed one of the red stones. If he went to the emperor now…

"Trust me," Philokrates said in his ear. "Trust what your instincts tell you, Watcher."

Cian shivered. Philokrates asked him to trust the beast, not the man. Instinct.

He met Geleon's gaze. "Yes," he said. "I will defend him."

"Then we must let him go——" he raised his hand at Shahriar's protest "——if the Watcher swears to serve our cause."

"My first obligation is to my people," Cian said.

"It is doubtful that many remain alive. The priests will be hunting you. Your only hope of survival lies with us."

"Even if all the Ailuri are dead," Cian said, "I must find my companions."

"That you may also do…with our help."

"Then I agree to your terms. But I will see Philokrates away from this place—alone."

Geleon nodded. "Go back the way we came, as far as the Street of Weavers and no farther. Do not let yourself be seen by anyone. If you haven't returned within the hour, we will come after you."

Cian turned to Philokrates. "If the mob finds you before the guards do..."

"It's a risk I must take." He squeezed Cian's arm. "Let them help you, but do always as your instinct bids." He started for the door.

Geleon intercepted him and put his ear to the wood. "Go now," he said.

Cian led the way into the alley. Geleon closed the door. Violent sounds and the scent of blood assaulted Cian, and for a moment he was paralyzed. Philokrates hurried toward the Street of Weavers, but Cian caught up with him at the corner.

"You're safe from the rebels now," he said. "We can return to the inn. I'll find a way."

Philokrates raised his device so that its glow illuminated his face. "It is too late. I should have been better prepared. Sooner or later I would have been recognized—if not by the rebels, then by someone from the emperor's court, I had hoped..."

"Why did you not tell us who you were?"

"And earn your contempt before I could do anything to help?"

Cian took the old man by the shoulders. "You would truly go to the emperor? You would serve him again?"

"You cannot believe I would serve him, or even you would not let me leave. If I stay in the lower city, the rebels will find and kill me. They believe they have just cause to do so."

"Do they?"

Philokrates smiled, though his eyes were expressionless. "Perhaps one day I will tell you. Now, go back to the others."

"And if I should stop you?"

Philokrates thumbed the crystal head of the metal rod. Light flared. "Once I remove the crystal, the pneumata within will be set free. They will seek the closest living bearer of the metal from which they derive—the special alloy of the armor worn by the emperor's troops. The pneumata will be compelled to lead the soldier or soldiers they find directly to me—or to whomever is near enough to be touched during their release. If you remain when I open the device you also will be marked."

"I won't believe you threaten me, old one."

"Yet I will do this, unless you leave me. Move away." Philokrates gave the crystal a sharp twist.

The beast in Cian responded instantly. He cast off the cloak that was his sole garment and leaped up the side of the nearest house, scrambling up the mud-brick walls to the roof on the second level. A tile slipped and shattered on the ground at Philokrates's feet.

Cian saw the magic happen, watched as the pneumata, like a handful of golden dust, burst out of the rod and swirled in a wide arc about Philokrates's head. The old man glanced up through the veil of tiny particles and met Cian's gaze. He lifted his hand in farewell and walked out of the alley.

Cian grabbed a handful of tiles and tore them from the roof, flinging them in every direction. He roared. Somewhere voices answered, echoing his rage. He crossed the roof, jumped to the next building and kept running, easily leaping the alleys and narrow streets between.

In time he came to a place where the street was too wide to traverse. He crouched, panting, on the edge of the roof. He smelled dawn in the air, besmirched with blood and sweat. The unmoving body of a naked woman sprawled in an alley across the lane.

Sense cleared the savage haze from his mind. He'd given his word to help the rebels and accept their aid in return, but Rhenna…she could be that woman in the street, stinking of death. Gentle Tahvo was alone. The rebels would delay, thinking to protect him while his friends suffered for his stupidity.

Festival ended at dawn. Soon the sun would rise. He would collect Tahvo and take her to safety among the rebels, then convince them to search for Rhenna. If they refused...

A new scent came to him on a fresh wind from the citadel. His hair stood erect. He looked down into the street.

What he saw was impossible. The woman was Rhenna's height. She wore Rhenna's scent like the cloak concealing her face. If she spoke, he knew he would hear Rhenna's voice.

She lifted her arms. He leaped to the ground. She sang to him in a sweet, inhuman voice and opened her robe.

The ugly thing he had been holding within himself broke loose. All urges fled but one—burning, brutal, uncontrollable lust. He would take her in any place, by any means, brand her as his and blot out every memory of Farkas. She was his, by all the gods— yes, even by the Stone God itself.

He snarled. She laughed, but still he couldn't see her face. He prepared to seize her, and she slipped from his grasp.

Then she changed. The gray cloak floated to the ground, and from its folds emerged a being of surpassing beauty, black as onyx, golden-green eyes alight with answering hunger.

She could not exist, yet she was real. She was Ailu. Female. Undeniably, deliciously female, and eager to mate.

Cian became what he was meant to be.

"You took what is mine. Return it to me, sister. Give it back, or I will never let you rest."

Tahvo struggled to see her brother's face. He was the age he should have been, if he'd lived; his hair was silver, like hers. But his features were a blur, a masculine version of her own, reflected in dirty, broken ice.

"You stole my life," he said. "Now you will suffer as my spirit has suffered."

He showed her the things she most dreaded: Rhenna dead, her throat slit like a gaping second mouth; Cian chained and beaten to a whimpering husk of himself; Philokrates given to the Stone God's fire with the in-

fants and aged…and Quintus, defeated by the Stone, willingly corrupted, marching with the emperor's conquering armies.…

"You cannot stop it," her twin said. "The spirits have abandoned you. Your visions come no more. But the dreambark comforts you, does it not, my sister?" He laughed. "Sleep. Dream." He withdrew a huge bag of dreambark from within his coat. "Take it, sister. Take it all."

He threw her the bag. She caught it, unable to resist the sweet smell and honeyed promises of peace. Here was enough dreambark that she need never hoard again, painstakingly counting out the grains on her tongue. She would never again miss her coat and her drum, or hear the cries of dying spirits.

Only sleep. But no dreams, not if she took enough.

"Yes," her brother encouraged. "If you take enough, you will not even feel it when I reclaim what is mine."

Tahvo dropped the bag. She crawled toward him on hands and knees, helpless as a babe.

"My friends," she begged. "I cannot find them. Let me see them, brother."

"But you *have* seen them, my sister. You have seen what they will be." He grinned, his full lips and straight white teeth vivid in the smudge of his face. "Is it not you who have led them to this end?"

"No. I will give all I have if you will save them. I will die so that you may be born. My life for theirs." She stretched flat, fingers straining to touch his feet. "Brother!"

"It is not enough," he said. "Not enough, sister. Not enough." The words echoed over and over again, dwindling as he vanished.

Not enough. Not enough. Not enough…

Tahvo woke with a start, sprawled facedown on the floor. Her feet were twisted and tangled in the blankets, and her thrashing had shoved the pallet to the wall.

The room was dark. She had slept through the day and half the night without a single dream or vision. Until her brother had come to her.

As a child, she had seen him sometimes, walking beside her in the wood or reflected in a pool. He hadn't spoken then. She had been afraid, knowing that his spirit had not found peace.

Only once had she reported these visitations to Grandfather, and he'd told her never to mention them again. If others knew, he said, some might believe her cursed and unfit to wear a noaidi's robes. But her brother stopped coming when she grew into a woman's body.

Tahvo pulled her feet from the blankets and sat against the wall. The room was very warm, even at night; the mist had been part of the dream, an illusion, like the great sack of dreambark.

She felt under her belt for her pouch and remembered that Rhenna had taken it. Her heart leaped into a frantic beat of terror. The dreambark was all she had. Without it...

Without it, she might feel too much, know too much. She had lied to Rhenna and to herself, claiming that the dreambark helped her to see. It did not. It dulled her senses, gave her fragments of images and insights but denied her complete understanding.

She had forsaken her duty when it became too painful to bear. But dreams brought warning in her brother's guise. *Is it not you who have led them to this end?* He had shown her what would be if she did not find her courage again—real courage, not the false confidence the dreambark brought with its gentle deceptions.

The spirits had guided her until she ceased to listen. Some must survive even here, like the spring in Hypanis, clinging stubbornly to existence.

Tahvo crossed her legs and closed her eyes. It was much harder without the drum to keep rhythm, but she began the chant, tapping her fingers on an imaginary skin painted with sacred symbols. She emptied her mind of all doubt, all fear. She felt beneath the earth where deep waters ran, opened her heart to the distant sky where particles of moisture danced in the air—places so remote that no ordinary power of good or evil could encompass them. She stretched so far that she began to break apart.

But the Stone God was everywhere, the essence of endless, malevolent hunger, so absorbed in its feeding that Tahvo knew some terrible sacrifice must be taking place at this very moment. People were dying, not singly but by the dozens. The dreambark had made her deaf to the screams, but now they pierced her body like needles.

In the midst of the horror she found Cian's shadow, imperiled and unaware of his danger. She could not reach him when her own perceptions were choked with blood. The more she fought, the more thoroughly she was drawn into the carnage.

Cian chained and beaten to a whimpering husk of himself. . .

She had made a promise to her brother, who had been but an evil dream. *"I will give all I have if you will save them."* She made that promise again, and since she could not find a spirit to hear her vow, she gave it to one whose gifts she had used so poorly.

Slahtti.

She fashioned the spirit-wolf out of dreams and prayers and wishes, shaped him with such fervent hope that he seemed to materialize in the hot and murky room. He had told her he could not come to the South—even he, so much stronger than any other spirits she had met, could be harmed by the Stone God's power. But she made him real, real enough to accept what she offered.

Everything.

A chill of winter streaked the sluggish air. White teeth flashed in massive jaws, and blue eyes blinked in solemn affirmation.

Tahvo, Slahtti said.

She bowed her head to her knees. "You are here."

He sat on his haunches and stared at her. *Do you know what you say?*

"I know," she said humbly. "I have little, yet this body and this spirit I would trade for the power to save my friends."

Do you not already possess such power?

"I have squandered the gifts of the spirits," she whispered, "because I was afraid."

Slahtti flattened his ears. *Yet now you would give your life, your senses, all that you are, for the sake of your companions?*

"Yes."

Then listen well. Like the water that is your element, you will become the reflection of those who would help you on your journey.

"I...do not understand."

He rose and paced toward her, and she saw her own reflection in his eyes. All at once her features became those of some other woman, red-haired and berry-lipped. Soft, pale skin gave way to a menacing, masculine face, and then to a second man whose eyes were black and fathomless. There were many more: woman and man, dark and light, people Tahvo did not know, people who were more than human.

Gods, Slahtti said. *Spirits, daimones. The names do not matter. Some chose at the beginning of time to blend with the elements of the earth, like your spirits of forest and stream, unseen and unheard by all but the wisest of humans. But others chose to walk as men do, taking mortal shape at will and speaking in mortal tongues. The adoration and worship of men made them great, and sometimes arrogant.*

"The Exalted," Tahvo whispered.

"No. Only a few of the darkest and most ambitious chose that name to set themselves apart from their brothers and sisters. But they, like the rest, learned that human form lessened their powers and even threatened the perils of mortality. Most of the gods became spirit again, their former bodies remembered in carved wood and stone.

"The statues near Hypanis," Tahvo murmured. "The spirit of the spring."

Still these gods bore some love for men and answered the prayers of shamans and priests, while they in turn were kept strong by human reverence. But then the Stone God came, to destroy men and spirits alike.

Tahvo covered her eyes. "Yes."

After so long the spirits have forgotten what it is to fight for life itself, yet they fear death. As the Stone's sickness spreads, many gods who survive have chosen to hoard their strength rather than aid mankind. They will retreat until no place remains for them to hide.

"I have seen spirits die to save men," Tahvo protested.

Simple elementals, generous as children who will show great courage and yet do not fully understand what they sacrifice.

"The gods of the Skudat wished to save the chief—"

Like the Skudat themselves, they are close to the wild and easily dispersed. They and other lesser spirits will assist you in the task that lies ahead—elementals of water and air, earth and fire. Some may die for your sake. But times will come when you must beg the help of the greatest.

Tahvo held her head between her hands, certain that it must surely burst. The spirits had guided her from the beginning, through visions and dreams—spirits not of one land but of all. But Slahtti spoke as if the spirits worked in darkness, not joined in understanding and purpose, but separate and ambivalent.

Not entirely separate, Slahtti said, *but not all-seeing. The gods must be shown that their fear and selfishness will end only in obliteration. If you agree to accept this trial, you will become the voice and the body of the spirits whose primal powers may decide the course of this war.*

War. A word, like *evil,* that had once been all but unknown to her. "Tell me what I must do."

You will not die, and yet you will surrender your life. You will sleep long and wake in places you do not know. You will forget your own name. You will be feared by many and loved for what you can never be. You will be given that which you most desire, only to lose it. You will be tempted again and again, but if you falter . . . He shuddered, shaking his fur from nose to tail. *Do you agree?*

It was useless to tell Slahtti again that she did not understand. Wisdom would come in time. The decision must be made on faith alone.

"You will save my friends?"

"You *will save them*."

"Then I agree."

As soon as the words left her mouth, a new flood of strength filled her body. She knew it came from Slahtti, and that he was about to show her exactly what she had promised.

She held out her hands. He rested his muzzle on her shoulder. Strange and alien images raced through her mind. Two hearts beat inside her chest, out of rhythm with each other.

Forget your own name.

She took a last breath and released her memories to the spirit-wolf. She who had been Tahvo became very small and very still. Awareness dimmed, and she no longer felt her hands and feet. *I am a reflection,* she thought in wonder. *I am not real*.

But Slahtti was with her. She was not afraid. This was joy, perfect union, ecstasy beyond the puny comfort of dreambark.

And then it ended. She sat alone in the hot room, gray with dawn light. Footsteps shook the floor. Dazed, Tahvo turned toward the door flap. The one who entered wore the robes and hood of the Stone priests, and with him came two soldiers and the innkeeper.

"I knew there was something wrong about these newcomers," the woman said, wringing her hands. "The other three left at dawn, but they didn't return. I thought, with Festival——" Her eyes rolled in terror. "Then I heard the screaming."

"Two men and a woman," the priest said, gazing into the face of his crystal pendant. "One man had yellow eyes?"

"Yes, like a cursed cat." She glanced at Tahvo and hastily away. "Holy One——"

The priest ignored her. "It is here," he said. He looked down at Tahvo. "Stand up."

She obeyed, recognizing that there was no escape. "I am a visitor," she said. "I have come to——"

"Silence." He extended his pendant. "Place your hand upon the stone."

As if in a dream, she did so. The crystal flared under her fingers. At once the soldiers fell into step on either side of her and grasped her arms.

The priest tilted his head, and Tahvo glimpsed the rot that had eaten his upper lip and widened his mouth into a skull's grin.

"You are fortunate, heretic," he said, slurring the words around an ulcerated tongue. "You go to the High Priest himself."

Chapter Twenty-Six

Rhenna found the two swords in a neglected storage room in the back of the house, sheathes thrust into a cracked amphora surrounded by broken sticks of furniture. The design of the blades was unfamiliar and the hilts too ornate to be practical in a fight, but when Rhenna held one of the weapons in her hand she felt almost whole again.

She stepped out of the storeroom into the corridor, where she had room to practice. She swung the straight, short blade in a controlled arc and let the old discipline calm her agitated thoughts.

Danae's promised meal had been a veritable banquet, but Rhenna had had little appetite. She'd picked at her food while Quintus and Danae made casual conversation like very friendly acquaintances who'd met under the most ordinary circumstances.

Quintus behaved in a manner Rhenna had never seen before, courteous and elaborately respectful of their hostess. He'd gone from open suspicion to attentive respect in a matter of hours, and Rhenna looked from his face to Danae's with growing comprehension.

At the end of the meal Rhenna had gladly taken her leave. She hadn't tried to sleep. She'd wandered the garden, looked in on the sleeping girl and then paced the perimeter of the outer walls, listening to the noises from the lower city and waiting for dawn. Chance had led her to the storeroom, and the sword reminded her that she still had a purpose.

She sliced the air in a sharp vertical stroke and spun on her toes, meeting the attack of an imaginary enemy. The wind of the blade's passing lifted the edge of Quintus's cloak.

She snapped the sword to her side. "Did no one ever teach you not to approach a warrior at practice without announcing your presence?"

Quintus glanced from her face to the lowered sword. "Where did you find it?"

She snorted and put a safer distance between them. "Where it isn't likely to see much use against the empire." She gestured to the cracked amphora. Quintus walked around her and pulled out the other sword, weighing it with an expert's touch.

He could fight—she'd seen evidence of that during their battle with the mob. But he looked even less the warrior with his face freshly shaved of its dark growth of beard, wearing fancy garments fit more for a young lord than a rebel. A lord worthy of the beautiful Danae.

"It's nearly dawn," she said, shifting the sword from her right hand to her left. "Will you look for the Resistance, or have you found some new distraction?"

She regretted the words instantly, but it was too late. Quintus's hand clenched the hilt of his sword. "Did no one ever teach you not to impugn a Tiberian's honor?"

"Many of my people believe that males are incapable of

true honor," she said. "You and a few others have proven us wrong."

His jaw remained tight. "In my country, a woman's honor lies in keeping her home and children. I am not certain what you have proven, Rhenna of the Free People."

"Perhaps that not all women are the same."

"It is true that no two females could be more different than you and Danae."

"Or two males less alike than you and Cian," she countered.

He flushed, and she belatedly remembered how Cian had struck him just before they were separated by the mob.

"You and Cian—and I, and Tahvo, and Philokrates—face the same enemy," she said. "We have fought side by side—"

"Out of necessity," he said, recovering his dignity, "not loyalty or true allegiance." He gazed at his blade. "You have courage, Rhenna of the Free People, and some skill. But you also have weaknesses that will betray you when you least expect it."

"Weaknesses?" she repeated softly. "Perhaps you will enlighten me, Tiberian."

"What will you do when you leave this place?"

"Find Cian."

He grounded the tip of his sword. "I know that your people and his have an alliance of long standing. Philokrates told me that your Elders sent you to seek the cause of the Watchers' disappearance from your lands."

"I have found the cause."

"And you protect Cian as if he were necessary to your own survival. He is not merely an ally who requires assistance." He loosened a bit of tile with the sword. "How do women without men create new generations? Do your people keep the Watchers as slaves to father your children?"

Rhenna gritted her teeth. "We keep no slaves. You would not understand. The fates of the Ailuri and the Free People are one."

He nodded as if she had simply confirmed his suspicions. "Philokrates speaks of a separate fate for the Watchers. Cian resists the old man's prophecies and your attempts to keep him from danger. He has chosen his own way. But if he strays too far, you will try to stop him."

"If I must."

"For the sake of your people."

"And his."

"Even if the fate of the entire world rests in his hands?"

"You do not believe that, Tiberian. You believe it rests in yours."

"You find me arrogant?"

"You, too, have a weakness."

"There is no weakness in conviction. I am committed to my purpose. You do not even know yours."

For a moment she was struck dumb.

He shook his head as if in regret. "Courage and skill don't change the fact that you are a woman. It isn't duty or honor that moves you, Rhenna. Your heart rules your mind."

"*My* heart? Boy—"

"If you were given a choice between destroying the Stone God or saving Cian, which would it be?"

"It will not come to such a choice."

"Your voice betrays you, as Cian betrays himself. He is a man, yet it is the irrational beast that drives him in the end."

Rhenna returned the sword to her right hand. "Your hostility unbalances your mind, Tiberian."

"I do not hate you, Rhenna. But your sentiments may interfere with the work I must do. If you leave here and are caught—if Cian is taken—even your courage may not be enough to hold the priests at bay. You may betray me, or Danae—"

Her blade was at his throat before he could complete the sentence. "You go too far," she said.

He held her gaze without flinching. "I say what must be said. Tahvo claimed we must stay together to succeed. Now we're bound by dangerous knowledge, and only one can command."

"You?" She withdrew the sword. "The rebels already have a leader. You speak of others being driven by sentiment, yet you risked your life to set Geleon free."

"It was a calculated risk. I've proven myself to the Resistance, and now they'll trust me without hesitation."

"Was it a calculated risk to save the girl? How did that further your cause, oh mighty one?"

She had startled him. He nearly lost his grip on the sword and quickly firmed his hold. "Because of the girl we found refuge," he said, "and earned the favor of one who may be of great use to us."

Rhenna laughed. "And I suspected you of common male lust."

"If I take a lover, it will be to further the cause, not to fulfill my earthly desires."

"Then you are exactly like the Free People," she said. "We take our lovers for a single reason, and it has nothing to do with lust or affection."

"Is that why you would take Cian?"

She went hot and cold by turns. "I'll never win any battle with words. Does it serve your cause to help me find Cian?"

"If he is with Geleon and the others, yes."

"And Philokrates?"

"I did not ask him to come to Karchedon. I hope he survives."

"That isn't good enough, Tiberian. I'm returning to the inn to find Tahvo, and then I look for Cian. If that doesn't suit you, stand aside."

He braced his legs apart. "Only one can command."

"Then you must fight for the privilege."

He weighed the gravity of her challenge, his face without expression. "And if I am victorious, you'll obey me?"

"*If* you win."

He rearranged his cloak to free his right side and readied his weapon to meet hers. But, he hesitated, as if he were reluctant to engage a female.

Renna did not. She darted in with a sweeping attack, slicing with the edge of her blade. He batted it aside, relying on the advantage of his sheer male strength. He didn't hesitate a second time. He lunged with the point of his sword, direct and almost graceless. Rhenna parried as she danced out of his reach. Iron rang on iron. Rhenna rushed him with a series of spinning arcs meant to confuse and confound.

Quintus caught on quickly enough, but his method of assault remained the same. Again and again he deflected her blade like a bear swatting at angry bees, and chose the same method of attack: straight, short stabs aimed at Rhenna's chest or belly. She found it easy to dodge the thrusts, but she knew if she allowed him to grapple with her, she would lose the benefit of swiftness and finesse.

Quintus knew it as well, but he wouldn't use his left arm even when she misstepped within his grasp. Only the ferocity of his advances convinced her that he wasn't deliberately holding back. She forced him to retreat, feinting and whirling away as he struck again with the point of his blade.

As much as he tried to conceal his feelings, Rhenna observed the tightness of his lips and the flatness of the gray eyes locked on hers. He and Rhenna were a match because of his strength and her speed, but he would never give up, never concede. Forge straight ahead, look neither left nor right, pursue your single goal to victory or death. He was utterly, stubbornly, ridiculously…

She lost her concentration for a heartbeat as she realized what she saw in Quintus's eyes.

Herself.

Quintus jabbed at her midriff, and she felt the point press linen into flesh. She jumped back, crashed into a precariously balanced stack of amphorae and counterattacked. The tip of her sword caught a loose fold of Quintus's cloak with enough force to drag the garment up from his arm and shoulder. The cloak went flying. He moved his left hand to his side, but she saw what he had meant to hide.

His left hand was shriveled and twisted like a burned branch, the fingers misshapen, incapable of handling even the smallest weapon. He saw her glance, and leaped to attack. She blocked him and held fast with all her strength.

"Enough," she panted.

"Because of this?" He flung up his left arm. "Guard yourself, she-wolf."

She did, and he fought with such resolute fury that she was hard pressed to fend him off and still temper her response. She continued to feint and slip out of his path, slashing as she turned. He repelled her, recovered and doggedly edged forward, sword outstretched.

But it was no longer a match between equals. If not for the high stakes, Rhenna might have let him win. Instead, they fought to bitter exhaustion. Rhenna's muscles cramped. Quintus began to weave on his feet. They drew apart by wordless agreement and stared at each other, sucking in air like bellows.

The sound of applause cracked like a whip. Danae stood at the head of the corridor, Nefer at her elbow.

"Very good," Danae said. "A fine performance. But to whom do I award the victor's laurels?"

Quintus folded his left arm behind his back and bowed curtly. "No laurels today, my lady." He retrieved his cloak without haste and tossed it over his shoulder. A few deft motions arranged the folds to conceal his arm and hand. "I beg your pardon if we disturbed you."

"Disturbed? I do not believe I've been quite so entertained in many days." She glanced at Rhenna. "If only I had the time and skill to learn such an art. But I fear we all may have other concerns." She touched Nefer's arm. "You see, I have just learned that my maid is a rebel in good standing—which does not truly astonish me—and she has word of your lost companions."

"Cian," Rhenna whispered.

Danae lost her smile. "Nefer was given two names. I fear the news is not good."

Rhenna dropped the sword. "What has happened?"

"The ones called Philokrates and Cian were taken by a certain rebel leader to a place of refuge. Philokrates was recognized to be a man named Talos, once known as a builder of war machines for the emperor Arrhidaeos."

"Talos—?" Quintus said, his voice cracking.

Danae seemed to recognize his distress but pretended not to notice. "This Talos threatened to expose the rebels by magical means if they attempted to hold him for judgment of his former acts. He said he would go to Nikodemos rather than face death at the rebels' hands."

"This is not possible," Quintus said. "Philokrates was my—"

"That is not all," Danae said gently. "Cian assisted Talos in his escape. He swore to return to the rebel stronghold, but failed to do so."

Rhenna cursed. "You *are* with the rebels," Quintus accused.

"No," Nefer said. She glanced apologetically at her mistress. "We sometimes passed to my lady such information as would help her save children bound for the altar. That was all. But when we learned of Talos's return and his plan to go to the emperor..." She paused, biting her lip.

"Your rebels fear that Talos will create new war machines," Danae said. "They sent a messenger here to Nefer, who was to re-cruit me as a court observer—"

"Only with the blessing of Isis," Nefer murmured.

"But Isis was impatient," Danae said, "and the goddess led me to discover Nefer's clandestine activities at a most fortuitous moment." She smiled with only the slightest edge and turned to Rhenna. "My curiosity has ever been my downfall. I witnessed your conversation as well as your battle. I recognize a woman in love."

Rhenna choked. "You...you misunderstand—"

"You do wish to find your Cian and keep him safe?"

"Yes, but—"

"I have agreed to observe Talos's activities and make reports through Nefer. In return, the rebels will search for your lover until he is found."

"No," Quintus said. "Why should you put yourself at such risk for a complete stranger?"

"Have I not already done so?" She nodded to Rhenna. "Your Cian sounds most extraordinary. It's true that I have no knowledge of Watchers and prophecies, but it is also an unfortunate fact that my heart rules my mind."

Quintus flinched at her mockery of his own words. "You said you were loyal to your emperor, yet now you will betray him."

"I will merely watch, and if I find it possible to advise..."

"The emperor takes your counsel?" Rhenna asked.

"Did she not tell you?" Quintus said. "She is Nikodemos's mistress. His—" He broke off and turned back to Danae. "What if the rebels use your knowledge against your master? What if you're forced to choose?"

"The rebels know that I can expose them any time I wish. We all want to see the priests toppled from their altars." Her eyes gleamed. "It will be a very interesting game."

"Is that what this is to you, my lady? A game?"

"It seems we both enjoy our games, you and I," she said. "But it is far more dangerous for you. Once the city has...recovered from Festival, you may be sure that priests and soldiers will be searching for the escaped rebels and those who aided them. Were you seen last night?"

"Only at the temple, among other pilgrims, and by those who are now dead."

"But you were at the temple near the time of the fire. You would both be wise to remain here until I can arrange for the rebels to collect you."

Quintus and Rhenna spoke their denials at the same instant.

Danae sighed. "I thought you would not. At least the priests will be occupied this morning, and not at their most alert." She bent to listen to Nefer's whisper. "Nefer will lead us to a meeting place where we and the rebels will discuss how best to find your friend."

"Why accompany us?" Quintus asked. "Should you not return to your master?"

She gave a husky laugh. "I have the reputation of being most indolent of a morning, and the emperor has many pressing duties. Life at court teaches one to be…adaptable. As for choices, I will not borrow tomorrow's troubles. Today you have your own decision to make. You may accompany three lowly women on our quest, or you may brave the city alone."

"You won't take your guards?"

"We will be less conspicuous without them. You'll find that the morning after Festival is not like any other."

He answered her serious look with a face of stone. "I will go with you to meet the rebels."

"Then let us retire to our rooms and change into more humble garments. We'll meet in the outer court in an hour."

"Our companion at the inn," Rhenna said. "We must get her first."

"As you wish," Danae said. She left with a flutter of colorful robes.

Rhenna retrieved her sword and followed.

"If they discover you armed—" Quintus began.

"If they discover us at all, I would rather die fighting." Rhenna picked up his sword and tossed it to him.

He caught it one-handed by the hilt. After a moment he followed her, the weapon tucked under his cloak.

Rhenna, Quintus, Nefer and Danae, dressed in plain but serviceable clothing, left the house while the sun was still low over the horizon. The streets of the wealthy upper city were quiet, though a few servants diligently swept already spotless thresholds. The gates to the lower city stood open. Danae walked at a measured pace, looking neither to the left nor to the right. Rhenna gripped the sword beneath her cloak.

The mobs of citizens had dispersed with the morning light, but they had left ample evidence of their evil work. Bodies lay heaped like discarded trash on the sides of the street. The paving stones were splashed and streaked with muddy brown stains. Scraps of shredded clothing hung over a wall. A woman wept behind a shuttered window. Doors were firmly closed, but a few souls braved the horror: slaves; laborers and dockhands whose work usually began at sunrise; women fetching water.

And priests. They moved in small groups, hovering over the corpses like red-winged carrion flies. They carried poles bearing vessels of dark metal, and whenever they stopped to examine a body they seemed to collect something in the vessels.

"Pay no attention and you will draw none," Danae whispered. "They harvest the unfortunate psyches of those killed during Festival."

Rhenna remembered Timon, who had escaped such a fate because of Quintus. She saw the Tiberian shiver once and then move as if oblivious. He didn't even look up when they passed another band of priests escorting a pair of disheveled young women and a half-dozen dazed and frightened children.

Danae walked a little faster, leaving the priests behind. "All babes born of Festival are dedicated to the god," she said under her breath, "and so are the children left orphaned. Goddess protect them."

Rhenna ground her teeth until her jaw threatened to snap. *Asteria's blood,* what madness had brought her to this? Even with a sword in her hand, she was powerless to make a difference.

She had helped rescue a few rebels and one abused girl. A handful out of thousands. Cian was missing, Philokrates was not what he had seemed, and Quintus, for all his potential, had his own impenetrable motives.

One way or another, she would help Cian determine the fate of his kin and then...then what else was to be done? The peoples of the North were in no wise prepared for the inevitable invasion of their lands. They had no conception of such evil. Unless Tahvo could give Rhenna a solid, rational reason why remaining here would truly change anything...

"We near the harbor," Danae said. "If you will describe the inn, I'll send Nefer to inquire about your friend."

"I'll go myself."

Danae lifted her hood so that Rhenna could see her face. "Nefer is clever, discreet and quick. She will make sure that there has been no...untoward activity since your departure."

"You said this part of the city was safe from your Festival."

"Ordinarily, yes." Danae spoke in low tones to her maid. "Please tell Nefer where to find your friend."

Rhenna gave a brief description of the inn, and the maid hurried off.

"Let us wait by the fountain," Danae suggested.

The docks were coming to life, showing few indications of last night's abomination. The streets were as clean as they had been the day before. Pilgrims nibbled on bread as they began their journey to the temple. Two black ships rode at anchor in the harbor, leviathans contemptuous of the minnows floating in their shadows. Save for their presence—and the complete absence of seabirds and animals scavenging the docks—the scene was almost benign. It seemed impossible that the blank, pleasant, incurious faces of Karchedon's citizens had become the snarling visages of frenzied killers.

Rhenna stared into the fountain, unable to bear the sight of them. Nefer's reflection joined hers in the cloudy water.

"Your friend is gone," the maid said, muffled under her hood. "She was taken by a priest and temple soldiers but a few hours ago."

Rhenna closed her eyes. "Why? What was the reason?"

"I could not ask without arousing suspicion," Nefer said. "But if they have taken her—"

"They may already know whom else to seek," Quintus said. He cleared his throat and looked away. "What will they do to her?"

"They will question her," Danae said. "If she survives and cannot be influenced by the stones, she will be given up for sacrifice."

Rhenna shook the tears from her eyes. "She insisted on remaining behind," she said, feeling for the pouch under her belt. "She said she would be safe."

"If she has the power of prophecy," Quintus said, "perhaps she predicted her own capture."

"She was a priestess?" Danae asked.

"A healer," Rhenna said. "A seer. And the Stone God's enemy."

"I am sorry," Danae said. She held out her hand, but Rhenna jerked away.

"I won't let her die."

"You'll never get near the temple."

"She's right, Rhenna," Quintus said. "The rebels may be willing—"

"They aren't fools." She grabbed Danae's outstretched hand. "Make them find Cian and keep him safe. Don't let him waste his life in an impossible fight."

"As you will?" Quintus demanded. "Is this to be your choice?"

I cannot choose. I cannot.

Oh, Cian.

"My thanks for all you have done," she said, pressing Danae's fingers. "I can't repay you."

"Repay me by staying alive."

"If they take me, I will not betray you." She glanced at Quintus. "Farewell, Tiberian."

"We haven't finished our bout."

"And you'll never know how it would have ended. Remember a woman's honor, Quintus."

She moved swiftly out of his reach and fell in among the pilgrims on their way to the upper city.

"You won't try to stop her?" Danae asked Quintus.

"I would endanger us all. Now, more than ever, we must reach the rebels."

Danae bowed her head. "Goddess be with her," she said. "Nefer?"

The maid set off the way they had come. As they left the harbor area, Quintus saw that work had already been done to wash the bloodstained streets of the lower city. The bodies were gone, and so were the soul collectors. Stalls and shops had opened their doors. The night's foul ritual might never have happened.

But there were other changes. Many more soldiers paced the streets, stopping passersby for questioning. A few hapless men were dragged off, not daring or able to protest. And priests stood by, waiting. Watching.

Nefer fell back to speak with her mistress. Danae slowed her pace and allowed the maid to walk ahead until she, like Rhenna, had disappeared into the crowd.

"She goes to learn if the meeting can still take place," Danae whispered. "It may be too dangerous."

"It will always be dangerous."

"But you will not find the rebels unless they wish it. We will wait here."

A priest and two soldiers stepped across her path, and she bowed with clasped hands. The Stone's servants continued into a side street without looking back.

Since the alternative was to pace like a madman, Quintus held his peace. The wait was uncomfortable, for he was acutely aware of every soldier or priest, and of Danae's vulnerability. Rhenna had proven able to take care of herself. But Danae's behavior was unfathomable. She took terrible risks for the rebels while serving, with apparent enthusiasm, as the emperor's mistress.

Quintus had hated the emperor long before he met Danae. To imagine such a woman lying in that butcher's bed...

Danae touched his twisted arm through his cloak, so distractedly that he was sure she didn't know what she did. "Nefer," she said.

The maid had stepped out of a side street some distance ahead. Danae started toward her. Quintus walked behind, his hand on his sword. Nefer turned as soon as Danae approached and scurried into the narrow street, deep in morning shadow.

Quintus caught the edge of Danae's cloak. "Are you sure of her?" he asked.

"Of Nefer? It is she who should fear me, now that I know what she is."

Quintus shook his head, unable to dismiss his unease. Streets became alleys, not quite so clean as the main road. Houses slumped against each other, their walls covered with crude scribbling and pictures.

Nefer tapped on the door of one such house, and paused for Danae and Quintus to join her. "They are here," she whispered. "Go in quietly, and wait."

"I'll go first," Quintus said.

Danae motioned him to precede her, but Nefer slipped in ahead. The room was very dark. Quintus freed his sword from the folds of his cloak. Nefer rushed across the room, where the light from a high window outlined five shapes against the far wall.

Two of the figures glinted with the metal of red-banded helmets, cuirasses and drawn swords. Two men in civilian's clothing stared at Quintus from bruised and bleeding faces.

The fifth figure wore the red robes and stone pendant of his breed.

Quintus pushed Danae back and glanced at Nefer, who cowered in a corner.

The priest touched his stone. "Take them," he said.

Chapter Twenty-Seven

Quintus was not certain what had happened, or how he came to drop his sword. He stepped over the weapon and pointed his right hand at the priest just as the soldiers moved to obey.

There was no sudden eruption of power, no burst of color or light. It started exactly as it had with Timon in Piraeos, when the effort ended so tragically. Quintus stared at the red stone with all the force of his hatred.

The red stone flared, and the soldiers stopped. The priest's hood quivered. He opened his mouth. His robes flattened to his body, cleaving to the shrunken lines of his frame.

Then the priest began to shrivel. Quintus had no words to describe what he saw, for all his mind was focused on the task of destruction. He might have said that the priest's red stone was like a drain in a bathhouse, sucking up fabric and flesh instead of water. The priest collapsed inward from the hollow of his ribs, turned to some vile liquid with a stench like rotted meat.

The priest screamed, but the sound was strangled by the rupture of his throat and the melting of his head into the hole where his neck had been. Legs contracted upward, blending into the red robes to become a single viscous mass. The pendant hung suspended in air with no body to support it. When the priest was gone, it simply hovered motionless, even its metal chain consumed in its ravenous hunger.

The soldiers jerked violently. Quintus reached for the stone. It resisted and then gave way, flying into his hand. He closed his fist around the stone and felt it die.

He let the blackened stone fall and picked up the sword, rising in time to block the attack of one of the soldiers. Iron struck iron with a shower of sparks. The soldier was both strong and relentless, but Quintus had no intention of fighting him long. He bent all his skill on holding the man at bay until he could strike a glancing blow at an angle precisely calculated to knock the soldier's helmet from his head.

The young, handsome face showed no emotion as Quintus lunged inside the soldier's guard and touched his fingers to the fragment of stone lodged in the man's forehead. The soldier's final blow would have riven Quintus in half had it not been for the bloodied man who threw himself at Quintus and sent them both tumbling to the ground.

The soldier toppled like a stump. His fellow guard was already down, dead from an expert slice to the throat that no mortal creature could survive. The second civilian lay on top of him, gasping for breath.

Quintus rolled free of his rescuer and looked for Danae. She leaned on the wall, face pale and fists clenched. The maid Nefer sobbed in her corner.

"You." A large hand grasped his shoulder. "You are the one Geleon spoke of, the man who saved him from the altar."

"This was a trap," Quintus said, moving closer to Danae. "Who are you?"

"I am Eochagan," the red-haired giant said, "and that is Kashta." He nodded to the dark man who had so efficiently cut the second soldier's throat. "Geleon told us to wait here for the ones Nefer would bring to us. This was one of our hidden places, but the priest found it before Nefer came."

As he spoke, Kashta crossed to Nefer's corner and pulled the weeping maid to her feet. "Traitor," he growled. "*She* led you to us. The priest let her go because she said she could bring him a great prize."

"Leave her alone," Danae said.

The men ignored her. "The priest was ready to burn us if we moved, but when you worked your magic——" Eochagan hesitated, staring at Quintus with respectful but wary blue eyes. "This is a strange and wonderful thing."

Quintus shivered. His stomach lurched as if he had eaten spoiled food, but at the same time he had never felt so sure, so powerful. He looked at Nefer. She shrank from his gaze.

"You intended to betray your mistress," he said coldly.

"No." Nefer turned pleading eyes to Danae. "It was only when I came and found the priest already here. He said he would give me to the fire——"

"So she bargained for her life," Kashta said with contempt. "She failed the first testing."

"I learned only today that she served your people," Danae said, gliding toward them. "But she always did so without betraying me." She caught Nefer's averted gaze. "Did you tell the priests of this place?"

Nefer fell to her knees. "No. No, my lady. I swear it."

"When the priest let you go, did you say whom you were bringing to him?"

"No, my lady. I said someone important, that was all."

"And now the priest is dead." Danae glanced at the cracked and lifeless crystal. "You are much more than you seemed, Quintus of Tiberia."

He briefly met her gaze, then addressed the giant. "How long until the priest and the soldiers are missed?"

"Not soon," Kashta said. "This one was not of high rank, only one of many hounds the High Priest sent to look for those who profaned the temple. We can dispose of the other bodies and hide the armor." He grinned at Eochagan. "We can save Nyx——"

"Wait." Quintus held up his hand, and all eyes fixed on him. "This lady came because your people agreed to find Cian, the one Geleon calls a Watcher."

"We know him," Eochagan said. "He came with you from Hellas?"

"We were separated during the Festival."

"And you also knew Talos?"

"Not by that name." Quintus hated to speak it, but he had already considered the worst possibility. "If this man is Talos as you claim, could he not have betrayed Cian to the soldiers?"

"It is possible."

"But you won't know until you've searched the city. This lady has promised to aid you in return for your help."

Kashta bowed mockingly. "We never expected the honor of my lady's personal appearance in our lowly kennels."

"Watch your tongue," Quintus warned.

Danae touched his arm. "You hate me for who I am," she said to the rebel, "yet that is what makes me useful to you. It seems that we need each other."

"What is the Watcher to you but an enemy of your emperor?"

"He is important to those whose welfare concerns me. If he is an enemy of the priests, I am content."

Eochagan shook his head. "Geleon has decided to trust you, lady, because of your good work with the children. But we trusted Nefer." He glared at the maid. "She cannot return with you."

Nefer buried her face in her hands. "You will not kill her," Danae said.

"Geleon will decide."

"She is my property," Danae said, "and I will go to the magistrates if any harm comes to her."

"Enough," Quintus said. "I came with the lady to find Geleon and the leaders of your Resistance. Will you take me to them?"

"Not with the priests hot on our scent like dogs after a bitch in heat," Eochagan said. "We must protect both you and our people, Destroyer of Stones. Even if Nefer did not lead the priests to this place, others will find it."

"I need no protection." Quintus kicked the black stone. It rolled and bounced like a pebble. "My purpose in Karchedon is not to sit and wait until some augur proclaims that the time has come to fight. I am here to find the Stone—the True Stone."

Both rebels stared at Quintus.

"It's said that only part of the Stone is here in Karchedon," Quintus said impatiently. "I must know where to find the rest."

"To destroy it?" Eochagan said. "The Stone itself?"

Quintus raised his right fist. "Of what other use is this?"

"No one knows the location of the original Stone. Not even our leaders. Only the priests, perhaps the emperor..." He glanced at Danae.

"I know nothing of this," she said. She avoided Quintus's eyes. "You have found the people you sought. It is time for me to return to the palace."

A sudden frisson of conviction shot through Quintus, absolute and irrefutable, like the supreme triumph he had experienced when he destroyed the priest and his stone. "Take me with you," he said.

"You're mad," Kashta said.

"Did I not hear you speak of rescuing Nyx?"

Eochagan tensed. "Geleon would not risk it, but we are willing."

"You're all mad," Danae said.

"The priests do not know my face," Quintus said. "Why would they seek rebels among your servants, my lady?"

She laughed. "They might notice your lack of appropriate humility. But why should either of us take such a chance?"

"Because my friend Tahvo and the woman Nyx are held in the citadel. I may find a way to set them free."

"Your modesty astonishes me," Danae said. "You will do this alone?"

"With your knowledge of the palace to guide me." He looked at Eochagan and Kashta. "You fear what Talos may accomplish in the service of the emperor. The man I knew as Philokrates was once my tutor, accepted as a member of my family. If he is an enemy to my people and yours, my family's honor is at stake. I'll make sure of him…one way or another."

"*If* I can arrange to get you into the palace, locate your Talos, and convince Baalshillek to allow one of my 'servants' to visit his prisoners?"

"Get me into the palace. That is all I ask."

"So little."

"It is no less than Rhenna attempts."

"I pray she abandons such foolish hopes before she goes too far. And you forget that your Tahvo must endure a most terrible questioning. The priests may soon know everything about you—your face, your powers, even what you hide under your cloak."

"I don't need two hands for what I do. Tahvo will not speak."

Danae covered her eyes. "Goddess look kindly upon all fools. Will you burn every priest in the temple and slaughter every guard?"

"I won't die in Karchedon."

She turned her back on him, wrapping her arms around her waist. "The emperor holds me dear, but if I am found helping you—"

"You won't be caught."

"How do you know these things?"

"How did you decide to help us, my lady? Why did you put yourself at risk for the sake of a woman you hardly know and a man you have never met? You enjoy dangerous games, Danae. How is mine any different?"

She shivered. "Because I understood the limits," she said. "Where are your limits, Quintus?"

"I have not yet reached them."

Danae tilted back her head, spilling golden hair over her shoulders. "Goddess have mercy when you discover them, my friend— upon you and everyone who has fallen under your influence."

For a moment Quintus thought only of taking those gleaming tresses in his hands and running them through his fingers. "You will help me?"

"Geleon won't thank us for letting you go," Eochagan said.

Quintus faced the giant, who averted his gaze. "If your people can't tell me how to find the Stone, I must seek elsewhere. Find Cian. Let me do what I can."

"And take good care of Nefer," Danae added. "Your leaders will arrange a way by which I may contact you. Can you show us how to leave this house without drawing attention?"

"Yes, my lady," Eochagan said.

She lifted her head and gazed at Quintus through narrowed eyes. "There is one condition upon my aid, and it is not open for negotiation. You will not harm Nikodemos, either directly or through any act you take against the Stone God and its priests. You will swear on your family's honor."

Quintus stiffened. "If I destroy the Stone, the empire will fall."

"I do not live by ifs, my friend. Swear that you will never raise a hand against my emperor."

He closed his eyes, imagining Danae in the emperor's arms, groaning and gasping as she whispered words of adoration. "I swear," he said. "I swear on the honor of my family and my ancestors."

Her shoulders dropped. "Very well. From this moment on, you are my servant, and you had best behave like one. You will take the necessary instruction from Aqhat."

Quintus bowed deeply. "At your service, my lady."

"I very much doubt it. But we shall see."

Their gazes met and locked. "There is much you have yet to see, my lady."

"And much you have to learn." She looked at the bodies of the soldiers. "Let us hope you learn more quickly than Baalshillek."

The soldiers dragged Cian inside the temenos walls, and though he felt the pain of their rough handling, he recalled little of how he had come to be their captive.

There had been a woman. A female. He remembered her laughter and her moans of pleasure. But then dawn became darkness, the female was gone, and *they* were all around him, striking with the butts of their spears while the priest wove a cage of red light.

That cage was not real, yet it held him just the same. This new one had bars of iron, and when he fell to the floor, he saw that the Stone's minions had brought him to the very place he had come across the sea to find.

The cell was stone on three sides and barred on the fourth, looking out on the same compound where he had helped to rescue the rebels. The naked men in the cage were scrawny, beaten and bruised. They didn't move to assist Cian as he struggled to his hands and knees, nor did they speak. But their golden eyes imparted a message he understood to the depths of his soul.

Welcome, brother. Welcome to despair.

He searched every gaunt face for one he remembered or who remembered him. His father might be here, or any one of a hundred men, young and old, he had known in the Shield.

So few remained. He counted twelve Ailuri hunched in the gloom of the cell. Twelve listless faces, twelve scarred bodies no longer capable of resistance or hope.

He had known it would be bad. He had known most of his brothers might be dead. But he hadn't been prepared, not for this.

He coughed to clear the rattle from his lungs and addressed the eldest, an Ailu whose lank gray hair hung in filthy knots around his ears.

"I am Cian," he said. "I have come from the Shield."

The Ailu blinked, and his eyes rolled in their sockets. "The Shield," he croaked. "Does it yet exist?"

"It exists," Cian said. He sat, resting his hands on his thighs. "The lands of the Free People are still free."

A groan rustled among the Ailuri. Cian sensed a new attention from them, as if he had spoken some magic word that lent strength to their broken spirits.

"Cian," one said from the shadows. "I remember a cub…left long ago."

"I left the Shield," Cian said. "When I returned, all the Ailuri were gone. Save one. And now——"

"You are the last," said the elder Ailu. "Our people. Our race…" He rocked from side to side. "Until the earth shook, we did not know any remained to be taken."

Cian scrubbed the tears from his eyes. "I escaped. I came here to find you. To set you…" His voice sank to a whisper. "Free."

At first he thought the sounds they made were snarls of rage, and that they would find enough strength to kill him where he sat. But that terrible noise was laughter.

"You came of your own will?" the eldest asked. He wheezed between his teeth. "Oh, my brothers, what have the devas wrought to mock us?"

Cian stood up, and the Ailuri went still. "I should have been with you," he said. "Now I am where I belong."

"To die," the old one said.

"No."

"I know you, Cian, son of Creag. You turned against the ancient ways. But there are none to keep them now, or to care." He closed his eyes. "The Free People survive?"

"They fight, but they survive. They sent a warrior to seek our people. She saved me from the Neuri and came with me to Karchedon." He swallowed, thinking of Rhenna, how he had been tricked into seeing her in an Ailu's body. He could still feel her beneath him, hear her voice urging him on.

She hadn't been real. But Rhenna...Rhenna was alive. Safe. She *must* be.

"We are not alone," Cian said. "Not even here."

"We have always been alone," the old one said. "Set apart from the beginning." He looked around the cell. "We could not tell the priests what they wished to know, for we did not remember it ourselves. And now that we remember..." He smiled. "They will never take it from us."

"Take what?" Cian whispered. "What are we?"

"They called us Watchers," the old one said. "Watchers who failed in their watching, very long ago." He sighed. "But we felt the earth shake the Stone's temple, and we knew it was one of us. The ancient powers are awakened too late."

"Or perhaps," a new voice said, "just in time." An Ailu of middle years crawled to the center of the cell. His eyes were white from corner to corner.

Cian knew him. He shuddered and flinched from the sightless stare. This one's claws would never rake tender flesh again.

"You fled the mountains," blind Teith said, "because you despised our ways. For this reason you were not taken with the rest of us. The powers have returned in you, Cian, son of Creag, the very powers the priests fear."

"The devas mock us," the old one repeated.

"Or they offer us redemption—we few who are left to redeem a race."

"It was the devas who failed us," said the old one.

"We failed each other. Over the centuries, the millennia...we lost too much."

"What did we lose?" Cian demanded. "Why do the priests want us? How do we threaten them?"

"Tell him," Teith said. "Before the priests come again."

"What will it serve?"

"I have come very far for the truth," Cian said. "If I am to die among you, at least let me know the reason."

The eldest bent his head. "Listen, then, to the tale of the Watchers."

The others drew nearer, as if they had heard the story many times and were eager to hear it again. Teith sank back on his heels.

"We all know," the eldest began, "that the Ailuri are children of devas. This we have been told for a thousand years. But our stories are but fragments of a whole, remnants of a greater truth we chose to forget." His gaze turned inward. "Our ancestors chose for us.

"The Ailuri are children of the gods, created for but one purpose—to build a cage fit to hold the most powerful of devas and to guard its prisoners through the centuries."

"The crystal cage," Cian murmured.

"The only barrier that stood between the Stone God and all the life of the Earth, mortal and immortal. The wall that is now sundered."

Philokrates's voice echoed in Cian's memory: *If the Watchers fail, the Exalted will rise again. They will come in fire and flood, in miasma and drought, to claim the Earth anew.*

"Long before the rise of Men and their cities," the old one said, "the gods fought a great war amongst themselves. Those who loved the creatures of earth and sky and water, sustained by the celestial fire, opposed the devas who wished to destroy all mortal life and recreate it in their own vile images. Twelve evil devas, called the Exalted by the Men who feared them, rose in power and malignance above all the others.

"In the end, the good devas were victorious. They could not destroy their fellow gods, but they sought to hold the Exalted in a place where they could never again harm the world. So they mingled their blood with that of mortals and created the Ailuri, who could mold and shape the very earth itself."

Cian stared at his hand, flexing his fingers in wonder.

"The Ailuri shaped a crystal cage which the Exalted could never breach. But before they could bind the evil ones, four escaped."

"What became of the four?"

"We do not know. But eight devas were sealed into the crystal, there to remain for eternity."

"Not *one* deva," Cian said, "yet they call it 'the Stone God.'"

"Eight gods bound in stone," the eldest said. "The Ailuri were set to watch the crystal cage in a vast and deadly wilderness where no mortal dared approach. We were created to live in exile, hardy and independent, maintaining the crystal so that it could never weaken or fail. As mortal Men grew more numerous, the Ailuri kept them away from the Stone and its evil.

"But after many centuries, the Watchers grew impatient. The crystal held fast. The Ailuri took no mates and sired no children. They were all but immortal, and weary of the bonds that chained them. At first only a few deserted the wilderness of the Stone, seeking lives of freedom in other lands. But as time passed more and more abandoned the duty for which they had been born."

Cian winced. The eldest might have been speaking of him, except that the fate of the world had never been in his hands. "Where did they go?" he whispered.

"To the Northern mountains, the Shield of the Sky, where they took mates among the women of the steppe and forgot that they were sworn to a far more vital task. Forgot their powers of the earth. Forgot the Stone God."

"Why did the devas not remind them?"

"Because the devas, too, had forgotten, or dismissed the ancient threat. They had become part of the elements, each deva bound to its own earthly realm, or had grown too dependent upon the reverence of Men. But the Stone God, the Exalted, did not sleep forever. It had grown in both strength and hatred. Without the Ailuri to watch, it drew Men to its place of exile and turned their wills to its own aims."

"Alexandros discovered it," Cian said.

"In some land far to the south, unknown to the peoples of Ta Thalassa. Alexandros gave the eight imprisoned Exalted their first taste of freedom. But it was Arrhidaeos who became the Stone God's true servant, who brought part of it to Karchedon, spread its influence and established its priesthood. Arrhidaeos gave his empire to the Stone, and his son continues its work—to subject every god and every race of man to its control, to steal the very breath of life from every creature—"

"To recreate the world by destroying it," Cian finished. "How?"

"We do not know," Teith said. "But when the Stone God and its priests rule all, our world will cease to exist. This is the failure of our people. This is our unspeakable dishonor."

Cian hunched on the floor, hugging his knees to his chest. This was the substance of the writings Philokrates had tried to explain, the inescapable destiny his words had implied.

"The priests discovered prophecies that told of our people and the powers we had once possessed," Teith said. "They sought us out so that they could control the ones who might threaten their god. They have tried to learn the secrets we have forgotten. We have died and given them nothing."

"But their torture is just punishment," the eldest said. "For it has restored our memories, but not the knowledge of how to shape the Earth." He stared into Cian's eyes. "That only you possess. Now they have you, and they will take it."

"But *I* know nothing. I understand nothing."

"They will twist your mind and your body until you have given up the secrets you deny with every breath."

"What can they do with such power, except turn it against their own god?"

"Whatever they touch is perverted," Teith said. "They will use it to make the Stone God invulnerable."

Cian pressed his palms against his eyes. "Then I have come not to save, but to betray. My kin. My friends. My—"

Rhenna. If he had gone home with her, he might have served some purpose for her people, even if not for his own. She would be with her kin instead of risking her life for his sake. For his shame, and his foolish dreams of expiation.

He scrambled to the front of the cage with its heavy iron bars. A dozen soldiers with red-banded helmets stood guard, spears crossed. Cian ran his hand across the floor of the cell.

"There is no escape," the old one said. "The cage rests on red slabs infused with the stone and does not touch the earth."

Cian closed his eyes. He could sense the soil beneath him, but the red stones were an impassable obstacle even if he could breach the floor. He had never tried to pass through anything save plain earth, and he had done so without any real command over his new-found skill.

There was no escape. He couldn't claim more courage than these his brothers, who had been reduced to broken shells by the priests' interrogation. But he knew another way to keep his poor gifts out of the priests' hands.

He looked from Teith to the old one. "Does any one among you have the strength to kill me?"

Chapter Twenty-Eight

The female was not what Baalshillek had expected. She was small and unimpressive, of no race he recognized, and yet as soon as he entered the room he felt her power.

His priests had been scouring the harbor inns for information on newcomers to Karchedon, but it was the Stone's favor that had led a lesser cleric to discover this peculiar creature. She had been working magic strong enough to affect his stone as he passed outside the building in which she thought to hide.

She must be ignorant indeed to wield her primitive witchcraft in Karchedon, but her stupidity had served the Stone well. The innkeeper had reported that she traveled with four other pilgrims—a woman and three men, one with golden eyes.

Baalshillek had no doubt that her former companion was the same Ailu who had jumped so readily into his trap—the Ailu who had been with the Annihilator in the temenos. The pieces had begun to fall neatly into place, and soon the whole would be in Baalshillek's grasp.

The barbarian female hung passive in her chains, her moon face as blank as one of the stonebound. But she was as invulnerable to the stones as the rebel scum or Nikodemos himself. And she was godborn.

Baalshillek lifted her chin with his fingertips. Her strange silver eyes rolled up and slowly fixed on him.

"What are you?" he asked. "From what land do you come?"

"I am Tahvo," she said. Her voice was hoarse, betraying the fear her face did not. "I am from the North."

"Where?" he said, squeezing her jaw. "How far?"

"I do not know what you call my land."

"What brought you to Karchedon? Who are the others with whom you traveled?"

She blinked, dull as an ox. "I do not understand."

"What is the source of your power? What gods do you serve?"

"I have no power."

Baalshillek let her chin fall and stepped back. He cupped his pendant. "If you do not answer, you will suffer."

She stared at the stone. "Why am I here?"

Baalshillek summoned stonefire, the least amount he could bring forth. It flew from the crystal like an arrow, piercing the barbarian in the center of her chest. She gasped as it burned a hole through her chiton and stole the air from her lungs.

"That was the smallest part of the god's power," he said. "But he is merciful to those who serve him. Those who come to him willingly."

The woman's head dropped to her chest, and she sobbed, her breath rattling. What air remained inside her seared the flesh and tissue of chest and throat, making every respiration fresh agony.

"How…how serve?" she whispered.

"Answer my questions. Forswear your petty deities. Surrender your power to the One True God."

She did not look up. She shouted defiance without making a sound.

Baalshillek considered a new approach. He focused his concentration even more precisely than before and launched a second attack. Stonefire started the linen of her chiton, peeling it from her body. Burns to her flesh could not be avoided, but they were insignificant; this work had a different aim.

When the last of the cloth had blackened and curled and dissolved to ash, the barbarian's body hung naked and exposed like a sow awaiting the butcher's knife. She was younger and firmer than Baalshillek had guessed, though far from beautiful. Her skin was a pale golden brown, slightly darker only on the hands and face. All her hair was silver.

She shivered in spite of the chamber's warmth. It was well known that few Northern barbarians ever removed their clothing, even to bathe. It was unlikely that this woman had appeared naked before any but her closest female kin. She would be shamed, vulnerable, perhaps even afraid that he might ravage her.

The mere thought sickened him. But there were others who would be pleased to accept such an opportunity.

"Now," he said. "We begin again. Whom do you serve?"

"I serve all spirits. And none."

"Spirits?"

"Devas. Daimones. Gods."

"Did these spirits send you to Karchedon?"

"Yes."

Baalshillek relaxed. He had found the key. "What did they demand of you?"

"Nothing."

He struck her across the face. Blood spurted from her lower lip. She caught a drop of it on her tongue.

"With what power do you serve them?"

"Only what the spirits have given me."

"What have they told you? That you can defy the Great Stone?" He pressed his crystal into the soft flesh of her breast, grinding down. "All the old gods are dead or dying. Show me what they have taught you."

Tears spilled from her eyes. "I am a healer."

Wetness splashed his hand, and he pulled his pendant away. The stone had branded her, and the lesion already blistered and seeped whitish fluid. Her tears sizzled on the wound.

Baalshillek wiped his hand on his robes. "You traveled with an Ailu, whom we now have prisoner," he said.

Real emotion crossed her plain features. "Cian."

"Is that his name? It hardly matters. He is ours now." He leaned close. "There were three others, two males and a female. One male helped the Ailu defile the temple grounds by freeing the Stone's lawful sacrifice. Who is he?" She shook her head, and he sighed. "We already know what he can do. We will find him. If you tell us where he is, you may yet be given a chance to serve."

"I do not know."

"You know who and what he is. Do you think he has the power to destroy the Stone? Is this the promise that brings other traitors to him, this false hope?"

"I do not know."

"All the Stone's enemies will fall. It is inevitable. Their souls will feed my god, and he will become more powerful than any being that ever lived upon this earth."

"And the others?"

A chill struck the perpetual fire in Baalshillek's heart. "There are no others."

"There were twelve," she said. "Twelve Exalted. Four escaped the stone prison. Eight remain. One would rule them all. He promises, but he deceives. Only fire——"

He struck, sending the stonefire into her bones. She screamed. He stopped before her skeleton melted from under skin and muscle.

He must not yet kill her. She had strength undreamed of, and his torments would only consume her body without breaking her spirit. If she possessed the gift of prophecy...if she could see so near the truth—

Ag stirred from his rest. The stone flared so brightly that it reduced everything else in the room to shadow. *What is this?*

An enemy. Baalshillek opened his thoughts, and Ag saw what had happened within the chamber.

Give her to me, Ag cried.

No. First we must go inside.

Ag raged against the confinement of Baalshillek's body, but he recognized the need for restraint. He could enter Tahvo's mind and tear it apart in his fury, but only his High Priest could guide the god's power to keep that mind alive.

The god subsided, threatening even as he let Baalshillek take control. Baalshillek returned to the woman's twitching body and laid his stone to her broad forehead. He forced his way in, channeling Ag's irresistible might to a narrow beam that penetrated the woman's skull and the vulnerable substance beneath. And he began to see.

He saw the vast Northland, with its teeming forests and waste of snow, as yet untouched by the Stone. He saw a people much like the woman, but dark of hair and eye, simple and unchanging. He saw a man's face—nearly identical to Tahvo's save in its gender—laughing as it promised ruin and suffering.

He felt the woman's fear. She was afraid of the man who was her reflection, and of the visions that came upon her uninvited. Baalshillek reached deeper and shared the images of death, the sure and relentless spread of the Stone over all the world.

The woman saw what would be, but she did not accept. She

heard the voices of her trivial gods, elementals who understood nothing outside their limited realm. She believed they sent her to find and oppose the great evil in the South.

Baalshillek laughed at the irony of her ignorance. Her faith in her spirits had carried her into lands her uncivilized nature could scarcely comprehend, yet always she believed. The gods would help her and those she selected as her champions. They might suffer and die just as men did, but they would join with humans in the great battle that lay ahead.

She didn't know what she was. She didn't realize she was god-born, the catalyst, her hidden gifts passed from generation to generation only to awaken when the old peril returned. She had been bred like the Ailuri. The visions came from within herself. The gods had forgotten, but her blood remembered. Everywhere she passed, her "spirits" also remembered and added their fragments of ancient memory to her own.

Everywhere she traveled the daimones of the wild lands and the elements, the feeble barbarian gods, roused from their long slumber and passed word to their divine brethren. The old evil had escaped its prison. Mortal and immortal must fight or die.

But she was too late. The lesser gods of the South had been devoured, the greater driven into exile, where their power would fade and wither. The Earth's as yet unconquered deities had no organization, no order, no plan; their former unity was millennia behind them. Their human tools would fail them, and they would fall one by one until the last was—

You are wrong.

The voice was not Ag's.

Baalshillek seized the woman's throat. No sound came from it. She was incapable of speech. But in Baalshillek's mind rose a new image, a blending of faces and forms he had already begun to know. Mortal visages of godborn, heroes created to wield the ultimate weapons.

First was the woman, tall and straight, with light brown hair and moss-green eyes. She wore barbarian garments, and in her arms she bore a bow and quiver. Her belly was swollen with child. Beside her stood an Ailu of black hair and golden eyes, naked save for the war hammer grasped in his fists.

Tahvo herself flanked the tall woman's other side, but she wore a coat of heavy furs and her face was obscured by a mask of ever-flowing water. She carried a sword whose blade was white and slick as ice, its hilt the snarling jaws of a wolf.

Last was a man who stood apart from the others, an ordinary dark-haired youth with iron-gray eyes. He bore no weapon. His right hand was raised, palm out, and in the center of his palm was a void without shape or color. It pulled at Baalshillek, ravenous as the Stone itself.

Reborn. Annihilator. Ag roared.

Baalshillek's body became a holocaust with the gods at its center. He opened his mouth, but only flames emerged.

Eight Exalted defeated. Four escape with the only weapons capable of defeating them. And four mortals to find and bear those weapons anew.

Baalshillek fell to his knees. He fought with Ag for control of his body, and as ever before, he won. But his robes were singed, and his chest ached with the new mark Ag had set upon it—the shape of the pendant, burned through cloth and into flesh.

The woman hadn't moved, but she still lived. She was one of the Bearers. She must die, and soon. Her godborn psyche would feed Ag well, if Baalshillek dared to save her for the fire....

Beware, servant of the Stone.

Baalshillek struggled to his feet. "Who are you?"

Tahvo heard the High Priest's question, as she had heard all the others. She could not answer. Her body was naked, her flesh seared and debased. She had been compelled to reveal what her own mind had not understood, memories of a future foretold and forgotten. Baalshillek had been warned, and he would act without mercy to stop what might be.

She could not permit him the victory.

Like the water that is your element, you will become the reflection of those who would help you on your journey.

Baalshillek could shatter her body, but her soul remained inviolate. *Times will come when you must beg the help of the greatest....*

Tahvo begged. She opened her heart as if it were the door to a lávvu big enough to contain all the Samah forest and the endless ice fields beyond. She made of herself an empty vessel, eager to be filled with clear sweet water.

It came not as a trickle but as a raging flood, washing away her name. The one who had spoken took possession of her limbs and her head and her voice. She stretched, snapping the chains that bound her, and laughed.

"We are those you thought vanquished," she said, her body changing, shaking her honey-colored hair so that it tumbled over her full, ripe breasts.

Baalshillek stared. "Ashtoreth," he said. "Impossible."

"That we speak through this mortal body?" The goddess ran her hands slowly over her voluptuous figure, taking delight in the touch. "We, so much less than your mighty Exalted." She closed her eyes, and suddenly her body changed again, still beautiful but undeniably masculine. The slim youth carried a caduceus, the herald's sign, and wore a traveler's broad-brimmed hat, a short cloak and a leopard skin. Winged sandals encased his feet.

"Is it impossible that we survived?" the youth asked. "Or that we stand here before you, murderer of infants?"

"I know you," Baalshillek said. "Hermes, messenger of dead gods..."

"Trismegistos, Guardian of Travelers, Patron of Children, Shepherd of Men and Beasts," the youth said. He dipped his caduceus like a club. "You trouble my people—"

"And mine." The youth's face changed to that of another

handsome young man bearing a crown of laurel wreaths and with a bow slung at his side. His fingers danced over the strings of a lyre.

"Do you know me, mortal? Apollon Thearios, Paian, Akesios, Lykios, Agraios—Apollon God of Oracles, Healer, Averter of Evil, Hunter, Apollon of the Wolves. I also live."

"So long as mortals seek justice." Apollon gave way to a stately, black-haired woman wearing a golden disk framed by curving cow horns.

"Isis," Baalshillek hissed. "You have no power here."

"Very little." The goddess narrowed her eyes. "But as you see, I am not dead."

Baalshillek raised his pendant. It lay quiescent in his hands. "You have nothing left," he said. "You subsist on dreams and memories."

"Perhaps," Isis said. "You do not fear us as you do the four Exalted who remain free, or the heroes who come. But we offer no battles, only warnings." She showed him the golden device she held at her side—the ankh, symbol of life. "The world does not yet belong to your master." Her voice became the voices of many. "'Twelve there were who sought to rule. Four times Four shall decide the fate of the Earth.'"

"Eight Exalted trapped in the Stone," Baalshillek said. "Four who escaped with Weapons they stole to avoid their siblings' fates. Four godborn Bearers to wield the Weapons anew." He stopped, arrested by some thought he did not yet grasp. "Two of the four Bearers are already in my hands. The other two cannot escape. They will never find the Weapons."

"So it may be," Isis said. "But hear us, creature of the Stone. If you bring about the deaths of any of the Bearers by your own hand or the hands of your priests or soldiers, in sacrifice or by the fire of the Stone, you too will die."

"How will you stop me, Great of Magic?"

"I will not. We will not. Try to kill this body before you and see what transpires."

Isis held up the ankh, and Baalshillek cringed. Apollon reappeared, striking a dreadful note on his lyre. Ashtoreth was last, altering her form to mimic that of the one Baalshillek could not resist.

And then the gods left their host, a plain and rather small woman who struggled to remember like one awakened from a glorious dream.

Hours might have passed, or days. But Tahvo knew that could not be so, for Baalshillek still wore his singed robes and his face was twisted with rage.

"So I am not to kill you, witch?" he said. "But there are many ways to die, and many ways to suffer without the release of death."

Tahvo heard more than anger in the High Priest's words. She heard uncertainty, an emotion with which the Stone's servant was unfamiliar.

Above all, she heard fear. *Four godborn to wield the Weapons anew.* She was one of those Four. In the dream she had held a sword in her hand, she who knew nothing of war. A sword of ice.

Godborn. She would have denied it if she could. But for one shining moment she had seen the prophecy the gods recited and known they could not lie, even to save themselves. This battle had been foretold when the spirits were young, written into the very bones of the Earth. No god or mortal could suppress it or predict how this game would end.

There would be sacrifice. Oh, most terrible sacrifice that burned in the fires of the soul and could not be extinguished with an ocean of tears.

You will be given that which you most desire, only to lose it. You will be tempted again and again, but if you falter…

Pain severed her thoughts. Baalshillek punished her, too skilled to bring death, and expert in the finest nuances of suffering. But the High Priest didn't see the one who came to share Tahvo's torment, who carried her to a land of cool stillness where stonefire dispersed into harmless mist.

Slahtti leaped across the ice fields, gathering stars in his silver coat. He found the little noaidi and swallowed her up without pausing in his journey. There, in the dark peace of his belly, she fell into a deep and dreamless sleep.

"You."

Quintus snapped to attention, his gaze averted, as Danae singled him out from the servant guards who had escorted her to the palace. Like them, he bore a whip in his belt, the only weapon permitted those who protected the favored courtiers of Karchedon. To the world he might appear a privileged and pampered slave, but he was keenly aware of Danae's veiled amusement.

"I have hurt my ankle," she announced in a voice pitched just loud enough for the palace guards to hear. She leaned on the frame of the litter, holding her delicate foot off the ground, and pointed at Quintus. "*You* will carry me to my chambers. The rest, except Leuke, go to your quarters."

With those words she dismissed all her servants save Quintus and her new maid to the dormitories kept for the slaves of courtiers when they visited the palace. There was nothing extraordinary or strained about Danae's approach that might attract undue attention; her party had passed into the citadel unmolested even by the red-banded Temple Guards who shared gate duty with the emperor's soldiers. Quintus hadn't received so much as a glance, though his left arm was bound from elbow to knuckle in an iron-studded leather brace made to hide his deformity. Danae's scheme had been successful...thus far.

Now, at the end of a tedious day of waiting and planning, they stood before the west doors of the palace, smaller and less elaborate than the main entrance, but still well attended by six watchful soldiers. Quintus moved to obey Danae's summons, but one of the guards reached her first.

"Allow me to escort you, my lady," he said with a bow.

Danae gave the guard her most dazzling smile. "My thanks, soldier, but I don't dare draw you away from your post when there are all manner of rebels and villains skulking about the city." She shuddered. "It is quite terrifying."

"You need have no fear, my lady. We hold one rebel in the palace dungeon, and I hear that the temple has taken two more. Soon we'll have the rest."

Danae wrinkled her nose. "Let us hope that the temple does not damage their prisoners before our lord emperor questions them."

"They won't, my lady. They've already given up their first prisoner on the emperor's demand. I hear this one is a female."

"A female. How dreadful."

"From Aithiopia, they say." One of his fellow soldiers cleared his throat, and the helpful guard backed away. "Only command us if you require any assistance, my lady."

"That I promise." She signaled to Quintus.

After a bow of exaggerated humility, he lifted her into his arms. Though his left hand was near useless, the muscles above his elbow were strong enough to support her back while his right arm cradled her knees. The guards saluted with their spears as he carried her through the high wooden doors, closely followed by the new and very frightened maid.

The hallway was decorated with frescoes of soldiers locked in deadly combat, and Quintus walked upon an intricate, many-colored mosaic. Lamps flickered in shallow alcoves set at regular intervals along the wall. Doors and archways led to other halls, but Danae gestured him to continue deeper into the palace. Not even a slave disturbed their solitude.

Danae weighed almost nothing in Quintus's arms, but her musky scent distracted him when he could least afford it. The Palace Guards had fallen all too readily under her spell.

"That man was one of the emperor's elite soldiers?" he whispered.

"I told you that Nikodemos does not allow his chosen to be tested by the priests," she said, "and that includes his hetairoi, his generals, palace troops and bodyguard, who owe him personal loyalty."

"As you do?"

She ignored his question. "Such men may not have the mindless obedience of the stonebound, but they have good reason to be grateful for the emperor's protection."

And such gratitude was a powerful weapon, a force to counter the temple's influence. "What of the troops in the field, the occupational forces in Tiberia and other newly conquered lands?" he asked. "Are they bound to the Stone or the emperor?"

"I know little of military matters, but I understand that most fighting troops are imperial recruits—"

"Conscripts, compelled to serve."

"I told you, I know little—"

"Conscripts are tested," Quintus said. "They are stonebound, like all common soldiers. Who controls the armies, Danae? The emperor or the Stone God?"

"Nikodemos is no fool," she hissed. "He—"

A plate-bearing servant rounded a corner, and Danae closed her mouth. She indicated several turns, directed Quintus into a colonnaded veranda opening into a large courtyard, and had him stop at a door framed by two fluted columns. Leuke opened the door, then barred it behind them.

Danae's chambers were beautifully furnished, as Quintus would have expected. The lamps had already been lit. An antechamber with chairs and a table led into the sleeping chamber, dominated by a large couch of ivory, cedar and gold, designed in the Aigyptian style.

"Put me down," she commanded.

He did so, insolently deliberate, and swept her another bow. "How else may I serve you, mistress?"

She snorted, briefly reminding him of Rhenna. "By climbing inside that couch and waiting quietly until I return."

He examined the couch. "Is that where you hide your lovers from Nikodemos?"

Her eyes struck at him more effectively than her hand ever could. "It's where you'll be safe while I seek news about the rebel woman and your friend Philokrates." She moved to the couch and touched a latch hidden beneath the mattress. The top swung open, mattress, pillows and all. The space within was just large enough for a man to fit if he lay curled on his side.

Danae patted the cedarwood bottom of the box. "My goddess also lies within," she said. "She will protect you."

"Your emperor permits the worship of other gods?"

"Not openly. But neither does he seek evidence of dissent. Now, quickly, get inside."

"How long?"

"Do you not trust me, now that we've come so far?"

He stared into the box and suppressed a shiver. He hated such small spaces, hated the vulnerability of them. "You will not lock it?"

"Of course not. And Leuke will remain here to watch." She touched his left arm. "You must trust me, Quintus."

His body was accustomed to flinching at any contact with his crippled limb, but with Danae it was different. She sent a rush of life into the withered muscles. He looked from her hand into her eyes.

"I trust you," he said. "But take great care, my lady."

"As much as you have." She ruffled his hair in a careless, playful gesture entirely at odds with their circumstances. He caught her wrist and turned her palm to his mouth.

"All games are not equal," he said. "And neither are all men." He kissed her hand and quickly let her go, stunned by his own impulsive act. He climbed into the couch before she had time to react.

The lid came down decisively. Quintus fought the urge to press up against it to make sure it would open.

Danae would not lie to him. If she had meant to expose him, she could have done so countless times. But as Quintus lay in that tiny space, his pulse pounding in his ears, he could not help but question his own sanity.

There was no measure of time, no change in the darkness. He heard the maid move about, once bumping into the couch but not attempting to communicate. His mouth grew dry. Sweat soaked his servant's tunic. He thought of Rhenna, Cian and Tahvo with regret and unaccustomed sadness. He hadn't valued them as allies, only considered them impediments to his great ambition.

The guard had spoken of two new prisoners. Tahvo was surely one of them, but the other...

Someone rapped on the frame of the couch. Quintus coiled his muscles to spring. The lid lifted, and Danae peered inside. She put her finger to his lips.

"All is well," she said. "It is as the guard reported—the woman Nyx is in a cell here in the palace. The emperor demanded that Baalshillek give her up, and soon he will demand the other prisoners."

"Tahvo."

"And Cian."

"How did you learn of this?"

She shifted, and a waft of musky scent drifted into the box. The smell of sex.

"Your friend Philokrates—Talos—is also here, given his own rooms but under guard."

Quintus closed his eyes. "Can you take me to him?"

"It is late, but much of the palace is still awake." She hesitated. "I have an idea of how we may get into the dungeon and see the woman Nyx. But there is no telling how soon Baalshillek will release his other prisoners. He will hold them as long as he can, and Nikodemos may not choose to press him immediately."

"Another game."

"A fragile balance. The emperor has been unable to claim some captives taken by the priests, but he does what he can."

"Out of the same great compassion he shows the peoples he conquers?"

She neglected to answer. "You must continue to be patient."

"Why am I here if I am to lie in this cage while you take the risks?"

"Because without my instruction you will be caught. Take this——" She lowered a cup of wine into the box. "Drink. Is there anything else you require?"

"The ability to act."

"In time." She took the wine from him and closed the lid.

Danae did not have to guess how much Quintus hated his confinement. She knew his feelings instinctively, in a way she had never known the emperor's. Her palm still tingled where he had pressed it to his lips.

Isis, she prayed, *keep me true to my purpose. And keep him safe.*

She paused outside the door to her chambers, watching and listening. Baalshillek was not in the palace, and lesser priests seldom invaded the emperor's domain. In spite of what she had told Quintus, most of the palace slept. Nikodemos sat in Council with his most trusted hetairoi and advisors, but he would soon retire for the night. She had already seen to his needs most thoroughly.

Quintus had known. She had felt his disgust and pulled away

in anger and... No, it was not possible that she should feel shame. She had chosen her life freely. Quintus could not judge what he entirely failed to grasp.

Shaking off her troubled thoughts, she started south along the moonlit hallway. She knew how to find Baalshillek's chambers, though she had prayed she would never enter them. Now she must. She knew about the secret passageways that ran beneath the palace, joining certain rooms with others, or with hidden staircases and mysterious doors.

One such passage ran between the emperor's suite and Baalshillek's quarters. Nikodemos kept it barred on his side, but Danae had seen him use it to meet with the High Priest and travel elsewhere in the palace. The emperor was aware of Danae's knowledge and completely unconcerned that she might use it against him.

And I will not. This rebel has already been questioned. It does no one harm to set her free.

If it could be done.

Danae found Baalshillek's door. It opened easily to her push. The antechamber was barren and filled with cold, the very opposite of the cloying heat the High Priest carried with him.

Just inside the door she began to feel along the walls with her fingertips. She discovered nothing but a profound chill in the first room, but in the second, furnished with a single chair and small table, she located the almost imperceptible crack in the stone that indicated a hidden entryway. She spent tense moments trying to imitate the way she had seen Nikodemos move the block in his own chambers.

She found the trick, and the door swung inward. A steep staircase led to the underground tunnel. The passage was, as she'd hoped, sufficiently lit by lamps that she need not stumble or feel her way in the dark. She had only a vague sense of direction to lead her.

She chose the passage she believed went nearest the dungeons and moved with caution, pausing at every branching to weigh her options and taking the time to memorize her path. Twice she took turns that led to blank walls. She tested a number of concealed exits, one of which opened to the outside. On several occasions she feared she was traveling in circles.

But Isis did not forsake her. She heard distant voices and pressed herself to the wall, only to realize that their nearness was an illusion. The next portal led into a dank, torchlit stone chamber, sealed by a thick wooden door at one end. The voices came from behind the door. On the far side of the chamber was a row of six barred doors set in a windowless wall.

Danae released her breath and dabbed at the perspiration on her brow. "Nyx," she whispered.

No answer. She moved nearer the cells, the back of her neck prickling with awareness of the large door behind her.

"Nyx," she repeated. "Do you hear me?"

A low groan issued from the cell farthest to the right.

Danae put her ear to the wood. "I am here to help you," she said. "Can you speak?"

"Who are you?"

"A friend. Are there other prisoners here?"

"I am alone."

"Good. Stand away from the door." Danae set all her weight to sliding back the heavy bar. The door creaked on its hinges.

The stench of fouled straw and rotten food struck Danae like a blow. She searched the fetid darkness, and at last her eyes picked out the figure it had concealed.

The woman in the cell was ebon-skinned and remarkably beautiful in spite of the multiple bruises and lacerations on her legs and arms. Her curly hair, matted with blood, had been cut close to her skull. Her stained chiton hung in shreds, barely covering her breasts and upper thighs. But she stood on her own two feet, pride in the set of her full lips.

"Who sent you?" she croaked.

"Does it matter? I am here to set you free."

The woman tried to laugh. "How?"

"Come with me, and find out."

Nyx hesitated, looking toward the big door. "The guards are just outside."

"We need not pass them."

The woman's eyes narrowed, but she stepped out of the cell, staggering as she crossed the threshold. Danae caught her arm to steady her. Nyx broke free.

"I will be all right," she said, peering into Danae's face. "I know you."

"This is no time for introductions." She hurried to the hidden portal. "There is a secret passage that leads outside the palace. It's still night. I'll take you as far as the outer door, but you must find your own way from the citadel."

Nyx watched Danae keenly as she triggered the mechanism that opened the portal. "You are the one who helps the children."

"When I can." She ushered Nyx through the portal and shoved it closed. "Quickly."

The woman kept pace in spite of her limp. "You know my friends? Were they taken with me?"

"Geleon escaped."

"And the Watcher? The Tiberian?"

"The Tiberian is safe."

Nyx was silent as Danae retraced her steps to the passage where she had discovered the exit to the palace grounds. The tunnel looked like all the rest, but its portal gave onto fresh air and dappled moonlight.

"Here," Danae said. "I don't know where you'll find yourself, but with the goddess's mercy you will reach safety."

Nyx leaned against the wall, breathing fast with pain and effort. "The emperor does not own you," she said.

"What I give, I give freely." She gestured toward the portal. "The night will not last forever."

"I was——" Nyx lifted her chin. "I *am* the daughter of kings. I will not forget what you have done."

"Isis go with you," Danae said.

Nyx slipped out and scurried away close to the ground. Her skin gleamed in the moonlight and then became part of the darkness.

Danae returned the way she had come. She stopped again to listen at Baalshillek's private portal, judged that his chambers were still empty and pushed through the stone door. She had just closed it when someone entered the antechamber from the hallway.

Baalshillek.

Chapter Twenty-Nine

Danae moved to the chair and sat, arranging her cloak and chiton to her best advantage. Baalshillek almost passed the inner room without seeing her. He paused, turned and stared through the doorway.

"You are very late," Danae purred. "I waited as long as I could, but now I fear I must return before I am missed."

The High Priest strode into the room. "What are you doing here?"

She pouted and looked up at him through her lashes. "If you must ask," she said, "I certainly shall not answer." She started to her feet.

He barely touched her, but that touch was enough to hold her still. "You go too far," he said.

"Is it too far to wish instruction in the way of the One True God?"

He released her and tossed back his hood. She immediately saw what she had missed before: the haggard lines about his eyes and mouth, the distracted movements, the underlying rage that contradicted his passionless face.

"You choose a poor time for piety," he said. "Why now?"

"Sometimes, in the night, I dream." She shivered most convincingly.

His expression almost softened. "Dream of what?"

"That I will fall and fall into darkness, and only one has the power to raise me up again."

He cupped her chin. "You dream truly." His thumb caressed her cheek. "Danae."

She held his gaze as if she were a tiny bird fascinated by the seductive stare of a cobra. "My lord," she whispered. "It is late. I must go."

"But you will return," he said. "You will have your instruction."

"Yes." She covered his hand with hers. "Soon."

He let her go. She escaped into the hallway like that same tiny bird, her heart stuttering in her breast.

She was safe. He had believed her…or he had deceived her far more thoroughly than she had him. But for now, she had won.

She entered her chambers, dismissed Leuke to her pallet and went to the couch. Quintus nearly bolted from the box when she opened the top.

"Where have you been?" he demanded. He glanced toward the high window, blinking. "It's nearly dawn. Nyx—"

"Is free." She grinned, unable to hide her triumph.

"How?"

"By means known to very few. She is out of the palace, and now you must leave, as well."

He could not have appeared more grim. "Why did you take such pains to bring me here if my presence was so unnecessary?"

She whirled away, losing a little of her jubilation. "I didn't know if I could do it. And if I had left you behind, you would have acted on your own and gotten yourself captured."

His jaw flexed. "What of Philokrates?"

"I will find some way for you to meet. Not today." She smiled coaxingly. "We'll return to my house. You'll be safe there—"

"Safe and protected—while a woman does my work?"

"I wouldn't dream of stealing your glory. No doubt you'll soon plunge into an ocean of peril deep enough to satisfy your monumental pride."

"Tahvo is still a prisoner."

"As long as she remains in the temple grounds, you cannot reach her. Perhaps in a few days—"

He caught her arm and spun her to face him. "You were with Nikodemos tonight."

"Let me go."

"Why do you stay with him—with a butcher and tyrant who permits the sacrifice of children?"

She jerked her arm from his grasp. "Because he is the man who will defeat the priests and the Stone God."

Immediately she regretted her outburst, but the damage was done. Quintus stared as if she had run mad.

"Nikodemos?" he said. "The emperor who sends priests to murder the helpless and turn his people into beasts?"

She despaired of ever making him understand. "He must use the priests. When Arrhidaeos died, many whispered that the priests would choose their own puppet emperor to replace him. Nikodemos was cunning enough to thwart their plans, but he is no fool. Baalshillek is powerful. Until the time is right, Nikodemos must keep the High Priest's favor."

"By spreading the Stone God's evil to the ends of the Earth?"

"By surviving. He lets the priests believe their god moves the empire. Arrhidaeos was weak. He gave the priests too much power from the beginning, but it isn't so easily taken away."

"Their power wins Nikodemos's wars. He attacked Tiberia—"

"Baalshillek threatened to depose him if he didn't continue to spread the Stone's holy word. Why do you think Tiberia has not been completely vanquished? Because my emperor sends his poorest soldiers to Italia. *He* allows the rebellion to continue. Or do you truly believe that Tiberians are so far superior to the men of every other nation?"

"The lowliest Tiberian slave is superior to the one who calls himself emperor."

She raised her fists. He seized her around the waist and pulled her against him.

Danae knew what was coming. She could have avoided it, or at least have resisted. She did neither. She let him kiss her, the gentleness of his lips belying his fierce words. She wound her fingers in his hair with mingled hatred and desire.

He held her away to search her face. His eyes blazed like a young god's.

"Leave this place," he said. "You will fall with the emperor. And he must fall."

"It is the Stone that will fall. And I'll be with my emperor when it happens. I love him."

"You deceive yourself in a thousand ways, Danae."

"And you, who believe you can defeat the Stone with your own hand…" She stopped, startled by the mist that flowed from her mouth with every word.

Cold. It was cold in the room, cold as Karchedon never was.

Quintus exhaled sharply and passed his hand through the cloud of his breath.

Danae ran to the window. The early morning light was not golden but white—white with a multitude of tiny flakes that poured out of a colorless sky.

Cian smelled the snow long before it began to fall. So did every other Ailu in the cage. Bodies that had lain quiet twitched into motion; heads lifted, and ears—shaped like human's though they were—quivered in amazement.

It was the smell of home.

"How is this possible?" Teith asked.

Cian knew of but one explanation. Even when the first snowflakes drifted out of the sky, he was afraid to hope.

But he clung to that hope when the priest walked out of the mist, the heat of his dark robes melting each flake as it touched the cloth. Steam rose from his shoulders and hood.

"Baalshillek," the old Ailu whispered.

Baalshillek. High Priest, Most Holy of the Stone God, dreadful tormenter of Ailuri and stealer of souls. The Ailuri cringed against the walls of the cells, crowding far from the barred doors.

Cian stayed. He watched the High Priest advance, sizing up his enemy. Baalshillek was neither tall nor overly large, but he radiated power and commanded respect with the sheer confidence of his stride. The faceted red stone in his pendant was more massive than any Cian had seen.

"He comes for you," Teith croaked.

"I know."

"It is too late for us. But you must survive and escape. You must carry on the work for which our kind was made."

"Destroy the Stone God?"

"Find a way to imprison it again, as our ancestors did."

Cian laughed, for there was nothing else to do. His brethren would not take his life as he had begged. He knew he couldn't resist the torture that had broken every other Ailuri. If he indeed possessed hidden knowledge that could aid the priests and gave it up to Baalshillek…

The High Priest stopped a few paces from the cage. He looked up at the sky, and his hood fell back to reveal the hairless skull and even, almost pleasant features. He spread his hand to catch the snowflakes, but they evaporated before they reached his skin. He glanced toward the cage door and signaled for the guards to open it. Soldiers took up new positions to either side, spears ready to thrust.

"Bring out the new one," Baalshillek commanded.

Cian had no desire to be dragged forth like a pig for the slaughter. He went to the cage door of his own free will. The guards seized his arms and hurled him onto the snow-flecked ground at Baalshillek's feet.

"So," the priest said.

One of the guards pulled Cian up by his hair and held his head back. Cian met Baalshillek's gaze.

"You are the one who came willingly to Karchedon," the priest said, his voice almost without inflection. "The last Ailu, they say. The one who made the earth shake with the old magic."

"I know nothing," Cian said.

Baalshillek raised his brow. "So said the others. But I think you are different."

Cian forced the guards to let him rise. "I am Ailu," he said. "I will die with my brothers."

He smiled. "Did you enjoy my gift to you, Cian? That is your name, is it not?"

"Gift?"

He raised his hand, and a woman appeared beside him. She wore a cloak as black as her hair, and her eyes were golden. The impostor who had seduced him into the priests' trap…

"There are no female Ailuri," Cian snarled.

"She is as much Ailu as you are," Baalshillek said. "Made of your own people's blood. And she is only the first. I will breed a new race of Ailuri to serve the Stone God." He stroked the woman's hair. "Perhaps you have already started a child within her belly."

Cian stared into the eyes so like his own. The female smiled, and he saw the red stone embedded in her forehead. He lunged at the priest. The guards beat him down.

"Is that why snow falls on your warm city?" he gasped. "To make your new slaves feel at home?"

Baalshillek's lip curled, betraying his displeasure. "If this is your work—"

"You don't know?" Cian laughed again. "There is magic you cannot control, Baalshillek, and it will be your god's undoing."

One of the guards thrust with his spear. The point pierced Cian's hand where it spread on the earth.

The Ailuri roared. As one they bellowed and shrieked, raising such a din that the guards staggered, and even Baalshillek pressed his hands to his ears. The female Ailu fled. Cian's brothers hurled themselves at the bars.

Baalshillek faced the cage. He palmed his red stone and flung out his hand. Streaks of fire shot from his fingers and struck the bars. They glowed white-hot. The Ailuri retreated but never ceased their screaming. Stonefire set hair and skin alight. Singed and burned, the Ailuri attacked the bars again and again until their weight on the heat-softened metal tore the bars asunder.

The Ailuri changed. Some leaped on the nearest guards; most ran, soot on snow, and an unfortunate few blazed like torches as their fur ignited. They, too, rushed the soldiers and took them down in a conflagration of heaving bodies.

"After them!" Baalshillek screamed at the remaining soldiers. "Hunt them down and bring them back alive!"

The soldiers obeyed. Dying Ailuri tore the helmets from their enemies' heads and bit through vulnerable throats. A badly burned Ailu writhed on the ground, pinned by a spear through the belly.

Cian tore the spearhead from his own hand and crawled to the Ailu's side.

"Teith," he groaned.

The Ailu opened his eyes and changed, still impaled by the

spear. Blood flowed on pale skin. "Go," he cried in the Ailuri tongue. "Live for us. Finish what our ancestors began." He hissed between his teeth. "Swear."

"I swear. Teith, I—"

But the Ailu couldn't answer. The snow fell with greater fury, sticking to earth that should have melted it instantly.

Cian shuffled around on his knees, cradling his injured hand to his chest. Baalshillek waited alone, so hot that he stood in a circle of bare, steaming ground. His stone pulsed on his chest.

"Do you truly believe you can stand against me?" he asked, tilting his head like a curious child. "The others will be found. They have nowhere to go, no spirit left to fight. And I have your companion, the woman named Tahvo."

Cian felt no more pain, only horror. He let Baalshillek see nothing in his face. "You think you have her?"

Something in his tone made Baalshillek understand. "This?" he said, waving at the sky. "This is her doing?"

Cian clamped his mouth shut and prayed that the healer was free. "*I* am the threat, priest. I can imprison your god forever."

The priest's eyes turned red as his stone. "Show me, beast-man. Godborn. Show me your power."

The snow was a blessing sent by the devas, and Rhenna was not about to refuse the gift.

She crouched at the base of the citadel wall where she had waited through the day and night, seeking some means of entrance. But the gate was well-guarded, and the thick ashlar walls held ranks of bowmen ready to let fly at any unwelcome guest.

Great caution and effort had brought her this far and no farther. But now the sky was filled with swirling white, the air grown so chill that Rhenna's arms and legs prickled with gooseflesh.

The shouts of men echoed up and down the walls—cries of consternation, amazement and fear. No strategist could have created a better diversion. Veils had fallen between every object and its nearest neighbor, turning the wall into a featureless lump and the men upon it into dim shapes scurrying to and fro.

Tahvo must be alive and well. Cian had better be.

Rhenna tested the cord that held her borrowed sword under her cloak and felt along the seams of the stone blocks. They offered just enough purchase for climbing, though she had to stretch to her full length and call upon all her strength to reach from one to the next. The wall itself remained dry under her hands, though snow had begun to accumulate at its foot.

She hung below the top of the wall and listened. Confusion had driven the nearest bowmen from their posts. Rhenna flung her arms over the edge and dragged herself to the raised lip. She tumbled into the space where the bowmen should have stood and caught her breath. Snow melted on her hair. No one came to accost her.

The way down the other side was more difficult, for Rhenna climbed with her back to potential attack, and her hands were fully engaged in gripping the stone. She dropped the last two bodylengths and rolled as she hit the ground.

The entire citadel was a dreamy world of floating voices and gray shapes. The beams of light from the red obelisk were feeble and dim.

Rhenna had no sun or stars by which to take her bearings. She estimated the location of the temple and started toward it, running low with the sword in her fist. She crashed into a metal-clad figure and caught the soldier's blade on her own.

They fought in ferocious silence. The soldier might have called out for assistance, but he didn't; perhaps he thought a female with a sword easy prey. He was strong and intended to kill. He protected the vulnerable points in his armor, under the arms, behind the knees and at the base of his throat.

Rhenna's sole advantage was the snow, which he didn't seem

to comprehend. He slipped on a patch of wet ground. She dived to slice at his hamstring. He righted himself and countered the blow.

Snow-laden wind gusted up between them. It blew into the slits of the soldier's helmet. He flailed with his free hand. For an instant he lifted his head, exposing a narrow line of throat. The tip of Rhenna's blade glanced off the bottom edge of his helmet, drawing blood. He swung at her. She took the brunt of his attack on an awkwardly bent arm and fell to one knee.

The ground gave a sudden, sharp jolt. The soldier lost his footing. Rhenna jabbed up, sinking the blade into the pit of his arm. He accepted the deadly wound with the same unnatural silence, and tilted sideways, giving Rhenna a second chance at his throat.

This time she hit her mark. The soldier gurgled, nearly beheaded her with his last assault and then collapsed.

Wind shoved at Rhenna's back. She jumped over the soldier's body and let the storm take her. When the next dark shape burst out of the veil, she struck without pausing. It dodged with a leap no human could make, sleek and twisting like a black-scaled serpent.

"Cian!" Rhenna cried.

The Ailu didn't stop. Golden eyes flashed and were gone.

Not Cian. Another Ailu. The captives, set free…

The wind offered no leisure for thinking. She ran before it, singing like an arrow released from the bow. The temenos walls were not so easily breached as the citadel, but Rhenna found the rear gate ajar and didn't question. The wind continued to lead the way, weaving between the temple buildings.

It did not take her to Tahvo. First she saw the priest, his robes flapping around him, and then the man he faced.

Cian was naked, and blood dripped steadily from his right hand. Black hair snapped like a banner.

Rhenna ran straight for the priest. Cian saw her, dropped to his knees and plunged his hand into the shallow layer of snow.

Rhenna gave the warrior's ululating cry and swung at the priest's bald head. He flicked his fingers, and the blade bounced from some invisible shield to strike the red stone pendant. Sparks showered from the contact. Edged iron bent like copper and carried fire to Rhenna's hand. She dropped the sword, letting a part of her skin go with the hilt. She clawed at the priest's face, and he backhanded her to the ground.

Dazed from the blow, Rhenna could only hope that she had bought Cian a little time. But of course he hadn't run. He crouched in the same position, his arm buried in the earth, his face a mask of agony. He was vulnerable now, and the priest knew it. Rhenna grabbed at the priest's robes.

Whatever you do, Cian, finish it quickly....

The priest kicked at her as he would a cur in the street, if any such creature existed in Karchedon. He stared at Cian. He touched his pendant, and the stone flared.

"Cian!" Rhenna shouted.

With a roar Cian pulled his arm out of the ground. In his hand he held a substance neither solid nor liquid that shimmered and sparkled as it shaped itself into a sphere. Cian squeezed the sphere until it shrank to half its former size.

The priest extended both his arms. Rhenna's hair began to singe. Cian threw the sphere directly at the priest's chest.

The sphere struck the red stone and instantly enveloped it, muffling heat and light in clear, faceted crystal. The priest grunted in shock. Cian tried to stand, but he had used the last of his strength.

Rhenna stumbled to his side. She supported him as the priest tore at the red stone's crystal cage, splitting his fingernails on the unyielding surface.

"Run," Cian gasped, clutching Rhenna's hand. "It will not hold."

The priest ceased his frantic efforts. "You will suffer," he said, looking from Rhenna to Cian. "You will know unimaginable pain before you die." He flung back his head. *"Ag!"*

His cry filled the air with the stench of burning flesh. The crystal's perfect shape distorted as if hammered from within, and its surface grew slick like melting ice.

"Run!" Cian snarled, hurling Rhenna ahead of him.

She dragged Cian's obstinate weight step by step, knowing he was spent. "Move!" she cried, pummeling his shoulders and back. He half fell, and she heaved him into her arms.

"Rhenna." He laced his hands in her hair and drew her so close that their foreheads touched. "This is not your fight."

"If it's yours, it's mine."

His hot breath wreathed her face in mist. "You don't understand. This was our doing. Now it is mine." He laid his icy cheek to hers. "I don't want you to die."

You will not.

The voice was in Rhenna's head.

Cian jerked and turned in her arms. The great wolf Slahtti rose out of the sleet for which he was named, huge ears cocked and tail high. His eyes were silver, and they spoke as his tongue could not.

Come. Touch my coat. Hold on, and do not let go.

"Tahvo?" Rhenna whispered.

Quickly. The wolf paced forward majestically, sparing not a glance for the evil power soon to be set free.

Rhenna took Cian's hands and pressed them into Slahtti's fur. She had no sooner taken hold when she felt her feet leave the ground. Flying snow gathered wolf, man and woman into its wild embrace. Rhenna could neither see nor hear, but she felt Slahtti's warmth and Cian's fingers touching hers. Earth and sky vanished.

They emerged into a place of clarity and warmth, where blossoms nodded on trailing vines and the stone pathways were clear of snow. Slahtti touched ground as lightly as a bird. He shook his fur to indicate that they had reached their destination.

Rhenna unclenched her fingers and looked about. She knew this garden, these trees and flowers flourishing amid so much death. Danae's courtyard was an island in the storm, walled by snow on every side but untroubled by so much as a single flake within its borders.

"Where are we?" Cian asked.

"A place of safety, I think." She left Cian in the courtyard and ran through the snow into the house. The main room was unoccupied and silent. She heard no footsteps in the halls.

"Danae?" she called. "Quintus?"

Her voice echoed, unanswered.

Slahtti came up beside her. *They are not here,* he said.

"Where are they? Tahvo…is she all right?"

The wolf lowered his great head. *Have no fear. Go to the Watcher. Wait.* He nudged her toward the courtyard. As soon as she had rejoined Cian, Slahtti turned and walked into the wall of snow.

"Slahtti!" Rhenna attempted to follow, but the barrier had fused to solid ice as firm as the wall of air she'd encountered after Sun's Rest. She could see nothing of the house beyond the columns that marked the courtyard's perimeter.

Cian laid his palm on the wall. "I don't think he wants us to leave," he said dryly.

Rhenna looked at his hand, and the retort died on her lips. In place of his smallest finger was a smooth nub of skin, a stump that ended cleanly just above his knuckle. She caught his hand and rubbed the stump with her thumb. No wound, no torn skin or severed bone.

"It was necessary," Cian said.

"Necessary." She released him, paced away and spun to face him again. "What happened in the temenos? That priest—"

"Baalshillek," Cian said, shaping the name with loathing. "High Priest of the Stone God."

"You fought the High Priest. Alone, and wielding some magic I have never seen. All because I let you out of my sight."

"It was better so."

"Better? Do you know what I've been thinking, wondering if you—" She clenched her teeth. "It was worse than either of us imagined."

"Yes," he said. "Much worse."

She steered him to the nearest marble bench and made him sit. Sunlight found its way through the high gray ceiling far above them, warming Rhenna's shoulders and dappling Cian's naked skin. She removed her cloak and flung it over him.

"Did you see Tahvo in the temenos?"

"She's no longer at the inn?"

Rhenna shook her head. "Danae, the woman who owns this house, rescued me and Quintus from the Festival mob. She was to help me find you, but we learned that Tahvo had been taken by the priests."

Cian swore. "Slahtti is here. She must be safe." He met Rhenna's eyes. "You went to the citadel to save her."

"I knew you would also go back to the temple. And you did free your brothers."

"No." He wrapped his arms around his belly. "They set me free, and died for it."

Asteria's blood. "You were captured?"

He nodded, unable to speak. Rhenna trembled with helpless anger. "Did Philokrates betray you?"

He jerked in astonishment. "Philokrates?"

"I know that Geleon took you and Philokrates to safety during the Festival. I know the rebels identified Philokrates as one named Talos, builder of war machines for the empire, and you helped him escape."

"They would have killed him——"

"Danae was told that Philokrates went to the emperor."

Cian shrugged, misery in every line of his body. "He didn't betray me. The priests laid a trap for me, and I entered willingly. They took me to my brothers. The Ailuri were beaten, Rhenna. Tortured. Nearly dead." He pounded his fist on the bench. "They knew I was in Karchedon when they felt the earth shake the night we helped Geleon. They believed I had the old powers...the powers given to my people by the gods. The powers we denied."

Rhenna enfolded his fist in her hands. "Cian——"

"We were chosen, Rhenna, but not to father the children of the Free People. The Ailuri were created to build and guard the cage that held the creatures men now call the Stone God."

"The Watchers," she murmured.

"Philokrates's ancient writings were true. There was a great war of the gods, and the evil ones, the Exalted, were cast down. Four escaped and fled, but the others were imprisoned in a cage of the Ailuri's making."

Rhenna remembered the strange substance Cian had pulled out of the ground and flung at the High Priest. "The pale crystal."

"It was our duty to watch and strengthen this cage so that the Exalted could never escape——a duty we abandoned. The Ailuri you knew in the Shield were only the remnants of a great people who had forgotten their purpose. Because of our negligence, men found the Stone and used its power to conquer and enslave——" His voice broke. "They slaughter children...."

Rhenna felt his pain like a knot in her chest. *Devas, how can I comfort him?* "If your people failed so completely, why did the priests send soldiers to find the Ailuri?"

"They believed we remained a threat as long as we continued to exist. But my brothers had no power to resist them."

"*You* do," Rhenna said. "I saw it."

"Not enough to save my people."

"You said they set you free."

He buried his face in his hands. "I am to finish what my ancestors started."

"Alone?"

He didn't answer. Rhenna jumped up from the bench and paced the perimeter of the courtyard, slashing at the lush foliage bent away from the wall of snow. "I saw an Ailu running from the temple. Some of the others must still live."

"Where will they go?" He laughed bitterly. "You had reason enough to despise my kind before. But now...to know we are responsible for such vile and monstrous evil..."

She stopped to face him. "Not you, Cian. You did not create the devas, good or evil. You didn't ask to be what you are."

His bleak gaze settled on her scar. "The one who gave you that...you need not hate him anymore."

She touched the ridged skin as if she had forgotten the scar's existence. "He was one of the captives?"

"His name was Teith. He saved my life. Now he is dead."

The memory of blazing eyes and tearing claws filled Rhenna's mind and faded away. "My anger died with him."

"You were right to question," he said. "Right to challenge the old ways. It was all false, twisted pride—"

"I was wrong." She returned to the bench and crouched before him. "Your people had a noble purpose. Ailuri did sire our greatest leaders, those who could speak to and understand the devas. The Free People couldn't have survived without them. This must have some meaning. I will not believe otherwise."

"You say this, Rhenna—you, of all your kind, who has such reason to hate?"

"I never hated you." She took his face between her hands and found that she was trembling. "I hated what was forbidden. I hated my own failure. I hated the brand I carried for all to see. Never you."

"Rhenna." He stroked the back of her hand with his palm and continued down her arm, drawing her shivers to new peaks of sensation. "I have lost everything…everything that ever mattered to me. Except you."

She gave him a gentle shake. "You will not lose me."

He closed his eyes. She could count every dark lash on his cheek, trace the slight curve of his brows, breathe the warm scent of his damp skin.

"Rhenna—"

She silenced him with her lips.

Chapter Thirty

Rhenna should have been hesitant and clumsy with inexperience, but the caress came to her as easily as riding a horse or wielding an axe in battle. The woman who kissed Cian was a stranger, and yet that stranger was too powerful to resist.

Cian did not even try. He growled and seized Rhenna in his arms, pulling her between his knees. He returned the kiss fiercely. His mouth and tongue pressed deep as if he could brand her more thoroughly than the sharpest claws had done.

Farkas.

She beat him off, striking his jaw with her knuckles. He grunted and leaped from the bench. They faced each other like enemies, he with his male weapon ready to thrust and she behind a shield of fear and rage.

Cian understood. The light went out of his eyes, and he bounded for the wall of snow. It rebuffed him. He pounded and kicked his way along every part of it until he returned to the place he'd begun, chest heaving with effort and emotion.

Humiliation. His anger was not for her, but for himself. And Rhenna looked with loathing at her own terror, at the hands that had assaulted and punished him for a sin he would never commit.

He was not Farkas. He was the very opposite. He was everything good a male could be and so much more than he believed.

And, devas save her, she desired him. She had felt this before and denied it, had driven such thoughts from her mind with the memory of Farkas's violation. Fear had kept her safe and duty-bound. Disgust had silenced the perverse hungers of her body.

To let a man, even this one, touch her again...

This one, Ailu, saved for the Chosen alone. If she continued, she would defile the laws and traditions of her people, make a mockery of her sacred oaths, merit the worst penalty the Elders could devise.

I recognize a woman in love. Danae's words, which Rhenna had dismissed with shock and incredulity. Desire was not forbidden in its proper place, but love was not for the Sisters of the Axe. Javed of the Skudat loved Klyemne of the Free People, and that was not permitted.

But Rhenna gazed upon Cian's tormented face and knew only one certainty. *I will not leave him again. Never again.*

"You are not Farkas."

Her voice was hardly more than a whisper. She squared her shoulders and raised her head high.

"You are not Farkas," she repeated. "Do you hear me, Cian? I know who you are."

He pressed himself to the magic wall, arms spread to embrace its cruelty. "I am worse than Farkas," he said hoarsely. "Forgive me."

"No." She went to him slowly, shaken by the frantic beating of her heart. "There is nothing to forgive. What I began I intend to finish."

"Stay away."

"Farkas took what I wouldn't give. Now I choose. *I* choose, Cian."

He spun about, warding her off with balled fists. "Don't touch me," he snarled. "If you touch me I may—I may not—" He choked on words he found too vile to speak.

"I don't fear you," she said. "Not in any shape."

"The beast wants too much. It cannot be controlled."

"You would never hurt me." She smiled, letting him see the wry edge of her own bewilderment. "Must I prove again that I am your match?"

He tossed his head, whipping black hair across his face. "Not in this. I have wanted you, Rhenna, and like a beast I would—"

He broke off as she touched his cheek with her fingertips. His throat worked. His muscles tensed, but there was nowhere to run.

"I see only Cian," she said. "Cian who is my friend, who would give his life for mine. Farkas was the beast. I will not let him win."

Suddenly Cian's eyes cleared, startling in their brilliance. "If you do this, you cannot go back. Your people—"

"—will not have me. I know. But you are not going home."

His skin burned under her hand. "My brothers...gave up all they had for my sake. When Teith died, he made me swear to use my people's gifts to stop the Stone God. For the third time I swore, Rhenna. I will not break this oath."

"I would expect no less."

He put his hands in her hair, loosening what remained of the braids with their bronze pins. His tenderness terrified her. She longed to shout for sheer joy.

"Why here?" he asked. "Why now?"

Devas, why wouldn't he simply accept? "We are together."

"And we cannot leave."

She refused to consider what he implied. "We've done all we can. Let Tahvo and her spirit-wolf do their part."

"You're so certain. But then, you always have been."

She couldn't bring herself to deny such a patently false statement. She took his right hand and kissed the smooth stump of his little finger. "There is a saying among my Sisters—'Tomorrow's axe for tomorrow's battle.' We fight today with the weapons we are given."

"Is it always war between us, Rhenna?"

She kissed him again, but this time she left no doubt that she wanted Cian as desperately as he wanted her. For all his fear of the beast, it did not take control. Rhenna did.

He stopped the mad thoughts twisting in his head and gave himself up to rapture.

Rhenna spread her cloak in a circle of miniature trees. She unpinned the shoulder seams of her chiton and let the light cloth slip down over her body to pool at her feet.

Cian had imagined her thus a thousand times, supple and strong in her nakedness, waiting with arms outstretched. She was nothing like his dreams. The skin of her face and neck was brown from the sun, her hands work-roughened, and every muscle from shoulder to calf was taut with exercise and constant training. But her breasts were high and firm, and her waist flared out into hips a Hellenish sculptor might covet for a goddess.

She was perfection.

She was Rhenna.

He stepped into her arms. They fell together, fingers tangled in each other's hair. He rolled her on top of him, still half-afraid she might feel trapped if he attempted another way. But she hooked her knee over his thigh and rocked him onto his side. They lay entwined, face to face, her nipples tight against his chest as she kissed his brow and his chin and his neck. She wrapped her legs around his waist and drew him inside.

Some peoples Cian had met in his travels claimed that paradise awaited the worthy after death. Cian felt far from worthy, but he and Rhenna died there under the trees and found their way to a paradise of their own creation. Zephyrs danced among the leaves and blossoms, and the earth rocked in time to the rhythm of their joining. It took them into its womb.

The Earth's lifeblood coursed through Cian's veins, nurturing him as a mother nurtures the child within her. From him the ancient strength poured into Rhenna, planting a seed in darkness where heat and water would make it grow.

A seed of new life...

Rhenna's lithe body became that of the female Ailu writhing beneath him, and Baalshillek mocked his shame: *Perhaps you have started a child in her belly.*

The Earth rejected him. He broke the surface, gasping for air, and felt Rhenna's lips restore him to the living.

"Cian?"

He had no words to explain. His body had finished its work, and it had known great pleasure. He was afraid to look in her eyes, to find that he was indeed no better than Farkas.

She cradled his face between her palms. "You didn't hurt me," she said.

Her eyes were moist, and he was humbled by the gift they gave him. All he wanted in that moment was to hide her away and keep her safe until...until...

"Cian," she said, muffled against his chest. "The snow."

He looked toward the perimeter of the courtyard. The opaque, icy veil had vanished, and he could plainly see the walls and doors of the house surrounding the garden.

Rhenna slipped from Cian's hold like a thief stealing his most precious possession. She shook out her cloak and threw it over him.

"Danae and Quintus aren't here," she said, pinning up her chiton, "but Danae has servants. Now that the snow has passed, we—" She broke off, staring across the courtyard.

Tahvo stood between two columns, clothed in an unbelted chiton cut for a much taller woman. Her body gave off a faint blue light, and her hair gleamed like highly polished metal. Her face was a mask of serenity and absolute authority.

"Tahvo," Rhenna said, taking a step toward her.

The healer turned her head, and Cian saw that her eyes were unbroken silver. Understanding extinguished the last embers of happiness. He rested his hand on Rhenna's shoulder.

"She's blind," he said.

"What?"

Tahvo smiled. "Do not be afraid," she said. "I am here. I am unhurt."

"Is it true?" Rhenna blurted, trembling under Cian's hand. "Tahvo, can you see us?"

"I see you," she said. "Not as I once did, but more surely."

Rhenna clenched and unclenched her fists. "I left you at the inn. They took you, and tortured—" She choked and caught her breath. "Oh, my Sister."

"Do not grieve for me," Tahvo said. "I am not alone."

"You and Slahtti became one," Cian said slowly. "You carried us to safety." *And trapped us here,* he thought, but did not speak the words aloud.

Tahvo smiled at Cian. "You have grown in wisdom, my child. You left the mountains as a boy, and so you were spared to continue your people's work." She turned toward Rhenna. "And have you seen your path, Rhenna-Once-of-the-Scar?"

Rhenna felt for the mark on her face. It was unchanged. "I know that I cannot go home."

"Not yet. You have a longer journey ahead."

"What journey? Where?"

"We must leave Karchedon," Cian said, searching Tahvo's face. "But not for the North."

"The things you seek will not come easily to your hands," Tahvo said. "But you must find them, no matter how arduous the quest."

"More riddles," Rhenna said with weary resignation. "Wherever Cian goes, he'll need a warrior at his back."

"Much more than a warrior," Tahvo said. "Your power will come."

Rhenna raised her hand as if she gripped an invisible weapon. "This is my power. I want nothing else."

"Even to save the world?"

Rhenna shuddered. It was all Cian could do to keep from taking her in his arms again, giving her comfort she was not ready to accept. And how could he ease her fears when he knew Tahvo spoke no less than the truth?

"Rhenna," he said. "Never doubt your strength."

She moved out of his reach. "This metal is flawed. Tell your devas to choose another piece for their forge."

"There is no choosing for one born of the gods," Tahvo said with profound sorrow. "Or for one who will bear—" Her eyes rolled up in her head, and she collapsed to the floor.

Rhenna raced to the healer's side, and Cian crouched beside her. Together they lifted Tahvo and supported her body, which seemed very small and ordinary once again. She blinked and opened sightless eyes.

"I am all right," she said in Tahvo's unremarkable voice. "What did you see?"

Rhenna frowned over the healer, examining her face for signs of injury. "I don't understand."

Cian did. "We saw *you,* Tahvo," he said. "But you were different."

She sighed. "This is very new to me. I heard the words. It will not always be so."

Cian stroked her hair. "Another spoke through you."

"Others. As I see through them."

"What others?" Rhenna demanded.

"The spirits. The wise ones. The hidden."

Rhenna glanced at Cian with eloquent and very familiar impatience. "Perhaps you can explain this to me someday." She gentled her voice. "Are you hurt anywhere else, Tahvo?"

She shook her head and tried to sit up. "They took me to the High Priest, Baalshillek. I do not remember how I escaped. Slahtti came."

"You spoke of finding things," Cian said. "Things to fight the Stone God."

"Weapons...stolen by the four Exalted who escaped imprisonment in the Stone. The rest has not been revealed to me." She looked directly at Rhenna. "Baalshillek knows who and what you are. He saw these things...in my mind, when he called upon his god. I am sorry."

"He knew about the Ailuri long before he caught you," Cian said.

"But he did not know that Rhenna was also descended from the spirits, one of the Four godborn."

"Nonsense," Rhenna muttered. "My mother was a Sister of the Free People. My father—"

"And Quintus," Tahvo interrupted. She turned her head from side to side. "Where is he?"

"I don't know," Rhenna said. She explained how she, Cian, Philokrates and Quintus had made contact with the rebels, helped set Geleon free and then been separated by the Festival mob. She told of Danae's intervention and their discovery that Tahvo had been taken by the priests. Finally she spoke of Philokrates and the identity he had concealed from his companions.

"Nothing is as we once believed," Tahvo murmured. "Baalshillek knew a Stone-killer walked within the city, but he had no face or name to guide his search. Now the High Priest will seek Quintus as well as the rest of us."

"And Philokrates can't be trusted," Rhenna said. "If Quintus has been foolish enough to enter the citadel for any reason…" She jumped up. "Some of Danae's servants must be here. I'll find out what they know." She strode off, leaving Cian and Tahvo alone.

"It is well with you?" Tahvo asked.

Cian understood the meaning behind her question. She was blind, but she—and Slahtti—had brought him and Rhenna to this place and trapped them within a wall of snow. All had been done with purpose, but whose? And why?

"You've always known my feelings," Cian said roughly. "And Rhenna's, though she would die before admitting them to anyone. Did you foresee what would happen?"

"I knew that you were bound," she said. "I did not, could not, control how that binding would be consummated."

But it has been. It is done and cannot be changed, even if Rhenna pretends it never happened.

Tahvo did not have the answers. Neither she nor her devas were all-wise or all-powerful. *We are being moved like pieces on a game board, men and gods alike.*

"Tell me more of Philokrates," Tahvo said.

So he did, relating how Philokrates had been exposed as the former Talos and had used his peculiar magic to escape the rebels' wrath. "He asked me to trust him. I don't believe he has turned against us, whatever he did in the past."

"Your instincts are sound, as they always have been."

He thought of the female Ailu and flushed. Tahvo touched his hot cheek.

"Each of us," she said, "sees but a portion of the whole."

"You spoke of the Four. Rhenna—"

"Quintus, you and myself." For just an instant she allowed him to see the terrible burden she carried. "There will be others, but we...we are chosen."

"Does this mean that you and Quintus are to...that you also—"

Tahvo laughed. The sound, weary as it was, loosened the cramped muscles in Cian's belly. She felt for his hand.

"Quintus and I are bound on different journeys. But we are Four, no matter what paths we walk."

"Will Rhenna stay with me?"

The subject of his question returned before Tahvo could answer. Rhenna's expression was grim.

"The servants are terrified," she said. "Most have never seen snow. I found one who was persuaded to tell me where Quintus has gone." She met Cian's gaze. "Danae took him to the palace. She disguised him as one of her personal guard. They went to find someone...on that point the servant wasn't clear."

"Quintus is not indestructible," Tahvo said, "even with his great power."

"Fool," Rhenna cursed.

"And of a more generous heart than he knows," Tahvo said. She tilted her head. "Someone comes who will help you. Go where he leads, and wait."

"Who?" Rhenna asked.

"You know him." She gathered her feet beneath her and tried to stand. Cian helped her up. "You will find him behind the house."

"You're coming with us," Rhenna said.

But Tahvo stepped back, and her eyes changed from flat silver to black-centered blue. Slahtti's gaze swept over them. A blast of icy mist drove Cian and Rhenna farther into the garden. When it cleared, Tahvo was gone.

"She'll be all right," Cian said. "Trust her, Rhenna."

"As much as I trust my axe…against any normal enemy." She looked narrowly at Cian. "There seems little point in finding you new clothes when you'll only ruin them again. Fasten that cloak and come with me."

She led him across the courtyard to what Cian supposed must be the rear of the house and out to a walled yard dominated by a crumbling miniature temple. Snow was dissolving into slush even in the deepest shadows. The mid-morning sun hung hot and red in a cloudless sky. Only hours had passed since Slahtti's appearance in the temple compound.

Geleon crouched half-hidden against the temple. He straightened when he saw them, relief in his eyes.

"We thought you were taken," he said to Cian, "or that you had gone to the emperor with Talos."

"The former," Cian admitted, "but as you see…" He shrugged. "You remember Rhenna."

He nodded to her briefly. "I will not ask how you come to be in Danae's house at such a strange time. I know you were here with Quintus and Danae the night of Festival."

"I left them soon after," Rhenna said. "I have not seen them since."

"Then you will not know that Nefer betrayed Danae to a priest and soldiers who had caught two of my men, and Quintus killed the stone bearer."

Rhenna pounded her fist in her palm. "And still he went to the palace."

"To rescue Nyx, so my men say. He also spoke of finding Talos and another prisoner, Tahvo."

"Tahvo is safe. She escaped by…other means."

"I rejoice for your sake, but Quintus has been very foolish." He kicked at a puddle of slush with the toe of his sandal. "Everything in Karchedon is turned on its head. There is powerful magic afoot, and it does not all belong to the priests."

"Some of the magic is Tahvo's," Rhenna said. "Devas know where she's gone."

Cian touched her arm. "She'll find us when she needs to."

"We can't get near the palace now," Geleon said. "I hope the Watcher, at least, will accept our protection."

"He will," Rhenna said. She met Cian's gaze, and her eyes reflected that strange and remarkable moment out of time when they had truly been together. "Lead on, Geleon. But don't expect any help from gods or men if we're taken again."

Quintus knew he had stayed too long and even the snow would not save him.

If he had left the palace in the first frantic moments of confusion, he might have reached the citadel gates. But he hadn't reckoned the passing of time until shouted commands replaced cries of panic and the tread of soldiers' boots echoed in the hallways.

Danae slipped from the room and returned to report that the entire citadel was being closed off. Foreign magic had invaded Karchedon, temple prisoners had escaped, and every corner of the palace was to be searched for traitors.

"I've heard no more of Nyx," Danae said, rattling her bracelets as she paced the room. "They may not know of her escape. But Baalshillek is in a rage because of the others."

"Tahvo?" Quintus said, sifting for a grain of hope.

"If the names are known, no one dares to speak them." She whirled on Quintus. "The soldiers will not disturb my chambers until they've searched everywhere else in the palace save the emperor's own suite. I'll go to Nikodemos—"

"No." He took her arm in his good hand. "Not that way. Never again."

She touched his cheek. "It is too late. It was always too late for us."

"You care for me."

"I would not see you given to the Stone. If I can distract attention away from this section of the palace, I may be able to take you to one of the hidden passages."

She tried to shake him off, but he refused to let her go. "We must do something—unless you wish to die."

"I said I wouldn't die in Karchedon." He bent his face near hers. "If they find me here, or with you, what will the emperor do? How much does he love you?"

Her breath came swift and shallow. "I can take care of myself."

"You lie. If you are found to be a traitor, he won't spare you." A clamorous banging sounded from the corridor. "You said they would come here last. I think you were wrong."

"Quickly. Get into the couch, and keep silent. I'll—"

He kissed her again, almost punishingly, absorbing the taste of her with all his senses. Then he turned her about so that her back was to his chest and wrapped his right arm around her neck.

"Quin—"

He cut off her protest, despising the necessity of hurting her to save her life. "Be quiet. Now you are my prisoner, Danae of Karchedon."

He pushed her ahead of him to the door and worked it open with his twisted hand. He kicked the door closed and dragged Danae down the corridor. She struggled just as a captive should, lending credibility to his performance. He had reached the nearest corner when a soldier spotted him. The man snapped a single command.

"Stay back!" Quintus shouted. "Or I'll break her neck."

Danae sobbed. Her tears splashed his arm. The soldiers started toward him cautiously, and Quintus recognized the red bands on their helmets. They were of the temple, not the palace. They wouldn't stop to save the emperor's mistress.

Quintus pressed his lips to Danae's ear. "I am about to turn coward," he said, "and you will be a heroine. When I give the command, kick back with all your might. I'll let you go and run." He breathed her in for the last time. "Say nothing, Danae."

The soldiers were very near, spears leveled to strike.

"Now!" Quintus whispered.

Danae hesitated and then suddenly lashed out with her foot, striking him on the shin and foot. He groaned and released her. She half fell, deprived of his support, and he deserted her just as he had promised.

He didn't get far. Two soldiers in palace armor met him at the next turning. Their spear tips pierced his thin chiton and drew beads of blood from his chest. Stains spread across the wheat-colored cloth.

"Hold," one of the soldiers said. "What are you called?"

"Sometimes 'Tiberian,'" Quintus said, "but only by my friends."

"He is the one," a second, toneless voice said behind Quintus. "The emperor's hetairai was his hostage. Baalshillek will question her later, but this one goes to the temple now."

"Not before the emperor sees him," said Quintus's captor. "Where is the Lady Danae?"

"Unharmed. Give the man to us."

"We have this prisoner, temple slave."

Hidden stares locked. Quintus watched the silent exchange with an almost detached interest, wondering which side would prevail.

In the end he was not surprised. The palace soldiers retreated, pulling their spearheads from Quintus's tunic. Four temple guards moved up to collect their booty. As they hustled Quintus away, the palace men strode in the opposite direction, doubtless to report their failure to their royal master.

At least Danae was safe. She was far too intelligent not to avail herself of the emperor's immediate protection and tell her side of the story before Baalshillek got anywhere near her. Gods grant that she had sense as well as intelligence.

You have done this for a woman, a part of Quintus marveled. *You.*

But he felt no regret. He felt very little when the guards marched him into the sunlight and through the shrinking puddles of melted snow. The soldiers took him directly to the temple, empty of supplicants, and into the altar itself. The presence of the Stone was like an overwhelming stink of corruption.

Quintus noted every step of the way through hidden portals, down steep staircases and into corridors carved out of the very earth. He heard the clash of weapons and the groans of men and women. He counted the doors to one where the soldiers finally stopped and dragged him into a room fitted with chains and manacles and all manner of devices made to give pain.

A hooded priest waited there. The size of his stone declared his high rank, but Quintus would have recognized his power even if he wore nothing at all. The guards forced Quintus to his knees.

"It is you," the priest said in a soft, measured voice. "Just as in the vision. Quite unprepossessing." He signaled to the guards, who backed out the door and closed it.

"You are Baalshillek," Quintus said. He rose, keenly aware that the soldiers had left his hands free.

"We recognize each other," the High Priest said, "though I have not yet learned your name."

"A man should always know his enemy's name."

Baalshillek reached up to his hood and drew it from his head. He was not what Quintus had expected. His features were pleasant and ordinary, neither those of a monster nor those of a vicious murderer.

"Are we truly enemies?" he said. "Or are we brothers?"

Quintus spat at Baalshillek's feet.

"Eloquent," the High Priest said, "but hardly effective. You must understand your position. You have a unique ability, my young friend, and you have used it without discretion. You have interfered with the One True God's lawful sacrifice and killed servants of the Stone. There is no punishment sufficient for such crimes."

"You fear me, priest."

"Perhaps. Yet you will die. It is simply a question of how lingering a death, and whether or not the god devours your soul."

"Your god would choke on me."

Anger, brief as lightning, flashed across Baalshillek's face. "You overestimate your worth, boy. Such is the arrogance of youth. But my god can be merciful to those who serve him. Even to one such as you."

Quintus thought of Tahvo, who might have been brought to this very room. He dared not reveal that he knew her or any of the others. "You hope that I'll turn against my own people?" he asked. "You do not know Tiberians."

"You think not?" Baalshillek displayed his hand, palm up, and closed his fingers as if he crushed something in his fist. "You are like disobedient children who must be taught a lesson. You will help me to teach that lesson to your countrymen."

"It won't matter what you do to me. My people—"

"Will lose the one asset that might have been of some use to them." He raised a brow. "Did they know, I wonder, what they had? Did they let you go?"

Quintus controlled his expression with rigid discipline. "They have others."

"Others like you?" He shook his head. "If you are the Annihilator, the Reborn—and time alone will prove or disprove that prophecy—there can be only one."

He babbled on, so sure of himself and his victory. Quintus felt anger begin to slip its leash. "How will you prove it, slave of the Stone? Will you let me test myself against you now?"

Baalshillek went very still, as if he were communicating with someone or something Quintus couldn't see or hear. His eyes narrowed to slits.

"You ran away, didn't you?" he said. "Your countrymen knew you were their greatest weapon. You came to Karchedon to demonstrate your worth, to show that no man nor god should rule you. You, Herakles and Achilleos and Gilgamesh and all the fabled heroes reborn in one flesh."

"I am Quintus," Quintus said. "I have no other name."

"And you would make that name legend." The priest's body loosened in the way of a warrior preparing for battle. "How did you get into the palace?"

Quintus stared straight ahead. "I forced the woman Danae to help me."

"Indeed. That must have been most…pleasurable."

"She wished to stay alive."

"You were either very wise or very foolish to choose the emperor's mistress as your tool."

"She was convenient."

"I fear the emperor will not find it so amusing." His mouth trembled, and Quintus saw what the High Priest sought to conceal.

"You want her," Quintus said. He laughed. "You lust after the emperor's whore."

Baalshillek snatched at his stone, and his body cast off heat in shimmering waves. "I have had enough of your child's mewlings," he said. "You wished to test your power against mine. Very well. Show me, child of Tiberia. Show me and my god what we should fear."

Quintus struck before he drew another breath.

Chapter Thirty-One

The boy's power was potent, of that there was no doubt. But Baalshillek was ready. He and Ag repelled the smothering force of Quintus's attack, and from the instant it began, Baalshillek observed and examined and analyzed.

It was said that only fire could fight fire. Ag was the very essence of all-consuming flame, the conflagration that eradicated whatever fell within its burning grasp. He was the mightiest of his Exalted brethren; sooner or later he devoured all that opposed him. Even those he favored were changed forever, and his most tender benediction brought the corruption of flesh too fragile to serve his divinity.

But if Ag was the ultimate holocaust, Quintus was his very opposite. It was not fire he wielded, nor any of the elements Baalshillek understood. It was a dampening, a draining, a suction that pulled at the being of the Stone as the Stone absorbed the psyches of those it took in sacrifice. The core of the Tiberian's power was complete and utter nothingness.

Annihilator.

Baalshillek's concentration wavered, and a trickle of Quintus's magic splashed through his shield to touch the stone. Baalshillek knew pain like that he had felt facing the witch Tahvo, who had so miraculously escaped while he was occupied with the Ailuri. He knew astonishment as deep as the shock of seeing snow fall in Karchedon. He knew fear as he had known it when the Ailu Cian had attempted to create a cage for his stone. And he knew rage— rage that so many had defied him and escaped with their lives.

But his rage was cold where Ag's was hot. Baalshillek saw how raw and unfocused was the young Tiberian's grasp of his power. He was a child clutching the reins of an unbroken stallion, believ- ing it would prance and caper at his command.

Baalshillek loosed Ag to counterattack, directing the god's blast to the stone wall behind Quintus's left shoulder. Globules of liquid flame, red and black, burst against the wall like putrid sores. Boiling drops rained upon the boy's left arm, eating at the iron and leather band wound from his biceps to the boxer's thongs over his hand.

The boy staggered, holding the arm away from his body. But the fire could not be stopped. It was sufficient to incinerate the armband, reducing it to a handful of ashes that fell from the Tiberian's singed flesh.

Baalshillek stared at the twisted forearm and clawlike hand, stunned first by memory and then overwhelming comprehension.

Twenty-one years ago. A joyful day in the palace of the em- peror: the healthy birth of Arrhidaeos's third son to his favored mistress, a full ten years following the stillbirth of his second son to his discarded Persian wife.

It had been a great day for Baalshillek, as well. After sixteen years of service to the Stone God—service unmarred by the

physical deterioration that claimed so many——he had been pro-
moted to the coveted position of the High Priest's chief assistant,
honored to aid him in the rituals of consecration and sacrifice.

Until that day, all of Arrhidaeos's hetairoi, courtiers, generals
and servants had been tested by the priests like every other citizen or slave in the empire. Arrhidaeos's eldest son and heir,
Nikodemos, was unaffected by the Stone and thus dangerous, as
was the emperor himself. But this new child might be the one the
priests had prayed for: a boy of royal blood fully susceptible to
the Stone God's control.

Arrhidaeos, for all his flaws, had been no fool. He knew the
danger of having such a son in the line of succession. The fragile balance between secular and sacred rule would be lost, and
the heirs of Alexandros would become mere puppet kings under
the priesthood.

And so the emperor had used trickery and the distraction of
opulent festivities to prevent the testing of the child, whom he
had named Alexandros in honor of his brother. The boy had been
guarded night and day by soldiers loyal only to him. Arrhidaeos
had defied the Stone God, trusting that the High Priest was not
prepared to risk an open confrontation.

He judged correctly. The High Priest, like his predecessors,
was beginning to fail, consumed from within by the Stone God's
fire. He clung to his power by a thread, yet he could not ignore
the emperor's blasphemy. With bribes and threats, he finally
worked his way into the guarded nursery.

Baalshillek was at his side when he brought forth the red stone
and placed it before the mewling babe's wrinkled face. At such
an age no child could focus its eyes or grasp an object in its tiny
fingers, yet Alexandros seemed to look directly at the shining
crystal. His features had grown distorted with infant rage, and he
had opened his mouth to wail in protest.

The High Priest had silenced him with a lash of pain, but then the extraordinary had happened. The babe flailed with one chubby hand and touched the High Priest's pendant.

Baalshillek had felt only the periphery of the blast that struck the priest, but he had seen his master fall and the red crystal sputter and die like drowned embers. Then the second miracle occurred.

Ag had entered Baalshillek. The god had deserted his dying host and leaped into another strong enough to carry him, displacing the lesser Exalted who resided in Baalshillek's stone. For a time Baalshillek had been helpless, overflowing with the god's power and presence, fighting for his own existence. But he had looked down on the babe and seen the blackened flesh of the boy's left hand and forearm, heard his screams of anger and agony.

Baalshillek had fled, leaving the High Priest to gasp out his last breaths alone. Later, when Baalshillek had recovered and proclaimed himself High Priest with the awful might of Ag's power behind him, he had demanded that the babe, Alexandros, be given over for sacrifice.

By then it was too late. The child had disappeared. The rumor spread that he had been sacrificed to the Stone God, and Arrhidaeos allowed the rumor to go unchecked. His beloved concubine vanished. Finding no trace of the babe, Baalshillek had been compelled to accept the emperor's private claim that both mother and child had drowned in an attempt to escape Karchedon by boat.

Baalshillek never found cause to believe the child had survived. But he had seen with his own eyes that a stone and its priest could be destroyed. If a mere babe had such power...

He pulled himself out of the past and gazed at his enemy's face. He recognized now what he had so egregiously missed. He'd met the elder Alexandros only once, but Quintus was the very image of his grandfather. His hair was darker and his eyes a different hue, but the features...ah, yes.

Quintus held his trembling left arm cradled in his right. The limb had grown in proportion to his body, but the deformity should have marked him for sacrifice long ago.

Unless he had been hidden away in unconquered lands...

During his childhood Tiberia had been free, a safe enough refuge until Nikodemos became emperor. Perhaps Arrhidaeos had intended to recall his son one day. Or perhaps he had simply been satisfied to thwart a new and untried High Priest.

But the boy did not know who he was. He had grown up as a Tiberian of good family, recruited to fight among the rebels and against his own elder brother.

Reborn. Quintus had been reborn into a new life in a new land. Yet he was mortal.

...if you bring about the deaths of any of the Bearers by your own hand or the hands of your priests or soldiers, in sacrifice or by the fire of the Stone, you too will die.

Baalshillek cursed Isis with her portents of doom, and Ag's defiant rage brushed aside the goddess's warnings as if they were cobwebs in a plundered tomb. Quintus must not die yet. He must be preserved from all harm until the prophecies were interpreted to the last glyph. Isis had said nothing of his well-being, only his life.

One other complication remained: Nikodemos. The emperor must never know that his younger brother had survived. He was capricious enough to defy Baalshillek's most careful calculations—he might repudiate the boy as an impostor, have him killed outright...

Or he might acknowledge his bastard brother just to spite the High Priest of the One True God.

"You have failed," Baalshillek said, meeting the boy's pain-scalded gaze. "You will have much time to think upon your error and admit your heresy."

"Kill me now. I will not change."

"You may choose otherwise when we find your companions. I

know them now, as I know you." He walked to the door, displaying his indifference to the boy's power. His men waited outside.

"Summon Orkos," he ordered one of the soldiers. "You three are to guard the prisoner with your lives until the commander takes personal custody. Under no circumstances are you to kill this man, but you may take any other measures necessary should he attempt to escape."

The men signaled acknowledgment, and the fourth set off to find Orkos. Baalshillek saw the door barred and turned down the hall toward the library. If there was any means by which the Annihilator could be safely eliminated, he would find it.

And when next he met Danae, they would have a most interesting conversation.

Tahvo woke in a room she did not recognize. It smelled of stone and sweat, wood and incense. She could no longer see with Slahtti's eyes, but fleeting memory revealed images of a chamber furnished with chairs and tables and a couch for sleeping.

She was inside the emperor's palace in the citadel of Karchedon, and she had found the one she sought.

"Tahvo?"

"Philokrates." She felt the air with outstretched hands. He caught her fingers in his warm, wrinkled palm.

"By Zeus's hairy thighs," he whispered, "how did you get here?" He paused, and she felt his sudden realization. He guided her to a chair and made her sit.

"This is not possible," he said. "The palace is under constant watch. How did you find me, when…" He sucked in his breath. "I called you seer, but you are far more than that. What are you?"

"A messenger," she answered softly. "No one will hear us?"

"I am not yet trusted with my freedom," he said, his voice harsh with irony, "but the Palace Guard have more pressing duties than

to watch over an old man who may be of some use but can surely
do no harm."

"A man once called Talos," she said.

"Then you know."

"Talos is not Philokrates."

He laughed. "But he is. He can never escape his past. He can
only hope to use the small value of his former reputation to assist his friends in their time of need."

"And that is why you left Cian."

"You have spoken to him? I had heard rumors that an Ailu was
captured in the city."

"It was true, but he is free."

"My fault," Philokrates murmured. "I feared too much for my
own life. What of Rhenna?"

"She is well."

"I am grateful. But you cannot remain here. Any influence I
may wield with the emperor will be undone if you are caught."

"I will not be. Have you seen Quintus?"

"No." He cleared his throat, and his feet shuffled back and
forth across the floor. "But I know where he is...in the hands of
the High Priest Baalshillek, deep in the bowels of the temple itself."

Tahvo slumped in her chair. She was not shocked at the news,
but it would be no simple matter to rescue him, even with all
Slahtti's power and the help of the spirits. Each use of magical
power, such as that which had transported her into the palace,
drained her allies' strength at a time when they must hoard every
particle of it merely to survive.

"He was found here, in the palace," Philokrates went on in
a near whisper. "They say he held the emperor's mistress
hostage, but the Temple Guard took him from Nikodemos's
men. Once Baalshillek realizes what Quintus can do..." He
shifted something heavy on a wooden surface. "I must find a

way to get him out of the temple. With Nikodemos he has a chance, but the emperor has not yet granted my request for an audience."

"The emperor will not kill him?"

He hesitated and sat down abruptly. "There is something I never told any of you, and it may be the key to his salvation. Quintus is the emperor's half brother."

Tahvo listened and absorbed his words, letting them sink into her mind like stones to the bottom of a well. The ripples they made spread far indeed.

"He was born with the ability to damage the red stones," Philokrates said, "and he faced death from the priests every instant he remained in Karchedon. His father, Arrhidaeos, sent him to Tiberia to be raised in secrecy. When Arrhidaeos learned that I, too, had fled to Tiberia to avoid serving the empire, he offered me a bargain. I could keep my freedom if I looked out for the boy and saw to his education. So I introduced myself to Quintus's adoptive Tiberian family, and I tutored him from the time he was ten until Nikodemos began the conquest of Italia."

"But Quintus did not know who he was."

"It was too dangerous. If Arrhidaeos planned to recall him, he wasn't able to do so before he died and Nikodemos took the throne. Quintus had every reason to hate the empire, and I left Italia after the conquest. I dared not trust Nikodemos. I could not guess how the emperor might react to such a revelation, or if he would protect Quintus from the priests."

"Yet now you must speak the truth."

"If there is any chance of saving Quintus's life." The chair creaked as he rocked it back and forth. "After the conquest, the Tiberian rebels recognized what they had in Quintus. They sought to keep him as their weapon of last resort, to be wielded only in the final battle for freedom. But he was far too headstrong, too proud, too afraid of becoming a mere tool in the hands of others who regarded him as less than a man. He chose to believe he could confront the Stone God alone."

"It was not chance that brought him to you in Hellas, or you to us."

The creaking stopped. "I had been studying ancient writings I gathered or stole during my service to the empire—secrets the priests kept locked away for fear that the empire's enemies might find a means of fulfilling their prophecies. The texts mention one called the 'Reborn,' a man capable of annihilating the Exalted and all their works. But I dared not tell Quintus anything that would encourage his reckless plans. Then the Watcher came, and I was so certain. I thought I had enough influence with Quintus to… Oh, gods. I am an old, stupid man…." His voice trailed off and he began to weep.

Tahvo rose and felt her way to his side. "You could not stop him."

"But if I had revealed his identity, made him understand the nature of his peril…"

"Baalshillek will not take his life."

He gripped her hands. "How do you know?"

"The spirits tell me."

"The daimones speak to you, not I."

"It is you who have seen the writings. You must give them to me now."

"Why?"

"So that we may fulfill the prophecies."

"You?" he croaked.

"The Four godborn, and the others who will aid them."

Philokrates shook so violently that he nearly upset his chair. "I have a thing…a device that contains knowledge. It is the only one of its kind, the chronicle of all I have learned in thirty years of study. It can be used but once, and then all it holds will be lost forever."

Tahvo heard the pain in his voice and knew that this device was more than a treasure to him. It was the token and symbol of his atonement for the evil in his past. "Will you give it to me?" she asked.

He got up, brushing her with his robes. "If I am wrong," he whispered. "If he is not the one…"

"We cannot escape the cost," Tahvo said. "It must be paid in full."

She waited in silence for Philokrates to decide. Many heartbeats later he opened her fingers and placed a smooth, cool object in her hand. It felt like a tube pinched at both ends.

"I call it a mnemosyne, after the goddess of memory," he said. "When you twist this cap to the left, you release the pneumata that hold all the speech I have given to it, my recording of the ancient texts."

Tahvo shuddered with pity. "You force the spirits to do your bidding?"

"These are not daimones, but fragments of what might have been living spirits long ago. They do not suffer. Once they have served their purpose, the pneumata will become one with the ae-ther and cannot be recalled. If they are released out of my pres-ence, their message will be disarranged beyond any interpretation. This was my safeguard so that the priests should never learn what I know."

"Then I cannot take it to the others."

"No. But you are a seer—and more. If you can listen now, and remember—"

"I will."

"Can you get out of the palace as you came?"

"Yes."

"Then release the pneumata now. Carry the message to those who must hear it, and let me help Quintus. I will do whatever is necessary to keep him alive."

"His destiny is not in our keeping." She smiled. "Do not be afraid, Philokrates. Your time will also come."

"I think I would rather not know." He squeezed her shoulder and briefly touched his magical device, murmuring some prayer or incantation. "Tell the others…tell them that I wish them well. May your gods attend you."

"They are with me always." Even as she spoke, she felt Slahtti returning and the other spirits gathering near. The spirit-wolf's eyes gave her a glimpse of the old man's anguished face. Then she twisted the tube as Philokrates had taught her, and his words rushed into the minds of those with whom she shared her body.

When it was finished and the pneumata were free, Tahvo faded into a dreamworld of gentle motion as Slahtti carried her away.

Nyx arrived at the rebel safe house not long after Geleon had gathered his council to discuss the incredible events that had so lately overtaken Karchedon.

The young woman, trembling with exhaustion, passed the street sentries and immediately reported to Geleon. She told a tale of unlikely assistance and an escape aided by clouds pouring from the sky. It was clear that she, like many of the rebels, attributed the freakish snowfall to the intervention of benevolent gods.

In that assumption, Rhenna thought, she was not far wrong. Much good had come of Tahvo's false winter. But though Nyx spoke of Danae's part in setting her free, she had no word of Quintus save Danae's claim that the Tiberian was safe.

Geleon and his council feared that Quintus must inevitably be taken if he remained in the palace, and Rhenna could not but agree. She hoped against hope that Tahvo and Slahtti were on their way to fetch him. The rebels considered and rejected the idea of sending agents into the citadel. They debated Quintus's importance to the cause, and some went so far as to suggest that he would betray them the moment he was caught.

Rhenna and Cian stood apart from the discussion, more like prisoners than allies. Tahvo had insisted that they accompany Geleon. That had been a mistake. They had to get out of the city, but Rhenna doubted the rebels would let their Watcher go without a fight.

She tried to concoct some plan while her mind spun with images, sensations and bits of conversation gleaned from the past few hours: lying beneath Cian as he moved inside her, giving pleasure she could not accept; fighting the tender emotions she had no right to feel; rejecting Tahvo's bizarre revelations of power and destiny.

There is no choosing for one born of the gods. Rhenna snorted. Born of the gods indeed. She'd never heard such foolishness from the mouth of one so wise.

Your power will come…

She heard Tahvo's voice so clearly now that it seemed only right when Slahtti appeared before her eyes, chasing startled rebels from his path with a sweep of his silver tail. He shook his coat, and white wolf became woman. Tahvo collapsed. The rebels crowded around her, some with weapons ready to strike.

"Stop!" Rhenna bellowed.

Every head swung toward her. Geleon raised his hands for silence.

"You know this creature?" he asked.

"Tahvo," Rhenna said, shouldering men and women aside. "Give her room to breathe."

"Do as she says," Geleon commanded. He moved closer, peering at Tahvo's prone form. "This is the woman Quintus sought at the palace? She has magic indeed."

"More than you know."

"You vouch for her, then?"

"She saved our lives," Cian snapped. "No one hates the Stone God more than she."

Tahvo lifted her head. "Rhenna?"

"Here." Rhenna pulled her up. "Must you always exhaust yourself with these comings and goings?"

The healer rested her head against Rhenna's breast. "I had to decide," she whispered.

"Decide what?" Cian asked, kneeling beside them.

Blind silver eyes welled with tears. "Quintus was taken to the temple. I did not have the strength…"

Rhenna hugged her fiercely and glared at the muttering rebels. "Is Quintus alive?"

"Baalshillek cannot kill him," she said. "But his path is not ours. I had to come back, to tell."

"If Baalshillek has Quintus," Geleon said grimly, "then hope is at an end."

"No." Tahvo indicated her wish to stand, jaw tightened with effort. Rhenna and Cian supported her between them. "You will listen."

Several men began to protest. A woman approached Tahvo with a look of pity on her face.

"You will listen."

The profound authority in Tahvo's voice brought all sound and movement to a stop. Rhenna's skin tingled as if a thousand tiny thorns pressed into her flesh. Cian grunted in surprise.

Tahvo grew. Bright light radiated from her body, and Rhenna was sure she would have flown up into the air if she had not been held to the earth. To Rhenna's eyes the healer became the wisest of Earthspeakers, gray-haired and handsome, her headpiece richly adorned with fur, leaves and feathers.

The woman Nyx murmured a reverent word in her own tongue and fell to her knees. Others spoke names Rhenna had heard before: Isis, Serapis, Ishtar, Melquart, Tabiti.

"What do you see?" Rhenna whispered to Cian.

He shook his head, speechless, and Rhenna understood that

Tahvo was no longer Tahvo but a different being to each man and woman who gazed upon her. For a moment Rhenna caught a glimpse of what the others saw: a tall, black-haired woman crowned with a blazing golden disk and cow's horns; a dark-skinned woman draped in brilliantly colored garments, vivid jewels and animal furs; a youth with winged sandals.

"I have come," the deva said, "to tell the story so many of us have forgotten. I have come so that you will remember and act accordingly. I have come to speak of the end of the world."

Chapter Thirty-Two

The deva smiled like a mother upon her children, and several rebels who had failed to show proper respect began to weep. Cian sank into a crouch at the Earthspeaker's feet. Rhenna closed her eyes.

"In the beginning," the goddess said, "there was only Earth and Sky, Water and Fire. From these elements sprang the gods, who gave their fecundity to the world. Mighty beasts now unknown grazed upon the fruits of the soil, the seas were fertile with life, and nurturing fire leapt from the mountains and ran in the veins of the ground.

"But many of the gods were not content and wished to shape a new creature with the wisdom to recognize and praise the gods for their bounty. They selected a beast to raise up above all others and gave it the name of Man. But each clan desired to form Man in its own image——Fire in fire, Water as water, Earth of earth and Air of air.

"The clans quarreled among themselves most bitterly. Many gods were destroyed in the battle, and the pieces of their bodies were scattered to the farthest corners of the world. The remaining gods agreed that Man should be shaped by all the elements equally, and swore sacred oaths that no god or element should seek to rule the others or claim sole rights to Mankind.

"At first the numbers of Men were small. There were no temples, no priests and no holy rites, no cities and no kings. Men sought the gods in the wild places where they had always existed—in caverns that reached into the earth, in springs and rivers, and in the high places. The gods gave Men the favor of the elements, and in turn Men sustained the gods with their devotion.

"For countless ages Men and gods lived in harmony. But the numbers of Men grew, and they began to quarrel as once the gods had done. The cleverest discovered the bones of the dead gods and learned how to reawaken the magic hidden within them. They offered this magic to the living gods in exchange for greater power over their fellow Men.

"Remembering their oaths, most of the gods refused. But three of each clan accepted the offerings of the clever Men, and began a secret rebellion led by the most powerful among them, Ag of Fire. They became the Exalted. Together they taught these Men the arts of growing grain, of brewing beer, of building walls of stone and brick, of channeling the rivers, of taming the beasts and of forging metals.

"In gratitude, Men built a great city on a fertile plain and erected a temple to these twelve gods. They raised mighty statues of obsidian, crystal and stone to focus and contain their magic. The more Men came to the city on the plain, the greater the Exalted became. The wild places were deserted. Too late the other gods realized that they had become weak from neglect and ignorance. They commanded the Exalted to remember their oaths.

"But the rebel gods had learned that the violence of Men against Men made them stronger than the old ways. With every metal weapon forged in flame, with every sacrifice, they grew more arrogant.

"But when they demanded that Men burn all the wild places, the other gods rose up to fight. They possessed the bodies of Men to sire half-divine warriors who could stand against the Exalted and created four Weapons that only such heroes could wield.

"In the end, the Exalted became mad and could not be stopped by any means save the total destruction of their city and their temples. The old gods and heroes joined together and leveled the city in flame and flood, quake and gale. Four of the twelve Exalted escaped to the four corners of the Earth, stealing the Weapons that could destroy them. The other Eight were captured and imprisoned forever in a Stone forged of all the elements and bound with the bones of the gods cast down in this most terrible of battles.

"When the war was finished and Men were left to rebuild with the scraps of their former glory, the gods vowed never again to take human form in the cause of divine quarrels. Great and small, they withdrew to their caves and streams, high peaks and hidden springs, charging one race of their half-divine children to guard the Stone prison."

"The Watchers," Geleon whispered, and stared at Cian.

"Even as time worked its healing magic on the Earth, it made both Men and the children of the gods forget the age before. The Stone prison was buried in the most desolate wilderness, and none remembered where it lay. But the Eight imprisoned in the Stone were not dead, nor had they forgotten."

"We failed," Cian said, touching his head to the goddess's feet.

The deva laid a gentle hand upon his head. "They have awakened, the Eight," she said, "but they are not yet free. Those who were captive seek to shape new bodies strong enough to hold them. Until they succeed, their power is limited, and their priests and soldiers may be opposed."

"We have no magic to match theirs," Geleon said.

"Four times four shall decide the fate of the Earth—eight lords of destruction, four Exalted who escaped, and four to wield the Weapons—four called the 'godborn.'"

"Who?" Geleon asked, sinking to his knees. "Who, Mighty One?"

"The Warrior, the Watcher and the Seer," she said.

"What of the Fourth?" Geleon asked.

"Three will leave the city, and one will remain."

Quintus, Rhenna thought. "These Weapons, What are they?"

"The Hammer, the Arrow, the Sword and the one who is Reborn."

"How are we to use them?"

"This you will learn—in time."

"Where can they be found?" Cian asked, forestalling Rhenna's testy response.

"In the farthest corners of the Earth, where no mortal of the empire has ever trod. And those who guard them will not relinquish them easily."

"You expect us—" Rhenna's voice hitched on the word "—to fight the devas who stole the only means capable of defeating them?"

"You were ever stubborn, my daughter," the Earthspeaker said, gazing at Rhenna. "The free Exalted may be formidable opponents, but none is invincible. You must find the Weapons and return before the final reckoning."

"Are the 'good' devas such cowards that they send mortals on such a quest rather than risk themselves?"

Someone gasped at Rhenna's effrontery, but the Earthspeaker only shook her head, heavy with sorrow. "We are bound in our way, Rhenna-of-the-Scar, as mortals are bound to walk upon the

Earth. The Weapons are not ours to hold. Yet Men will not suffer and die alone. Through the Four godborn, all that resist evil become one. For this struggle the children of the gods were made long ago. Their gifts still run true."

"And if we refuse? Or fail?"

"Everything we know will cease to exist," Cian whispered.

"The Eight will return the world to its original elements," the deva said, "and, in the end, Ag will have his way."

Its fire is everlasting, Tahvo had said on the black ship. It was too terrible a prospect for Rhenna to imagine. But she remembered…remembered a boy burning on an altar, a girl brutally raped, the torn bodies of farmers and weavers slaughtered like sheep in their peaceful village.

Cian got to his feet. "I swore to my brothers," he said. "The Ailuri will not fail again."

"You know where you must begin?" the deva asked.

"South." He smiled, humorless. "Always South."

"And what are we to do?" Geleon asked. "How do we serve, we of Karchedon who resist the Stone God?"

"However you must to aid the Four."

"Then help us," the rebel leader begged. "How do we get them out of the city? Every gate will be doubly guarded. No one will be permitted to enter or leave as long as——"

He halted in mid-sentence as three dark shapes flew into the room, pursued by rebel spearmen.

"No!" Cian shouted.

Black shadows resolved into beasts with golden eyes and bared teeth. They bounded to Cian's side and crouched around him.

"Ailuri," Rhenna cried.

The Earthspeaker goddess shed light of blinding brilliance. Rhenna moved to catch Tahvo as she fell. Half the rebels pressed close to witness this new transformation, while the rest exclaimed over the Watchers' astonishing appearance.

Rhenna put her ear to Tahvo's chest. "Are there any healers among you?"

A beak-nosed man came forward. "I know something of the art. There is another room with a couch." He offered to take Tahvo, but Rhenna carried her into the adjoining room and laid her on the bed.

The male healer sat on the edge of the couch and examined Tahvo, feeling her forehead, prying open her eyelids and smelling her shallow breath. He wet a scrap of cloth to bathe Tahvo's face and tried to make her drink. The water dribbled untasted from her lips.

"What's wrong with her?" Rhenna asked.

"She was a vessel for the gods," the man said. "It is no wonder her body suffers."

And I blamed her powder for her illness. "Will she live?"

The man laid his fingertips on Tahvo's wrist and frowned. "Her pulse is weak, but if she rests…" He sighed. "Her fate lies with the gods."

"Then they won't let her die. She is one of the Four who'll save the world."

The man gazed at her from dark, serious eyes. "I was born in the Two Lands," he said. "The gods have spoken to my people for millennia. Do not mock what you have not learned to understand."

"I have no wish to be chosen by any gods. Would you go in my stead?"

"Not for a pharaoh's crown."

"Then I'll care for Tahvo. Send Cian to me."

He bowed profoundly and left the room.

Cian came quickly, his face flushed with excitement and worry. He brushed Tahvo's forehead with his fingertips.

"She should recover," Rhenna said, "but I doubt her chances if she continues to let the devas use her like this."

"It is her choice," Cian said softly.

Rhenna shook her head. "What of the Ailuri?"

"The few that escaped tracked me here." He crouched beside her, hands dangling between his knees. "They have offered to help, though they've suffered...." He bent his head.

She squeezed his shoulder. "What does Geleon say?"

"That we—we three, and my brothers—must get out of the city immediately."

"And Quintus?"

"The rebels still argue."

"I can't leave Tahvo now. Report to me what they discuss, and I'll speak to Geleon later."

He laid his hand over hers. "You will come with us to the South?"

"Do you believe what Tahvo's devas told us?"

"Yes."

Asteria's blood, he does. With all his heart. And I'll be spending every day and night at his side.

She had thought to rid herself of unnatural desires and the taint of Farkas's touch with a single frantic coupling, a one-time surrender to madness. But she was not cured. Cian touched her, and her body went strange and weak. She had tasted the mating of friends, companions...lovers...and she longed to taste it again.

Lover or guardian. She couldn't be both on the journey that lay ahead. She had broken her people's covenants, but she was still a Sister of the Axe. This thing she had shared with Cian would inevitably drain her fighter's strength and will, just as carrying a babe in her belly made the finest warrior clumsy and dull. Love, lust— whatever these Southern females chose to call it—could only make her useless to Cian and to the devas' grim venture.

She removed her hand from Cian's shoulder. "I've seen enough," she said. "We'll go on with Tahvo's plan until it becomes clear that the whole thing is complete and utter lunacy."

"Tahvo will have more to tell us."

"At this price?"

"She's strong, like you," he said. "She will survive."

"Is that enough?"

He stood and backed away slowly, holding her gaze. "It will have to be."

But Rhenna knew he lied, just as she lied to herself.

Ag screamed in Baalshillek's head, and he woke from the communion with the voices of gods, light and dark, ringing between his ears.

The Stone throbbed in nauseating waves, and the lesser priests writhed on their backs like worms exposed to the desert sun.

Disaster.

Baalshillek found his legs and leaned on the platform surrounding the Stone. Ag raged so violently that he couldn't make sense of the god's warning, but he knew that something had gone terribly wrong.

A beta priest entered the sanctum and flung himself at Baalshillek's feet without pausing to genuflect before the Stone. "Holy One," he gasped. "The emperor's Guard have invaded the temple and demand the prisoner Quintus."

Baalshillek kicked the priest aside and ran from the chamber. Temple Guards marched down the hall toward the stairs beneath the altar, already moving to confront and detain the intruders. Baalshillek passed them and strode up to the barred door of his most extraordinary prisoner's cell. Orkos was among those who stood watch outside.

"Is he safe?" Baalshillek snapped.

"He is, my lord," Orkos said.

"The moment we have dealt with Nikodemos's men, send all

available troops to the city gates. No one is to enter or leave Karchedon."

"The outer gates are closed, my lord. I will reinforce the guard."

"As soon as this prisoner is secure. Open the door."

Orkos and his men obeyed. The Tiberian blinked at them from the darkness.

"Take him to the sanctum," Baalshillek said. "This man is not to be released."

Orkos grabbed the young rebel and half carried him out the door. Shouts and the clash of metal on metal sounded from the stairway. Orkos and his men dragged Quintus in the opposite direction.

"Baalshillek!"

The High Priest turned. Orkos stopped, reacting with instinctive obedience to a voice of unquestioned authority.

Nikodemos walked into the stonelight, his personal guard before and behind him. Of the temple soldiers there was no trace. The emperor smiled as if he had not just broken a solemn compact between palace and temple. As if he owned the holy ground he trod upon.

"Baalshillek," he said in a milder tone, raising open hands as he would to an old friend. "What is that you have there? Another secret prisoner?" He sighed with mock regret while his men formed a tight circle around him, bristling with weapons.

"Go, Orkos," Baalshillek commanded.

"Stay," Nikodemos said, "or I will be compelled to have my men search every chamber of this passage."

"Blasphemy," Baalshillek said. "You have broken the agreement sworn before the Stone. The god will—"

"No doubt he will, but I remember that our agreement also bound the temple to inform me of every rebel prisoner taken by the priests or Temple Guard." Nikodemos cocked his head like a mischievous boy. "First you were slow to tell me of the Aithiopian female, and now I hear there were others, as well. Including that one."

He didn't need to point. Quintus had wrenched about in Orkos's iron grip and faced Nikodemos.

"This prisoner," Baalshillek said softly, "is of no interest to the emperor."

"Of no interest?" Nikodemos laughed, profaning the very air. "I know he was one of those who freed the rebels' leader—"

"Rightful property of the god, not—"

"—*and*," Nikodemos interrupted, "he was caught within the palace itself and taken from our lawful custody by your servants." He studied his varnished nails. "I understand that he is a young man of most extraordinary abilities."

Baalshillek clasped his pendant. Red light glowed through his hand. "You have been misinformed, My Lord Emperor."

"Indeed," Nikodemos said. "Let me see his face."

"If you will leave now, the god may forgive this intrusion."

"I have come for what is mine under our agreement," Nikodemos said, half yawning. "Surely the Stone God keeps his holy word."

Baalshillek controlled Ag's murderous impulse. The god would destroy Nikodemos here and now, heedless of the consequences. He had the power. But the Exalted were not ready to assume direct leadership of the empire. Nikodemos was still useful. And still too powerful.

"Bring the prisoner forward," Baalshillek told Orkos. "Show the emperor his face."

Orkos did as he was told, betraying neither fear nor concern. Quintus stepped into the stonelight. His deformed hand was clearly visible, but Nikodemos seemed not to notice.

"So," he said. "I never saw my grandfather, and few live who served under him. But I kept a few of the old coins, and they do not lie."

"You are the emperor," Quintus said, his voice strangled with hatred, not yet beginning to understand.

Nikodemos raised his brow. "And what are you?" He looked at Baalshillek. "Long ago I lost an infant half brother. Today I discover that there was a witness to my brother's fate...when he was saved from your kind by my father. It seems the babe had certain talents the priests did not wish to see survive."

Quintus jerked in shock. "I regret that the emperor is misled," Baalshillek said.

"Did you ever meet a man called Talos?" Nikodemos asked.

Baalshillek knew the name. Who did not? When Talos served Arrhidaeos, Baalshillek had been a beta priest, indistinguishable from the rest save by his unfailing health. But he had never met the inventor, nor learned what became of him after the Persian rebellion.

"Perhaps you have heard the name Philokrates?" Nikodemos said. "He recently visited the palace, offering the service he gave to my great father."

Baalshillek had known nothing of this. So many of his men had been occupied hunting rebels in the city—looking for the witch, the escaped Ailuri and the Annihilator himself....

"How strange are the ways of the gods," Nikodemos mused. "You detain my kinsman, Baalshillek. You have no right to keep or punish him. Give him to me."

Ag roared. Baalshillek coldly weighed his options. The last thing he dared do was warn Nikodemos of the extent of Quintus's power.

"The god holds you in his favor," he said quietly. "What will become of your empire if he turns his face from Nikodemos?"

"There is no empire without the emperor."

Baalshillek had never doubted the emperor's strength of personality and will, so markedly absent in his father. But circumstances were changing. One day even the loyalty of Nikodemos's handpicked troops and generals would not save him.

As long as Quintus remained in Karchedon, he could be taken again. Better to hand him to the emperor than to give Nikodemos's men an excuse to explore the underground chambers. If the emperor suspected any part of the priesthood's clandestine activities, he chose to ignore them for the sake of peace. That neutrality would not survive a full disclosure.

Nikodemos would undoubtedly hold the boy's powers as a threat to the priesthood. He knew of the Ailuri and the rebels, but he did not have access to the documents hidden within these walls, nor enough information to grasp the significance of what was occurring in the city this very moment. He didn't know of the other Three, and how close they were to escape.

What belonged to the Stone God must return to him sooner or later.

Baalshillek bowed his head and signaled for Orkos to release Quintus to the Palace Guards. "Guard him carefully, My Lord Emperor. He may prove more trouble than you anticipate."

Quintus walked stiffly from one set of captors to the other, staring into his half-brother's face. Nikodemos smiled.

"Brother," he said. "I understand that you have caused much disturbance in our city, but I've been assured that you had no knowledge of your true birth. You fought for those you believed your kinsmen, though it was treason to your emperor. Both your ignorance and your knowledge may spare your life."

Quintus was remarkably calm for one whose world had changed so irrevocably. "I will not betray those with whom I have fought," he said.

"We shall see." Nikodemos glanced at his brother's withered hand. "I must determine a fitting punishment for such rebellious activities. And there is a certain lady to whom you owe a most humble apology."

"I regret any pain I gave to the innocent."

"There are no innocents."

"A few may have yet survived your slaughter."

Baalshillek considered how simple it would be for the boy to provoke his half brother into killing him. If Quintus died by the emperor's hand, his threat would be ended with no risk to the Stone.

But his powers might still be turned to the god's service—to secure the Stone's dominion rather than destroy it.

Nikodemos lost his smile and addressed the commander of his guard. "A few nights in the dungeon may soften my brother's tongue. He is to have no visitors without my permission."

"At once, Lord Emperor." The commander and his men turned smartly and herded Quintus back to the stairway.

"I leave you to your devotions, priest," Nikodemos said. "May they strengthen the empire."

And may the Stone feast on your royal blood. Baalshillek bowed again, and the emperor took his impious presence from the holy precincts.

"To the gates," Baalshillek ordered Orkos. "Send every man you can summon, but do not alert the emperor's servants.

"Bring me the Three."

Chapter Thirty-Three

The plans, such as they were, had been laid. Cian had agreed to them, though by doing so he deceived both the rebels and his fellow Ailuri. He had no intention of staying out of the fight.

It was suicide. No one spoke the thought aloud, but everyone knew. Many of the rebels who attacked the west gate would die, either on the swords and spears of the soldiers or by the priests' stonefire. Geleon had warned his followers not to underestimate the vigilance of the Stone's servants. It must be assumed that Baalshillek knew almost everything that passed in the city and expected his former captives to attempt escape.

Rhenna didn't know the details of the reckless scheme. Cian wanted her and Tahvo outside the gates no matter what else happened this night. Tahvo was far too weak to produce a convenient snowfall, let alone whisk them all out of Karchedon.

Men and women waited inside the door of a warehouse near the west gate, which opened to the Karchedonian countryside on the other end of the city from the harbor. To the south and west lay the tilled fields and groves and pastures that fed the populace, a soulless land like the chora surrounding Hypanis or Piraeos.

Beyond the cultivated earth were wild hills and desert and territory that had once belonged to barbarian princes conquered by Arrhidaeos. Men spoke of ever greater deserts and lush forests and raging rivers in places where no man of Ta Thalassa had ever ventured, of fantastic beasts and mysterious, savage gods. No one knew how far the Southern lands extended.

Cian couldn't think so far ahead. He watched the gate, manned by armed troops and red-robed priests, and wondered if any of the allies would make it past the high ashlar walls.

Metal rattled behind him. Cian knew the men inside the stolen armor, as he knew the naked Ailu who hung prisoner between them. His brother didn't meet his eyes. Their farewells had already been made, a second reunion quickly and bitterly ended.

The other two surviving Ailuri had hidden themselves as close to the gate as possible, though there was no real shelter within twenty paces of the wall. When the false soldiers brought their prisoner to the priests and created their distraction, the Ailuri would be first to attack. They would go directly for the priests.

Rebels armed with swords and axes, staves and knives—anything they had been able to steal during the years of resistance—shifted nervously and wiped sweating palms on their tunics. Most were men, though a few women had demanded the right to fight; they were of nearly all races and peoples known to the empire, from pale-skinned Kelts to the dark folk of Aithiopia. Each and every one had volunteered for this assault. Many had wives and children. But they believed what the gods and Tahvo had told them; they believed that the hope of the world lay with four called the godborn who could end the Stone God's reign of terror.

Cian wished he could deny their faith. Rhenna would surely do so. But he could not, and Rhenna trusted him to lead while she protected Tahvo.

He flexed his icy fingers, sick and terrified.

The attack had been timed to coincide with the very end of the day's watch, when new soldiers and priests came to relieve their predecessors. Even so, Geleon knew, as Cian did, that some who served the Stone God were more than human. The rebels couldn't count on weakness or hesitation.

Someone passed a signal, and the fraudulent soldiers prepared to make their appearance. Cian loosened his cloak, ready to throw it aside. He didn't look for Rhenna and Tahvo; they were with Geleon, whose sole purpose was to get them out the gate.

"Do not fight, Watcher."

He turned to face Nyx, who regarded him with the same mix of awe and wary hope he had learned to expect from the others.

"I know you intend to fight beside us," she said, "but you must save yourself."

Cian looked away. "My people have died for me," he said. "I'll share their final battle."

"But the Hammer is yours to carry," she said. "Who will bear it if you die?"

He had no time to ask her what she meant. The false soldiers walked out into the open space between the outermost buildings and the city wall, their Ailuri prisoner suspended limp in their arms. Immediately one of the three priests on the wall descended to confront the men with questions. The rebels, concealed by the red-banded helmets, gave the Ailu a vicious shake and answered the priest at length. The priest summoned another of his brethren, and four soldiers came with him.

When two of the priests had descended from the wall, Geleon gave word to strike. The Ailu prisoner sprang up between his supposed captors and changed, leaping for a startled priest's throat.

The rebel soldier to his right stabbed at the second priest with his spear just before he was himself cut down by the priest's escort. His fellow rebel sliced at the soldier's legs and barely dodged the searing flash of the third priest's stonefire.

The full attack began. Cian charged, discarding his cloak and changing as he ran. He tried to watch for Rhenna and Tahvo, but that soon became impossible. For a short time he was aware of Nyx at his side. Then the beast took him.

He followed the scent of his brothers and bit through the ankle of a soldier about to sever an Ailu's head. Golden eyes met, but there were no words. Only blood.

Blood dripped from Cian's claws and coated his tongue. Stonefire singed his fur, and he snapped brittle human limbs between his teeth. He peeled armor from bodies as easily as skin from bone. The screams of men were like music. Instinct alone marked friend from enemy and spared the allies who got in his way.

He felt it when one of his brothers died, burned through the heart by a priest's beam of fire. A second Ailu, his fur striped with gaping wounds, fell from the top of the wall locked in a fatal embrace with a priest whose exposed face was a mass of putrid sores. Some life remained in the priest after he hit the ground. Cian extinguished it, choking on the vile taste of the Stone's poison wherever his fangs pierced flesh.

A subtle change in the air told him when the rebels had opened the gate. Cian jumped over dead and dying bodies, alert for the only scent that could overcome the stench of death and the lust to continue killing long after the need was past.

Rhenna and Tahvo stood on the threshold to freedom, Nyx and a few of the surviving rebels grouped around them. Rhenna held a sword in one hand, and her eyes searched ceaselessly for the one she couldn't find. A streak of blood sullied her unscarred cheek.

Cian roared and batted aside the injured soldier who thought to stop him with mortal weapons. He paused for an instant as he passed the man he had once known as Shahriar, gazing blindly at the darkening sky. Then he ran to Rhenna and changed.

His eyes and nose told him that Rhenna and Tahvo were unhurt. The rebels had done their work well, but they had suffered for their courage and loyalty. There were many dead—men and women Cian recognized by face if not by name.

"They wouldn't let me fight," Rhenna whispered.

Cian gripped her shoulder, unable to ease her grief when all he could think was that she was *alive*. Tahvo lay insensible in her arms.

"More will come," Cian said. "We must go."

"Who will sing their last rites?" Rhenna asked, tears running down her stern warrior's face. "Who will remember—"

"Out!" Geleon shouted from the wall. "Run!"

Cian snatched Tahvo from Rhenna and pushed her away from the gates. Most of the rebel escort fell back to block pursuit, but Nyx remained at Rhenna's side as if she might use her long spear to prod the warrior. Cian heard shouts as a new contingent of priests and soldiers took up the chase. He prayed that the rebels had sense enough to realize that they'd done all they could. Let them live to fight another day.

The road from the west gate of Karchedon was straight, well paved and very much exposed. "This way," Nyx said, waving her spear to the south.

They cut away from the road and raced cross-country, unimpeded by the farmhands and slaves finishing their day's labors.

The sounds of organized pursuit kept pace just behind them. Cian saw well in the growing darkness, but he had no doubt that the priests had their own sorcerous methods of creating ample light by which to hunt their prey.

"Is there a place to hide?" Cian asked Nyx between breaths.

"Not here."

Cian glanced at the ground under his running feet. He could

move the earth. He could make it shake and split open like an over-ripe melon. He looked at his missing finger, the small sacrifice of his own substance given to strengthen the spirits of the earth so that they might aid him in his battle with Baalshillek.

He would gladly sacrifice more to save his friends. But he was a child playing with a weapon he didn't understand and couldn't wield without the risk of hurting those he loved.

He stopped, and Rhenna stopped with him. Nyx dashed ahead for several strides until she realized the others hadn't followed.

"What are you doing?" she demanded. "The red jackals snap at our heels!"

Cian thrust Tahvo into Rhenna's arms. "Go with Nyx."

The tears had dried on Rhenna's face, freezing her features in an ominous and all-too-familiar determination. "I said I wouldn't leave you."

"I may be able to slow them, but not if you and Tahvo are nearby. The risk—"

"No," Tahvo said weakly. "We must stay together."

Rhenna flashed Cian a look of triumph. "Work your magic," she said.

In grim resignation Cian knelt and laid his palm against the soil. He reached with his heart and his mind. The earth did not give. His fingers sank no farther than the length of his nails and struck an implacable surface, like the hardest stone.

"I'm not strong enough," he said, scratching at the soil until his fingertips bled. "Nyx, lead us where you will."

"It's too late." The dark woman stared into the night, her spear aimed at the thunder of approaching footfalls.

Rhenna eased Tahvo to the ground. She lifted her sword in both hands. She closed her eyes. And Cian glimpsed something in her face he had never seen.

She hummed deep in her chest, some song of her people both fierce and coaxing, a warrior's prayer. A breeze started up at her feet and swirled around her, lifting the frayed hem of her chiton. She let the sword fall as the breeze became a wind and tore her hair loose from what was left of its braids.

Nyx swayed, eyes wide. Tahvo turned her face into the rising gale. Cian braced his feet and listened to the wailing voices of those who answered Rhenna's call.

They were many, and afraid, but they came together and made such a storm of dust and debris that even the light of moon and stars was obliterated. A whirlwind was born with Rhenna at its heart. But the choking clouds didn't touch her or her companions; they spiraled outward, carrying everything before them.

There were other voices then, cries from very human throats.

Rhenna picked up her sword, faced south and started forward again. The storm parted before her, leaving a clear path ahead. Cian helped Tahvo rise and followed Rhenna as close as he dared. Nyx took up the rear.

The wind didn't let up until the stench of the Stone God's city was far beyond the reach of an Ailu's senses.

Epilogue

Alone in the sanctum, Baalshillek knelt before the Stone and prepared to work a most terrible magic.

If there had been time, he would have journeyed to the core, the resting place of the Great Stone, the very heart kept hidden from all but a few. But there was no time. Three of the four Bearers had escaped, and even the temple's finest and deadliest Children were not sufficient to bring them back.

If you bring about the deaths of any of the Bearers by your own hand or the hands of your priests or soldiers, in sacrifice or by the fire of the Stone, you too will die.

But the Four could be killed by those who were neither priests nor soldiers but were sprung from the gods themselves, created for one purpose alone.

Baalshillek straightened from his bow and arranged the vials of fleshly substance on the table before him. Only two Children to make this day, but their creation would tax all his strength. And if he lost control, Ag would consume his work before he could complete it.

Eight babes had been given to the Stone to appease the Exalted and feed their constant hunger. Now the Stone would receive a taste of its enemies, and from these particles of skin and blood the union of god and mortal could commence.

Baalshillek chanted the sacred prayers and emptied one of the vials on the pulsing red surface of the Stone. Fetid steam clogged the air. Ag screamed, and the other seven Exalted fought among themselves. Each time a god gave up a piece of its being—for the Children, the altars or the stones carried by the priests—that god grew a little weaker. And yet such a sacrifice also meant freedom, no matter how limited or confined in a single form. It was a fine balance the Exalted could not entirely accept.

But ultimately like must be drawn to like. Because the witch Tahvo was of Water, so must be the Exalted who shared its essence with the new creation. As the thing Tahvo feared most was male, so must be her counterpart.

Baalshillek sank back on his knees and waited for the alchemy to proceed. Once the shape began to materialize above the Stone, he guided its formation with incantations and directed his stone-fire with the precision of a physician's lancet. The thing writhed and shrieked as it grew.

When it was finished, it stepped down from the platform on two human feet and stared at Baalshillek out of tilted silver eyes. It did not bow, for part of it was a god. But it was not yet fully mature, and must act under Baalshillek's guidance until it had achieved understanding. In days it would be ready, but the training must begin at once.

"What is your name?" he asked it.

"I am Urho."

A foreign name, from the Northlands. It was acceptable.

"Who is your enemy, Urho?"

"The one who stole my power."

"Your double. Your sister."

Urho snarled with as yet mindless hatred. Baalshillek commanded him to stand aside, then retrieved the second vial.

Again there was smoke and the nauseating odor of sorcery. This creation was born of air, air tainted by the fumes of poison aethers and the miasma of disease. It descended like its brother, a taller figure of dark and handsome aspect. Its lips curved in a smile, for it was drawn from something more than fear. It *remembered*.

"I am Farkas," it said.

Baalshillek gestured it to join its companion, and summoned the last of the three. She glided from the shadows, already whole and eager to hunt. Yseul, the first female Ailu, made of Ailuri blood and bone.

"You do not carry his offspring," Baalshillek said.

She would not meet his gaze, but a goddess walked within her, savage and proud.

"I will find him," she said. "I will take him."

"You will do as you are told," he said. "But you will have your pleasure."

She grinned with all her sharp white teeth. The new male godborn stared at her, capable of lust when there was no greater objective to distract them. But each would have his own, in due course.

Three of four. The pattern was almost complete. They would not go alone into the South; highly trained Children would watch them and report to Baalshillek, lending aid where they could and rousing new enemies to hinder those who thought to vanquish the Stone.

As for the fourth counterpart...Baalshillek advanced to the

Stone and laid his hands on its radiance. The last of the Four remained in Karchedon; only one could bring him down.

And you will fall, Alexandros, son of Arrhidaeos. You will fall, and the world will be mine.

* * * * *

Look for Hammer of the Earth,
the next volume in Susan Krinard's new fantasy series,
"The Stone God,"
coming in October 2005.

Author Note

Shield of the Sky is set in a fictional alternate history of the ancient Mediterranean circa 290 BCE. I've taken liberties with both history and geography, and this novel is not intended to accurately portray historical events.

In "real" history, Alexander the Great conquered much of the known world, including a portion of India, between 336 and 323 BCE. He never conquered Carthage—Karchedon—nor did he or his successors attempt to invade the nascent Roman Republic. His "empire" didn't long survive his death. His brother, Arrhidaeos, was considered a half-wit and never attained any political prominance.

Tiberia is based on the Roman Republic, which in 290 BCE was not the powerful state it would become under the emperors. But its people had already repelled the invasions of Celts and other Italian tribes, and the Romans proved their ingenuity and resilience many times in the following centuries.

Karchedon is Carthage, which was the Roman Republic's most formidable enemy. Rome defeated Carthage in the Third Punic War, which ended in 146 BCE. Historical Carthaginians did engage in human sacrifice, specifically of babies and young children—a practice that disgusted the Greeks, Romans and other contemporaries.

The Free People, based on the legendary Amazons, did not actually exist except in stories of the ancient Greeks. But the Scythians—Skudat—were a real seminomadic culture based in the region surrounding the Black Sea. They were eventually displaced by the more easterly Sarmatians. The Neuri were barbarians described by the Greek historian Herodotus. They may or may not have existed under some other name.

The Samah of my story are drawn from the living Sámi culture of northern Finland, Norway and Sweden, but I have taken considerable liberties in altering source material. Little is known about the pre-medieval Sámi world. More information about the modern and historical Sámi can be found at the Web site of Siida, the Sámi Museum in Finland:

www.samimuseum.fi/english/info/en_index.html

**Bestselling fantasy author Mercedes Lackey
turns traditional fairy tales on their heads
in the land of the Five Hundred Kingdoms.**

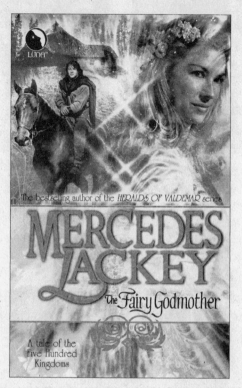

Elena, a Cinderella in the making, gets an
unexpected chance to be a Fairy Godmother. But being a
Fairy Godmother is hard work and she gets into trouble by
changing a prince who is destined to save the kingdom,
into a donkey—but he really deserved it!

Can she get things right and save the kingdom?
Or will her stubborn desire to teach this ass
of a prince a lesson get in the way?

On sale November 2004.
Visit your local bookseller.

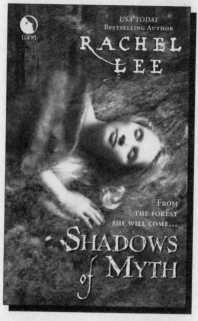